THE
LIGHTHOUSE
KEEPER

DISCARD

ALSO BY CYNTHIA ELLINGSEN

Marriage Matters

The Whole Package

THE LIGHTHOUSE KEEPER

CYNTHIA ELLINGSEN

LAKE UNION
PUBLISHING

Text copyright © 2017 by Cynthia Ellingsen
All rights reserved.

Published by Lake Union Publishing, Seattle

www.apub.com

Amazon, the Amazon logo, and Lake Union Publishing are trademarks of Amazon.com, Inc., or its affiliates.

ISBN-13: 9781477822821
ISBN-10: 1477822828

Cover design by Michael Rehder

Printed in the United States of America

To Hudson, the light of my life

CHAPTER ONE

The lighthouse in Starlight Cove filled the television screen, its red door vibrant against the midnight blue of Lake Michigan. The familiar theme music of News Tonight rang out to the cheers of the friends gathered in my living room before the announcer gave a brief teaser about treasure hunting and the show cut to commercial.

I let out a pent-up breath. My parents' part in the show was supposedly small—just two quick interviews—but I never knew what to expect with my family.

My best friend, Libby, hit me on the leg. "Starlight Cove was the first shot," she squealed. "Your parents are going to be the star of this thing!"

I pulled an embroidered throw pillow across my chest. "Please don't say that," I mumbled. "The show is about famous lost treasures. *Not* my parents."

Thank goodness.

It was hard to believe that even though I was now thirty-two years old, they still had the power to embarrass me. Some people are raised by lawyers or bankers. My parents specialize in historic shipwrecks. To put it more aptly: they're treasure hunters.

I typically avoided talking about their irresponsible lifestyle altogether, but Libby has known me since I was a kid, so I've never hidden it from her. Now that my parents were on national television, it would be hard to hide it from anyone.

"Is it too late for me to wait this out in my room?" I reached for my glass of pinot grigio. It sat on a silver coaster, sweating profusely.

Libby giggled. "You have to be here. This is the first time Todd gets to meet your parents."

I flushed. Todd and I had been together for more than a year. There was a good chance he was The One, but every time he mentioned meeting my parents, I changed the subject. They wouldn't understand his pressed khakis, starched shirts, and interest in the stock market, and he was sure to have strong opinions about how I was raised. Until the two worlds were forced to collide, it was much safer to keep them apart.

Todd caught my eye and lifted his glass of scotch. I raised my glass back, hoping he couldn't see that my hand was shaking from nerves.

My eyes wandered over my apartment. Entertaining ranks last on my list of fun at-home activities—bingeing on home improvement shows is much more my style—but Libby had invited everyone for a potluck and screening before I could stop her. To make it bearable, I'd texted out a list of acceptable dishes so there would be an actual meal instead of fourteen varieties of spinach and artichoke dip sitting on the table.

The *News Tonight* music started, and Libby called, "Here we go!"

Todd and Jack, Libby's fiancé, came over to join us on the couch. Todd took my hand. His was cool from the ice in his drink, and I pulled away, embarrassed my hand was warm and sweaty.

He tucked a strand of blonde hair behind my ear. "You okay?"

I gave a tense smile. "Ask me when this is over."

Was it too late to cut the power and pretend I hadn't paid the electric bill? Probably. And no one would believe that I could be that irresponsible.

"There he is!" Libby cried as my father loomed on-screen. In the lower right corner, it read PROF. WARD CONNERS, TREASURE HUNTER. "I know him!"

"He looks great," I admitted. "Sean Connery, watch out."

My father was as distinguished as ever with his short white hair and close-cut beard. He sat in a mahogany chair against the backdrop of my parents' enormous library, sporting a captain's blazer over a gray turtleneck sweater.

The host, Greg Norten, said, "I'm sure everyone in America wants to know: How does one become a treasure hunter?"

The camera zoomed in on my father's face, and he flashed his familiar charming smile. "I got a metal detector for my tenth birthday. There were some stray quarters in the yard, I scrounged 'em up, and I was hooked."

The story wasn't true, of course, but it didn't matter. My father is a master of showmanship.

He went on to explain that he obtained a degree in archaeology before working as an apprentice on several fishing boats and, later, wreck dives. He reminisced about the first dive he went on with my mother and waxed poetic about how that led to the discovery of the *San Arabella*. He forgot to mention that it took at least a decade for them to find anything at all.

"The *San Arabella* was a Spanish ship, missing for centuries," the host said. "That find came with a huge payout. It made you one of the most famous treasure hunters in the country."

More than one person in the room sneaked a look at me, and I shifted, uncomfortable. My friends would certainly Google the *San Arabella* that night, if they weren't already doing it right there in my living room.

"Yes." My father looked pleased with himself. "The *San Arabella* was quite the coup."

"Your grandfather was also a ship captain," the host said.

My father's expression became guarded. "He was indeed. Now, if I could—"

"Captain Fitzie Conners was responsible for a very large shipwreck," the host said. "A lot of men lost their lives."

Libby shot me a nervous look. In general, my father loved talking about treasure hunting and his work as a ship captain. But after years spent trying to clear his grandfather's name, he didn't talk about Captain Fitzie with anyone.

Sure enough, his tone turned low and dangerous. "The weather caused that wreck," he said. "It was nobody's fault."

"What about the missing treasure?" the host persisted.

I bit my lip. If Greg Norten valued his hair plugs, he'd drop this line of questioning.

When my father didn't answer, the host continued. "If that treasure is still out there, I'm surprised one of the most famous treasure hunters in the country hasn't found it yet. Have you looked?"

"I'm not discussing that," my father growled. "And this interview is over."

I jumped as he ripped the microphone out of his lapel and stormed out of the view of the camera. The show cut to commercial break, and an awkward silence filled the room.

"Snap!" Libby lifted her glass in a toast. "Your father shut him down."

Everyone laughed and applauded. Libby patted me on the knee and got up for more wine. I gave her a grateful look.

"Is that true?" Todd turned to me. "About your great-grandfather?"

"Which part?" I asked, fiddling with the diamond stud in my ear.

To my relief, two of his fellow accountants cut in to coordinate a golf game. I escaped and headed to the dining room to wrap up leftovers.

Armed with foil and a fat Sharpie, I wrote today's date on Post-it Notes and stuck them to each dish, hoping to look industrious instead of upset.

The interviewer had made my father seem grumpy and uncooperative, which was hardly the case. I wasn't sure what to think; I had texted with my mother after my parents filmed the interviews, and she said everything went fine.

The theme music rang out, and Libby paused the show. "Dawn, it's back on!"

"Go ahead," I called. "I'm watching."

I was wondering if I should sneak off to call my parents when Greg Norten's voice boomed through the room, measured and dramatic over a lilt of mysterious music.

"It wasn't a surprise to us that Professor Ward Conners ended our conversation when we began to dig into the history of his family." I set down the Sharpie. The host stood on the beach of Starlight Cove, his ridiculous hair blowing in the breeze. "So, we did some investigating of our own."

I walked back to the couch and sank into the soft leather. A montage of old photographs flitted across the screen: Lake Michigan in the height of a storm, the wreckage of a ship smashed against the shore, and a wiry ship captain in front of the American flag.

My phone lit up: *Mom.*

"Hi," I said, in a low tone. "What is this?"

"Dawn, we don't know." She sounded panicked. "They told us this was about lost treasures. We assumed that meant the *San Arabella.*"

My blood went cold. "It's not?"

"I don't think so, baby. I think it's an exposé on your great-grandfather and the legend of *The Wanderer.*"

"Mom, I—"

My father's shouts echoed in the background, followed by the sound of something crashing to the ground. It might have been the television.

"Honey, I have to go," she said, and hung up.

I stared at my phone in disbelief.

This was exactly what I was afraid of. The reason I didn't want to watch the show with a roomful of people.

"What's wrong?" Libby whispered.

Shaking my head, I stood up. I walked to my bedroom and shut the door.

Voices murmured out in the living room, the television clicked off, and people gathered up their things while saying good-bye. Someone knocked on my door—probably Todd—but I was too upset to answer. Instead, I locked myself in the bathroom and turned on the hottest shower I could handle.

I came out a half hour later, in a waft of steam and peach shampoo. I wrapped my hair in a white towel, put on a silk robe, and padded out to my bedroom. There, I listened.

Silence.

I risked opening the door. The living room was spotless, as if no one had been there at all. A piece of paper rested on the counter, probably a note from Libby. Something along the lines of *Sorry I bullied you into having everyone over to witness your family get humiliated on national television.*

In the kitchen, I put on the kettle and picked up the phone to call my mother. Their landline beeped and beeped, as though someone had taken the phone off the hook.

I pictured my parents' cozy country kitchen in Northern Michigan. The place was filled with antiques and treasures from their travels around the world. Even though I hadn't been there in ages, I wished I could sit in that kitchen with my mother now, my toes buried in the bright-red Persian rug beneath the table, sipping coffee from the hand-crafted pottery she loved.

Instead, I put together a plate of macaroons and poured milk into my tea. Setting up the spread in the living room, I let out a deep breath.

"Okay." I cued up the DVR. "Let's see how bad this is."

It was worse than I could have imagined.

The first segment of the show was indeed about *The Wanderer*, the ship commissioned to transport silver coins, fur, and illegal whiskey from Chicago to Canada. It sank a mile and a half outside of Starlight Cove on April 29, 1922, under my great-grandfather's command. The wreck can still be seen in Lake Michigan, but the silver was never recovered. Pretty much every person with a pulse has tried to find it since.

When the ship sank, the price of silver was weak, but there was enough on board to make it valuable. Today, the imprint of the lost Morgan silver dollars is rare and worth more than ever. Treasure hunters have calculated the lost coins to be worth somewhere in the millions.

Theories surrounding the silver have existed for decades. Some people continue to believe the coins rest on the floor of Lake Michigan alongside my great-grandfather, Captain Fitzie Conners. Others think he survived and disappeared with the very treasure he was commissioned to protect. My family has always believed he was innocent. Clearly, that didn't matter to *News Tonight*.

They painted my great-grandfather as the one most likely to have stolen the treasure, especially since he trafficked illegal whiskey. Worse, they questioned whether my parents' vast fortune really came from the discovery of the *San Arabella*. The entire segment was inflammatory, embarrassing, and sold in a way that sounded plausible.

They made it sound like the Conners family was up to no good.

I barely slept, which made it harder than usual to go for a run at 5:00 a.m. The streets of Boston were quiet, and I looked up at the sleek buildings, wondering how many people watched *News Tonight*. I didn't want it to be a trending topic at the watercooler, along with the usual Sunday night shows.

Back at my apartment, I found a text from Todd.

Can we meet for coffee?

I hesitated. I liked to stick to my routine before work. Still, considering the way I'd acted the night before, I owed him the courtesy of a conversation and, maybe, an explanation.

Thirty minutes later, I walked into Buzz, a coffee bar in the business district. The tables were chrome, and the waitstaff wore white jackets. The smell of fresh-roasted coffee hung thick in the air.

Todd sat at a corner table. He wore a tailored navy suit with a light-blue shirt and a burgundy tie that worked well with his tortoise-shell eyeglasses. He wasn't handsome in the traditional way, which was fine by me. I've never felt comfortable around attractive men—I have a gift for embarrassing myself in front of them. It started in the first grade, when I laughed during snack time, only to have chocolate milk come out of my nose. It sprayed all over Bucky Branson, the cutest boy in class.

Todd stood up as I approached. "How are you?" He studied me from behind his glasses.

"Fine." I settled into a cold, metal chair.

To be honest, I wasn't fine. I felt shaky inside, as if the wrong words might break me. Still, I didn't want Todd to know, so I kept our conversation centered on the news headlines, the stock market, and the cleanliness of the restaurant.

The waitress dropped off our coffees—a French press for Todd and a chai latte for me. She swept away before I could ask for honey, so I riffled through the collection of condiments in my purse to find a stray packet. Todd watched as I squeezed it into the mug, an unreadable expression on his face. Then, he took off his glasses and sighed.

"This isn't . . . working," he said.

I assumed he meant the French press. I pushed down the plunger and poured him a full cup of coffee. He added cream before shaking his head and pushing the cup away.

"I meant us," he said.

The din in the restaurant went quiet.

"What do you mean, exactly?" I asked.

Todd reached for my hands. "Dawn, you know I care for you. But last night I realized I don't know a thing about you, your family, or your past." He dropped my hands. "That show shocked me."

"That show was a completely fabricated version of the truth," I told him.

"I don't want to pass judgment on you or your family," he said, in a tone that indicated he was absolutely passing judgment on me and my family. "I just can't be a part of that type of sensationalism."

Sensationalism?

He got to his feet and patted my shoulder.

"Good luck to you, Dawn," he said, and headed out the door.

On the walk to work, I called Libby. I was so stunned I couldn't even cry. Not that I would have on a public street, but still.

"Forget Todd," she said, furious. "I never liked him."

I stood outside the elevator in my building. "Really?"

"Well, I don't anymore," she said. "Are you okay?"

I stepped into the elevator and studied my reflection in the faded metal of the walls. My gray pantsuit was perfectly precise, hair up in a neat French twist, and makeup flawless. Everyone around me probably thought I seemed just fine.

"Not really," I whispered.

"Call me after work," Libby said. "We'll get drinks. And, hon?"

"Yeah?"

"Hang in there."

I swept into my office on the fourteenth floor, where I worked as a corporate loan officer. The moment I shut the door, I sank to the floor and pressed my fists into my eyes, fighting back tears. I couldn't believe this.

Just last Friday, Todd and I had talked about what it might look like to get married, move to the suburbs, and raise a family. It sounded so good, so *normal*, that I should have known it could never happen to me.

The phone on my desk rang. I forced myself to get up but didn't trust myself to answer. Instead, I waited for the red light to flash, indicating a voice mail.

When I went to check it, I found that I had fifteen new messages—about fourteen more than usual.

"Hi there," sang a brisk, overcaffeinated woman. "Katie Marina here from the *Goodmorning Post* . . ."

I skipped to the next message.

"Bob Cadaglia from 98.1 Talk Radio . . ."

I flipped through the entire series—each from a reporter—and finally hung up. The phone rang again and I jumped, then immediately felt silly. It was just my boss on the internal line.

"Good morning, Gail."

Typically, she liked to exchange three pleasantries before getting to business. Her go-to topics were the weather, the line at Starbucks, and the slow elevator. Today, she breezed past them all.

"Dawn, come to my office, would you?" she asked.

Something in her tone made me want to head back to the coffee shop for another breakup with Todd. No matter how much that hurt, I imagined it would be easier than hearing what she had to say.

"I'll be right there."

Gail was dressed in hot-pink and purple workout wear. She always ran on the treadmill by her office window, making calls and dictating plans. She beckoned me in, wiped sweat from her forehead with a towel, and gestured for me to take a seat.

I remembered the first time I ever set foot in this office, ten years ago. It was a clear day, and I could see the Boston Light out in the harbor. The lighthouse seemed like a sign that, after a life at sea, I had somehow ended up in the right place. As Gail swigged her kale-and-blueberry smoothie, I hoped that was still true.

"So." She gave me an upbeat smile. "We just need to wait for . . ."

The Human Resources director walked in the door.

Gail launched into a speech the moment the HR director took a seat. *She* didn't care that my family looked like common criminals on national television, but it made some executives at the firm "nervous." She spun phrases like "regroup," "rethink your game plan," and "rebuild trust within the financial community." From there, she cited the mistakes I'd made during the past decade.

The HR director produced a file of my cases that had defaulted, as well as a recent filing mistake. He acknowledged that it could have happened to anyone. Then he launched into the details of my severance package.

Afterward, I sat on the concrete railing next to the building in shock. I'd spent my entire life striving for security, and for what? I may as well have lived like my parents: drifting on the ocean, hunkering down to fight the storms.

Staring at the harbor, I watched the seagulls ride the wind. I studied the lighthouse for a long moment before dropping my head into my hands.

Despite repeated phone calls to my parents, I didn't hear from them. The phone was off the hook in their house, it went to voice mail at their antique shop, and their cell phones were off. My mother finally called back a week later while I was out on a walk, taking a break from submitting my résumé online.

"Where have you been?" I demanded, ducking into the doorway of a coffee shop.

It smelled like freshly baked bread and coffee. I'd barely eaten a thing all week, but it would be a waste of money to buy a croissant or a muffin. I was too stressed out to eat, so half of it would wind up in the trash.

"Dawn, we had that camping trip, remember?" she said. "Reception was terrible."

Now that she mentioned it, I vaguely remembered. But would it have killed them to try to send a text?

"Your father's still in the woods," she added.

"How is he doing?" I asked.

Silence stretched over the line.

Not okay. Well, that made two of us.

The bell on the door jingled. I stepped out of the way for a couple leaving the restaurant. They held hands and I felt a pang, remembering all the times I'd refused to hold Todd's hand in public.

My mother continued. "The insurance company that represented *The Wanderer* has opened an investigation."

I whipped off my sunglasses. "About *what*?"

"They want proof your great-grandfather didn't run off with the silver. If we can't provide it in ninety days, they plan to comb through every financial record we have, looking for who knows what. The lawyers said they plan to place a lien on the house, since the property can be traced back to Fitzie."

I took in a sharp breath. "You can't let that happen."

Thanks to my parents' life at sea, I attended eight elementary schools and spent half my life living out of a suitcase. The one certainty was our summer visits to see my grandparents in Starlight Cove. The rambling old house built by my great-grandfather was the only place I ever considered home.

"We can't lose the house," I told her. "You'll have to pay off the lien."

"According to the lawyers," my mother said, "paying it off would be an admission of guilt. We'd be on the hook for the lost silver."

I blinked, staring out at the busy city street. Cabs honked, bike messengers scurried down the block, and people walked from store to store. How could life around me seem so normal when the world was crumbling at my feet?

"This can't be possible," I told her. "There has to be some sort of statute of limitations on this type of thing."

My mother sighed. "It's amazing what loopholes people can find when they're chasing after money."

"What are you going to do?" I demanded, sliding my sunglasses back on my head. "You have to do something!"

"I thought you could come home for a little while," she said. "To help."

I fell silent as she went through all the reasons a visit might do everyone good. I promised to think about it. Then I went into the coffee shop, drank a chai, and Googled Starlight Cove on my phone to remember what I was missing.

The news feed popped up first. *The Wanderer* was at the top of the list, along with links about *News Tonight*. Below that, there was an article that made me sit up straight: the lighthouse in Starlight Cove was for sale.

On the General Services Administration's auction site, the listing sat between a list of lab equipment and medical, dental, and veterinary equipment. The white, cylindrical structure was exactly as I remembered it, with its red door, black stripes, and outdoor gallery at the top. I sat back in my chair, studying the pictures.

I had loved that lighthouse since I was a little girl. Every lighthouse, actually, as they were the markers I searched for while out to sea with my parents. But the one in Starlight Cove was personal.

What if I bought it? I thought, suddenly. *Not to keep it, or anything, but to remodel?*

The opening bid for the public auction was $10,000. Based on the pictures, the lighthouse was hardly move-in ready. I couldn't imagine too many people would have the freedom to sink their savings into something like this.

I looked around the coffee shop. It was practically empty. The only people not at work at two o'clock on a Tuesday afternoon seemed to be seniors, sipping at their coffee and reading the paper. I was the only one my age, with no plan other than to submit résumés and hope for the best.

I looked back at my phone, debating.

Not only would I love to own the lighthouse in Starlight Cove, but the time spent remodeling it would give me time to hunt for answers about *The Wanderer*. My parents might let some insurance company place a ridiculous claim on our family home for something that happened a century ago, but I'd already lost enough.

The theme music of *News Tonight* flitted through my brain, reminding me of the struggle it would be to keep my head above water in Boston. My eyes drifted to the picture of the lighthouse. Then back to the bright-red button that read "Place Bid."

With a trembling finger, I pressed it.

Chapter Two

I stood on the beach of Starlight Cove and stared up at the lighthouse. Over a hundred years of wear and it still stretched strong toward the sky. Iron balustrades circled the thick panes of glass at the top, and a lone seagull rested on the railing, its feathers ruffling in the early morning breeze.

Shielding my eyes from the sun, I called, "How does it look from up there?"

The seagull gave me a disdainful glare before soaring across the inky blue of Lake Michigan. I secured a loose strand of hair and let out a deep breath. I couldn't believe the lighthouse belonged to me.

When I was in Boston, buying the lighthouse at auction had seemed like a good idea. Now, I couldn't help but think I'd made the biggest mistake of my life. The lighthouse seemed sturdy on the outside, but who knew what it looked like—or smelled like—inside?

Maybe there was still a chance the second-highest bidder could take it off my hands. I was scheduled to meet with the General Services Administration agent later that afternoon to get the keys and do a walk-through. I could tell him I had changed my mind and hope for the best.

"Dawn Conners?" a voice called.

I snapped out of my reverie and stared.

A gorgeous guy in his midthirties dragged a rickety rowboat through the water. His dark hair was windblown, cheeks rough with stubble, and his navy T-shirt clung to a strong upper body. He flashed me a smile I felt all the way down to my toes.

"Are you Dawn?" he called.

"Yes," I said, smoothing my hair.

Who on earth was *he*?

I was at the beach because I had a meeting set up with Kipling Whittaker, an older gentleman who frequented my parents' antique shop. According to my mother, he wanted to discuss my "family history." I was eager to talk with him because, while I was in town, I planned to prove my great-grandfather's innocence to the insurance company. I figured it would be helpful to talk to someone close to his generation. So I was a little confused to see some guy with bulging biceps calling my name.

I watched as he tossed a bowline knot over a metal pole and cinched it with a firm tug. The rope went taut, along with his upper arms. Then he jogged across the sand and came to a halt next to the boardwalk.

Midnight-blue eyes surveyed my fitted linen dress, bare legs, and low pumps. In a voice much too husky for polite conversation, he said, "You always wear high heels to the beach?"

I flushed.

Even though Libby liked to say that my fitted dresses and pinned-up hair made me look like a candidate for public office, I didn't expect to hear it from a stranger.

"Depends on the day," I shot back. "Do you always look like you just rolled out of bed?"

He grinned. "You're already thinking about me in bed?"

"I have an appointment with Kipling Whittaker," I said. "If you don't mind, I'd like to—"

"You can call me Kip."

Arrgh. I couldn't believe this.

The fact that my mother had led me to believe that this guy was a gentleman of a certain age meant she was up to one thing: matchmaking. In her mind, I came to Starlight Cove for a fun, relaxing summer vacation. That assessment could not be further from the truth. The last thing I wanted to do was waste time flirting with some rumple-haired playboy.

Especially one named Kip.

"Sorry for the confusion." I straightened my shoulders. "My mother made it sound like you were more mature."

His blue eyes sparkled. "Ouch."

"Older," I clarified. "She said you were older."

"Maybe we should go straight to breakfast." He gave me another once-over. "That dress wouldn't last long on my houseboat."

Even though I was 99.9 percent sure he didn't mean it like *that*, I was mortified. He had to know my mother was aiming for a love match. If he was even—I glanced at his hand, no ring—yes, he was single.

I decided to clear up the matter right away.

"I don't know what my mother told you," I said. "But I'm not here for a hookup."

"A *hook*up?" Kip laughed. "Do you mean a setup?"

"It's the same thing."

He raised his eyebrows, and I realized my mistake. I felt like milk was coming out of my nose all over again. With as much dignity as I could muster, I said, "You know what I mean. Either way, I didn't want you to get the wrong idea."

"It didn't even cross my mind," he said cheerfully. "Most of my hookups don't happen at nine in the morning. But if they did, your lovely blonde hair wouldn't be stuck up into that bun." His eyes met mine. "It would be fanned out against my pillow."

As I struggled to find something, anything, to say to that, he said, "Come on, Fancy Pants. I know just the place we can talk."

~

Even though I was tempted to chalk up the meeting as a complete disaster, I followed Kip Whittaker to Main Street. I still wondered what he knew about my great-grandfather. Besides, based on the insulting things he'd said—*fancy pants!*—it was clear he'd made a snap judgment about me.

I looked forward to proving him wrong.

Walking down the cobblestone sidewalks, I forced myself to turn my attention away from Kip Whittaker and on to Starlight Cove. Just being here made me feel like I'd stepped back in time.

Starlight Cove was built in the early eighteen hundreds on money from the lumber industry. Lake Michigan served as a thoroughfare for vessels transporting logs from Canada to Chicago, and downtown Starlight Cove served as a port. The buildings were designed to withstand the tough Northern Michigan winters, and they hadn't changed a bit over the years. Maybe Starlight Cove was too solid to change; or perhaps it was so steeped in history it couldn't move on.

My favorite store as a child was—of course—the candy shop. The fudge was produced with the same fervor as whiskey during Prohibition, and I could smell it all the way down the block. I remembered the colorful batches of candy poured onto marble slabs in dark browns, pale pinks, and creams. The lady behind the counter always slipped me a piece of Rocky Road. Now that I was back, I'd have to make a visit to the candy store a priority.

Kip came to a stop in front of a restaurant with a yellow-and-white-striped awning. The wooden sign above the door read TOWBOAT.

"Look good?" he asked, pointing.

I peeked through the front window. The single-room restaurant was crowded. Old fishing nets and paintings of ancient ships hung on walls of rustic wood. In the back, a huge window offered a spectacular view of Lake Michigan.

"Perfect," I said, particularly interested in the size of the servings. The plates were piled high with pancakes stacked with butter and thick maple syrup. I'd gone for a run earlier that morning and now I was starving.

Kip held open the door. "Be careful." He pointed at the series of stone steps that led down into the restaurant.

I gave him a questioning look.

He nodded at my feet. "In those shoes."

Giving my best glare, I stalked down the stairs into a cool, bustling cavern. It felt good after the heat of the early morning sun on my shoulders. My stomach growled as the scent of freshly brewed coffee and smoked bacon hit me.

A teenage girl with trendy purple hair gave an enthusiastic wave before pointing us to a wooden booth in the corner. On the way, I stopped in surprise. In between an etching of a ship and a painting of a sunset hung a black-and-white photograph of my great-grandfather.

I took in the old-fashioned clothing and stiff posture of Captain Fitzie Conners. He stood in front of the lifesaving station, silhouetted against the American flag. He sported a wiry mustache, close-cut hair, and a confident gleam in his eye.

A strange emotion tugged at my heart. Growing up, I considered Captain Fitzie a romantic hero. Someone who loved my great-grand-mother and protected her at all costs. It was strange to think he was also the reason my entire life fell apart.

"Did you know this was here?" I asked Kip.

"Captain Fitzie's picture is everywhere." He patted it with affection. "Thanks to *News Tonight*, the tourists have been taking selfies with him."

"His picture is up for tourism?" I demanded.

Kip shrugged. "Every small town needs a good outlaw."

Irritated, I followed Kip to the corner booth. It had an incredible view of the lake. I tried not to look right at the lighthouse. The purchase was supposed to be confidential, at least until I got the keys.

What would Kip say if I told him I was the person who bought it? I was sure he'd think I was kidding.

A lanky busboy rushed up to our table. He held a pot of coffee over the ceramic mug on the table. "Coffee?"

I smiled at him. "How about a chai latte?"

He looked at me in confusion.

"Ginger tea?" I tried.

The busboy glanced at Kip, who shrugged.

Embarrassed, I said, "I'll just take some hot water, please."

Kip opened his mouth to speak, but before he could, our purple-haired waitress bounced up to the table. She had Kip's eyes, a freckled nose, and a moon-shaped face. Despite her wild hair, she wore a conservative polo shirt, tan shorts, and white Keds, along with plain silver studs in each ear.

Kip beamed. "Dawn, this is my niece, Sami. Her mother owns this place."

"It's nice to meet you," I said.

"Dawn's parents own Shipwreck Antiques and Treasures," he told Sami. "As for Dawn . . ." He rested his chin on his hand and studied me for a long moment. "Well, she just likes high-heeled shoes."

I fought off the urge to kick him. On the other hand, I was relieved Sami didn't bat an eye at the mention of my parents. Maybe my family wasn't as notorious around here as Kip said. Or, more likely, Sami was too young to care.

Kip and Sami chatted about the last few days of her junior year. I liked her enthusiasm. She was excited about design but not a big fan of precalculus. Kip even offered to help her study for the final exam.

It struck me as sweet but unexpected. Kip Whittaker seemed like the type of guy who would rather hang out with his buddies than act like a role model for his niece.

"You guys ready to order?" Sami asked.

Kip requested fried eggs, bacon, hash browns, and butter pecan pancakes with real maple syrup.

I handed her the menu. "I'll get that, too."

They both looked at me.

"It's a lot of food," Sami warned. "My mother gets a little crazy with the pancakes."

If there is one thing I am not afraid of in this world, it is a lot of food. Particularly if that food happens to be a good, homemade breakfast. The servings did seem a little large, though, and Sami seemed genuinely concerned.

"Bring me a to-go box," I suggested. "If I need to, I'll pack up half and give it to a homeless person."

Kip gave a little cough. "Last time I checked, everyone in Starlight Cove had a home."

"Oh." I flushed.

I hadn't been the new kid in school for so long, I forgot what it felt like to be an outsider. Now, the feelings came roaring back. Both Sami and Kip studied me with a mixture of amusement and pity, and I wished I hadn't said a thing.

"I'll keep the same order," I managed to say.

Sami scampered away, and the busboy returned with a mug of hot water.

Thanking him, I reached into my bag and pulled out my collection of condiments. I riffled through Tabasco sauce, packets of dried cranberries, A.1. steak sauce, vinegar, spiced jerky, a whole lemon, and several mints before finding a packet of chai tea. Ripping it open, I dropped it in the mug.

I looked up to find Kip staring at me.

"What?" I asked, raising my eyebrows.

"I'm surprised you didn't order your pancakes with the pecans on the side." He rubbed the dark stubble on his cheek. "Like Meg Ryan in *When Harry Met Sally.*"

Basically, he was calling me difficult. It wasn't the first time I'd heard that from a guy. I've also heard I'm regimented, scared to take chances, and too particular to open myself up to love. The night the guy laid that one on me, I went home and cried.

Part of the reason I fell in love with Todd was that he didn't push me to be something I wasn't. He accepted the fact that I only wanted to get together on Tuesdays, Thursdays, and Saturdays and that I didn't like public displays of affection or sentimental gestures. I already missed the security of being with him and couldn't help but hope that, once he found out I was gone for the summer, he would miss me.

"Go ahead and make fun," I told Kip, who was still laughing at my portable collection of condiments. "I wanted chai and now I have it. What's the big deal?"

He hid a smile behind a big swig of coffee.

"So," I said. "You watch romantic comedies. That's interesting."

He held up his hands. "*When Harry Met Sally* was on at my sister's house. I didn't watch it."

Right.

I bet he *did* watch romantic comedies, which hardly matched up with his whole smoldering, outdoorsy look. It was nice to have that piece of information at my fingertips for the next time he made fun of my shoes.

I turned my attention to the water. I must have been staring at the lighthouse, because Kip noticed. He raised an eyebrow and said, "Nice view."

"It is," I said, taking a sip of tea.

"Too bad some moron out-of-towner bought it at auction."

"Some moron out-of-towner?" I bristled. "Is that what you think of everyone who's not from here?"

Kip laughed. "Only the dumb ones." Looking out at the lighthouse, he shook his head. "The buyer has no idea what they're getting into. A few locals have a bet they'll take one look and run away. It's got to be filled with mildew. Or the seagulls have torn it to shreds."

Based on photos posted on the auction site, Kip could be right. But I also knew how the lighthouse used to look, before it fell apart. When my mother learned about my purchase, she filled my in-box with pictures from the local historical society.

It used to be beautiful, her e-mail read. *It could look like this again!*

Scrolling through the pictures was fascinating. The lighthouse was six stories, complete with a spiral staircase, wooden floors, and stone walls. The interior was rustic and inviting, completely different from the dilapidation apparent on the auction site. So much had changed.

But—and maybe it was my irritation at Kip Whittaker that made me think this—so what if it had?

I could wield a hammer. Sand and stain some boards. How hard could it be to bring the lighthouse back to its original form?

"The lighthouse is a part of Starlight Cove's history," I told Kip. "It shouldn't just sit there, falling apart."

"Few lighthouses in Michigan make it up for private sale," he said. "I don't think the buyer bought it to preserve Starlight Cove's history. I think he or she plans to remodel the interior and sell for a profit."

Maybe Kip Whittaker was more perceptive than I gave him credit for. Between this and the whole "moron out-of-towner" insult, there was a good chance he knew I bought it.

"What's wrong with making it look good?" I asked, to test him.

"Nothing, if it's not exploitive." He leaned forward on his elbows, drawing unnecessary attention to his upper arms. "But if it is, the buyer will have some explaining to do."

"To whom?" I demanded.

"The people of Starlight Cove."

This guy was really unbelievable.

If "the people of Starlight Cove" wanted the lighthouse, they should have bought it. Kip Whittaker made it sound like they planned to show up at the door with pitchforks to try to steal it back. He probably planned to lead the charge.

A parade of servers saved him from getting a piece of my mind. Led by Sami, they delivered plate after plate of food. The pancakes smelled rich and buttery, with the sweetness of maple syrup.

I cut my pancakes into neat little squares, followed by my sausage. Then I shook ten drops of Tabasco on my eggs, added one more dash of creamer to my tea, and dug in. The pancakes were slightly crunchy and sweet, definitely the best I'd ever tasted.

"So, what do you do?" I asked.

"Consulting." He picked up his fork. "Nautical research. That sort of thing."

"Who do you do work for?"

"Some ecological, some commerce." He popped a piece of bacon in his mouth. "The most interesting people I work with are the treasure hunters."

"Ah." I fidgeted with my fork. "How well do you know my father?"

"Pleasantries at the shop, but that's about it," Kip said. "Everyone knows of him, of course."

"They do now," I said. "I heard he wouldn't meet with you about this, even before *News Tonight*. Why not?"

"I found a letter from Captain Fitzie to my great-grandfather. When I brought it up to your father, he told me to go jump in the lake." Kip considered the stretch of water hugging the horizon. "The water's still a little cold this time of year, so I declined."

"Do you have the letter?" I asked, curious.

Kip slid his cell phone across the table. "Take a look."

I squinted at the sleek screen. It showed a picture of a yellowed piece of paper. I wiped my fingers off on a napkin and zoomed in. My pulse quickened.

"Fitzie definitely wrote this," I said. "I recognize his handwriting."

I hadn't seen it in years, but I knew it well.

Back when Fitzie captained long journeys, he passed the time by writing love letters to my great-grandmother. The man wove phrases with the grace of a concert pianist. I used to read the letters when I was a teenager, sipping on cherry cola and dreaming of a love like the one my great-grandparents shared.

Based on the things Fitzie wrote, it was clear he adored his wife, which made me certain he was innocent. No man who felt that way would abandon his wife and his unborn child.

Squinting, I leaned in to read.

> Sunday, May 7
> Dr. Whittaker,
> Thank you for treating this matter with discretion. I am surprised by my actions, but, given Madeline's condition, I have chosen the only possible option. I ask for your assistance in protecting her and providing her with the help she needs. I will contact you shortly to make arrangements.
> Capt. Fitzie Conners

I reread the letter three times, trying to understand what I was missing.

"Okay . . . ," I finally said, setting the phone down. "I don't understand."

"Look at the date." Kip reopened the screen and zoomed in. "I only caught it because I was doing research, comparing my great-grandfather's office records to his journal. May seventh fell on a Sunday the year the ship went down. Madeline was pregnant at that time."

"The ship sank in April," I said.

"So, unless Captain Fitzie was writing letters from the other side . . ."

The clatter of silverware and the buzz of conversation seemed to go silent. I couldn't believe it. Kip Whittaker was trying to prove that my great-grandfather was still alive after the wreck; it was the exact opposite of what I wanted to hear.

If I didn't like Kip before, I definitely didn't like him now. I'd only met with him because, based on what my mother told me, it sounded like he was on our side. Clearly, that couldn't be further from the truth.

"That is completely ridiculous," I said, shoving his phone back across the table. "It's much more likely that he wrote the wrong date or the wrong day."

"His livelihood relied on planning a route down to the very last degree. Remembering the days of the week would not be a problem."

I shook my head. "That's the stupidest theory I've ever heard."

Kip glowered. "Didn't you grow up on a ship?"

I did, but how did Kip know? Oh right. My mother probably told him, while planning for us to have glowering little babies.

"Regardless of the date or day on that letter," I said, "there's no way Captain Fitzie was alive after the wreck."

Kip sat back in his chair. "You're pretty confident about that," he said. "Do you have proof?"

That's what I was here to find. But Kip Whittaker didn't need to know that.

I glanced at the photo of Captain Fitzie hanging on the wall. The emotion from the love letters shot through my heart.

"My great-grandmother," I said simply. "There's no way he would have left her."

Kip groaned. "Ah, a romantic. Fooled into believing true love always wins."

"Funny to hear that, coming from you," I shot back. "Don't you spend your time watching *Titanic*? Or do you prefer Nicholas Sparks?"

I was not about to sit here and let some overconfident playboy tell me the rules of love. It was obvious from my relationship with Todd that true love didn't always win, but I knew it was possible. I'd read the words myself, from a man who believed in it.

Taking another bite of pancakes, I said, "No offense, but . . ."

"Every time someone says 'no offense,' the person says something truly offensive."

"No offense," I repeated, "but I have no reason to trust you. We just met, you insulted the way I dress, and you whip out some picture of some letter to try and prove my great-grandfather was a criminal? Sorry, but that doesn't cut it with me. I'm not saying you faked the letter . . ."

Even though that was something to consider.

"But if it *is* authentic, it still doesn't prove anything." I stabbed a piece of pancake and popped it into my mouth. "I'm surprised you didn't get airtime with *News Tonight*. Your theory would have fit right in with theirs."

Kip sat back on the bench, looking every ounce the frustrated explorer. "Look, Dawn. There's more to the story. You know it and I know it. So can you cut me some slack?"

I looked at him in surprise.

"My great-grandfather kept meticulous records," Kip said. "If he did help good ol' Fitzie, as this letter seems to indicate, there will be a record of it. But all that's tucked away in the attic at the big house."

I folded my hands. "I assume you mean your family home. Not jail?"

Kip's eyes crinkled at the corners. "Nice one, Fancy Pants," he said. "Let's search the attic. Look through some old office paperwork and see what we can find."

Spending more time with Kip Whittaker did not appeal, but the idea of visiting the Whittaker home certainly did. It was an impressive

Victorian mansion perched on the edge of a bluff, and I'd admired it since childhood. The house was there long before Fitzie's time, so it was very possible a secret or two hid inside.

Still, I couldn't help but wonder at Kip's motivation. *News Tonight* had done an impressive job of slandering my great-grandfather, but that didn't stop them from suggesting that part of the treasure might still be hidden in Starlight Cove. Plenty of people were searching for the Morgan silver dollars. Kip could be one of them.

"What's in it for you?" I asked.

He considered the expanse of the water. "I've always been interested in the story. Now that it involves my family, I'm invested."

Reluctantly, I nodded. "I can meet tomorrow evening."

"You can handle seeing me again?"

I took a final sip of tea and got to my feet. "I suppose that's up to you."

Tomorrow, Kip Whittaker would know I was the "moron out-of-towner" responsible for taking the lighthouse from the people of Starlight Cove. I had no doubt he'd have something to say about that.

I punched my number into his cell phone and hit the "Call" button. I waited for my cell to ring, then handed back his phone.

"Call me if something changes," I said, dropping some cash on the table. "Otherwise, I'll see you at six tomorrow."

Even though I was not looking forward to spending more time with Kip, I hoped he wouldn't cancel when he found out about the lighthouse. Because even though the letter to his great-grandfather didn't mean Captain Fitzie was a thief, it definitely meant something.

I was determined to find out what.

~

My mother was dusting a pistol from the 1890s—nonworking, I could only assume—when I walked into Shipwreck Antiques and Treasures.

She seemed younger than her age in a loose, multicolored silk dress and several beaded necklaces. People say I look just like her, but I don't see it.

My mother is a natural beauty, with wide cheekbones, an easy smile, and wild blonde hair. She smells like lavender, won't touch a highlight, and never wears makeup. Personally, I can't imagine leaving the house without mascara.

"Well, I didn't expect you back so soon," she sang.

The store was busy, with several middle-aged tourists in brightly colored clothing browsing collectibles, ancient furniture, and trinkets. I perched on the edge of a Victorian fainting couch near the cash register.

"Why?" I asked. "You expected Kip Whittaker to drag me off to a cave and make me his bride?"

"Dawn." She bounded over and tucked her arm in mine. Leaning in, she whispered, "It's a small town."

Even though the majority of the customers in her store appeared to be tourists, Starlight Cove's winter population was just forty-five hundred. The odds were good that someone in the store knew Kip.

"Sorry," I mumbled. "But I can't believe you tried to set me up with him."

"You should thank me. He's practically royalty here." My mother made a big deal out of fanning herself. "*Everybody* likes Kip Whittaker."

I remembered the moment I saw him on the beach. I liked him, for a total of about ten seconds. Then he spoke.

My mother patted my knee. "How are you feeling about the lighthouse?"

I glanced at the antique clock on the wall. One hour to go until I got to see it.

"Kip said whoever bought it was a moron," I said. "So, that was encouraging."

My mother laughed. "Isn't he a hoot?"

I decided to change the subject. "I wish Dad was coming to the walk-through. How long is he planning to stay in the woods?"

My mother frowned. I noticed dark circles under her eyes and a tightness to her mouth.

"Who knows?" She shrugged a thin shoulder. "You're going to have to go see him. I thought the lighthouse would draw him out, but it turned out to be just another thing that got him worked up."

"What do you mean?" I asked, surprised.

"It reminds him of his grandmother. Madeline became obsessed with the lighthouse and everything it represents when Fitzie died."

"What does it represent?"

My mother ticked the words off on her fingertips. "Loneliness, misery, desperation . . ."

"Do you think *I'm* lonely, miserable, and desperate?" I demanded.

"No, no, no." Her laugh trilled through the store. "It's a completely different situation. You needed a change, and the opportunity was there. I'm glad you bought it. It got you to move here, didn't it?"

"I didn't move here," I said. "I'm visiting for the summer. That's all."

"We'll see," she sang.

I rolled my eyes. My parents had been trying to get me to move to Starlight Cove for the past five years. They were convinced small-town charm was just what I needed, but I had no intention of sticking around. I planned to find out what I needed to know about *The Wanderer*, sell the lighthouse for profit, and get back to my real life.

"Don't get your hopes up," I told her. "I'm not going to live in your guest bedroom for the rest of my life."

"I doubt any of us will be living there for much longer," she said lightly. "But that's the way the cookie crumbles." Getting to her feet, she gestured at a man studying a painting of a ship. "Be right back," she murmured. "I have to charm a customer."

Drumming my fingers against the couch, I switched my thoughts to my father. I was disappointed he wasn't coming to the walk-through. Like my mother, I'd thought my purchase of the lighthouse might be a way to cheer him up, especially considering he was the reason I fell in love with lighthouses to begin with.

In one of my very first memories, I'm running toward him across the wooden deck of some ship, waving my arms at a flock of seagulls. I had a handful of saltines crushed in my tiny fist. The seagulls swarmed around, pecking at my hand. Panicked, I scattered the crumbs on the deck. The birds descended in a flurry of screams and feathers, and I promptly burst into tears.

My father scooped me up in his arms. "What's wrong, little bumpkin?"

I told him I was scared of the birds, the ship, and the fact that my parents disappeared underwater every day. He nodded, deep in thought. Then, he showed me the endless stretch of water beyond the bow and told me about a beam of light in the night.

"It shines like your very own star," he said. "Every time you see it, you won't have to be afraid. You'll know that you're not alone."

The next time I felt scared, I searched for that beam for three days. I finally saw it: a pure, white light flashing against the night sky.

From that moment on, I searched for lighthouses everywhere we went. I loved the unique structures, all alone on the water. The way the beams lit up with a simple, rhythmic flash or an arc of light that swept across the water like a pair of arms. No matter how far we traveled, or how lost I felt, I could always count on the fact that a lighthouse would be there.

To me, lighthouses didn't represent loneliness or desperation, like my mother said. They represented a port in the storm.

My very own star, waiting to guide me back home.

Chapter Three

Even though I had placed my bid for the lighthouse online, I contacted an agent in Starlight Cove to help me with the final process. I knew enough about the world of mortgages and real estate to want a professional on my side. At two thirty, my mother and I headed to the office. It was a small cottage with a white picket fence, just a few blocks off Main Street.

Freshly baked cookies greeted us from under a glass dome on a table in the entryway. Steam clouded the lid and the cookies were warm and gooey. I took two and offered one to my mother.

"Thanks." She took a big bite. "Chocolate's good for stress."

The small entryway led into a large main room with hardwood floors, glistening windows, and a desk with neatly organized stacks of papers. A fern hung from the ceiling, its pale-green leaves lively in the afternoon sunlight.

"Be right there!" A friendly voice called from the back. "Grab a seat."

My mother and I settled into a pair of green leather chairs in front of the desk. The stack of paperwork made the situation feel a little too real.

"I don't think I can go through with this," I whispered.

Four weeks ago, I had sat on the fourteenth floor of a financial building, crunching numbers, confident I would spend the rest of my life doing the same thing. Now, I was sitting in some random office in Starlight Cove, about to sign off on a dilapidated piece of real estate.

At what point had I lost my mind?

"Of course you can." My mother patted my knee. "It will be fun."

Fun? Her word choice, coupled with her free-spirited tone, irritated me. I knew that tone. It was the same one she used to agree with my father's schemes, no matter how outlandish they were.

"I'm thirty-two years old," I whispered. "I don't have time for fun. I should go back home, get a job, any job, and act like a grown-up. Not hide out here, wasting time failing at this."

"You'll be just fine," my mother said. "For the first time in your life, you're following your—"

I held up my hand. "Do *not* say it. I hate that expression."

Sorry, but I did. I spent my entire childhood in the company of parents who cared more for joy than responsibility. Besides, I hadn't come here because the idea made me happy. I came here because, like always, my parents refused to act like grown-ups.

"Just let me panic in peace," I told my mother. "I think I have a good reason."

"Dawn, I really don't know when you got to be so uptight. It's time you—"

Her hippie-dippie lecture was interrupted by a cheerful voice. "Sorry to keep you waiting!"

A woman about my age bounced into the room. She was heavyset, with smooth, brown hair; wide, green eyes; and a deep dimple in her right cheek. She wore a green shirt and a pair of navy shorts, along with a turquoise necklace and at least ten bracelets. She looked like a hard worker and completely sane—something I needed at the moment.

"Hello." I got to my feet and extended my hand. "Dawn Conners."

"Kailyn." She bustled forward in a waft of apple-scented perfume and shook hands before I could blink. Then, she leaned against the desk, crossed her arms, and said, "So, *you're* the sucker who bought the lighthouse."

I almost passed out.

Kailyn broke into peals of laughter. "I'm just teasing! You've been thinking it, so I figured I'd just come out and say it! Seriously, I am so jealous I can hardly breathe. You own a *lighthouse*. How wild is that?"

It was "wild," no doubt about that.

"If I were in your shoes," Kailyn continued, "which I wish I *was*, I would be sweating bullets. That's why I got you this . . ." She rushed behind her desk and held up a bottle of Captain Morgan, followed by an enormous basket. "And this! Happy housewarming."

She lugged the basket around the desk and dropped it in my lap.

"The rum's a joke, *obviously*," she said, "but I thought it was a good one since you'll be living on the water. Like a pirate. If you're allergic to chocolate, I know someone who can take it off your hands." She pointed at herself with two thumbs. "This gal."

My mother laughed.

The basket weighed about a thousand pounds, was wider than my lap, and was piled high with survival supplies, including a fleece blanket, a kerosene lamp, an enormous flashlight, batteries, a portable burner, and a thick bundle of rope. It also offered a book about lighthouses, a package of chocolate-covered cherries, fudge, coffee, cocoa, and tea from the shops in Starlight Cove.

"Goodness," I said. "Thank you."

"Thank *you*." Kailyn flipped a strand of hair over her shoulder. "Everyone was shocked when I got to be a part of this, since you didn't really need to use an agent. To be honest, I wasn't quite sure what to think of it all, but you made me look like a superhero."

I paused. She seemed sweet as candy, but there was something sharp behind that comment. I bet Kailyn watched *News Tonight* and had her own opinions about my family and our history in Starlight Cove.

Well, whatever. It wasn't like I'd be here long enough to worry about making friends. It was a shame, though, because I liked her. In some ways, her upbeat attitude reminded me of Libby.

Taking a seat behind her desk, Kailyn slid on a pair of purple glasses. "Before we meet with the GSA agent, I want to go over some basics with you about the lighthouse," she said. "It's important to know that you can make changes to the interior, but not the exterior. In particular, those two black stripes painted at the top."

"The daymark," I said. "It's there so it can be seen during the daytime, against the shore."

She raised her eyebrows. "You know your lighthouses," she said. "I figured, but you never know. Now, it only went up for auction because the Coast Guard periodically reviews all the lighthouses in the country. If it doesn't make sense to maintain them, they get offered to nonprofits. If that doesn't work, they go to private auction. So, here we are."

"There wasn't a nonprofit that wanted it?" my mother asked.

Kailyn clicked her tongue. "Their application was denied. They bid in the private auction, but as we all know, Dawn snatched it away."

Great. I could just imagine what the people in town would say about a Conners "snatching" the lighthouse away from a nonprofit. Maybe I should call *News Tonight* and offer them the chance to do a story on that, too.

"From what I understand," she continued, "there was only one private bidder that you really had to battle."

"Who?" my mother asked.

She seemed to hesitate. "That, I don't know."

I doubted Kailyn would tell us even if she did know.

"Now, the Coast Guard will have keys to your house," she continued. "You're an active aid to navigation, so it's their job to maintain the light and all that. I'm so jealous, because I'm currently stalking someone in the Coast Guard." She grinned. "If Ronnie comes over, you have to call me."

"Is he your friend?" I asked.

"He's my future husband. He just doesn't know it yet." Pushing her chair away from the desk, she hopped to her feet. "You ready?"

I shook my head. "Let me just . . ."

I reached into the housewarming basket, grabbed the bottle of Captain Morgan, and took a ceremonious swig. I hadn't touched hard liquor in ages. The alcohol seared the back of my throat and left a sharp caramel taste in my mouth.

"Okay." I tried not to choke. "Let's do this."

Kailyn and my mother burst into peals of laughter.

"She's tough," Kailyn said, as we headed toward the front door.

My mother nodded. "She's going to be just fine."

The beach was bustling with tourists by the time we arrived. The GSA agent, Bud, stood on the rocky point, holding a clipboard. He was tall, with round cheeks and close-cropped black hair.

"You must be Dawn," Bud said when we reached him. "Or, as I'll call you, our new steward."

"Hi." I shook his hand. "Is it too late to back out?"

Bud laughed. I considered telling him it was a serious question, but before I could, he handed me a large iron key and pointed at the lock on the door.

"I'll let you lead the way," he said, smiling.

I swallowed over a dry lump in my throat. The lighthouse was so tall, so iconic. I could feel tourists watching us from the beach, and probably some locals, too. Kip Whittaker was probably out there somewhere, glowering away.

There was an iron ladder that led up to the main door. I grabbed onto the bottom and started to climb the narrow rungs, grateful I'd changed into starched shorts, a button-up shirt, and loafers. Once I got to the top, I inserted the key in the lock and turned it with a loud clang. Pushing the door open, I stepped inside, and let out a deep breath.

"All right," I whispered. "This is it."

The main room was about fifteen feet wide and dim, like a cave. The sunlight cast eerie shadows, illuminating the stone floor and dirty walls. The moment was surreal. I'd spent so many years of my childhood obsessed with lighthouses. It was hard to believe one finally belonged to me.

To my surprise, my eyes smarted with tears. Blinking furiously, I let out a slow breath. My mother stepped into the main room, followed by Kailyn and Bud.

"Whoa." My mother laughed. "What's that smell?"

I breathed in. The air smelled sour and sharp, like a damp basement mixed with something else.

"Bird crap," Kailyn said cheerfully.

Bud noted something on his clipboard. "Birds and bats have a way of taking over, when left to their own devices."

"Wait." I held up my hand. "What do you mean, bats?"

Bud chuckled but didn't answer.

Fantastic.

Bats freak me out. The fact that they sleep upside down is weird enough, but the way they swoop and dive without warning? I hoped he was kidding.

To gauge the situation, I swept the flashlight on my phone across the ceiling. No bats, but the walls were a mess. Dirt and spots of mold covered everything.

The romanticism I had felt moments before faded away.

"This place is filthy," I murmured.

"It still has its merits." Bud pointed at an iron apparatus on the wall and pushed against its hinge. "For example, this is unique to the structure."

The stone wall gave a loud scrape as dirt fell away in a rectangular pattern. The heavy stone moved outward, into the open air, and sunlight streamed into the room. The midnight-blue water of Lake Michigan stretched for miles.

"Look at that," I breathed.

I knew that the top of the structure had windows, but I hadn't realized the lower level did, too. The lighthouse was certain to have plenty of secrets like this. I tried to focus on that thought, instead of on the mess around us.

"Ready to go up?" Bud asked.

Our group followed him to the curved staircase hugging the stone wall. The steps were black-painted steel with small, star-shaped holes.

"Bud, I noticed the old pictures of the lighthouse had wooden steps," my mother said.

He nodded. "The Coast Guard replaced them about ten years ago. Back in the day, there were only fifty steps. There are eighty steps now. Less steep and a lot safer."

I recognized the walls on the next floor from the pictures. They were a beautiful combination of brick and stone. There were also two small iron shelves. I could imagine copies of *The Rime of the Ancient Mariner* or *Treasure Island* resting there, to be read by oil lamp as the lake raged outside.

"Where does the power come from?" I asked Bud. "A generator?"

"There's an electrical power source that runs from the basement," he said. "You won't have to worry about waking up every few hours to keep the light lit."

The kitchen was on the next story. I was instantly drawn to the dramatic frame of the ancient wood-burning stove. The black chimney ran up the wall and out into the open air.

Even though the kitchen seemed hopeless, it had possibilities. Back in college, Libby and I had turned the portable hot plate and kettle in our dorm room into a full-service dining experience. We cooked a gourmet dinner each week for our latest boyfriends and served it on a blanket in the middle of the floor.

I was long past the days of sitting on the floor to eat—especially a floor as filthy as this one—but the kitchen could be turned into something decent. The edge of the sink had plenty of room for a cutting board and a set of knives. The stove had large burners and the oven's main compartment might even work for baking.

I pulled it open to see whether it was meant for food or wood. It was impossible to tell, considering that the only thing in there was a nest that moved. I screamed, slammed the door shut, and ran across the room.

Everyone stared at me like I'd lost my mind.

"You open it, then," I said.

My mother sailed over. "Aww," she said. "Those little mice just had babies. How sweet."

"Bleh." I shuddered.

Bats were bad enough, but I really can't stand mice. I've always hated that scene in *Cinderella* where the mice make the dress. I sincerely doubt that someone destined to be a princess would fight for a dress sweatshopped by little pink paws.

"Take the stove and sell it in the antique shop," I told my mother. "I will never touch it again."

"It's original to the structure," she said. "It's staying."

Bud looked relieved. Walking over to the sink, he demonstrated how to unhook the latch on the pump handle. "Now, the water system for your lighthouse is pump operated. It pulls water from the cisterns in the basement."

"Water's a good sign," Kailyn said. "So, where's the baño?"

I turned to Bud expectantly.

"Well . . ." He tucked his thumbs into the loops of his khakis. "The previous keepers used an indoor porta-potty system. You'll just have to figure out what works best for you."

I blinked. "There's no bathroom?"

Bud scratched his head. "No, not really."

Kailyn giggled. "Well, this definitely qualifies as a fixer-upper."

No kidding.

I'd imagined the lighthouse might need a good cleaning. Some repairs. But a complete lack of bathroom plumbing hadn't crossed my mind. That would be expensive to install but was a must for resale, which was not good news.

Upstairs, my spirits sank even further.

The large window in a room that could be a bedroom was shattered. Feathers, bird crap, and broken glass littered the floor. When we walked in, an entire family of birds flew out: grandparents, cousins, and even a few family friends.

Bud frowned. "I wish we would have known about that window," he said, walking over to take a look.

The mold had seemed bad downstairs, but up here the humidity and open air had caused serious damage. The room was speckled from the top to bottom. Huge sections of the floor were absolutely covered in splotches of angry-looking spores.

I didn't know much about home repair, but I did know that ripping out moldy floorboards would not be cheap. Up until now, I'd never paid to get anything fixed in my life. I suddenly longed for Terry, the on-site repair guy with the sagging tool belt who skulked around my building in Boston.

"This is a disaster," I whispered to my mother. "What am I going to do?"

"Fix it up." She patted me on the back. "It's just going to take some hard work."

"This isn't just work, though," I said. "It's a health hazard. It's condemned. It's . . ." My eyes darted from the bird mess to the mold to the broken glass. "I don't have the first clue how to do this."

"But it *can* be done." Her voice was firm. She put a hand on my shoulder and guided me to the staircase. "Let's head up."

The watch room was just below the lantern room. A stream of sunlight from the shaft increased the heat of the day. Our group stood in cramped silence, my mind still on the mess below.

"How are you feeling?" Bud asked. "Think this is something you can manage?"

"It's a mess," I said. "But I guess it's my mess now."

Bud smiled. "You might be surprised at how many people will want to get involved," he said. "The lighthouse belongs to you now, but the community loves it, too. They'll want to help."

I wasn't so sure that would be the case. I was afraid the people of Starlight Cove really would show up with pitchforks. First when they discovered the lighthouse was bought by a Conners, and then when they found out how ill equipped I was to handle the renovations.

"Now, the lantern room will get a little tight," he informed us. "I think only Dawn and I should head up."

Kailyn gave an eager nod. "Good call. This gal's scared of heights."

Bud and I walked to the ladder in the center of the room. He went first and pushed open the trapdoor. I climbed up behind him. The rungs felt sticky but secure, and they led us to the most magnificent light I'd ever seen.

"Dawn, I'd like to introduce you to your Fresnel lens."

The Fresnel lens resembled a beehive made of prisms. Large, horizontal slivers of glass were stacked in curves with a mazelike circle in the center. Miniature rainbows danced across the room, reflected in panes of glass overlooking the water.

"It's incredible," I whispered.

Bud tilted his long neck back. "The Fresnel is an antique and something we don't always leave behind. This one belongs here, though. It shines for miles," he said, indicating the view. "Want to head outside?"

He pushed open a small door. With a tentative step, I followed him out to the lantern gallery, the concrete balcony guarded by an iron railing. The sudden rush of wind whipped my hair around my face as I surveyed the scene.

From where I stood, I had a 360-degree view of the lake, the hills, and—through the part of the lantern room unobstructed by the light—Starlight Cove. The colors were so vibrant from up above: the patchy green vegetation on the foothills of the sand dunes and the turquoise water that darkened to deep navy as it reached the horizon.

Bud rested his arms against the railing, tilting his face back in the sunshine. "Do you have any questions?"

"Hundreds," I admitted. "But with this view, I can't think of one."

"I'll head back down then." He gave a slight nod. "Enjoy it."

The door clicked shut.

I gripped the iron railing and walked around the top. I could see the bustle of Main Street and the tree-lined residential avenues. From up above, Starlight Cove looked as perfect as a painting.

Down below, the waves shifted and roiled. I looked out across the water and spotted a few boats anchored about a mile and a half out. That had to be . . . Yep. People were diving down to *The Wanderer*. It was a clear enough day that I could see its ghostly shape hidden below the surface.

It was so strange seeing it from the lighthouse. I imagined the violence of the storm that night, the sound of the ship groaning and cracking as it went down. My great-grandfather and his crew, desperate to make it to shore.

I stared at the formidable shape in the water. The wind picked up, and the ship disappeared in the whitecaps of the waves. Shivering, I wrapped my arms around myself and headed back inside.

Chapter Four

Both Kailyn and Bud said their good-byes in the main entryway. They promised to check in with me over the next few days.

My mother glanced at her watch. "I need to head back to the store. Will you be home for dinner?"

"We could eat here," I said. "Mold stew? Pigeon-feather soufflé?"

Laughing, she gave me a quick kiss on the cheek. "I'm excited for you, honey. This is going to be great."

I watched as my mother climbed down the ladder. It brought to mind all the times I watched her and my father drop into the ocean for a dive. They used to treasure hunt for hours while I sat on the deck, dodging offers to play Go Fish with weird-looking deckhands.

"Don't be too late," she called up. "We're having grilled swordfish."

Grilled swordfish? When I was little, we ate tuna from the can.

Growing up, I loved everything about being at sea.

I wore a necklace of pirates' gold, a bracelet of magical rope, and clothes sewn by a mermaid. I dove off the bottom of the ladder into a sea of salt, made friends with dolphins as they leapt by, and dozed on the deck, staring at my very own sky full of stars.

My world was idyllic until school came along.

Instead of sending me to a traditional school, my parents wanted to hire a tutor to bring on the water. Tutors, they soon learned, were expensive. So, they had no choice but to settle on land.

I started kindergarten in Oregon, where my parents could hunt for treasure off the coast. But by the time winter hit, they moved us to San Diego and, soon after, San Francisco. In the beginning, I was eager to make new friends. I'd come home babbling to my parents about this girl or that. But it only took two new schools for me to decide it was pointless to get to know the other kids at all, since I'd just have to leave them behind.

By the time I was in fifth grade, I had attended eight elementary schools, and my parents were failing to survive as treasure hunters. Desperate for money, they accepted a job cataloguing a shipwreck off the coast in Florida. We were scheduled to stay for two years—far beyond anything I had experienced before.

In Florida, I made my first true friend.

Everyone liked Libby because she had long, black hair that fell in ringlets down her back. She wore a backpack that lit up and fluorescent shoes that sparkled. On my third day at school, she cornered me in the science lab during recess. Plunking onto a stool, she chewed on a red gummy worm and stared me down.

"Is your dad a pirate?" she asked.

I was tempted to lie. Kids were a lot nicer when they thought my family was normal. By the time they found out the truth, it was time to move again, anyway. But something about Libby made me want to be honest.

"He's not a pirate," I said. "He's a treasure hunter."

"Has he ever found gold?"

"Not a lot." I shrugged. "Sometimes, we eat tuna from the can because we don't have any money."

I regretted the words the second I said them. They gave Libby information that could make my life in school miserable. To my surprise, she said, "Come to my house. My mom makes lasagna, and we have ice cream every night." Then she pulled a green worm out of her pocket and handed it to me.

I loved Libby's normal life. Her mother packed lunches and cooked dinner. Her father read the paper at the dinner table. Her house was warm and cozy, with comfortable chairs and chocolate chip cookies in the jar on the counter.

I never wanted to leave.

When my parents finished the job in Florida and decided to move to the Carolinas, I dug in my heels. I hid under Libby's bed without telling anyone—not even her—and was missing long enough for my parents to call the police.

I had a meltdown, of sorts, when I finally came out from my hiding spot. I sat in Libby's mom's lap and told her how hard it was to go from school to school, changing my friends, my home, and my life. I was desperate for stability, but it was nowhere in sight.

Libby's mother must have had a talk with my parents, because things started to change. For the first time in my life, my mother didn't join my father on the dives. She started working part time at antique shops, offered to help with homework, asked me about my day, and started to get on a schedule for dinners.

It sounds ridiculous, but knowing that Monday meant tuna casserole; Tuesday, pasta; Wednesday, tuna melts; Thursday, soup; and Friday, chicken tacos gave me something to hang on to. I even helped my mother cook, for fear she'd try to switch things up. This gave me a sense of security that seems sad now but meant everything back then.

A year into our life in the Carolinas, my father discovered the shipwreck that made him famous. He was offered a job at a university in

Boston, along with the freedom to accept fellowships all over the world. We moved to Boston, and, since my father didn't want to take on the fellowships without my mother, they signed me up for boarding school.

I loved boarding school for the same reason I loved our dinner schedule. I finally got to stay in one place. I made friends, studied hard, and spent time with my parents when they were in town.

It wasn't like we lived some white-picket-fence existence or anything. But we never ate tuna from the can again.

The sun was barely up when I climbed into the cab of the truck my parents used to haul antiques and headed out to visit my father. With the windows down, my hair whipped across my face as I zipped past the pine trees lining the winding roads of Northern Michigan.

My father's campsite was nearly two hours north of Starlight Cove. He gave me the latitude and longitude coordinates, but that's all I had to work with. I hoped it wouldn't be too difficult to find him—whenever he escaped to the woods it was like he turned into Thoreau.

I was worried about seeing him. Even though it was important to me to find out the truth about *The Wanderer*, I couldn't help but be annoyed that I was the one scrambling to find evidence to appease the insurance company. Like always, my parents refused to accept responsibility for anything.

Still, I could only imagine the struggle my father was going through. He'd had his family, his history, and his professional reputation trampled, all within the span of a televised hour. I could understand why he wanted to stay far, far away.

Turning on my blinker, I pulled off the main highway and followed a gravel road back into the woods. The hickory scent from the smoke of a campfire blew through my hair, and the road became narrow. Just as tree branches started to scratch against the paint of the truck, the path opened up to reveal a clearing at the top of a hill.

I let off the gas and smiled.

My father's tent sat in an enormous clearing in the woods with a spectacular view of Lake Michigan. There was a hammock strung up between two trees and a perfectly polished, silver Aston Martin convertible parked to one side.

"Dad?" I called, stepping out of the truck and onto the moss-covered ground. Silence. "Dad!" My voice echoed across the bluff. The only other sound was the trees creaking in the breeze.

I walked over to the tent and noted the dying embers of a campfire nearby. Based on the bag of trash hanging up on the tree, he'd eaten Spam and eggs for breakfast. So gross, but he loved Spam. It reminded him of being out at sea.

Careful not to slip on the pine needles, I followed a makeshift pathway to the edge of the bluff. The lake reached as far as the eye could see. The outline of a barge loomed against the horizon.

My father strolled along the edge of the shore. With every step, he swept a metal detector over the sand.

Cupping my hands around my mouth, I called, *"Dad."* It took two more shouts, but he finally heard me.

"Dawn!" His face lit up.

Aw. My dad could be a serious pain in the ass, but I loved him something fierce.

Grinning from ear to ear, I picked my way down the trail to the sand and hugged him. Immediately, I was hit by nostalgia at his signature scent: Carmex, vanilla tobacco, and heavy wool sweaters. The temperature didn't matter; when he was outdoors, he always wore a wool sweater over his shoulders on the chance of a breeze.

"How's my favorite child?" he asked, his voice deep and gravelly.

"Your *only* child," I reminded him.

"Hmm . . ." He scratched his beard. "You might have a few brothers and sisters in Scotland. The women up there are brutes."

I laughed. *"Dad."*

He set down the metal detector, linked his arm in mine, and led us to a piece of driftwood. Plunking down, he patted the seat next to him. I sat down on the wet log, even though I was wearing a pale-blue dress. That's the thing about hanging out with my father: normal rules don't apply.

He studied me. "I heard you bought the lighthouse," he said. "What in the name of bologna did you do that for?"

He's also not one to beat around the bush.

"The lighthouse went up for auction the second I lost my job," I said. "I thought it might be a sign."

He pulled his wooden pipe out of his pocket, along with a weathered pack of vanilla-flavored tobacco. "I'm surprised you didn't try to get another job in Boston." He glanced at me. "You've never been the type to run away."

Picking up a handful of sand, I let the warm grains sift through my fingers. I felt like my father was waiting for me to admit that I came here to look after him, which I was not about to do.

"Do you remember my friend Libby?" I asked.

He struck a match, and the scent of the spark filled the air. "Liked gummy worms," he proclaimed. "Has incredibly dull parents."

"Her mother died," I said. "Last year."

The words sounded unreal. I had been there the moment Libby learned of the heart attack. I helped make arrangements, and I even spoke at the funeral. It all still felt distant, like an event that happened to someone else.

"I'm sorry, Dawn," he said. "Truly." Reaching over, he gave an awkward pat to my knee. "You were close with her mother?"

"Pretty close."

Before I had left Florida, Libby and I promised to stay best friends forever. We kept that promise, writing weekly letters to each other and plotting to be roommates in college. Once we were in college, my parents were always off on dives over the holidays, so Libby invited me home every Thanksgiving and even some Christmases.

Her parents had so many traditions I loved, like hiding a present at midnight and seeing who could find it first, or starting the Thanksgiving meal with an original poem about a turkey. Her mother and I often stayed up talking long after the rest of the family fell asleep.

Once Libby and I got jobs in Boston, I barely saw her family or mine. The trip to Florida was long, and I had my apartment, my routine, and I didn't like to leave it. Travel was the last thing that appealed to me, especially after the way I was raised.

I rolled a grain of sand between my fingers.

"Libby had a hard time," I said. "Losing her. Then, a few months ago, she tells me life is short and that she's always dreamed of seeing the world by sailboat."

"Ha!" My father laughed, rubbing a hand against his beard. "I knew I liked that girl."

"I told her it was a terrible idea," I said. "But she and her fiancé plan to do it this summer." Her smile had been huge the day her office agreed to let her work remotely. "Maybe the whole 'life is short' thing was in the back of my mind when I decided to buy the lighthouse. I don't know, really."

My father nodded. Wisps of smoke from his pipe blew past me like clouds along the horizon. For a moment, I felt lost in time. I could have been any age, sitting by the water with him.

"So, I don't know when you're leaving for your next dive . . ."

He grunted. "Not anytime soon. The one I had this summer cancelled."

"What do you mean, cancelled?" I said.

Dive teams from all over the world fought hard to get my father on board. They wanted an investment in their project, yes, but they also wanted his expertise. I couldn't believe someone had dared to cancel. It proved how badly the allegations on *News Tonight* had hurt his reputation. Still, I couldn't stand the fact that he refused to fight.

"Is that why you're hiding out in the middle of nowhere?" I demanded.

My father frowned. "Steady on, Dawn. I'm fine."

"Well, I'm not," I said. "I need your help with the lighthouse." I remembered what my mother had said about my great-grandmother's obsession with it. "I was surprised Madeline was so interested. It must be in our blood."

My father puffed madly at his pipe. "You can see *The Wanderer* from up there. It's easy to spot, when the wind is right."

"I know," I said. "When were you up there?"

"Madeline used to take me over there all the time when I was five or six," he said. "She sweet-talked the keeper into letting us climb all the way to the top. She had to be into her eighties by then, but you'd never know it by the way she climbed those stairs." He kicked at the sand. "We used to sit up there for hours. She kept her eyes on the wreck, talking about Fitzie's journeys. She was pretty old, so it was hard to tell what was fantasy and what was reality. But she was crazy about him."

I sat in silence, scraping my fingernail over the damp wood of the log. Kip had basically called me a hopeless romantic. He would have said the same thing about my great-grandmother.

"I ended up talking to Kip Whittaker about his great-grandfather's connection to *The Wanderer*," I said.

"What did you talk to him for?" he asked.

"Mom told me about the insurance company."

He shook his pipe at me. "You don't need to worry about that!"

Someone needs to, I wanted to tell him, but of course I didn't.

I studied his profile against the light-blue sky. His weathered skin and strong nose could have been taken straight from a painting of a sea captain, but the pain on his face made me think of a man searching for something he had yet to find.

Turning back to the water, I said, "Dad, I want to know what really happened. It doesn't seem right that people get to make up whatever story they want when we're the ones who have to deal with it. I just . . . I want to know."

My father let out a deep sigh. "You and me both, kid."

His words were unexpected.

"Really?" I said. "What changed your mind?"

He puffed away, lost in thought. Finally, he dumped the ash from his pipe in the sand.

"I don't know." He looked out at the water. "It seems to me, there's just no escaping these types of things until you face them."

Chapter Five

I climbed into the truck and waved at my father as I drove away. The ride home was at least two hours, and I spent most of it listening to sea shanties—something I hadn't done in years. I stared out at the water along the edge of the highway while driving, the mournful melodies swirling around me like a storm cloud.

My father had agreed to wrap up his camping trip in the next few days and help me with the lighthouse. When I described its current state, I expected him to hand me the number for a good contractor. Instead, he listened to my report on what needed fixing and helped create a list to tackle the project.

It reminded me of the days when I was little and would sneak into his office to watch him prepare for his role as captain on dive expeditions. He would sit in his office for hours, researching coordinates, star patterns, and maps of the ocean floor. He liked to say the treasure he found in the Carolinas was not dumb luck, but hours of research with a little stardust thrown in.

I was relieved he was interested in learning more about *The Wanderer*, even though he refused to admit he was doing it to satisfy the claims of the insurance agency. I invited him to help Kip and me search for information in the Whittaker attic, but he wouldn't go that far. He agreed to analyze any worthy data that came his way.

Emphasis on *worthy*.

Drumming my fingers against the edge of the open window, I worried about my meeting with Kip. I still planned to show up at his parents' house at six, but I was scared of what we might find. What if we discovered more evidence that Captain Fitzie was still alive after the wreck?

When I told my father about the letter to Dr. Whittaker, he shook his head, like it was old news. He had to be tired of hearing theories like that one. He didn't want to discuss anything that would support the idea of Fitzie as a criminal and neither did I, especially when I knew he wasn't.

A few miles outside of town, I slowed to take in the view of Starlight Cove. It was nestled below the hills like something out of a picture book, seagulls soaring overhead and sailboats skimming over the surface of the water. The lighthouse sat in the center of it all.

I gripped the steering wheel, feeling stress set in. The remodel would require so much from me, and I barely knew where to start. I decided to make cleaning the first thing on my list.

There were a few hours until the meeting with Kip, so I had plenty of time to stock up on cleaning supplies. Figuring out exactly what I would need and lugging it to the lighthouse was going to be a big job, and one that required plenty of caffeine. I parked the truck behind the store and walked down Main Street to try to find a cup of coffee.

The first place that caught my eye was Chill Out, a shop with a spearmint-and-white-striped awning and a pink front door. Glittering pictures of ice cream sundaes and coffee mugs hung in the window.

Inside, the air conditioning was cool, and the room hummed with business. Cloth-covered tables were crowded with tourists, groups of teenagers in swim cover-ups, and families with kids. Nearly everyone nursed a sundae, ice cream cone, or iced coffee drink, and it all looked delicious.

I stepped into the long line, breathing in the rich scent of chocolate. The sporty-looking girl behind the counter had ash-blonde hair and a friendly smile. Her name tag read JAMIE.

When I got to the front of the line, she tried to place me. "Do you live around here?"

"Just for the summer." Before thinking it through, I added, "My parents own the antique shop."

"Ah." A definite chill settled over her demeanor. "What would you like?"

I hesitated. "I can't decide between ice cream and coffee."

"Maybe you should step out of line while you figure it out."

"No, no," I said. "I meant . . ." Quickly, I glanced up at the menu. "I'll get the espresso milk shake."

Turning, she scooped up vanilla ice cream and dropped it in a blender with a cup of milk and an old shot of espresso. She squeezed in chocolate syrup, gave a disdainful press of the button, and leaned against the counter, watching the machine whir. Then, she dumped the entire concoction into a Styrofoam cup and shoved it down the counter.

"Pay over there." She pointed at a teenager standing at a cash register, then turned to the next customer. In a much friendlier tone, she said, "Hi there! What can I get you?"

I took a sip of the milk shake, eyeing her. The drink was delicious, a perfect combination of thick, vanilla-bean ice cream and sharp espresso. Too bad, considering I would never set foot in the place again. I couldn't believe the girl went from friendly to hostile the moment she figured out my family name.

Once I'd paid and turned away from the counter, I noticed a well-dressed woman a little older than my mother sitting at a corner table and staring at me. Her dark hair fell in a severe bob, and she wore diamond earrings big enough to blind someone. Crooking her finger, she beckoned me over.

I imagined she wanted to know what concoction Jamie had whipped up. In Boston, I never would have walked up to a stranger, but I was not about to be as rude as the barista.

On the way, I studied the series of framed, black-and-white photographs lining the walls. There were pictures of the shop when it first opened, old-fashioned photos of Main Street, and the same picture of my great-grandfather that was in Towboat. Kip said every town needed an outlaw, and I felt a fresh flash of annoyance at the reminder.

When I reached the well-dressed woman's table, I held up my drink. "It's an espresso milk shake," I said. "It's really good."

"I'm Maeve Weatherly." Her voice was sharp, like the bark of a Chihuahua. "Is it true you purchased the lighthouse?"

"Yes," I said, startled by her tone. "How did—"

"Don't you dare interrupt me!" she snapped.

A hush seemed to ripple across the ice cream shop.

"I'm sorry, what?" I said.

Was this a joke?

She got to her feet and took a menacing step forward.

"There's something you better get straight," she hissed. "The Weatherlys built this town. You have no business swooping in here, taking something that belongs to us all."

I couldn't believe it. This woman was telling me off, in the midst of wrought iron tables and ice cream sundaes. I felt like I was back in junior high, being ridiculed in the middle of the cafeteria.

"It was a public auction," I stuttered. "You . . . you had as much of an opportunity to buy it as I did."

Based on the size of her earrings, maybe even more.

"It shouldn't have *gone* to public auction." Maeve's small, black eyes bored into mine. "It should have been awarded to our town. We planned to use it for water conservancy and to educate the public. But just like a Conners, you took a treasure that didn't belong—"

Just like a Conners?

I held up my hand. "You can stop right there," I said. "You have no right to judge my family for something you know absolutely nothing about."

"Everyone knows about it," she said. "Since your family decided to make a public display of themselves on that television program and in the process give Starlight Cove a bad name."

I stared at her in disbelief.

"Do you think my parents had any idea what that show was about?" I demanded. "The entire thing was filled with lies."

Maeve Weatherly sneered. "I think it's perfectly clear your great-grandfather was a criminal. Not the type of lineage we want here."

Back in the day, the same group of girls that made fun of me in the cafeteria made me a target because of what my parents did for a living. They showed up to school wearing pirate patches and calling me "matey." It was embarrassing, but I was older now and less willing to let people walk all over me.

"My great-grandmother lost her husband when that ship sank," I said. "She was left to raise her child on her own, like so many of the other women who lost their husbands. It was an accident and a tragedy. I don't know how the people of Starlight Cove got it so twisted."

Maeve sniffed. "So, you came here to get revenge?"

This woman had to be insane.

"Look, lady," I said. "I don't know if the size of your earrings is interfering with your brain function, but why don't you pull the stick out of your ass and leave me alone?"

Maeve Weatherly's face turned as red as a cherry. She seemed ready to spew another sharp retort, but I didn't give her the chance. I stalked out of the coffee shop, the bells on the door clanking behind me.

I stood outside on the sidewalk underneath a manicured tree, shaking with embarrassment. It was so strange—I'd gotten dumped, lost my job, and learned I might lose my family home, but getting berated by a stranger in the middle of an ice cream shop felt more humiliating than any of that.

I didn't know why I was surprised. Kip Whittaker had set the tone for the people of Starlight Cove, and so far they lived up to his gold-star standard. Even Kailyn, with her effusive personality, seemed a little reluctant to be on my team.

I squinted through the sun at my parents' antique shop. People were coming and going. It didn't seem like the rumors about my family had affected business there. On the other hand, the majority of the customers could easily be tourists, not locals.

I was just about to head over to the shop to tell my mother what happened, when the front door of Chill Out opened. A wiry, dark-haired guy poked his head out. Spotting me, he waved and rushed over.

Something about the guy made my hackles go up. It wasn't like I was on the street alone, as plenty of tourists were strolling by in their pastels and golf shorts. But for some reason, I still felt cautious. Maybe it was his outfit. His black sunglasses looped in a thin band across his face, and he wore a white guayabera shirt with khaki cargo shorts. His look was right for a tropical beach town, but something about it rang false here.

"Dawn Conners?" he said.

I crossed my arms. "Yes?"

"Sorry to bug you." He glanced over his shoulder, as though looking for someone, then back at me. "I was in the coffee shop and heard that wretched woman use your name. I'm Sal Reynolds."

The fact that he called Maeve Weatherly "wretched" won him a few points, so I shook his outstretched hand. "It's nice to meet you."

Sal's skin was weathered, and he seemed close in age to my father. As we shook hands, I noticed he had a compass tattooed on his wrist.

"So, I'm not going to beat around the bush," he said, sliding his sunglasses back on. "I saw *News Tonight*, and I wanted to tell you I'm working on a documentary proposal for some investors."

I drew back. "You're a reporter?"

"No!" Sal shook his head, cackling. "A thousand times, no. I'm a filmmaker. Whatever that means anymore, right?"

Filmmaker?

He ran his hand through his thinning black hair. "Listen, I want to shoot a historically accurate portrayal of the legend of *The Wanderer*, not the slop that was on a few weeks ago."

I gripped my milk shake. The sun shone down, tourists bustled by, and I struggled to reconcile what was happening. Everything about this moment was so far from the life I was living just a few weeks ago that I didn't know whether to laugh or cry.

"My investors really want your input," Sal said. "I was hoping I could sit down and talk with you about some things."

"Sorry," I said. "I'm not . . ."

I blinked in the sunlight, unable to find the right words.

This guy claimed he was interested in being historically accurate, but I had no reason to trust him. His interpretation could be as bad as *News Tonight*'s. My family had endured enough humiliation already.

"This is all too strange for me, Sal," I said. "So, thanks, but no thanks. It was nice to meet you."

Raising my drink, I started to head toward the antique shop.

"Wait!" He rushed forward and pressed a small, black card in my free hand. It had his name, title, and contact information, as well as a sour stench of cologne. "I'll be doing research a few towns over for the

The Lighthouse Keeper

next few weeks. Give me a buzz when you're ready. I really want *your* story to be told."

"No." My voice was firm as I handed the card back to him. "Please. We just want to be left alone."

∽

The antique shop was busy when I walked in. I stopped and surveyed the scene.

Just like a Conners? Based on the activity in my parents' shop, the Conners family offered quite a bit to this town.

My mother was chatting with a group of customers, making them laugh at some story. Today, she wore turquoise, silk balloon pants, a form-fitting pink tank top, and at least ten strands of turquoise around her neck. She looked like a genie let loose from a bottle. The moment she got a free second, she swept over with a puzzled look on her face.

"What's wrong?" She smacked my cheek with a kiss. "You look pale."

I started to speak but, to my complete surprise, choked up. Mortified, I mumbled, "Give me a minute," and headed to the storage room.

The room was dim, dusty, and cluttered from floor to ceiling with antiques. The chaos made me feel worse. I pulled a wet towelette out of my purse.

My mother rushed in as I wiped down the chair. "Dawn, what's wrong? Did something happen with your father?"

"No, he's fine." I sat down and buried my head in my hands. "Go back out there. You have customers."

"Brad's here and he can handle things," she said, speaking of the college kid they had working in the shop for the summer. She settled onto a couch in some weird yoga pose. "Now, let's talk this out. What's wrong?"

59

"Nothing." My coffee shake was cold and bitter on my tongue. "Some stranger just asked me to help him with his documentary."

My mother laughed. "That's funny."

I glared at her. "How is it *funny*, exactly?"

Her expression sobered. "That's what upset you?"

"I also had a run-in with Maeve Weatherly."

She sat up straight. "What do you mean by a 'run-in?'"

By the time I finished the story, she was up and pacing the room. She picked an old lantern off the shelf and brushed the dust off the glass before setting it back down. Her pretty face was troubled.

"Dawn, the Weatherlys are powerful people," she said. "They own this building. They could pull our lease at any time."

"There are laws against that type of thing."

"You'd think." My mother shrugged her thin shoulders. "But I've heard of it happening to more than one person."

Maeve Weatherly's beady stare flashed through my mind. It wasn't hard to imagine her causing trouble, just because she could.

"You could find another location," I said. "If it came to that."

"Not on Main Street. People have these places locked down for years." She fiddled with her necklaces, and they made a sharp, clicking sound. "I guess I could speak with her mother. Beulah has a barn on her property packed with antiques, and she's sold me several pieces. Maybe she'd talk some sense into her."

I snorted. "Is Beulah anything like her daughter? Because . . ."

My mother's face brightened. "Kip could help! He's close with Maeve."

That didn't shock me. I bet the two got along like thorns and weeds.

"I'm supposed to research *The Wanderer* with him in a few hours."

My mother clasped her hands in delight. "Really?"

The rapturous look was so out of touch with reality that I wanted to shake her. Granted, I hadn't told her much about Todd, but she knew enough. One would think she wouldn't be trying so hard to push me toward the next available guy.

"I don't want to hear it about Kip," I said. "He's probably the rudest person I've met in Starlight Cove, and that is saying a lot."

"Dawn, get the chip off your shoulder," my mother said. "The people here are nice, if you take the time to get to know them."

"They haven't been nice to me."

"It takes time." She lifted her curly hair off her shoulders and let it drift back down. "They were suspicious of us when we first moved here, and they definitely got upset when the show aired. But most of the families that live here have been here for a long time. Everyone has a story. This time, the story just happened to be about us."

I rolled my eyes. "You give this place too much credit."

"What's wrong with that?" When I didn't answer, she said, "I doubt Maeve would come after the shop, but it wouldn't hurt to mention it to Kip. He's pretty diplomatic."

"*I'm* diplomatic," I said. "I had a whole list of things I wanted to say to Maeve Weatherly, but didn't."

My mother laughed. "I'm glad you refrained. I've lived here for several years now, and during that time I have learned one thing."

"What's that?" I asked.

She raised her eyebrows. "Don't piss off a Weatherly."

Chapter Six

I'd planned to find cleaning supplies for the lighthouse, but it hit me that before I could clean, I needed to get the debris out of each room. There were six stories full of random stuff like driftwood and loose hardware that I needed to move out.

Did I really want to carry bags of trash up and down all those stairs, though? And at some point, I would also need to transport water, cleaning solution, and all sorts of materials, too. I probably needed to figure out a way to do that where I wouldn't break my neck.

Back in the day, lighthouse keepers brought the oil for the lamps to the top using a pulley system. Maybe I could set up a modern-day version. Of course, I didn't have the first clue how to do that.

I stood outside my parents' store, chewing on the straw of my drink. On a whim, I pulled out my phone to call Kailyn. She'd recommended a hardware store, but I couldn't remember if it was in Starlight Cove or the next town over.

"Hi," I said, when she picked up. "It's Dawn Conners. I'm sorry to bother you, but—"

"No bother." Her tone was brisk. "How can I help?"

"I need to get the name again of that hardware store you recommended?"

"Henderson Hardware," she squealed. "I would *totally* go with you, but I have a showing that will take hours."

Huh. I thought she didn't like me, but she'd go to the hardware store with me?

"I'll be fine," I said. "Thank you."

"Take pictures, okay?" she said. "Sneak me at least one."

"Pictures?" I gave my phone a funny look. "Of the work I do on the lighthouse?"

"No." Her voice went wistful. "Of the Henderson brothers."

~

The hardware store on Main Street was as stoic as could be, nestled in an ancient wooden building with a single-pane, mirrored storefront window. **HENDERSON HARDWARE** was etched on the glass in a simple, gold font. The poor store. It probably saw a ton less traffic than the ice cream or antique shops.

I was proven wrong the moment I walked in. There was a steady hum of activity. Men stood by an endcap display talking tools, as expected, but plenty of women were there, too. An older woman clutched a lightbulb, a teenage girl studied swatches of paint, and at least five women puzzled over this project and that, all while biting their lips and smoothing their hair.

I stood in the doorway, unsure what to do next.

The run-in with Maeve at the coffee shop and the conversation with Sal had made me nervous. I didn't want to announce that I bought the lighthouse and risk another scene. Since the store was so crowded, I decided to come back at another time.

As I turned to leave, a gorgeous guy in his early thirties headed right for me. Worn jeans cupped strong thighs, a pair of worker boots suggested rugged competence, and a white T-shirt snuggled against his broad upper body. Small lettering above his right pocket read HENDERSON.

When he got closer, I noticed his handsome face was covered in freckles.

"Carter Henderson." He extended a calloused hand, all business. "What can I do to help?"

"Uh . . ." I shook his hand. "I don't quite know how to explain it . . ."

"Sounds mysterious," a deep voice echoed. "Now you have to tell us."

I looked over at the cash register. The line had thinned, revealing the cashier. He was an even better-looking version of Carter, with the same cleft in his chin, sparkling eyes, and fitted T-shirt. Sandy hair curled around his ears, making him look like a Renaissance poet.

"That's my little brother, Cameron," Carter told me. "He'll tell you he knows something about home repair, but he learned it all from me."

"Dirty, dirty lies." Cameron leaned against the counter. "The customers know I'm much smarter and much better looking. Isn't that right, Mrs. Holt?" he asked as an older woman with white hair approached the register.

Mrs. Holt set a single pack of lightbulbs on the counter and gave a winsome smile. "It depends on who's in charge."

"In other words . . ." Carter gave me a freckled smile. "She wants a discount." He strolled behind the register, pushing his brother aside. "Mrs. Holt, I can give you ten percent off."

"Oh, Carter," she cooed. "You're the smartest and best looking of the bunch."

Cameron shook his head and took a sip of a Coke. "It's the only way my brother can get women," he said. "Such a sad state of affairs."

"Why isn't anyone working around here?" a thunderous voice boomed.

My jaw dropped as yet *another* Henderson—clearly capable of wrestling lions with his bare hands—strutted out from the first aisle. His neck was the size of his head, and he was pure muscle, from top to bottom. He strolled up to the counter, every eye in the place on his bulging biceps.

"Mrs. Holt, let me carry that bag for you," he said.

The woman with the white hair had only bought the small package of lightbulbs, but she gave an eager nod. "That would be mighty fine, Cody," she said. "Mighty fine."

"Now, Cody, on the other hand . . ." Cameron waved the Coke bottle. "He has no problem getting girls. Until they find out he waxes his chest."

The lion-wrestling guy let out a roar. "Not true." He held open the door with one muscular arm. Shooting me a meaningful look, he said, "I'm confident in my manhood, but not enough for that."

Carter walked back over to me. "Did we scare you off yet?" he asked with a grin.

My head was spinning. There were so many of them; so many muscular, flirty Henderson brothers that I barely knew where to look. No wonder Kailyn wanted a picture.

"Not at all," I lied.

To be honest, I was a little nervous. The Hendersons seemed like a good, solid group of guys. It made me sad that they would probably turn on me, too. I couldn't help but imagine the long trips I'd have to take to the next town over every time I needed a new paintbrush.

Carter gave me his full attention. "So, what's the project?" he asked, crossing his arms. "Painting? Refinishing furniture?"

I fiddled with the light-blue strap of my dress. "I need to construct a pulley system to make it easier to clean the lighthouse."

Carter drew back. "You bought the lighthouse?"

I held up my hands. "I completely understand if you—"

"Don't want to tell my brothers so I can see it first?"

Relief rushed through me. "Something like that."

"Good deal." He rubbed his strong hands together and gave a smile that belonged on a home improvement show. "When do you want to get started?"

Chapter Seven

It turned out Carter knew and liked my father. He even seemed a little protective of him, asking how the antique shop was doing and if he had any new adventures coming up.

"I know he loves to dive," Carter said. "Where's he off to next?"

"He'll be here for the summer." It pained me to remember that a dive team had cancelled on him. "He wants to help out with the lighthouse."

"That's cool," Carter said. "I'm sure he wants to spend time with you, too."

From there, Carter asked me a hundred questions. We planned to meet the next morning to go over logistics for the pulley system. He suggested holding off on the cleaning supplies until then so that he and his brothers could help lug everything over all at once. I left the hardware store in a much better state of mind than the one I'd arrived in.

Since the trip to Henderson Hardware took longer than expected, I rushed to my mother's house to get ready for the meeting with Kip. I changed out of my sundress into a crisp, button-up, sleeveless shirt and fitted, navy shorts because I planned to ride a bike to his parents' house.

A lot of people rode bicycles around town. In Boston, I hailed a cab to go five blocks. Here, I wanted to be out in the fresh air.

Once I was ready to go, I hopped on my mother's bike and pedaled toward town. The sky was so clear, the air clean, and the lawns brilliant green. Flowers dripped from window baskets, birds chirped, and the fresh air felt unique to small-town life.

I picked up the pace, breezing past the shops on Main Street. The restaurants were full of tourists tired and burned from a day out on the beach, and the air was thick with the smoke of hamburgers cooking on the grill. Out past town, I breathed in the scent of honeysuckles and freshly mown grass.

The bike ride was a challenge on the hill up to Kip's house. The grade was steep and I stood up on the pedals and pushed hard. Once I made it to the driveway, I rested my hands on my legs for several minutes, gasping for breath. Then, I pushed the bike through the tall gate and stared at the Whittaker estate.

The house resembled a yellow ship, with a strong front mast and several decks on each level. Three towers with port windows stood above the trees like watchtowers, and two stone chimneys flanked each side. An enormous wraparound porch somehow made the house seem homey. Flower baskets were draped over the railings, lush with wildflowers in pink, purple, and blue.

I leaned my bike against a tree and started up the walk. I tried to imagine my great-grandfather visiting Dr. Whittaker back when they were schoolmates and friends. It felt poetic, somehow, to think that I was walking the same path, so many years later.

"You showed up." A gruff voice cut through my thoughts and I squinted.

In the shade of the porch, Kip Whittaker sat in a rocking chair. He looked every bit the aristocrat in a pair of rumpled khakis and a black linen shirt, his signature glower firmly in place. He was a lot more attractive than I remembered—probably because he'd only spoken three words.

I climbed the steep steps at the pace of a snail. Now that I was so close to learning more about my great-grandfather's history, I was eager to get started, but that meant figuring out a way to get along with Kip, first. I decided to address the issue of the lighthouse right away.

"Listen, Kip." I wiped my sweating palms on my shorts. "I—"

He gestured at the wicker chair next to him. "Sit."

In a flash, I remembered exactly why this guy irritated me. He was bossy. It was like he expected everyone to agree with whatever he said, as though he was a prince or something. He might be royalty in Starlight Cove, but that didn't mean I had to bow down to him.

Crossing my arms, I said, "I prefer to stand."

Kip locked eyes with me. For a second, it seemed like he was going to tell me to leave. Instead, he picked up a glass of water from the wicker side table and held it out.

"I saw you bike up that hill," he said. "Thought you'd need this."

"Oh." I fidgeted, not quite sure what to do. The glass was heavy crystal and awkward to hold. It wouldn't take much to drop it and watch it shatter into a million pieces.

I settled into the chair next to him. "Maybe I'll sit."

He gave me a sidelong look. I ignored him and took a drink of water. It was exactly what I needed.

"No lemon?" Kip asked.

"Sorry?" I said, looking at him.

"I thought I saw a lemon in your purse yesterday."

"It's for salad," I said. "I don't like lemon with water."

"Ah."

The birds chirped in the trees and squirrels ran through the front yard. In the distance, a sailboat skimmed across the surface of the lake. Setting the glass on the table between us, I took a deep breath.

"Kip, I have something to—"

"You bought the lighthouse." He frowned. "Is there a reason you didn't mention that at breakfast?"

"You called me a moron! It wasn't the time to start sharing secrets."

He scoffed. "I didn't call you a moron."

"Yes, you did. You said some moron out-of-towner bought the lighthouse," I told him. "It's not exactly the type of thing you want to hear when you've taken the biggest risk of your life."

With a huff, I stared out at the lush greenery of his landscaped front yard. When I turned my gaze back to Kip, a small smile played at the corner of his lips.

"Laugh all you want," I said. "But I didn't need to hear that the whole town is against me. Buying the lighthouse was . . ."

I bit my lip to stop talking. I'd already said enough about it being a risk. I did not need to add how scared I was to find myself doing something practically guaranteed to make me fall flat on my face.

Changing the subject, I said, "You'll be pleased to hear I bumped into Maeve Weatherly yesterday. She's as mad as you are that I bought it."

Kip stretched, his shirt hugging his strong shoulders. "She's a force."

"She's a pain in the ass." I took a gulp of water. "My mother was hoping you would talk to her. To make sure she's not planning on doing anything to get revenge, like pulling the lease on my parents' store."

He seemed surprised. "She threatened to do that?"

"Not in so many words." Then, because Kip wasn't exactly a friend, I added, "You're not the person I'd pick to ask for help, but my mother seemed to think you could do some good."

Kip rested his elbows on his knees. "Thanks for that vote of confidence," he said, locking his gaze onto mine.

My stomach fluttered. "You're welcome."

The flutters were unexpected.

Yes, Kip was attractive, but I was hardly in a place to notice a man other than Todd. Besides, Kip was a complete jerk. Even if I hadn't been nursing a heartache, I would not be interested in his rumpled hair and five-o'clock shadow.

We sat in silence for a moment. Then, Kip said, "I'll talk to her. It's the least I can do for calling you a moron."

"Thanks." I took a quick sip of water. Then, just to have something to say, I added, "I'm starting to think Maeve Weatherly bid against me."

Kip got to his feet. "You ready to take a look at the attic?"

The sudden change in conversation unnerved me. Or maybe it was the rush of electricity I felt as he walked by. Getting to my feet, I smoothed my shorts and followed him to the front door.

He held open an ornate wooden door. I slid past him into a formal entryway. There, I came to a complete stop.

Dramatic staircases framed an enormous hall with a chandelier hanging from the ceiling. Oil paintings graced the walls, including life-like portraits of the Whittakers through the generations. Oriental runners in vibrant blues, yellows, and greens perfectly complemented the floral arrangement centered on a priceless antique table.

"Wow," I said. "You sure *your* great-grandfather didn't steal the silver? This place is pretty swanky."

Kip rested his arm against the stair railing, a faint look of amusement on his face. "It's crossed my mind."

"Really?" I said.

He gave me a dry look. "No."

"Bummer." I shrugged. "That would help to take the heat off Captain Fitzie."

Kip led the way up two flights of stairs past a port window that offered a view of the lake and lighthouse. At the top of the second flight, we stepped out onto a landing much too small for two people.

I stood back as Kip pulled down the attic door, guiding an attached wooden ladder to the ground. He turned, and we stood eye to eye in the small space. Slowly, he ran his gaze over me.

"What?" I asked, suddenly nervous.

His dark eyes settled on mine. "Just making sure you didn't wear high-heeled shoes."

I glared at him. "I rode a bike."

"Which would have been impressive in heels," he said, turning to the ladder.

"I almost brought a pair," I told him. "To put on when I got here."

"That would have been a sight to see." He started to climb. "Watch your step, Fancy Pants."

I followed him up the ladder, determined not to smile.

The Whittaker attic was impressive. The enormous space looked as though someone came in once a week to give it a good scrub. I planned to whip the storage room in my parents' antique shop into similar shape, the moment I had a chance.

"It's like a museum in here," I said.

Kip shoved his hands in the pockets of his khakis. "It's pretty big," he said. "My sister and I used to come up here when I was little to roller skate."

I imagined a glowering little Kip stomping across the floor in skates. "I bet you were a terror."

"That's what my sister claims, but she's two years older." He grinned. "Memory loss is a problem at her age."

I'd always wanted a brother or a sister. Someone to tease, share memories, and discuss the poor decision-making skills of our parents with. Libby ended up being like a sister, but it wasn't the same.

Kip headed across the attic to an area that included a rolltop desk, stacks of old books, and a black physician's bag. Several trunks were stacked from floor to ceiling. He gestured at them.

"Divide and conquer. We're looking for any type of paperwork or journal or anything, really, from nineteen fifteen on."

The thrill of possibility ran through me. I loved mysteries. One of the things that intrigued me about treasure hunting, even though I wanted nothing to do with it, was the possibility of discovering something that could otherwise stay lost forever.

I unhooked the latch on the trunk nearest to me and opened it up. It smelled like mothballs and metal. The trunk held all sorts of interesting artifacts, like old medical instruments, used pen quills, and ancient pairs of reading glasses.

I spent the first half hour creating a detailed list of everything I found. It made me feel productive, like I was getting somewhere. I was just about to review it when Kip walked over and eyed me with suspicion.

"What are you doing?" he asked.

"Documenting." I showed him my work. "I'm a very organized person."

He raised an eyebrow. "The point is to search records, not create new ones."

"I'll do it my own way, thank you."

He studied me for a moment. "You seem to be good at that."

I tucked the pen behind my ear and gave him my full attention. "Good at what?"

"Doing things on your own." He walked back over to his area. "Don't let me interrupt."

I couldn't tell whether he was complimenting or insulting me. Either way, I picked up my pen and got back to work, all too aware of the ninety-day window I had to prove my great-grandfather's innocence. But a few minutes later, Kip's words still rang in my ears.

I'd put a lot of effort into my list, but maybe he was right. It had nothing to do with what we wanted to accomplish. I waited until he wasn't looking, then set the notebook aside and starting hunting through the paperwork.

The search did move a lot faster. Still, I felt compelled to put a little tick mark on my list for every page I reviewed. We settled into a quiet rhythm and spent the next hour poring over records and letters.

I stopped, suddenly, recognizing my great-grandmother's name.

"Kip," I said, feeling a rush of excitement. "I think I found something."

He came over and settled on the floor next to me. He smelled like cedar and musk. I forced myself to focus on the pages in front of me instead of those darn flutters in my stomach.

"It's an office report, I think." The page was as thin as parchment, with handwriting that matched Dr. Whittaker's.

Kip skimmed through it. It was a report on the birth of my grandfather. The birth was breech and my grandfather almost didn't make it. My great-grandmother caught an infection and almost died in the days that followed.

I rested my fingers against the handle of the leather medicine bag sitting nearby. It could have been the very same bag Dr. Whittaker used to nurse my great-grandmother back to life. Gratitude rushed through me.

"It sounds like he saved her," I said. "Regardless of when that letter was sent, Dr. Whittaker did what Fitzie asked. He took care of her."

"He did," Kip said, quietly.

"Did you find anything?" I asked.

"Not yet." He stretched. "But yours is motivating."

We went back to work. I didn't look up for an hour. When I did, Kip was reading through a leather journal with intense concentration. Outside the window, the sky had turned to a sultry shade of evening.

I had a crick in my neck from squinting at the ledgers. Dr. Whittaker's office records were neat and precise, but dry as bone. They didn't give any further clues as to whether or not he offered continued assistance to my great-grandmother. We had so many trunks and boxes to look through that I couldn't help but wonder if it would take weeks for us to find anything at all. Considering the insurance company's deadline, that was time I didn't have.

"How's it going over there?" I asked.

I didn't want to stop the search, but my focus was shot. I was ready to head home, take a shower, and fall asleep between a clean set of bedsheets.

"Good, depending on your point of view. I found something, but . . ."

"You did?" Rushing over, I settled on the floor next to him. "What is it?"

Kip sighed. "I think we need to set up some meetings and start asking questions." He flipped through the pages of the journal. "Because according to these journal entries, your great-grandmother had a best friend." He rubbed a hand against the stubble on his cheek. "The friend is long gone, but she had a daughter."

"Who?" I asked, holding my breath.

Kip frowned. "Maeve Weatherly's mother."

Chapter Eight

I took the journal from Kip's hands and skimmed the pages.

"I can't believe this," I breathed, feeling sick inside.

How was it possible that the one person in Starlight Cove that I already disliked happened to be connected to my great-grandmother?

Madeline, I thought. *I wish you could have planned a century or so ahead when you picked out your friends.*

Kip rubbed his temples. "Maeve would not be happy if we talked to her mother about this."

I got up and walked to the attic window. Starlight Cove covered the valley. Lights twinkled in the windows. I started, noticing the beam of the lighthouse shining against the water.

Flash flash—five-second pause—flash flash flash flash—five-second pause—flash flash—five-second pause—flash flash flash flash.

It was the first time I'd seen this lighthouse at night in years. I turned to Kip, wanting to explain to him about the rhythm, called the character of light. The moment I looked at him, I changed my mind.

I was not about to let him in on something so special. He didn't think I should own the lighthouse in the first place. Why would I share my excitement with someone so eager to take it away?

Instead, I said, "I'm not scared of Maeve Weatherly. I just don't want her to cause trouble. If you think it's fine, then set up the appointment with her mother."

Kip studied me and silence fell over the attic. He had dust all over his black shirt and smudges of dirt on his nose. He frowned. "Do you have a light on that bike?"

The question caught me off guard, and I had to think about it.

I doubted my mother had a light because the front part of her bike was ornamented with a woven basket. I saw what Kip was saying, though. It would be a challenge to navigate the roots and ruts on that hill in the dark. I'd probably have to walk my bike all the way back home—a process that sounded exhausting.

"I don't know," I said. "Don't think so."

"What kind of a lighthouse keeper forgets a light?"

I waved my hand. "I'll be fine."

My words sounded much more confident than I felt.

Kip gave me the same look he did when he saw my high heels on the beach. "I'm heading back to my houseboat," he said. "I'll give you a ride."

"It's not necessary," I told him.

He shook his head. "Yes, Fancy Pants. It is."

The next thing I knew, we stood in a massive wooden shed outside the Whittaker home that smelled like sawdust and motor oil. Despite its obvious age, the smooth stone floor was as pristine as the attic. The space housed a pontoon boat, speedboat, and Jet Skis.

Not to mention some metal contraption Kip seemed to think I would ride in.

"What is that?" I asked, crossing my arms.

"A dune buggy."

He jumped behind the wheel and waited.

"Its wheels are specifically designed to handle sand," he said when I didn't move. "I could take it down to the beach or up in the sand dunes and get around just fine."

"Like one of those machines in the desert in *Star Wars*?" I asked.

He gave me a blank look.

"Sorry," I said. "I forgot you like romantic comedies."

I eyed the dune bug . . . whatever he called it. The metal frame sat low to the ground, with four enormous wheels, two front vinyl seats, and a big bench seat in the back. There were no side panels, but two large headlights perched on the front.

I drummed my fingers against the metal frame. "Does it have air bags?"

Cicadas chirped in the woods.

"It has headlights," Kip said.

"Right, but—"

He turned a key and the machine roared to life. I coughed in the sudden cloud of exhaust.

"Get in," he called.

I hesitated. Then, because there really wasn't another option, I hopped in. The seat vibrated under me, and my teeth clanked together.

"Cozy," I shouted.

He winked. "Hang on."

Gunning the engine, Kip sped out onto the gravel driveway. Instead of doing circles in front of the shed, which I half expected, he drove straight to the tree where I'd left my bike. He jumped out, hauled the bike over his shoulder, and threw it into the back of the buggy. Then we sped down the hill toward Starlight Cove.

The headlights cut through the darkness, bugs and dust darting through the beams. I gripped the edge of the door, squinting against the rush of the wind. Sneaking a look at Kip, I studied his profile in the dark.

I was curious about him. He came from the Whittaker fortune but lived in a houseboat. He was grumpy and judgmental but determined to get me safely home. He claimed not to be interested in treasure but was motivated to learn the truth behind *The Wanderer*.

"Check out the stars," Kip called.

Speckles of starlight pushed through the ink of night as far as I could see. Suddenly, there was a burst of light and a white streak zoomed across the sky.

I made a wish.

Please let me prove Captain Fitzie was innocent.

The dune buggy rumbled to a stop in front of my parents' house, and I rested my hand against the car door, studying our family home. It was built in the early nineteen hundreds by my great-grandfather out of sturdy logs and the stones still visible in two enormous chimneys.

My father remodeled the house when my grandparents passed away in the nineties. It was well done, in that it was hard to tell where the original structure ended and the additions began. Every detail, from the sunroom to the front shutters, was unique, charming, and chock-full of memories. I couldn't believe a place with so much history was at risk over something that happened almost a hundred years ago.

What would Kip say if I told him? I didn't dare. I still didn't know whose side he was on.

Kip hopped out of the dune buggy, grabbed the bicycle, and leaned it up against the garage. I climbed out, half wishing the ride weren't over.

"What do you think?" He met me in the driveway, his eyes warm in the reflection of the headlights.

I straightened my shirt. "I think I'm lucky to be alive."

"That's how it should be." He smiled. "I'll let you know when I set up an appointment with Beulah."

"Great," I said quickly. "Talk to you then."

I headed up the path and gave a jaunty wave when I reached the front door. To my surprise, my heart was pounding.

It took some work to convince myself it was only because of the ride.

Chapter Nine

My mother and I made breakfast together the next morning. Well, she made breakfast while I went through her pantry and put the canned and boxed goods in alphabetical order.

"It's a logical system," I told her, sliding a box of wayward brownies into the *B* section. "You'll sleep better at night if you can find the bacon bits when you need them."

My mother turned the heat off on the stove. "Whatever floats your boat," she said, pushing her hair off her neck. "How was searching the attic with the mysterious Kip Whittaker?"

I thought of him sitting behind the wheel of the dune buggy, telling me to look up at the stars.

I slid a can of peas into place. "He's hardly mysterious. In fact, he's pretty predictable."

The charming smiles he sent my way, the well-timed winks. Kip Whittaker was a Charmer with a capital *C*. I could understand why the women in town liked him, but that didn't have anything to do with me.

"We discovered Beulah's mother was Madeline's best friend," I said. "It was in some journal."

My mother put a hand to her chest. "That's amazing. Life connects in ways we could never even imagine."

"Uh-huh," I said, shelving a can of ravioli.

It was pretty obvious she'd spent the morning doing yoga.

"Well, this is about done . . ." She whisked the pan of scrambled eggs off the stove and added them to plates with sliced kiwi and strawberry and buttered toast. "Voilà!"

"Looks good," I said, rinsing my hands.

My mother fluttered past me in her flowing purple dress, multicolored silk scarf, and armful of bangle bracelets. She grabbed two pottery coffee mugs from the cupboard and filled them with steaming coffee.

"*Now* it looks good," she said, settling in at the table. "Do you have big plans today for the lighthouse?"

I took an eager sip of the coffee. She made it with chicory, which added a sharpness that I liked. "Carter Henderson is going to rig a pulley system to help me haul trash. I figured there's no way to manage those steps otherwise. So I'm going to get that set up. Then I'll walk around in a mask and gloves and start picking stuff up."

"Sounds like a good plan."

I sprinkled ten drops of Tabasco sauce on my eggs.

"Where do you think I can dump trash?" I asked. "It's not like I can rent a dumpster to set up on the beach."

"Use the one behind the store," she said. "The truck could help you transport the trash bags."

I shook my head. "The wheels would get stuck in the sand."

My mother laughed. "That's why you're project head, not me."

I'd only thought of it because of the ride in the dune buggy the night before. That thing would come in handy but, of course, I'd never ask Kip to borrow it.

I chewed on a piece of toast. "Any chance you own a wheelbarrow?"

~

My mother didn't own a wheelbarrow but loaned me a wagon-type contraption belonging to one of her neighbors. It was about twice the size of what people might use to haul kids around in. I planned to load it up with trash bags, wheel them up the boardwalk, and transfer them into the back of my parents' truck.

My mother was headed to the store, so she dropped me off at the boardwalk. I lugged the thing onto the wooden slats and dragged it down to the water. It wasn't easy, but it would be better than carrying each bag on its own.

I spotted Sami, Kip's niece, down by the water. She was with a group of friends, kicking a soccer ball around.

"Hi," I called, waving at her.

I regretted it the second I did it. Since the ride in the dune buggy with Kip, I no longer saw him as the enemy, but that didn't mean his niece would want to acknowledge me. To my relief, she shouted, "Hey!"

Sami jogged through the sand to the boardwalk. She wore a colorful one-piece, board shorts, and a purple bandana tied in her hair. She was taller than she seemed when I first met her. Like most teenagers, she was as lanky as could be.

"What are you trying to do with that thing?" She squinted at the wagon. "It looks ready to roll over and die."

I laughed. "I know, right? I'm going to haul some trash out of the lighthouse."

"Oh." Sami frowned, scrunching up her nose. "You're the new owner?"

I glanced at the majestic structure by the water. The lighthouse had been there for so long that it was hard to imagine anyone owned it, really. Still, I felt proud to say it.

"Yup," I said. "I'm pretty excited about it."

Sami shoved her hands in the back pockets of her board shorts but didn't comment. Even though I didn't know many teenagers, I imagined home improvement projects were last on their list of hot topics.

"So, what are you up to today?" I asked.

"Me?" Sami looked back at her friends. Mainly guys, I noticed. One kept looking over, as though eager for her to come back. "We're about to go sailing, I think."

"That sounds fun." I smiled at her. "Have a good time."

"Yeah." She scrunched up her nose again. "Good luck."

Sami jogged over to her friends. She jumped right back into the game, giving the soccer ball a furious kick.

The lighthouse looked stoic in the early morning sun. It was the size of a small high-rise, but I was determined not to let that intimidate me.

Leaving the wagon at the base of the ladder, I climbed up and unlocked the door. I stood in the main cavern for a moment, took a deep breath, and climbed down the stairs to the basement to find a rope. My skin started to crawl the second I was down there.

It was dark and cool and smelled like the underbelly of a ship. Cobwebs hung from the ceiling like clouds of dust.

I'd hoped the lighthouse wouldn't have any spiders, being on the water, but I should have known better. After all, I once heard about a lighthouse on a cluster of rocks in the middle of the ocean that had its very own *species* of spiders. They evolved specifically for that rock, so as not to miss an opportunity to torment the human race.

I used the flashlight on my cell phone to scan through a collection of rusted shovels, cans, and hardware. Sure enough, I found a piece of rope. It was rough, filthy, and covered in cobwebs, but it would do the job.

Holding it at arm's length, I headed up to the main floor and dropped the rope out the front door onto the sand. I climbed down the ladder, ready to tie up the wagon with some tricky sailor's knots. But when I hopped to the ground, the wagon was gone.

"No," I said, out loud. "No, no, no."

I used my hand to shade my eyes from the sun, looking in every direction.

The boardwalk bustled with tourists carrying beach bags, but the wagon was nowhere in sight. I turned to the lake, somehow thinking it might have rolled in. It wasn't floating in the water. Besides, the waves were small, and there were rocks on the edge of the shore. It would have taken a serious gust of wind for it to end up in the lake.

Did someone steal it?

Fear prickled the back of my neck.

Yes, I had gotten a rope to secure the wagon, but that was only because I was used to city living. I didn't *really* think anyone would steal in Starlight Cove. But obviously, I was wrong.

Maybe someone stole it to send a message: *The lighthouse belongs to us, so why don't you just go home?*

I felt sick.

Was this what it was going to be like? A summer of feeling like a target, like someone who didn't belong?

Yes, plenty of time had passed since the many times I was the new girl in school, but being an outsider still hurt. Besides, I didn't even know where this new insult was coming from. The coward with my wagon took it and ran away.

Calm down. I imagined what my mother would say. *You don't know that's what happened.*

Maybe I was jumping to conclusions.

Why would someone steal a wagon? It was much more likely that someone took it as a prank. Or a tourist thought it was public domain or something. I looked around for Sami and her friends to ask if they saw anything, but they'd already left. Probably headed to one of the many sailboats in the harbor, eager to enjoy the day.

I wished I could do the same.

It was still possible. There was a chance—maybe a very good chance—that the theft was not intentional. The wagon would turn up. If it didn't, I'd have to replace it, but that wasn't the end of the world.

I turned the key with a loud clank and set off for the hardware store. The sun was shining, and the pale sky stretched over the sandy beach in a way that made it impossible to be in a bad mood. I turned my thoughts to what I planned to accomplish, refusing to give in to the wave of dread threatening to crash over me.

~

The Henderson brothers weren't officially open when I showed up, but they let me in anyway. They were planning a big sale on rakes, trowels, and gardening equipment and putting together a display in the front of the store.

Carter, Cameron, and I debated which type of wagon I should buy. When we agreed on one, I asked if they had chains and a padlock to lock it up.

"City girl," Carter teased. His hair was in a square buzz cut, reminiscent of the fifties. It added height to his face and made his jaw look even more defined. "People don't steal things around here."

"Contraire, my friend." Cameron pointed at him. "I stole your breakfast bar. Right out of the break room. I didn't even throw away the wrapper."

Carter punched his brother in the arm three times. "I was going to eat that!"

I shoved my hands in the pockets of my shorts. "You guys, it was stolen. It didn't just disappear."

"I sincerely doubt it," Cameron said, taking a sip from a bottle of fruit-infused water. "Some kid with a runny nose probably took it, thinking it was up for grabs. Or . . ." He gestured at the back office. "I bet Cody nabbed it. He's all about supply and demand."

"I heard that," Cody roared from his office. "Dawn, don't try to return our wagon when your shitty wagon turns up."

Cameron raised his eyebrows. "How shitty was it?"

I laughed. "Pretty shitty."

"Don't listen to Cody," Carter said, as serious as ever. "If your wagon turns up, we'll take ours back. Deal?"

Talking to them made me feel better. I wanted to believe Starlight Cove was a safe place with friendly people. The Hendersons matched that description. Even better, they seemed to appreciate what I wanted to accomplish with the lighthouse.

Carter helped me pull the new wagon down the boardwalk and chained it to the ladder. When I let him into the main room, he whistled.

"You have a serious mold problem," he said. "I can smell it from here."

"Thanks," I said, pretending to be hurt. "You're the first guest I've ever had. Tell me how you really feel."

His freckled cheeks colored. "Sorry. My brothers keep telling me to work on my bedside manner."

I patted his arm. "I'm kidding."

There was something sweet about Carter. He seemed like the type of guy who would make dinner for his mother or bring flowers to a first date. It hit me that he might be a good match for Kailyn and her big personality.

"Do you know how it happened?" Carter asked.

"The upstairs window is broken."

Carter shined a penlight up at the ceiling. "The mold probably spread quickly because of the heat and humidity. We should fix the window first. Then you need to do mold treatments."

"Is that going to cost a fortune?" I asked.

I didn't want to spend everything I had battling mold. I had to think about trying to make a profit when I sold it. That wouldn't be possible if I blew my whole budget on fixing a problem like this.

To be fair, I had a decent budget to work with. Back when my father found the *San Arabella*, he received a huge payout. He put some of that into investments and savings, and then he set up a trust fund for me.

Having a trust was a strange thing. I would have traded every penny for a normal childhood with parents who were around. I never touched it, until the lighthouse went up for auction. On some level, I think I finally used it out of anger at the accusation that my parents' fortune didn't really come from the *San Arabella*.

The suggestion that my parents didn't earn that money infuriated me. I was there for all the painful years leading up to that find. They'd earned every penny, and I'd decided not to let it keep sitting in the trust.

Still, I didn't want to waste it battling mold.

Turning to Carter, I said, "I want to do what it takes, but I don't want to throw money away. My father's the famous treasure hunter, not me."

"Understood." Carter grabbed a chunk of loose white paint off the wall and tugged at it. It fell away from the brick in a moldy sheaf. "Did the mold get into the wood anywhere?"

"The floor upstairs with the broken window."

The bedroom. I planned to remodel the lighthouse to feel like a home, to be more appealing for resale. That is, assuming I could find anyone crazy enough to live there.

"Hmm." Carter scratched the cleft in his chin. "We might have to rip that floor up. But you can probably handle the mold treatments on your own."

He suggested getting a face mask, as well as a hazmat suit of sorts to protect my hands, body, and lungs. Breathing in mold spores was, apparently, a bad thing.

"The bleach treatments are pretty basic," he said. "You'll need to seal everything off and let it dry out for at least three days after you finish up."

"Sounds like a plan," I said. "I want to set up the pulley first. It's probably not smart to carry gallons of bleach up and down those stairs."

Carter nodded. "Agreed."

He studied the build of the staircase and started to walk up. I was just about to follow him when he came back down and restudied the angles from the bottom. Then, he whipped out a measuring tape and a small notebook.

"I'll need some time," he said, jotting something down. "Then we'll see what we're talking about."

~

Hours later, Carter walked back down into the main room with his shirt off and his tool belt low over his jeans. His upper body was tanned and built. If Kailyn were here, she would take a picture.

"That should do it." He tugged his T-shirt back on, wiped his face on it, and gave me a shy smile.

Earlier, Carter had listened to my plan for a block-and-tackle pulley system with interest. We returned to the store, gathered materials, and headed back to the lighthouse. It took several trips and deliveries from Cody, but by late afternoon Carter had rigged a fully functioning pulley system.

On each floor, a shiny new contraption looped with fresh white rope was secured at the top of the staircase. It was so new and perfect that it gave me hope that the rest of the lighthouse had the potential to look that way.

"Ready to give it a try?" Carter passed me a gigantic brick in a canvas bag. I almost collapsed under the weight, and he laughed. "Cody would tell you to drink a protein shake."

I hooked the bag onto the rope with a grunt. Then I grabbed the opposite rope and gave it a firm tug. The initial tug brought resistance, but then the bag lifted and started an easy ascent up the stairs. The rope remained taut until I had the bag positioned over the dropping place on the next floor. Then, I secured it and raced up the stairs.

"It works!" I cried. "You're a genius."

"Will you say that back at the shop?" Carter called up. "My brothers need some convincing."

Laughing, I unhooked the bag with the brick. Then I connected it to the next system and hoisted it up to the next floor. Instead of carting bags up and down the stairs, the only challenge would be rehooking the items and sliding them up or down with the pulley.

"Thank you so much," I told him. "This is exactly what I pictured."

He gave the rope an affectionate tug. "What else do you need?"

During one of our trips to the hardware store, I'd bought the heaviest trash bags available, gloves, goggles, brooms, and a mask with a respirator. While Carter rigged the pulley, I'd spent the morning filling the bags with debris. Unless Carter wanted to help, his work here was done.

"I'm good to go," I said. "Unless you want to become a professional cleaner."

He snorted. "I'll pass. Oh, and don't use the water just yet," he reminded me. "Cameron needs to get over here and take a look."

Cameron's Renaissance-era looks did not stop him from being an expert in plumbing. He was booked up for days but had agreed to come over later in the week. The delay didn't matter, since it would take time to sweep up dirt and remove debris.

"Cody's stopping by to fix the window tomorrow, right?" I said.

Carter looked worried. "Do you need me to be here? That guy's an operator."

I laughed. "I'll be just fine."

"Good deal," he said. "I'll swing by in a few days to see what you need."

He headed toward the door, and a silly thought struck me. It was a little ridiculous, but the type of thing that might help Kailyn let down her guard with me.

"Hey," I said. "Do you mind if I grab a picture of you standing by the pulley? I think I might document the before-and-after process of the remodel."

"Sure," he said. "That's a good idea."

Carter adjusted the pulley to lift up one of the bags and pretended to be holding the weight with one hand. Laughing, I snapped the shot with my cell phone.

"Thank you," I said. "You don't care if I show this to people, right?"

"Not at all."

"Thanks," I called as he headed toward the front door. "I appreciate your help."

He lifted a hand as he climbed down the ladder. "No problem. There's a high priority this summer for people remodeling lighthouses."

Once he was gone, I texted his picture to Kailyn, along with the caption: The Henderson brothers are awesome. Thanks for the recommendation.

Not only were they nice people, they knew what they were doing. Thanks to them, the lighthouse might not crumble down around me. The floors would be solid, the window fixed, and the walls, mold-free.

As for bringing the lighthouse back to its original splendor . . . well, that was up to me.

~

I made some serious progress hauling debris. The way my muscles ached the next day proved it. To loosen up, I decided to go for a run. Tugging on a pair of tennis shoes, I jogged from my mother's house to the beach, feeling the tension loosen with every step.

I ran past the lighthouse and marina, and out to the part of the lake that was pure wilderness. The sand transformed into a rocky coast and, finally, swampland. I came to a stop and breathed in the silence of the morning.

The fog had lifted, and the birds called out to one another from the nearby forest. I wondered that I didn't feel scared, alone in the middle of nowhere. In fact, it was a relief, after years of taxicabs and a constant crush of people. I might have done well as a lighthouse keeper in the olden days. With a smile, I turned and headed back toward civilization.

Just as I passed the marina, a chocolate Labrador blurred across my path. He leapt up and caught a Frisbee with strong, white teeth. He landed on all fours like a cat before bounding back over to his owner, a man with silver hair in a military cut that matched the frames of his mirrored sunglasses.

The man threw the Frisbee across the water and laughed as the dog bounded into the lake. I came to a stop, resting my hands on the top of my knees. The dog seemed to revel in fighting the waves to get back to shore. The Frisbee was clamped firmly in his mouth, and he snorted out of his nose as he swam.

"He's a braver soul than I am," the man said to me. "That water is cold."

Harsh winters and deep waters kept Lake Michigan from ever getting truly warm. I could only imagine the chill of the icy water crashing over the men on *The Wanderer* as they had struggled to manage the lifeboats.

The lab bounded out of the water and streaked toward us. He came to a halt in front of his owner and shook icy droplets all over him. I burst out laughing.

"That'll teach me." The man wiped off his sunglasses. "You want to throw one out for him?"

"Sure," I said, surprising myself.

I'd always wanted a dog. Of course, my parents were never in one place long enough to have one. Libby and I had planned to get one back when we shared an apartment, but once we started work, we decided it wouldn't be fair to make a dog sit indoors waiting for us to come home.

"Here." The man held out the red Frisbee.

Tentatively, I took the worn piece of plastic, only vaguely grossed out by the bite marks in the surface. I threw it out over the sand. The lab brought it right back, dropping it at my feet.

"Uh oh," I said. "Looks like I made a friend."

I threw it again, this time out over the lake. The dog hit the water like a cannonball.

The man strolled over to shake my hand. "Steve Kingsley." Pointing out at the Lab, he said, "That's Captain Ahab. My daughter named him when she was reading *Moby-Dick* in high school. My wife and I both agree it's a terrible name."

"It's cute," I said. "I'm Dawn Conners."

Steve frowned. "As in Captain Fitzie Conners?"

I shrank inside. "That would be the one," I said. "He was—"

The official-looking radio on Steve's belt started to crackle. He picked it up to listen.

"We have to get back." He gave a sharp whistle for the dog. "Listen, I know your father. Feel free to drop by Search and Rescue anytime. We have a team of five dogs. Most of them live with local volunteers, but Captain Ahab here is at our main facility. We have people that come to hang out with him, since we're always out and about, taking calls."

"Thanks," I said, scratching Captain Ahab's ears.

It sounded fun. Besides, I was already in love with the dog. I gave him one last pat and told Steve I'd keep it in mind.

Heading back down the beach, I calculated the distance of my run. I planned to go by the lighthouse, cutting across the back way to the residential streets and my parents' house. That would come out to about five miles. But on the way past the lighthouse, I screeched to a stop.

"What the . . ."

The red-painted steel door dripped with a message written in black paint.

Go Home!!!

I stood in the early morning sunshine and stared in disbelief. My earbuds were still in, my legs shaking with exertion and my skin damp with sweat. The world around me seemed to come to a complete stop.

It was one thing to imagine someone being rude, wishing me harm, or stealing a wagon. It was quite another to stare at the evidence as it dripped down the door like blood.

Go Home!!!

I sank down on the edge of the boardwalk. Tears pricked the backs of my eyelids. This lighthouse was connected to my great-grandfather, yes, but it belonged to me. The fact that someone could do this—make it so clear that I was unwanted—was humiliating.

Even though more than one person had made me feel unwelcome, I suspected Maeve Weatherly had something to do with it. She'd made it perfectly clear I had no business owning the lighthouse. Still, it was hard to imagine her getting revenge with a can of spray paint. Maybe she'd enlisted help?

I wanted to know who did it, but at the same time, I was tempted to just give up. Get back on a plane, back to my old life in Boston, and leave my parents to fend for themselves.

My phone vibrated against the holder on my arm. I didn't recognize the number. I picked up, half expecting some stranger to hiss something terrible at me.

Instead, a distant voice said, "Dawn? Can you hear me?"

"Libby!" I gripped the phone like a life raft.

Leave it to Libby to call at the moment I needed her most.

She gave her familiar, husky laugh. "I'm calling from out in the middle of the ocean. I think we're somewhere off the Caribbean, but I missed you. How's it going up there?"

I clutched the phone, fighting against tears. I was so, so glad to hear her voice.

"Great." I pushed my tennis shoes into the sand and stared at the spray paint dripping down the door. "If you like small-town bullies mad at the girl who stole their lighthouse away."

For a second, I thought I'd lost the connection. Then, her voice came back on the line. Strong, sure, and furious.

"Tell me everything."

By the time our conversation was over, I felt more hopeful. Not only was she having a great time with Jack out on the water, she told me they were thinking about coming to visit.

"It won't be for a while," she said. "But we might have some time when we get back. I'd love to see the lighthouse."

"I can't guarantee I'll still be here," I admitted. "I'm going to find what I need to do to help my parents and get out as soon as possible. I'm not here to fight."

Her voice turned serious. "Do you know why I wanted to be your friend? When we were little?"

I bit my lip, blinking fast against hot tears. "No."

"Because you have fire," she said. "Not everyone has that, but I could see it in you. You deserve to live a big life, Dawn. Don't let a little spray paint scare you away."

~

I stood on the top rung of the ladder to the lighthouse, a scrub brush in hand. The paint was still wet, so at least it came off easily, leaving only a slight stain underneath. Once that step was complete, I painted over it with red paint from Henderson Hardware that was a perfect match. It worried me that someone from the Coast Guard would think I was trying to change the exterior, but I had to fix this.

It was still early, so I didn't have much of an audience. That didn't stop me from shooting mean looks at passersby, as if they were all somehow the guilty party.

"Hey," a voice called as I dipped the brush into the paint. Sal. He wore the same black sunglasses, but this time his shirt was a khaki guayabera. "What are you doing up there?"

"Touch-ups." I didn't want a story about vandalism in his documentary.

"You alone?" he asked.

It unnerved me to realize that, in a sense, Sal had me trapped. The only exit route was to head into the lighthouse and bolt the door. I gripped the paintbrush a little tighter.

Sal must have sensed my unease, because he added, "I just mean I want to talk to you, not your parents. Want to grab some coffee?"

"No, thanks," I said. "I have a lot of work to do."

"I found out some interesting history," he said. "Did you know your great-grandfather used to be a logger? Before he became a ship captain?"

I did not know that, actually. The tidbit was interesting. But I was not about to get tricked into a conversation with a filmmaker.

"Tough job." I indicated the fact that I was balanced on a ladder, holding a can of paint. "Like this."

Sal adjusted his sunglasses. "So, you haven't changed your mind about talking to me?"

"Nope." I added pressure to the paintbrush. His confidence irritated me. "Sorry."

"No worries." He laughed. "Have a good day, Dawn." Lifting his hand, he headed down the beach.

Ugh. He was the type that wouldn't take no for an answer. It would be a pain trying to avoid him, but given the creepy-crawly feeling he gave me, I still planned to try.

~

That afternoon, I stopped by my parents' house for lunch. I stripped my bed in the guest bedroom and popped the sheets in the laundry. I liked to sleep in fresh sheets each night and I'd already used the entire stack my mother kept for the guest bedroom.

I was glad she was at the antique shop or she'd tell me to lighten up.

After a quick sandwich, I headed back to the lighthouse to get to work. The temperature was getting hotter outside, and the paint on the front door was dry. The air inside was stuffy and the smell of animal droppings more pronounced. I needed a nose plug to add to my gloves, goggles, and mask.

Pulling up iTunes on my phone, I turned it to shuffle. The first song was a sea shanty, and I turned it up as high as it would go. Then I got to work.

I worked steadily, sweeping up feathers and scraping up dried bird crap. I also picked up random things like small pieces of wood, crumbling pieces of stone, and rusty nails. The work was slow and messy, but somehow I made it up to the bedroom.

Everything was going fine until I got to the middle section of the floor and heard a sharp crack. I looked around, trying to figure out where the sound had come from. Was the other window about to go? Another sharp crack sliced through the air, and the ground split and crumpled beneath me.

With a squawk, I fell through the floorboards, all the way up to my thighs. I squeezed my eyes shut, convinced the wood had sliced my femoral artery and this was the end. When I didn't pass out, I tentatively investigated the situation.

I was really and truly stuck. I could move my arms, but my legs were wedged in between the floorboards. Lifting myself out would be impossible. The sharp splinters holding my thighs in place would flay me like a fish. Claustrophobia set in, along with panic.

The beams under my feet held up the kitchen ceiling. How long would it be before that gave out? It stood at least fifteen feet high, and, the last time I checked, I wasn't wearing a parachute.

"Help," I shrieked. "Help!"

I hoped someone on the beach could hear me. Doubtful, considering that the broken window faced the water, but it was worth a try. Taking a deep breath, I shouted, "Is anyone out there?"

Silence.

Suddenly, I remembered my cell phone and almost cried in relief. I carefully pulled it out of the pocket of my shorts and called my mother at the antique shop, but no one picked up. If she was with a customer, she'd let the phone ring all day.

Kailyn! I hadn't heard back from her after my text, so I still doubted she was on Team Conners, but that hardly mattered at the moment. Looking through my records, I pressed her number. It went straight to voice mail, which meant she was probably with a client, too. I racked my brain for another option.

Kip Whittaker.

The name popped into my head and I groaned.

Kip was the only other person in Starlight Cove programmed into my cell phone. It was either Kip or 9-1-1. I would have preferred the emergency number, but I didn't want the authorities to declare the lighthouse condemned.

Letting out a frustrated breath, I called him.

Some people get pleasure in a job well done. Others find joy in doing things for others. Kip Whittaker, I soon learned, found delight in the sight of me wedged in the floor of the lighthouse.

He let himself in through the front door, raced up the stairs, and poked his head into my bedroom. Then he burst out laughing. He threw his head back and laughed long and loud, leaning against the wall as though he would crumple to the floor without it.

"I knew you were not a nice person the moment we met," I snapped.

"Fancy Pants, how could you say that?" He ran a hand through his rumpled hair. "I'm your knight in shining armor."

"Then could you please help me?" I demanded. "Before the rest of the floor gives out?"

"I'll give it the old college try." He tiptoed over, testing the floor-boards as he walked. Then he peeked down into the hole, concern on his handsome face. "That doesn't look very comfortable."

"Odd," I said. "Since comfort was my only object when *I fell through the floor.*"

"Ah, the troubles of home ownership." He gripped me by the arms. "Hang on."

I breathed in his spicy cedar scent and decided it would become my favorite smell if he could only get me out of this. But as he tried to lift me, the wood cut into my leg, and I screeched.

Kip dropped my arms. "We might need a saw." He laughed at my horrified expression. "I'll go see what the Hendersons have."

"Don't leave me here!" I begged. "Call Carter and have him bring something. Don't go!"

"Well, well." Kip locked his dark gaze on mine. "I thought you didn't like me. Now you're begging me not to go." He gave an exaggerated sigh. "Women. Ever so fickle."

I tried to understand how it was possible to be attracted to him and want to punch him all at the same time.

"Call Carter," I said. "He'll know how to get me out of this mess."

"*I* know how to get you out of this mess," Kip said. "I have some tools downstairs."

"Really?" I said.

He glowered. "What kind of man shows up to rescue a woman who fell through the floor without any tools?"

It took a crowbar, hammer, and a couple more scratches, but Kip managed to extract enough of the moldy floor to get me out. Then he grabbed me by the hand and pulled me out of the room altogether, as if the whole floor might sink beneath us. I walked with him down to the front door, examining the scratches on my legs. They weren't too bad, but I definitely needed a shower and some disinfectant.

"Thank you," I told him. "If it weren't for you, I would've been trapped there for days."

"True." He stepped onto the ladder, the toolbox in one hand and a rung in the other. "I'm just impressed you called me for help."

"I'm new in town," I said. "You're the only number I have in my phone."

Kip was halfway down the ladder. Looking up, he shot me a sexy grin.

"Keep telling yourself that, Fancy Pants."

Chapter Ten

I was not about to go back to work on the lighthouse until Carter had a chance to check the structural integrity, so I decided to pay a visit to Captain Ahab.

The Search and Rescue building was stark and official, with a white stone floor, painted white walls, and wooden chairs lined up in the waiting room. Nautical photos hung on the walls. Steve sat behind the desk, looking authoritative with his short gray hair and starched navy shirt.

Getting to his feet, he gave me a pleased smile. "You came to see us!"

I felt a little awkward, just dropping in. Still, Steve had invited me even after he knew the identity of my great-grandfather. I figured I should accept kindness where I could get it.

"You asked," I said.

I studied the photographs on the wall. There were photographs of ancient ships, rescue boats, and Main Street. The buildings looked the same, only in black and white. Right next to those photographs hung the picture of my great-grandfather. Tourists wouldn't be passing through this building, and I was curious why it was up.

Before I could ask, Steve said, "Do you like bad coffee?"

I laughed. "Not really." I held up a waxy, white bag. "I brought a hamburger for Captain Ahab. If that's okay."

"You met the little charmer once and you're already bringing him takeout?" Steve chuckled. "I don't know how he does it."

We walked out the back door, and a dark streak flew across the yard. Captain Ahab practically tackled Steve with sixty-five pounds of pure puppy love. Then he sat down in front of me and held out his paw.

"It's nice to see you, too," I said, shaking his paw.

His face was handsome, if there could be such a thing for dogs, with a strong snout and a touch of distinguished gray around his nose and whiskers.

"I brought something for you." Reaching into the bag, I pulled the extra hamburger patty out from the bun. Captain Ahab's nose twitched, and his tail thumped against the grass.

"Should I just give him the whole thing?" I asked Steve.

"Break it up into chunks. You can put it in the palm of your hand, or we can put it in his food bowl." He winked. "Captain Ahab doesn't like to eat food off the ground."

I hesitated, trying to decide whether or not he'd take my hand off with his teeth. Probably not, considering he was in the business of helping people. I broke off a couple of chunks and stuck out my hand.

Captain Ahab didn't make a move. Instead, he gave a little whine and thumped his tail even harder.

"Do you want this?" I asked, waving it at him. "It's for you."

"He's well trained." Steve shoved his hands into the pockets of his pants, after rubbing the dog's head. "I just wanted to show you how good he was. Say h-e-r-e b-o-y."

"Here, boy," I said.

Captain Ahab leapt to his feet and gobbled up the hamburger. I laughed in delight as he nuzzled my hand, looking for more.

"You're pretty smart." I got the rest of the burger out of the bag. He stared at me with longing. "Oh. Sorry. Here, boy."

He seemed to smile at me, and then went in for the burger. He was the perfect man—handsome, charming, and polite. Captain Ahab won my heart.

Once the burger was exhausted, we tossed around a ball in the yard. The ball was covered with spit, but it made the dog so happy that I couldn't help but keep throwing it.

Steve settled in on the back porch with a mug of coffee. "Looks like it's going to storm."

The sky was a threatening shade of blue, with clouds gathering like soldiers on a battlefield. The air felt hot and sticky, but there was a chance the temperature would drop when the storm hit.

"It's supposed to be a big one," he said. "We're expecting some action here in a few hours."

I settled in next to him on the stoop. "Do you go out with the Coast Guard?"

Every time I'd been at the lighthouse, I noticed the boat patrolling the shore or heading out to the open water. The town was small, but the lake was busy, with a lot of tourists on speedboats and Jet Skis. I imagined the Coast Guard had plenty to keep it on its toes.

"Search and Rescue is on a volunteer, as-needed basis." Steve gestured at the sky. "In situations like this, we'll probably get called to help out."

Captain Ahab took a sloppy drink from a metal water bowl and lay next to me.

"It would be interesting to see the storm from the lighthouse." I imagined the beam of light sweeping over the water and felt a thrill of responsibility. "I'm the one who bought it, in case you didn't know."

Steve's eyes twinkled. "That type of news doesn't stay quiet in Starlight Cove."

"Have you lived here long?"

"My whole life," he said. "I grew up with your father. He was a grade or two above me. Older and therefore much cooler. He's a good guy. Played a mean game of baseball."

That was interesting. I'd never known my father to be the sporty type. By the time I rolled around, he was obsessed with sailing, scuba, and, of course, shipwrecks.

"I'll have to tell him I met you," I said.

"Get him to come over here," Steve said. "I haven't seen him in a while."

"I will." I fiddled with a blade of grass. "I noticed you have a picture of Captain Fitzie in the main room."

Steve took off his cap and folded it in half. "It's a good reminder to stay diligent. The night of that wreck, Starlight Cove could have done a better job."

"What do you mean?" I asked. "The lifesaving service helped bring the lifeboats into shore."

"Yes, but they failed to get the first two." He shook his head. "The light wasn't on, and the horn didn't sound. The only thing the ship had to go on was Captain Conners's expertise and the navigation bell on the buoys. No one knew help was needed until the houses onshore heard the shouts and cries from the sailors in the lifeboats."

I blinked. "The lighthouse light wasn't on? That's the first time I've heard that."

"No one talks about it." He took a sip of coffee. "There are much more exciting things to talk about, like the lost treasure. Around here, though, we're interested in the lives that could have been saved."

Captain Ahab thumped his tail as he rested his head on his paws.

"Why wasn't the light on?" I asked.

"Well, legend has it that the keeper was an alcoholic," Steve said. "It's not documented well, but stories get passed down through the generations. He spent all his time off in the speakeasies and I guess that carried over. Do you know how he died?"

"He got struck by lightning on the balcony?"

Steve laughed. "No, but close." His face grew somber. "He got drunk and fell down the stairs."

I was just about to scratch Captain Ahab's ears when the magnitude of that hit me. "Really?"

"I'm afraid so."

I sat in horrified silence.

"The steps were replaced, since then," he said. "It's not a safety factor."

I wasn't thinking about the safety factor. I was thinking about the poor lighthouse keeper and the fact that he died in my lighthouse. Even though it happened nearly a century ago, it was still spooky.

Steve took another sip of coffee. "Rumor has it, he was so distressed about the crash of *The Wanderer* that his drinking took a turn. It happened soon after that. There are rumors it was a suicide, because he felt responsible for the wreck."

"People blamed him?" I asked. "The only blame I've ever heard about fell on my great-grandfather."

Steve swatted at a bee buzzing around Captain Ahab. "That's because no one knew the light was out. By the time the rescue boats showed up, it was on. The men on the ship were probably too disoriented to realize what happened, but the first mate knew. He didn't say anything until a few years later. The focus was on Captain Conners by then."

That seemed unfair.

"Why didn't he say it right away?" I demanded.

Steve shrugged. "The keeper was from here," he said. "They probably wanted to protect him."

"So was my great-grandfather."

Steve gave me an apologetic smile. "Captain Conners wasn't born here. Plus, he started with nothing and rose in the ranks to marry Madeline LaGrange. Your great-grandmother was from a good family and one of the great beauties around here. The locals were mighty protective of her. They turned on her husband's memory the moment he left her behind."

"That's terrible," I said. "I know it would have hurt her, too."

Steve squinted. "The scandal was too much for her parents. When the heat got to be too much, they moved down South. Madeline believed Captain Conners would come back to her, one day. She walked the beach at night, waiting for him. Some say she still walks the beach today."

I rolled my eyes.

He chuckled. "Take that for what it's worth."

"Do any of these families still live here?" I ran my hand over the rough cement of the stoop. "The keeper's family? The first mate? I wouldn't mind talking to them."

Steve dumped the rest of his coffee in the dirt. "Seems like the great-grandson of the first mate stuck around. I don't know if you should contact him, though."

"Why not?"

"Let's just say he hasn't always been on the right side of the law. I don't think it would be wise for you to meet with him."

With only a few weeks left to find some type of evidence to prove Fitzie's innocence, I was willing to risk it.

"Could you get me his contact information?" I asked. "I'd really like to talk to him. I'd bring someone with me. I wouldn't go alone."

Steve seemed to debate for a long moment. Sliding his hat back onto his head, he nodded. "I'll see what I can do."

The phone rang indoors, and Captain Ahab perked up his ears. Steve got to his feet. "Excuse me." He strode inside and said in an official tone, "Search and Rescue."

I rubbed Captain Ahab's ears one last time, and then stood. The air was quiet, and even the insects were still. The calm before the storm.

"Enjoy it while it lasts," I told the dog.

Based on the chill running through me, it felt like I was saying it to myself.

~

Carter spent over an hour checking the lighthouse for structural integrity, one floor at a time. When he was finally finished, he walked back down the stairs, a smile playing at the corner of his lips.

"It's pretty impressive," he said. "You managed to find the one rotted part of the whole place. Everything else looks fine."

"Well, at least I lived to tell the tale," I said, embarrassed. "You're *sure* I'm not going to fall through anywhere else?"

"Pretty sure." He grinned, tucking his thumbs in his belt loops. "I'll patch that area for now. It will hold until we get a new floor in. Just be careful to work around it."

"If you don't hear from me for a few days," I said, "send a rescue team."

He laughed. "What are you up to today?"

"Picking up trash," I said. "I only got as far as the bedroom the other day."

"It looks good so far." He nodded. "You're making progress. Keep it up."

With his words in mind, I worked steadily through the day, but it didn't feel like I was getting anywhere. I decided to keep taking photographs to document the changes. I liked having a record of the work I did.

I was taking shots of the kitchen when the door downstairs banged open. The bang was followed by a cheerful "Toodle-oo!"

I stopped in surprise. It had to be Kailyn, since she was the only person in a three-mile radius who would say "toodle-oo" and mean it.

"Up here," I called. "In the kitchen."

Kailyn was breathing heavily by the time she poked her head around the corner. She wore a sleek lemon suit, and her hair was pulled back. I could picture her driving around in the light-blue convertible parked outside her office, showing clients beach properties.

"Haven't these people ever heard of central air?" she cracked.

"How are you?" I took off my mask, brushing my fingers over the indent on my nose. My entire body was sweaty and sticky from a day of hard work. "Sorry, I'm a mess."

"This looks great!" She surveyed the room. "I wanted to stop by and follow up. It looks like you have things under control."

I'd made a lot of progress, but piles of dirt and debris were everywhere. Ten stuffed trash bags already lined the room, thanks to my pulley.

"Look at this," I said, walking over to the staircase and showing her the system. "You were right. The Henderson brothers are great. Carter's a genius."

"Hold up." Kailyn put a manicured hand to her chest. "Carter Henderson was in this room?"

"I texted you a picture of him," I said. "Didn't you get it?"

She looked puzzled. "No."

I pulled up the text. It read Send Failed.

I showed her the shot. "I guess the reception's spotty in here."

Kailyn grabbed my phone. "That is hilarious!" She smiled. "I can't believe you did that. Carter Henderson has been my ultimate fantasy since I was five years old."

The vision of Kailyn in pigtails, cornering Carter on the playground, made me laugh. I could imagine him blushing and looking down at his tennis shoes, trying to decide whether or not it would be rude to run away.

"I think you and Carter would be a good match," I said.

She grinned, fanning her damp face. "It's hard to resist a Henderson brother."

I thought of the three of them, in matching T-shirts and body-hugging jeans. "They're something."

Kailyn's voice went low and earnest. "Cody—he's the oldest—he was my first kiss. We played spin the bottle at a party at my house, and I totally rigged it." She whacked me in the upper arm. "Are you totally in love with Carter now?"

"I'm not in love with anybody."

To my annoyance, an image of Kip Whittaker danced through my head. I quickly replaced it with a picture of Todd. The memory was faded, but I could easily remember the moments when he said he loved me. Each time, he took off his glasses and kissed me.

"Well, I'm starving," Kailyn said, looking at her watch. "Would you want to grab dinner?"

"Really?" I said, delighted.

"If you already have plans, I can—"

"I don't," I said quickly. "I'd love to go."

I definitely wanted to go to dinner with Kailyn. Maybe the invitation was part of her client appreciation follow-up, but I hoped she was starting to think I wasn't so bad, after all.

"Do you care if I take a shower first?" I dared to ask. "I'm pretty filthy."

Filthy and sore. I was not used to lifting so many bags of stuff. Or climbing so many stairs. Or falling through floors.

Kailyn made a silly face. "I wouldn't let you come with me if you didn't." She patted her bag and turned back toward the stairs. "Meet you at the Harbor Resort in an hour?"

"See you then," I called.

I wadded up my dirty cleaning mask and brushed my hands off on a paper towel. Cleaning would have to wait.

❧

The Harbor Resort was a fixture in Starlight Cove. It was over a hundred years old and still in immaculate condition. The grounds were perfectly manicured, and the white-painted wooden deck offered an impressive view of the sun as it set over Lake Michigan.

I had a vague memory of coming to this restaurant as a child. I'd sat outside with my parents, drinking Shirley Temples and counting the ships as they floated by. My father always ordered a huge bowl of the New England chowder and polished it off with a loaf of homemade bread. I thought it might be fun to bring my parents here for old times' sake, but as I took a closer look, I realized the restaurant was much fancier than I remembered.

The tables were covered in white cloths, silver vases held fresh yellow flowers, and the gleaming silverware was perfectly lain out. The clientele seemed to be the upper crust of Starlight Cove, decked out in seersucker and breezy linens. I hoped the menu wasn't over the top—I had a lighthouse restoration to pay for.

I was about to call Kailyn and ask to get a burger somewhere instead when I spotted her at a corner table, a fluorescent-green martini at her lips.

"Hi," I said, pulling out a chair and taking a seat. "This place is swanky."

"Isn't it?" she whispered. "My father's the manager. We'll get everything half-off."

That was a relief. Still, it seemed like just the type of place I might bump into Maeve. I ordered a glass of chardonnay and decided to warn Kailyn.

"Thanks for asking me to dinner," I said. "But I don't want to hurt your business or your reputation, so if you just want to have drinks, that's totally fine."

Kailyn eyed me over the rim of her martini. "What are you talking about?"

"Because of the thing with *The Wanderer*," I said. "It's a bit of an issue around here."

Kailyn looked vaguely guilty. "People might be cautious at first, but once they get to know you, they won't care." She frowned. "Why, did something happen?"

I took a deep breath and explained the incident at the coffee shop with Maeve. It was tempting to add in the vandalism of the lighthouse, but I hadn't even told my parents.

"I'd hate it if she made a scene here," I said, looking around the restaurant. Soft music played over the speakers, and the vibe of the porch was cool and relaxed.

"Pshhh," Kailyn scoffed. "She wouldn't dare try that with me." She furrowed her brow. "I should have guessed Maeve Weatherly would throw a fit. She's so bitter her group didn't get the lighthouse."

I sat up straight. "She was the nonprofit?"

"Yup," Kailyn admitted, slathering a pat of butter on a slice of bread. "She headed up this movement to start a water conservancy program. The group submitted a letter of interest within the sixty-day window. They got to do a walk-through of the property with the Coast Guard and the GSA."

"Wow," I said. "She was really going for it."

Kailyn took another sip of her drink. "Right, but she didn't have the money. Maeve's husband planned to be a long-term donor but not to fund the entire project. She needed a big community push but couldn't get it together in time."

Interesting. That certainly gave her the motivation to vandalize the lighthouse—or to have someone do it for her.

The waiter returned with my wine and went into a long description of the nightly specials. Everything sounded good: a tart and creamy tomato bisque with chunks of blue crab; fresh trout pan sautéed with garlic and white wine; a salad with every garden-fresh vegetable imaginable . . .

"Take a moment to consider." He scraped breadcrumbs off the table and swept away.

Kailyn handed me a menu. "Get the fried clam strips. I am doing you a serious favor."

I was happy to note that a white wicker basket on the table held plenty of condiments, so I wouldn't have to whip out my travel bag. Harbor Resort might frown upon that sort of thing. Besides, I didn't want Kailyn to think I was weird.

Once the waiter took our order, the sun started to set. Streaks of pink, red, and orange lit up the sky as she and I swapped stories about our professional lives. The more we talked, the more we discovered we had in common. Her anecdotes about local real estate were hilarious, and I shared a few good mortgage stories from Boston.

When the waiter arrived with our plates, Kailyn clapped her hands in excitement. "You will *love* these," she promised.

The clams, it turned out, were a lethal combination of grease, sea, and salt. They were served with a side of fries with five dipping sauces and a plate full of corn on the cob, dripping with butter. She squeezed fresh lemon over both of our plates, and we dug in.

Healthy? No. Heaven? Yes.

"So." She polished off her martini and waggled her eyebrows. "*You* had breakfast the other day with Kip Whittaker."

The moment I heard *Kip Whittaker*, my stomach did that flutter thing. My body seemed intent on betraying me every time his name was mentioned. I tried not to think about how his arms felt against mine as he pulled me out of the floor.

"How did you know I had breakfast with him?" I asked. "Is there some sort of Starlight Cove hotline that sends out updates on outsiders?"

"There is," Kailyn said. "If you stay here long enough, I'll give you the number."

I must have looked horrified, because she burst out laughing. "I'm kidding! I saw you that morning before I knew who you were, silly. I noticed because I always notice Kip Whittaker. He never has breakfast with anyone other than this girl he dates."

I crumpled up my cocktail napkin.

It wasn't like I thought Kip Whittaker would actually be interested in me, but some moments, it seemed like he was. Like the time he said, "Keep telling yourself that, Fancy Pants," from the ladder and gave me that special grin. Not that *I* was interested in him—he was much too pompous—but after my recent heartbreak, the attention was nice. It was disappointing to think I'd imagined it.

"I didn't know he had a girlfriend," I said.

"Eh." She waved her hand. "It's hard to tell. Cassie VanDeCamp. She's local royalty, just like he is, but she's never in town. The Hamptons are more her style." Kailyn clapped her hands. "I know exactly what you are going to do!"

I shook my head. I was not about to make some play for Kip Whittaker. Cassie CandyCamp, or whatever her name was, sounded like his mirror match.

"I'm not going to do anything," I told Kailyn. "I'm not interested in Kip."

"*Every*one is interested in Kip. But I'm talking about Maeve." She beamed. "Give me a few days. I have something in mind."

"I think I'm going to need another glass of wine for this." I signaled the waiter. "It's nothing too dramatic, is it?"

Kailyn gestured at our plates and grinned. "I haven't steered you wrong yet."

Chapter Eleven

Kip called early the next day to say that Maeve's mother would be happy to talk to us, so I agreed to meet him at her house. I didn't want to deal with Maeve once she found out, but I was here to discover the truth about my great-grandfather. She wasn't about to stop me.

It was a beautiful day outside. The sky was clear and the flowers lush and blooming. I rode my bike over and met Kip at the bottom of Beulah's driveway. My heart did a little jump at the sight of him. He was dressed for work, in a button-up shirt and fitted slacks, his hair as rumpled as ever.

"Hey," I said. "Where's the dune buggy?"

He grinned. "I left it at home. Didn't want the poor woman to think she was under attack." He studied me with his sharp gaze. "You ready for this?"

"Depends." The image of spray paint dripping down the lighthouse door flashed through my mind. "I hope this meeting doesn't cause any more trouble."

Kip squinted at me. "Is Maeve still causing problems?"

Whether or not she was behind the vandalism in some way, I knew it wouldn't make her happy to learn her family history was connected to mine.

"Ask me tomorrow," I said, and headed for the steep driveway. "You ready?"

Beulah's house reminded me of a smaller version of Kip's family home. It was also a Victorian, complete with the turrets and lake view, but the difference was the upkeep. The old barn my mother mentioned sat on the edge of the property, the roof sagging in the center. The gray trim was faded and peeling, the hedges overgrown.

"If Beulah gives us some good answers, I'll get someone to come up here and take care of all this," Kip muttered, tugging at a weed that practically swallowed the path up to the house. "There's no excuse for this type of neglect."

"You'll do yard work?" I asked. "Guys who live on boats don't have to do yard work."

It was a joke my father used to make whenever I teased him about the fact that we would never own a lawn mower or have a dog.

Kip laughed. "I said I'd send someone to do it. There's a difference."

"The aristocratic way of solving problems," I said. "Hire someone."

"Isn't that what you're doing with the lighthouse?" Kip asked. "I heard the Henderson brothers were over there again."

"They've been great," I said. "I just met with Cameron this morning."

Earlier in the day, Cameron had checked the water supply, determined the pipes were in good working order, and discussed options for indoor plumbing. When I asked what it would take to install a bathroom, he suggested a compost toilet. It wouldn't use any water and would be easy to maintain.

I must have looked scared, because he started laughing.

"Relax," he said. "You don't use the compost for anything. It's just a dry toilet method that relies on sawdust instead of water. It's better than trying to manage some chemical septic system like you'd find in a motor home. Can you imagine lugging that thing down the ladder? Nightmare."

Cynthia Ellingsen

Cameron went on to explain that the compost toilet would be completely sanitary. It wouldn't smell, either, if properly vented outside. Plus, water supply and mechanical problems wouldn't be an issue.

"I'd like to install it as soon as possible," he said. "When do you plan on moving in?"

I didn't want the Henderson brothers to know that I planned to put the lighthouse back on the market. It's not that I wanted to deceive them, but I doubted they would be as committed to helping out. I planned to tell them eventually, but not yet.

"I don't know," I said. "It's hardly habitable."

"Still, I imagine you'll want to camp out?" Cameron pressed.

Hmm. Even though I liked my creature comforts, it might be fun to stay there for a night. When else would I have the opportunity to sleep in a lighthouse?

"Yes," I said, surprising myself. "I'll probably do that at some point soon."

"Well, the plumbing should be there when you are," Cameron said. "Trust me, you do not want to traipse out to the public restroom in the middle of the night. It's not safe."

"You and your brothers said Starlight Cove is the safest place on earth," I said. "Now you're telling me it's not?"

"Tourists leave trash in the can by the bathroom, and there's a family of raccoons that gets a kick out of dumpster diving. It's the perfect storm." He stretched his fingers and grinned. "Do you really want to trip over a masked crusader in the middle of the night?"

I was already tired of traipsing to the public restrooms in the middle of the day. I told Cameron to go ahead and set it up as soon as possible. If it ended up being too . . . rustic, I'd figure out another option.

Not that I was about to discuss any of this with Kip.

We climbed up the sagging steps to Beulah's front porch two at a time.

Beulah answered right away, as though she had been waiting by the window for us to arrive. "Welcome." Her face glowed. "It's so nice to have visitors."

She was in her eighties but didn't look a day over seventy. She was small and sprightly, with bulging brown eyes magnified by a pair of thick glasses. I could see a vague resemblance to Maeve, but instead of the sharpness, Beulah's cheeks were round and soft, and she was quick to offer a smile.

"It's nice to meet you," I said, accepting her enthusiastic hug. "My mother sends her regards."

I had told my mother about the meeting the moment we set it up. She'd been in Starlight Cove a lot longer than me, and she'd tell me if I should call the meeting off altogether. Instead of protesting, she said it sounded like a great idea.

Beulah pulled her lilac sweater tight. "Tell her I have some more things for her. I need to empty that barn out. It has so much history I don't know what's there anymore."

Kip shot me an eager look, and I shook my head. I was not about to ask an eighty-year-old woman if we could sort through her barn in hopes of finding who knows what. I doubted we would find a thing other than the antiques my mother had already described.

"Come in, come in!" She led us into the entryway and down a dark hallway.

The lack of lighting felt creepy, like someone might jump out from the shadows at any moment.

The parlor was old-fashioned. The ancient pale-pink wallpaper had a hypnotic silver diamond pattern. Curtains in striped green and a yellowed cream ornamented the windows, while pastels of floral arrangements lined the walls. The room was old and faded, as though lost conversations still lingered in the corners like dust.

"Have a seat." Beulah gestured at a tiny love seat.

Somehow, Kip and I squeezed onto the small couch without touching. Still, he sat close enough for me to feel the heat from his body and smell his woodsy scent. I had to remind myself that I didn't like Kip Whittaker. Every time I saw him, it became harder to convince myself of that fact.

I didn't know what it was that drew me in. He was attractive, but, more than that, he seemed to care. The moment I mentioned not wanting to cause more trouble, he was quick to ask what was going on. He seemed almost . . . protective, which was a surprise.

Or maybe I was just feeling soft toward him because he pulled me from the lighthouse floor.

Beulah bustled over with a tray of cookies, followed by a pot of coffee. She poured it into pink-and-white china cups for the two of us before settling into a straight-backed chair with her own cup. She regarded us with a serene smile.

"I'm happy you're here," she said. "It's rare I have an opportunity to entertain."

Beulah and Kip launched into a conversation about Starlight Cove, his family, and a bunch of people whose names I didn't recognize. As Kip talked, he gestured animatedly with his hands. His elbow brushed against me every other word, which was more than a little distracting.

A sudden silence in the room caught my attention.

"What?" I swallowed a bite of cookie. "What did I miss?"

"She said you look like your great-grandmother," Kip told me.

I blushed. "I do?"

Beulah gave an eager nod. "When you came to the front door, that's all I could think about. You look just like her. Strong, pretty . . . I thought to myself, well, she could be Madeline all over again."

I hadn't seen a picture of my great-grandmother in years. They were with my great-grandfather's love letters in a chest in my parents' attic. I'd have to pull them out and take another look.

"It was such a shame all she went through," Beulah said. "She always thought he would come back, you know, after that one . . ."

"After that one what?" Kip asked.

The older woman took off her glasses. "Nothing. I . . . I get lost in my conversations these days." Briskly, she changed the subject.

I could feel Kip tense alongside me.

What was she about to say?

Beulah launched into another modern-day story about Starlight Cove, but it seemed scattered. She kept looking at me, as though confused.

I was about to ask her a follow-up question when Kip said, "Beulah, just a few weeks ago, an inflammatory documentary aired on television about Captain Conners. It claimed he was alive after the shipwreck. You just made it sound as though you knew something about that."

I leapt to my feet. "It's time for us to go."

Beulah stared at me from behind her glasses. "Madeline, I haven't told anyone."

I froze, my hand on the back of the loveseat. "Sorry?"

"That he came back for you."

My hands went cold. This was exactly what I did not want to hear.

"What do you mean?" I whispered.

She covered her face, like a little girl. "I wasn't supposed to listen, but I hid under the table. I was a naughty girl, spying and reading my mother's journal. But she found me and . . ." She closed her eyes, as though in pain. "I'm sorry."

"It's okay," I whispered. "Beulah, it's okay."

Silence crackled in the air.

"I know what he said, but I won't tell." She fidgeted. "If I tell, people will get hurt."

Kip went tense. "Who would get hurt?"

She looked right at me. "You."

I shivered. Beulah looked pale and tired. Even though I wanted to ask more questions, Kip put his hand on my arm.

Be patient.

I swatted his hand away. "Beulah, thank you so much for meeting with us."

Kip nodded. "We appreciate your time." He kissed her on the cheek. "If you need anything at all, just let us know. I'll send someone up to trim those hedges."

"No, no," she said, quickly. "My son would not like that."

Kip opened his mouth as though to say something. Then, he seemed to change his mind. "It was nice to see you."

Beulah was back on her feet, all smiles. She ushered us to the door and gave a cheerful wave.

"Such a pleasure to see you, Madeline," she said. "Do tell your mother I said hello."

The door shut behind us, and we walked down the porch in silence. Shadows from the trees fell around us while the birds chattered and cawed. The sky was overcast, like it might rain.

I wrapped my arms around my body to fight off the shivers. "What do you think it means?"

"I don't know." Kip's expression was dark. "But I doubt her son would get mad about lawn care."

"She seemed pretty insistent that he would."

"That's impossible." Kip shook his head. "He died thirty years ago."

Kip and I sat on a bench on downtown Main Street. He grabbed us burgers and French fries from the local hamburger joint. I sipped on an ice-cold Coke, trying to stop shaking.

"You okay?" Kip asked.

I didn't answer.

News Tonight was right. Not about all of it, maybe, but about the fact that Fitzie had survived the shipwreck. Which meant a real chance existed that my great-grandfather stole the silver and abandoned my great-grandmother—two things I was not ready to accept.

If Fitzie was a crook, my parents were going to have to pay for it. With the only home I'd ever known. I should have just stuck my head in the sand, like they had. Instead, I had played the role of dutiful investigator, only to discover our history was not what I wanted it to be.

"What's on your mind?" Kip asked.

I didn't answer.

He had to be delighted to learn that his hunch about the date on the letter was, most likely, correct. I was sure he'd spend some time patting himself on the back for that one.

Letting out a sigh, Kip unwrapped his burger and took a bite. "Look, the whole thing was strange," he said. "Then there was that comment about her son . . ."

The point did not make me feel better. Even if Beulah had dementia, too much of what she said matched up with the evidence stacked up against Fitzie.

I wasn't hungry, but I pulled out the bag of French fries and searched my purse until I found a packet of A.1. steak sauce and a mini-jar of Dijon mustard. Setting them on the bench, I dipped my fries in the sauce and ate in silence.

Tourists strolled by. My gaze settled on a couple that was holding hands and exchanging loving looks. Nearly a hundred years ago, my great-grandparents could have strolled this very street, looking at each other in the same way.

"The whole thing was strange," I said.

Kip seemed relieved I was talking. "I'll give you that. And she *didn't* say he walked away with the treasure."

"No." I ate a fry. "She didn't."

I licked some salt off my lip. Kip's dark gaze follow the move. Embarrassed, I wiped my mouth with a napkin.

Clearing his throat, he said, "The thing that got me was the part where she said her mother kept a journal." He took a bite of his burger and chewed it thoughtfully. "If we found it, it might help."

"You want to go back and ask her if we can search her attic?" I took a sip of Coke, relishing the sharp blast of cool sugar against my tongue. "That's not going to happen."

"No. But we could ask her if she still has the journal and see what she says. It might be better than pummeling her with questions about a memory she would rather not revisit."

"She got so scared when we asked about Fitzie," I said. "I don't want to push her too hard."

"If she's hiding something," he said, "we need to know about it."

"She's a little old lady."

"She's Maeve's mother."

The comment threw me. "Meaning . . . ?"

"Family feuds run deep here," he said. "But when it comes down to it, blood is thicker than water. She has a pretty good motivation for not giving us information."

Kip's cell phone buzzed. Checking it, he frowned. "It's Sami," he said. "FaceTime. I can call her back."

I waved my hand. "No, go ahead."

He picked up the call. "Hey, what's up?"

"Why are there trees in your office?" Sami asked.

"I'm not in my office." Kip turned the phone toward me. "I'm having lunch with Dawn."

Embarrassed, I waved.

His niece glowered. For a moment, she looked a lot like her uncle. I could tell she was not happy with the sudden intrusion, so I pushed the phone back to Kip.

He peered into the screen. "What's up?"

"Private things," she said. "Ones I do not care to discuss on speakerphone."

Kip laughed. "Hint taken," he said. "I'll call you later." He hung up and shook his head. "Poor kid. She's been having a hard time. Her father jumped ship five years ago."

"That's awful." I might not have had a stable childhood, but at least I had the benefit of both parents. "She seemed to be doing okay the day I met her," I said, thinking back to that first morning in Towboat. "It's obvious she adores you."

"The feeling is mutual."

It was still a surprise to see how interested Kip was in his niece. I would have pegged him for a careless bachelor, but he seemed like more of a family man. I thought back to Kailyn's words, about Cassie Whatever-her-name-was.

"Do you want kids?" I asked.

"Eventually," he said. "Sami's enough to handle at the moment. I've been so busy with work that we haven't spent much time together. Plus, her mother's always so busy with that restaurant, I don't think she's giving her the time she needs." He frowned. "I think Sami has a boyfriend."

The expression on his face made me laugh. "What's wrong with that?"

"She's only fifteen," he growled. "But Kelcee—that's her mom—says that the kids hang out in a group, so there's always someone there. Still, I don't like it."

Sami had been hanging out with a group of guys on the beach. One definitely seemed more interested in her than the others, but I was not about to tell Kip.

"Find out where a group date is," I suggested. "Make a surprise appearance. That way, she knows someone is watching out for her but not hovering over her shoulder."

"That's not bad advice." Kip squinted at me. "Do *you* have ten kids or something?"

"No." The sky was overcast and the wind had picked up. I put my hand over my packet of fries to keep them from blowing away. "My parents were completely irresponsible, so I paid attention to see how the normal parents acted."

I brushed some salt off my hands, embarrassed by the confession. I'd dated Todd for more than a year, and I'd never said a word about my crazy childhood. I didn't know what prompted me to mention it to Kip.

He sat in silence, as though waiting for me to say more. When I didn't, he nodded. "That's understandable." Thunder rolled in the distance. "Looks like we're in for another big one."

"It was a perfect day," I said. "How did the storm come up so quickly?"

"It's just the way it is around here. That's what happened with *The Wanderer*, you know. They weren't ready for it. Not that it would have made much of a difference."

When I didn't say anything, he got to his feet. "I should get back." He studied me. "Since I didn't hear any objections, I'm going to follow up with Beulah about her mother's journal."

"Let me know what she says." I thought of what Steve said, about the first mate. "I've got a guy getting contact information for the descendant of the first mate. Do you want to meet him with me? See what he has to say?"

Since Steve said the guy might be dangerous, I figured it might be smart to have Kip come along.

"Sure," he said. "Let me know when."

He wadded up the bag with the extra burger and seemed ready to pitch it.

"Hold on." I held out my hand. "I'll take that."

I figured I could visit Captain Ahab on the way home and get the contact information from Steve, assuming the weather held. The clouds seemed thicker by the moment.

Kip gave me a look. "You're going to find a homeless person to give it to?"

"It's for a dog," I told him. "*Not* that I should have to explain myself."

"Uh-huh," he said. Then he turned and strolled off down the street.

My eyes settled on his broad shoulders. He must have felt me watching him, because he looked back. Lifting a hand in an easy wave, he continued on down the sidewalk.

That afternoon, my mother and I snuggled up under blankets on the couch and waited for the storm to hit. We had old-fashioned kerosene lamps on standby and books in hand. To my surprise, my father burst into the room like a tornado. He wore knee-high rubber fishing boots and rolled-up fishing pants, and his face was wild with excitement.

"Come on, ladies," he cried. "Let's watch this doozy from the lighthouse!"

My mother laughed in delight. "You're home." She rushed across the room and jumped into his arms.

I focused on the pages of my book as they kissed and canoodled. My parents were never really lovey-dovey when I was growing up. They were a good couple but not romantic the way my great-grandparents seemed. Now, it was like they hadn't seen each other in decades.

"All right, all right," I said, sliding in a bookmark and getting to my feet. "Break it up."

"Dawn!" My father strode across the room and gave me a kiss on the cheek. "I brought you a housewarming present." He produced a package wrapped in brown paper and navy string. "It seemed appropriate."

I tore into the wrapping paper. Inside it was a book with a yellow-green canvas cover and a title printed in faded-gold letters: *Instructions to Light-Keepers: July, 1881.*

"Where did you get this?" I breathed.

My father adjusted his wool sweater. "I have my sources."

I turned to a random page. It read: *The utmost neatness of buildings and premises is demanded. Bedrooms, as well as other parts of the dwelling, must be neatly kept. Untidiness will be strongly reprehended, and its continuance will subject a keeper to dismissal.*

I showed the passage to my father. "I think I'll hang this above the front door."

"You can do it right now," he said, rubbing his hands together. "We can still get to the lighthouse before it starts to rain."

Leave it to my father to show up unannounced, with big plans on how to spend the evening.

"Count me out." My mother padded back to the sofa and tucked herself under a cashmere throw. "I'm snug as a bug right here."

"What do you say, Dawn?" My father raised his fist to the sky, like a warrior. "Did you buy that lighthouse so it could fend for itself on a night like this?"

"Dad, I don't think it's . . ."

"Shake a leg," he cried. "Don't you want to be in the thick of it?"

I peered out the window. The sky was a bloated green and seemed ready to spill over. It seemed dangerous to walk right into the storm.

I wasn't wild like my father. I didn't need to do crazy things just because the option was there. No matter how fun it sounded.

I pulled my afghan more tightly around me. "I think I'm going to read."

"Quit dragging your anchor," he roared. "It's time to prove you're alive!"

My mother nudged me with her toe. "Go show him the lighthouse."

The message was loud and clear: *Stop being such a stick-in-the-mud. You're here to give him support.*

"Life isn't all beer and skittles, Dawn," my father said. "It's time to take a front-row seat."

I groaned. It took serious effort to peel myself off the couch, but I headed toward the bedroom to change.

~

The lightning streaked across the sky like the heated hands of a skeleton. My father and I stood up on the balcony, gripping the edge of the railing. Thunder roared in the distance, and we calculated the distance of the storm.

I watched my father with admiration. He hardly seemed like a man poised to lose everything. His eyes were bright and his cheeks flushed.

Electricity seemed to crackle around him, stronger than the charge in the air. He was alive and in the moment, thrilled to be in the eye of the storm. His wool sweater flapped against his shoulders in the wind.

"It's about ten minutes out." The short strands of his white hair stood up straight. "It's going to be a beauty."

The sky had changed from pea green to a dangerous pink, like a sunset lit from underneath. Thick clouds rolled against the sky like waves. Below, the water crashed and pummeled against the shore. I tried to imagine what it would be like to be on a ship during weather like this.

When I was out on the water with my parents, my father was meticulous about trying to avoid storms. He was convinced that he was destined to die in a shipwreck at the age of thirty-five, just like Fitzie. I imagined he enjoyed the power of standing over this storm, instead of fleeing for mercy.

He let out a sudden shout and I jumped.

"Jeez, Dad," I said. "What on earth—"

"You see it?" He pointed at the water. "You see *The Wanderer* out there?"

The beam of the lighthouse panned the water. It blinked across the surface, its reflection blurred in the churning of the lake. In a break in the violent waves, dark edges loomed below.

He ruffled my hair. "It's something, isn't it?"

I studied the sunken ship. It was tragic to think that it set out on a sunny day, only to encounter a night like this one.

"Why do you think he brought it in so close?" I asked.

"To bring the lifeboats to shore." My father rubbed his hand against his beard. "He knew it was going down and wanted his men to have a chance."

According to reports, there were four lifeboats. The first lifeboat was packed with the silver, and it sank so low that Captain Fitzie refused to allow his crew to board it. He waited until everyone was safely on the other lifeboats, and then climbed on with the silver. The third and fourth boat made it to shore, but the first two did not. The locals mourned the loss until the insurance agency started asking questions.

Was it possible, they asked, that Fitzie steered the boat to a remote area down the shore, hid the silver in the brush, and planned to return at a later date with the assistance of the men on the second boat? The seed of doubt did its good work. The people of Starlight Cove began to say that Fitzie led the men into danger because of his greed. The story wasn't based in truth, but it was enough to make people wonder.

I told my father what Steve said about the lighthouse not being lit.

"That shouldn't have mattered too much," my father mused, scratching his beard. "Fitzie could read his location, and he knew the coastline. I think the waves broke the boat apart."

"Not the sandbars?" I asked.

"I doubt he would have brought it in so close unless it was already falling apart."

We sat in silence, staring at the ghostly image just beyond the shore.

The first fat drops of rain started to fall, and my father let out a cry of excitement. "Here we go," he said, throwing back his head.

I blinked in the sudden onslaught of rain and pulled my raincoat tightly around me. The gigantic hood was no match for the deluge of water, and it streamed down my face.

"Let's go back in," I pleaded. "I don't want to get drenched."

My father started laughing. "Too late!"

The wind was wild, and my feet weren't steady on the ground. I wanted to be more like my father, ecstatic in the moment, but my mind was already moving ahead to walking home, putting my clothes in the dryer, and making a hot cup of tea so I didn't catch cold.

My father rumpled my damp hair, as though reading my mind. "You only live once, Dawn. Embrace it!"

"We're going in when the lightning hits," I insisted, determined to maintain some form of control over this situation.

"It's not here yet." My father raised his arms, gesturing at the lake around us. "Behold, the power of the storm," he shouted. "Isn't it magnificent?"

Sheets of water rained down around us. The wind howled, and the waves roiled and frothed below. It was an amazing sight. So, like my father said, I decided to embrace it.

I threw my head back and let the rain pound against my cheeks. An unexpected happiness bubbled up in me, and I started to laugh. When the water got to be too much, I buried my head against my father's arm, breathing in the wet wool of his sweater.

He grabbed my hand and raised it to the sky.

"This one's for you, Fitzie Conners," he cried.

A streak of lightning cut open the night.

We rushed inside, laughing and shouting. I looked over my shoulder one last time. I caught a glimpse of the broken bones of *The Wanderer*, sunk just below the surface of the water, and marveled at how quickly life could change.

⁓

My father and I waited out the remainder of the storm in the lighthouse. We sat in the watch room, just below the Fresnel light, wringing water out of our drenched clothing. He made us a makeshift blanket out of some trash bags, and we settled in on the floor, listening to the thunder crash and the rain hammer against the building.

It was cozy in the watch room, compared to outside, and I wished I'd put the housewarming basket from Kailyn in the lighthouse. It had blankets, a deck of cards, and plenty of survival supplies. When I mentioned that to my father, he produced a weathered Hershey's bar from one of his pockets and peeled back the foil wrapper.

He broke off half of the squares and handed them to me. "It pays to be prepared."

Nostalgia rushed through me. I'd forgotten that my father always carried a bar of chocolate with him. It was a habit he picked up as a ship captain, so he would always have some sort of food on him if he got stranded. I hadn't eaten a Hershey's bar in ages, and the smooth squares transported me right back to my childhood.

Of course, the second I started thinking about that, questions started cropping up. Why did my parents choose to live the way they did? Technically, I knew the answer: they were explorers. The actions they took led to the discovery of the *San Arabella* and several other significant finds. But couldn't they have waited a few years until I was out of school or, at the very least, found a way to give me a sense of security?

That lack of security as a child had affected me as an adult. I had some weird habits. Sleeping in clean bedsheets every night, the need for routine, the caution I used letting people in . . . My relationship with Todd had only existed on a surface level because I hadn't wanted to open up until I knew he was there to stay. In the end, that caution drove him away.

It made me sad to think so many things about my life could have been different if my parents had just settled down for a few years. I didn't think they should have given up their dreams for me, but they could have postponed them for a little while. Was I not worth it to them?

What if I'd asked them to make a change? I could have lived with my grandparents here in Starlight Cove. It seemed like such a clear solution now. Of course, I didn't really know how abnormal my life was until I became an adult.

"What's on your mind?" my father asked, as though sensing my confusion.

I hesitated.

As much as I wanted to talk about the past, needed to talk about it, I didn't want to upset him. He was already in a bad place. Besides, I barely saw him. Did I really want to spend the little time we had together getting into this?

Instead, I updated him on my research for *The Wanderer*. My father was interested in hearing about everything we'd found. He laughed out loud to learn Madeline was a friend of Beulah's mother.

He leaned back against the wall. "You must have searched stem to stern to catch that one," he said. "That family has a lot of history here. I'm not surprised they're involved."

I popped the last square of chocolate bar in my mouth and bit down. "Her mother didn't have much to do with the story."

"Are you sure about that?" he mused. "Maeve attacked you that first day you were here. It sounds like she has something to hide."

I shook my head. "No, she was mad about the lighthouse. She wanted it for her nonprofit group."

"Still." My father made an origami seagull out of the foil candy wrapper and handed it to me. "I'd follow up a bit more on the friendship between Beulah's mother and Madeline. Maeve's family has been around a long time."

"You think they stole the treasure?"

"Doubt it." He shrugged. "Supposedly, they made their fortune in shipping, long before *The Wanderer* went down. They were big into importing and exporting. They made a lot of money during the war, not to mention Prohibition." He raised an eyebrow. "If that tells you anything."

I fiddled with the silver wings of the bird. "Fitzie was transporting whiskey. Do you think losing it would have gotten him in trouble with the people he was smuggling it for?"

My father gave me a sharp look. "What do you mean?"

"Beulah said Fitzie was alive after the wreck," I admitted. "She overheard her mother and Madeline talking about it. She said Madeline would be in danger if anyone knew."

My father stood up and walked over to the window. He stared out at the lake for a long moment.

"I'm just telling you what she said," I told him. "That doesn't mean—"

"It's true." My father's voice echoed across the watch room.

I blinked. "Sorry?"

Lightning silhouetted his shoulders. Turning to me, he said, "Dawn, your great-grandfather survived the wreck of *The Wanderer*. Madeline told my father before she died."

I stared at him in shock. "You knew this?"

He shoved his hands in his pockets and turned back to the window.

"He stole the treasure?" I cried. "Where is it? Do we have it?"

This was too much. I had come up here planning to solve the mystery, prove Fitzie's innocence, and save the day, only to learn my parents knew he was guilty the whole time. This was so typical of them! They hadn't changed one bit.

"You should have told me," I said, my voice bitter. "I never would have come here."

My father spun away from the window. "He didn't take the treasure!"

"How do you know?" I demanded. "If he didn't, why would Madeline say anything about it at all?"

My father sank down next to me on the floor. "Because she wanted to know what happened. She begged my father to figure it out. He couldn't do it. Neither could I." Picking up the foil seagull I'd dropped, he squeezed it into a ball. "I've spent my whole life feeling like I let her down."

The sorrow in his voice echoed through the room. I sat in silence, trying to decide whether or not to be moved. I was still angry, but, finally, I reached out and touched his hand.

"Do you think he was in trouble because of the whiskey?" I asked.

Transporting whiskey was illegal in 1922. It could have been put on the ship by some dangerous people. It made sense they might blame the ship captain who lost it.

He shook his head. "The whiskey's still under the ship. It might be deadly to try and get it out. But if his employers wanted it bad enough, they knew where to find it."

"I wonder if someone attacked him," I said. "For . . . retribution or whatever."

"He was injured," my father said. "The night of the wreck, he . . ."

"There's more you didn't tell me?" I said in disbelief.

My father sighed. "He hid out here. In the lighthouse."

"Are you *kidding* me?" I jumped to my feet. "Why didn't you say anything?"

"You were starting your life over!" he said. "Did you really want me ranting about destiny and serendipity when you were searching for the coordinates to bring your ship to shore?"

It was my turn to walk to the window. I stared out at the violent waves and the streaks of electricity across the sky. I rested my hands on the edge of the windowsill. The stone was cold beneath my fingers.

I couldn't believe my great-grandfather had hidden out here, in the same place I bought almost a century later. I put my head in my hands and imagined the figure of Madeline walking the shore, waiting for Fitzie to come back home.

"Did he leave her?" I asked. "Did he abandon her?"

Silence stretched across the room. Finally, my father said, "I don't know."

Behind me, I could hear him get to his feet, gathering the garbage bags with him.

"Let's get home," he said.

"Not until you tell me what happened here."

I turned to face him. My father hadn't bothered to wear a raincoat, and he was soaked. Standing in his fishing boots and wet wool sweater, he looked like a man on the deck of a ship, fighting to keep his balance after the hit of a storm.

"What do you want to know?" he asked.

"All of it." I gave him a firm look. "Anything else that you know."

My father ran his hand over his beard. "Fitzie showed up here, injured, and the keeper called for Dr. Whittaker. It was all very hush-hush, of course. They planned a meeting for him and Madeline at Dr. Whittaker's home."

"What do you mean, injured?"

"He had a large gash across his head," my father said. "He'd gotten whacked by one of the boards from the boat, probably as it was sinking."

"So, Dr. Whittaker helped him," I said. "But why would he hide the fact that Fitzie was alive?"

My father shrugged. "Because he asked him to. They were good friends."

The letter to Dr. Whittaker proved that. Maybe Kip even knew this part of the story, about Dr. Whittaker and the lighthouse. If my own father kept this information from me, why wouldn't Kip do the same?

I had asked Kip that first morning why he was interested in *The Wanderer*. He didn't look me in the eye when he answered, but he said since his family was involved, he was invested. I couldn't help but wonder *how* invested.

"Do you trust Kip?" I asked.

"Your mother likes him. Thinks he's a good kid."

"Do you think he's trying to find the truth or the treasure?"

My father chuckled. "They both have their merits." He gave me a sharp look. "It sounds like you don't trust him."

It was complicated, because I was so attracted to Kip. Every time our eyes met, I felt a jolt of electricity. I wanted to give myself permission to like him, but something held me back.

"Trust has to be earned," I said.

My father shook his head. "No, it doesn't. I've met some bad apples in my time, but you've got to let people in, Dawn. They're not always going to let you down."

Hmmph. The information my father had kept from me was huge. It hurt me that he hadn't told me what he knew, but I understood. He didn't want anyone to believe the worst about Fitzie. Especially when he was determined to believe the best.

I followed him down to the main floor and unlocked the door.

My father put his hand on my shoulder. "Dawn, keep your head above water. There's a quote that says: The average man will bristle if you say his father was dishonest, but he will brag a little if he discovers that his great-grandfather was a pirate."

"Your point?"

"Either way, kid, you win."

~

The beach looked as chaotic as my emotions the morning after the storm. Pieces of driftwood had been thrown onto the shore, along with dead fish, strings of seaweed, and even a broken beach umbrella. The seagulls pecked in the sand while pelicans swooped overhead, looking for their next meal.

My father and I walked to the lighthouse drinking mugs of ginger tea. I wore a casual T-shirt and a pair of khaki shorts and was chilly in the post-storm morning. Clutching the travel mug for warmth, I looked out at the water, thinking about the things my father told me. I still hoped the pieces could fit together in a way to prove my great-grandfather's innocence.

I forgot all about the potential for more vandalism until we were almost at the lighthouse. The last thing I wanted was another threatening message, especially since it would require me to tell my father what had happened. I was keeping secrets, too. To my relief, the lighthouse sat in stoic silence, like a soldier at rest after battle.

My father stopped and peered up at it, as I did the first morning I arrived in Starlight Cove.

"Your great-grandmother brought me here again and again, but this was never my favorite lighthouse," he said. "Until now."

"What lighthouse could *possibly* be better than this one?" I demanded.

"Minot's Ledge," he said. "In Massachusetts."

The Minot's Ledge lighthouse was a cylindrical structure, just like mine, built in the eighteen hundreds. Because of its character of light, some of the locals said "1-4-3" instead of "I love you," for the number of flashes the lighthouse gave off and the number of letters in each word. I remembered my father holding me up on his shoulders when I was younger, pointing at the light and saying, "One four three."

"I can see how that's a close second," I told him.

Inside, my father went up to see if the new window had held up in the storm.

"Right as rain," he called, clambering back down the stairs.

I met him on the landing of the main entryway, holding the face mask, gloves, and loose-fitting hazmat suits Carter found for us.

"What's all that?" He eyed it with suspicion.

"Today," I said, sliding into my suit, "we are going to tackle the mold."

"It looks like we're about to go scuba diving."

The first time my father took me on a dive, I was terrified. It was a blast pretending to be a slippery seal up on the deck, but the moment I got down to thirty feet, I panicked. My father held my hands and made faces, calming me enough to keep me in the water.

Because of him, we made it all the way down to the floor of the ocean. We explored the rotting wood of *The Montague*, the shipwreck my parents were cataloguing at the time, and he showed me the funny fish that hid on the surface of the ocean floor. We stayed until the last possible moment and finally broke the surface with just a few minutes of oxygen to spare.

The time spent with my father was special, but I never fell in love with diving like my parents had. I didn't like the feeling of being trapped underwater. Much like in life, I wanted the freedom to make my own decisions, on my own terms.

What would it be like to stop dictating those terms? I felt it last night, standing up on the balcony in the rainstorm, and back when Kip sped down the drive in the dune buggy. Maybe it was just a matter of letting life happen to me a little bit more and planning for it a little bit less. That, of course, was easier said than done.

Once my father and I were geared up, he studied me over the rim of his protective glasses.

"I have something to say." His voice reverberated off the stone walls. "And I want you to hear me."

"What's up?" I said.

"Last night, we talked about some things that upset you," he said. "I know you might be tempted to give up. Don't. I need your help with this, Dawn."

I blinked, embarrassed at the sudden lump in my throat. "You do?"

He nodded.

135

Pulling his mask back up, he turned to the wall. "Watch out, mold," he cried. "We're coming for you."

I let out a small giggle and unleashed a stream of bleach. I doused the walls, imagining the mold just peeling away. The sloppy, messy work was incredibly satisfying.

"One four three, Dad," I cried, surprising myself.

My father smiled at me from behind his goggles.

"One four three, kid," he said. "One four three."

Chapter Twelve

That afternoon, I received a voice mail from Kip. I peeled off my gear and took my phone out to the ladder for some privacy. The fresh air was cool on my skin after the sweaty hazmat suit.

According to the message, Kip had set up a meeting with the great-grandson of the first mate for later in the week. I called him right back.

"How was he?" I asked, turning my face up toward the sun. "Did he sound normal?"

"No," he admitted. "He sounded rough. In fact, I think you should wear your high heels, so I have time to escape if he tries to attack us."

"Uh, if he came after us, I would throw one of my shoes at *you*," I told him. "That way, *I'd* have time to escape."

He laughed. "I have no doubt you would. See you Thursday."

Maybe my father was right about letting people in. I wasn't all the way there with Kip, but I was coming along. In fact, as I headed back into the lighthouse, I wondered when Kip and I had become friends.

~

Once the lighthouse was sprayed down with bleach, the Henderson brothers planned to work with us to set up fans and dehumidifiers on every floor.

I contacted the Coast Guard and informed them of the situation. They agreed to go into the lighthouse only in the event of an emergency. I also asked if the electric equipment we'd be bringing in was too much for the power source to handle, but the guy I talked to thought it would be just fine. So, the plan was to keep the lighthouse sealed for three days to help it dry out as the bleach killed the mold.

My father and I headed over to the hardware store, where he shook hands with the Henderson brothers and asked about the fishing season. Then he told a couple of stories about growing up with their father.

"He was a good man." My father's tone was somber. "A really good man."

Carter and Cameron already had the dehumidifiers and fans ready to go. We loaded them up into two flatbeds and transported them down the boardwalk. They walked behind us, trading insults.

"Did something happen to their dad?" I whispered.

"Single-engine-plane crash." My father rubbed his hand against his white beard. "Happened about eight years ago, on a trip to Massachusetts. Both parents were on board. Cody was supposed to be, but he had some stomach bug and stayed home. The crash was a tragedy, but the fact that the kids all survived was the silver lining."

The sunlight dimmed as I absorbed the news. I felt embarrassed to realize I never stopped to wonder why three brothers managed a hardware store without the rest of their family. It hadn't even crossed my mind.

On that first day, Carter had asked all sorts of small-town, friendly questions about me, but I was too used to big-city life to ask him anything. It wasn't like we needed some soul-searching conversation, but I could have asked. I waited until Carter and I were alone, setting up the fan in the kitchen, to bring it up.

"I'm really sorry to hear about your parents," I said. "I didn't know."

He focused on the oscillation of the blades. "Thanks."

"How old were you?" I asked. Since asking personal questions was foreign to me, I added, "If you want to talk about it."

Carter sat back on his heels. "It's been about eight years. I was twenty-two." His freckled face looked older than usual as he talked. "It hit Cameron the hardest, since he was just a kid. He's had some problems. But Cody . . . well, it made him turn his life around. It hasn't been easy, but we do what we can to stay a family."

"You guys seem so normal." An image of the three Henderson brothers with their perfect physiques and matching T-shirts rushed through my head. "That is, you seem like you're doing well."

"I like to think we're doing them proud," he said. "My dad was a carpenter and always wanted to own a hardware store. He'd be pretty happy about this."

Everything was set up and we were about to head back downstairs when something made me say, "Kailyn was really impressed by the pulley you built. You guys are friends, right?"

Carter paused. Maybe I imagined it, but his eyes seemed to flicker with interest. "Kailyn? Yeah, we went to school together. Don't see her much. She's pretty busy with the real estate."

In the past few days, I'd started to suspect Carter had a crush on Kailyn. Every time I mentioned her name, he blushed. So I decided to try a little matchmaking of my own.

"She's getting to be a friend of mine," I said. "I'm a little curious why someone so great is still single."

To my delight, the base of his neck flushed.

"I don't know." He adjusted another knob on the fan. "I think she's pretty busy with that job of hers. Besides, she . . ." He glanced at the stairs, as though worried one of his brothers would walk in and hear him talking about a girl.

"What?" I pressed.

He shrugged. "She never has much time to hang out. She comes to Maddie's when the kids from high school get together, but the rest of the time, she's working on something."

"What's Maddie's?" I asked.

"Local bar." He grinned. "Dive bar. Colored Christmas lights, sticky floors, jukebox from the eighties . . . Not too many of the out-of-towners go there."

Hmm. That was something to consider.

"You guys go on the weekends?"

I hoped my attempts at matchmaking weren't too transparent, but the more I got to know Carter, the more he and Kailyn seemed like a good fit. He was cute, respectful, and such a nice guy.

"Fridays, usually," he said. "You thinking of stopping by?"

"It might be fun." I squeezed my hands, hoping that what I was about to say would not end up being a huge mistake. "I could bring Kailyn."

His face lit up. "She's good at darts. Last time she was there, she kicked my ass. Tell her I want a rematch."

I hid a smile. "Will do."

∽

Once the lighthouse was closed up, I was faced with three days of freedom. It was a strange feeling. Back when I was in Boston, I typically let my vacation time build up until the end of the year, and then I'd lose most of it. Now, it was a luxury to have three whole days to do nothing but have fun.

I kicked off my first day by taking a run down by the water and then organizing the closets in my parents' house. There was no rhyme or reason to their current system, so I set up one closet for cleaning supplies, one for outdoor items such as boots and winter coats, and another for things like games and movies. Then, for good measure, I alphabetized the movies.

That took up most of the morning. After lunch, I stopped by the fudge shop for a box of Rocky Road. On impulse, I bought a box of peanut-butter fudge for Kailyn and stopped by her office. She was hard at work, sifting through the latest listings in an attempt to find a client a beach property. At the sight of the fudge, she clutched her heart.

"*Yes.*" She giggled, grabbing the box with both hands. "I haven't had lunch yet. This will do the trick."

According to my watch, it was well past two.

"I can't believe I'm saying this, but you need more than chocolate to survive," I told her. "Do you want me to go pick you up a sandwich?"

Kailyn shook her head. "I have to run to a showing in ten minutes. I'll pick something up when I'm out. I'm glad you stopped by, though, because I was going to call you today. Remember what I was saying about figuring out what you can do about your problem with Maeve?"

"What did you come up with?" I perched on the edge of one of the leather chairs.

"I mentioned you to one of the women in the historical society," Kailyn said. "They want to do a presentation on lighthouses, with you as the guest of honor."

My stomach dropped. "Yikes."

"Look, if you get those ladies on your side," she said, "you won't hear another word of trouble from Miss Maeve. Some of these women's families have been here longer than Maeve's family. That means they're pretty powerful."

I started laughing. "My family has been around forever. Does that mean we're powerful, too?"

Kailyn grinned. "If you weren't, your great-grandfather's picture wouldn't be hanging all over the place."

"How did it get up there?" I asked. "I've been wondering."

She took a bite of fudge and shrugged. "I heard a family member of one of the survivors put it up. Grateful and all that. Either way, it's pretty cool." She licked her finger. "He deserves to be honored."

"Kip said it was more of a famous outlaw thing."

"Maybe it's a little bit of both." She laughed. "Now, what do you say about this meeting? It's next Tuesday and if you don't come, they will hate me forever."

I hesitated.

Even though it was nice of her to set it up, I was scared. The meeting could turn into an ambush. I shuddered, imagining an entire roomful of women scolding me for taking their lighthouse.

But it was the historical society, which meant they must know their history. One of the women could have information that could help me. At this point, I was willing to try anything.

"Okay," I told her. "Sign me up."

~

Back at my parents' house, I settled in with Rocky Road and a show about home remodeling. The more I watched, the more I wondered what the experts would do with a lighthouse.

That, of course, got me thinking.

The lighthouse was still practically condemned—decorating seemed far along the horizon. Still, I couldn't help but fantasize about what it might be like to bring the lighthouse back to its original splendor.

I always liked those pictures my mother sent me of it in its earliest form, with the exposed brick walls and the crown molding in the center of the ceilings. The bones were there, hidden beneath the filth.

It could be incredible, I thought, *when it's all fixed up. Like a dream home.*

The sentiment surprised me.

When I bid on the lighthouse, it never once crossed my mind that I might want to live there. The idea was crazy, but . . .

I pictured the stillness of the summer nights on the water. Cooking meals in the quaint kitchen. Sitting up on the gallery with a glass of wine, watching the sun go down . . . It was a nice fantasy. But living there would be impossible once it turned cold.

Northern Michigan was brutal during the winter months. My parents told me stories of snowdrifts covering the front windows like curtains or giant ice balls floating onto the shore. Living on the water could be downright dangerous.

Kip lived on a houseboat and he was fine, though. I wouldn't have minded talking to him about that or . . . well, in general.

Only because he was one of the few people I knew in Starlight Cove. It wasn't because of the way he listened as I spoke, as though hearing every word. Or the way his glower could turn so quickly into a smile.

Kip was appealing. No doubt about that. But he was on my mind only because I had some free time and needed information.

Keep telling yourself that, Fancy Pants.

Letting out a deep breath, I picked up the phone and called him.

Chapter Thirteen

One hour later, Kip Whittaker rumbled up in front of my parents' house in a beaten-up Land Cruiser, kayaks attached to the roof. He sat behind the wheel in a pair of sunglasses and a navy T-shirt that showed off his strong arms. He looked tanned and sporty, and much more attractive than I remembered.

When I called him to ask about winter on the houseboat, Kip chatted with me about it in detail. Then he said he was about to head out for a kayak ride and asked if I wanted to come. I said yes, but the moment I hung up, I knew I'd made a big mistake.

It wasn't a good idea to spend time with Kip outside of our research on *The Wanderer*. His quick smile already flashed through my brain more often than necessary. It made me feel unsettled—an emotion I did my best to avoid.

I tried to call him back to cancel, but he didn't pick up. So, I changed into a one-piece, found some bug spray in the cupboard, and tugged on a pair of fitted white slacks and a long-sleeved white linen shirt. When I walked out of the house, Kip burst out laughing.

"Where do you think we're going?" he demanded. "Heaven?"

"The white will reflect the sun." I slid into the worn leather seat of his truck. "And mosquitoes love me."

"Do you at least have a swimsuit on under that getup?" Before I could answer, he reached over and pulled down the shoulder of my shirt, brushing his thumb over the strap of my swimsuit. "Good." He backed out of the driveway, oblivious to the blush spotting my cheeks. "You're going to need it."

Kip headed for the main road out of town—the one I took up to the woods to visit my father. The windows were down, and the warm wind blew his spicy scent in my direction. My shoulder tingled where his thumb had brushed against my skin.

We drove for about ten minutes before Kip pulled off the road onto a small, tree-lined path. The Land Cruiser rumbled down a hill and into a rustic parking lot. There were a few other cars parked there, and a family climbed up from an embankment, dragging red and blue kayaks behind them.

"This is a pretty popular spot," he said. "I know a couple of back channels, though, so we'll have some privacy."

I bit my lip. Spending time alone with Kip in a remote setting was a risk I wasn't ready to take.

"The main route's probably good," I said. "Not as many hungry mosquitoes."

He grinned. "Scared to be alone with me?"

I flushed to my toes. Kip seemed to have an uncanny ability to read my mind.

Before I could think of a good response, he hopped out of the car and pulled our kayaks off the roof. His was yellow and mine red. We walked down a worn pathway to a slow stream.

The view was lush with green foliage, lily pads, and sunlight sparkling off the water. It was also shallow enough to see the silt along the bottom. Birds sang in the trees overhead, and the stillness of the afternoon hung in the air.

Kip slid both kayaks into the water, holding them by their ropes. Then, he whipped off his shirt to reveal his tanned and built upper body. His stomach muscles were perfectly defined, and the broad sculpt of his chest was covered with a soft layer of dark hair.

Embarrassed, I rolled up my pants and started to wade into the water.

"Seriously?" He stopped me with a word. "Get on your suit. Otherwise, you'll just be uncomfortable."

I should have brought a wetsuit.

"I don't want to get bitten," I pleaded.

"The mosquitoes don't come out until dusk," he said. "You'll be fine."

With a huge sigh, I stepped back onto the shore. "Turn around."

He gave me a dark look. "Sorry?"

"I won't take this off until you turn around," I insisted.

He smirked but, to his credit, turned around.

I slid out of my slacks and long-sleeved shirt and rushed them back up to the truck. Tossing them into the window, I raced back to the shore. The soles of my feet stung with sharp sticks and nettles. Then I jumped into my kayak and pushed off.

Kip turned. "Is your chastity intact?"

"That's for me to know and you . . ." I stopped, remembering how that expression ended.

He grinned, paddling up next to me.

"Could you repeat that?" His gaze traveled over me, settling too long on my bare arms and legs. "I didn't catch the end."

The way he was looking at me made my knees weak. The world seemed to slow as his eyes met mine. His dark gaze made me shiver.

It's not that I didn't want to spend time with him. I did, more than I cared to admit. I just didn't want to risk getting to know him and, maybe, liking him. It was much safer to keep a distance, since I was heading back to Boston at the end of the summer.

"Skip it," I told him.

He cleared his throat. "I brought some dinner for us." Turning, he pulled a large lunch bag up from the cargo space behind his seat. He zipped it open to reveal two sandwiches, grapes, crackers, cheese, chocolate bars, and bottles of regular and sparkling water. "I figured we'd head to a private beach and have dinner there."

I reached for a water bottle and took a long drink. This was getting more difficult by the minute. It was one thing to make an effort to resist the charms of the notorious Kip Whittaker. It was quite another to resist a man who would think to bring chocolate on a kayaking trip.

We paddled in silence down the stream. Sunlight filtered through trees and thick brush, and once in a while we passed a couple or a family. I enjoyed listening to the steady tinkle of the stream, the croak of frogs on lily pads, and the shudder of birds lifting from the trees.

The sun was low in the sky by the time Kip veered off the stream into a thick set of bushes. He slipped easily through the brush. After surveying the area for spiderwebs, I followed.

We pushed out of the stream into the lake, just off the shore of a remote beach. Dunes loomed overhead. A few houses stood high up on the hills, but otherwise we could have been on another planet.

"This is so peaceful." I stepped out of my kayak into the spongy sand and pulled it to shore.

Looking around, I marveled at the incredible display of speckled stones and pieces of driftwood in the shallow water. Somewhere, probably in school, I had learned that Lake Michigan was a freshwater lake that recycled its water something like every ninety-nine years. It was pretty amazing to think the water was new compared to the relics hidden in its depths.

I turned to comment on this to Kip and found him watching me. His eyes grazed over my legs and the fit of my swimsuit. Then, he turned and rummaged in the back of his kayak, producing a faded-gray T-shirt.

"Here," he said, tossing it at me. "To protect your chastity."

Blushing, I slid on the soft material. I pulled it a little closer, breathing in his unique smell.

"I'm starving," he said. "Let's eat."

He pulled a folded-up blanket out of the cargo area of his kayak and shook it out. The red-and-white pattern turned the beach into a formal dining room. I helped him set up the food, putting the cheese and crackers on a plate and opening bottles of sparkling water.

"Dig in," Kip said, handing me a sandwich.

It was stuffed full of chicken and thick-sliced Swiss cheese, with frisée lettuce and sliced tomatoes. I was just about to take a bite when he said, "Wait! I almost forgot."

He reached into a side pocket of the lunch bag. "I whisked you away on this trip, and you're not stocked with your typical supplies. So, here you go."

Kip handed me a travel-size Dijon mustard, A.1. steak sauce, and wasabi mayonnaise.

I stared at the condiments in surprise. The tiny jars brought me right back to that first day at Towboat. I remembered riffling through my bag, feeling like the new girl in school. The fact that he brought me condiments made me feel accepted somehow.

"Thank you," I said.

He smiled. "You're welcome."

I cracked open the jars and searched the lunch bag for a knife. I stuck it into the mayo, smeared it onto the sandwich, and took a big bite. The wasabi mayo was delicious and perfectly spicy.

I blinked against a sudden spark of tears. "Whoa."

"How is it?"

"Hot," I cried, laughing.

He handed me a bottle of water and our fingers brushed. Heat—not from the wasabi—rushed through my fingertips.

"This spot is such a find," I said, to steady my thinking. "Everything's so clean. The sand, the lake . . ."

Kip ran a hand through his rumpled hair. "It's a hidden treasure. Just like our water."

"That seems to be a big topic around here."

"The Great Lakes are the largest freshwater supply on the planet." He looked out at the sparkling surface of the lake. "The world's water supply is so polluted, places like California are suffering water shortages, and some places barely have clean water at all. The Great Lakes are a big resource. It's a battle to protect them."

"Maeve's big on water conversancy," I said, remembering what Kailyn told me about the nonprofit group. "Were you a part of that project?"

"I consulted with her on it."

"Huh." I took a sip of bottled water.

Maybe he suggested using the lighthouse as the centerpiece. That would explain why he was so annoyed that someone other than Maeve had won it.

"Would you be a part of the group?" I asked. "If she got it up and running?"

"Definitely." Kip took a bite of his sandwich, his face earnest in the muted light of the evening. "It's a cause that's important to me and to everyone around here. I hope she figures out a way to do it."

"Without the lighthouse," I said.

He grinned. "Without the lighthouse."

I decided to switch the subject.

"So, how do you think the meeting will go tomorrow?" I asked. "With the first mate's great-grandson?"

Kip frowned. "It is interesting that the first mate waited so long to tell everyone the light was out in the lighthouse. So, he might have something that will point us in the right direction. But I can't imagine what."

I held Kip's gaze for a moment. I still wasn't sure why he was so interested in researching *The Wanderer*. Was he interested in the history?

The lost treasure? Or could it be possible that he wanted to spend time with me?

Even though I wanted to ask, I was too scared to hear the answer. Kip probably had his own agenda, something that had nothing to do with me. But I couldn't help but hope his interest had more to do with the present than the past.

Of course, there was still the pesky matter of the girlfriend. Nothing he said seemed to indicate he was with anyone, but there was still that possibility.

Glancing down at my sandwich, I said, "This is great. It must be from Towboat."

He grinned. "Lucky guess. You know, Sami was working tonight. She was not happy I was taking you kayaking. She's my typical boating partner."

"Tell her I owe her one."

"I will." He took another bite of his sandwich and chewed it thoughtfully. "I hope she's doing okay. I see a lot of my sister in her. I don't know if that's a good thing."

"What do you mean?"

"Kelcee had a hard time when we were younger." He took a drink of water. "She had Sami right out of high school and got married too young. But once she got divorced, she went to culinary school and really turned her life around. I'm proud of her, for the way she started Towboat and made it what it is."

"Best pancakes I ever tasted," I said. "I can see why it's popular."

Kip nodded. "Yeah, but before she got good, it was the locals that made it possible for her to stay in business. They rallied behind her. That's one thing about Starlight Cove. We protect our own." He gazed out at the lake. "There have been times I thought of leaving, that people tried to convince me there was something better out there . . ." He turned his gaze on me. "But this is my home."

The words impressed me. When I first met Kip, he seemed like some sort of Starlight Cove vigilante. I assumed he was committed to small-town life because he didn't want to believe there was a whole, big world out there that had nothing to do with him. Now, I could see he was loyal to the town that protected his sister when she needed it the most. Somehow, that made him even more attractive.

Dangerous thoughts. Not ones to keep having on a deserted beach.

"What do you think of Starlight Cove so far?" Kip asked.

I reached into the cooler and pulled out a chocolate bar.

"It's hard to fault a place with this much chocolate." I held it out. "I'll split this with you."

Kip chuckled. He accepted a few squares and I bit into my half. Dark chocolate and sea salt lingered on my tongue.

"It's from Macaroons," he said. "If you haven't tried the fudge there, you're missing out."

"Oh I have," I said, smiling. "I've loved that place for years."

We looked at each other, and his gaze wandered down to my lips. Quickly, I reached for another piece of chocolate.

Kip glanced at the sky. "We should head back," he said. "It's getting late. We don't want to get stuck out here."

I could think of several reasons why I wouldn't mind getting stuck in the wilderness with Kip Whittaker. Still, I got up to help him pack.

We folded the blanket and put the leftovers away. Then, I lifted his shirt over my head, preparing to give it back. He stopped me, resting a warm hand on my back.

"Keep it on," he said. "The mosquitoes will be out soon."

I pulled it back down, my skin tingling from his touch. Holding the material close, I climbed back into the kayak and started the trip back home.

Chapter Fourteen

I whipped down Main Street on my bike, fifteen minutes before the scheduled meeting time with the first mate's great-grandson. The wind tried to undo my pinned-up hair, and the scent of fudge and fresh flowers hung thick in the air. My phone buzzed just as I locked my bike in the bike rack.

Kip. Picking up, I said, "Hi."

"I'm stuck at work." He sounded grumpy. "I'm not going to make it."

My good mood faded. "Darn. I was looking forward to showing off my sunburn."

Apparently, the SPF 50 I'd slathered on was no match for the time we'd spent in the great outdoors. My chest and shoulders were as red as a cherry.

"Ouch," Kip said. "Well, I'm going to call this guy and cancel."

"Don't do that," I said. "I'm already here."

"Then be careful." Kip's tone went gruff. "He runs with a rough crowd. I don't like the idea of you there alone. People are . . . saying things."

"Like what?" I tightened the lock on my bike.

"That you came up here this summer to find the treasure."

I laughed. "That's not even close to the truth."

For a split second, I considered telling Kip the real reason I was in town. I only had a few weeks to prove that my great-grandfather didn't walk away with the silver, or we'd lose our family home. Of course, I wasn't sure revealing that much information was a good idea.

"Just be careful," Kip said. "If I've heard this stuff, this guy's heard it, too."

I leaned against the wooden wall of the restaurant and watched the tourists pass by. "Thanks for the warning. But if you were really worried, you wouldn't have stood me up."

Kip chuckled. "I'll find a way to make it up to you."

Even though he might not have meant anything by it, I couldn't help but feel a thrill of anticipation as I hung up the phone.

Inside Towboat, it was cool and dark. I claimed a table in the middle of the restaurant and ordered a Coke. It was busy, so Kip's worry over the great-grandson seemed silly. That is, until he walked through the door.

The dude was huge. He stood about six foot five, with arms bigger than all the Hendersons put together. He scowled at the diners as though deciding which one to fight first. When he spotted me, he licked his lips.

"Dawn Conners?" he asked, walking up to the table.

"Yes," I said. "You must be Dusty."

"There beer here?"

I handed him a menu. "It's more of a food place."

"There's a bar down the street." His beady eyes swept over me. "Let's go."

Crap.

I was not going anywhere with this guy. He was 275 pounds of pure muscle.

"Sorry." I opened my menu. "I'm meeting someone after this. The food's great, though, and lunch is on me. I appreciate you talking to me."

Dusty took a seat. When he put his arms on the table, it actually jumped, as though he'd hit it. He ordered two burgers with the works, a double order of onion rings, and a chocolate milk shake. My chicken sandwich seemed wimpy in comparison.

"So, what's this all about?" Dusty asked. He drummed his fingers against the table and cased the room.

"Well, since you're the great-grandson of the first mate on *The Wanderer* and I'm the great-granddaughter of the Captain, I thought we could compare notes," I said, in a lively tone. "Talk history."

Dusty gave a sharp sniff. "Bullshit. You're looking for that treasure."

I drew back. "I . . . I want to know what happened the night of the wreck."

"Dawn," said a familiar voice. "I didn't expect to see you here."

I looked up to find Sal standing next to the table, a black baseball cap pulled low over his eyes. Before I could stop him, he grabbed a chair and sat with his back facing the entrance of the restaurant.

"I'm Sal Reynolds," he said, extending his hand to Dusty. "You guys talking about *The Wanderer*?"

Ughh. Now was *not* the time.

"Sal, we're having a meeting—"

Dusty eyed him. "You the guy I talked to on the phone?"

"No," I said, my voice firm. "Kip couldn't make it. He—"

"Kip Whittaker?" Sal said easily. "He's been helping Dawn do research. I've been trying to sit in on one of their meetings, but so far I have yet to be invited." He grinned at Dusty. "Mind if I hang out? I'm making a documentary."

Much to my annoyance, Dusty's bloodshot eyes lit up. "That's cool, man."

Sal nodded, his hair shooting a waft of something like gasoline in my direction. "So, what's your play in all this?"

"My great-grandfather was the first mate of the ship," he said. "But I figured Dawn might have a lead on the treasure."

Sal laughed. "Do you?" he asked, turning to me.

I sighed. "I'm not looking for the treasure."

Dusty stuck his finger in his mouth and peeled off the tip of his thumbnail with his teeth. He spat it out. I cringed, hoping it didn't land in the salad of the woman sitting next to us.

"So, was your great-grandfather a big shot like Captain Conners?" Sal asked Dusty.

He gave a bitter laugh. "Yeah, right. Conners and my great-grandpop were loggers together. They were going to start a shipping business together, but Conners got too big for his britches. Forgot where he came from. They were supposed to be best friends, but Conners ran off with his girl."

"Wait, what?" I couldn't picture Fitzie with anyone other than my great-grandmother. "Who was she?"

Dusty shrugged. "Don't know. He married her."

"Madeline," I breathed. "She dated your great-grandfather first?"

Sal cackled. "Looks like you two could have been related."

The food arrived in a rush of onions and grease. Sal waved off the waiter's offer to take his order. I tried not to watch as Dusty tore into his burger like he hadn't eaten in a week. He polished off the first one and was onto the second before I'd picked up a French fry.

"Why do you say my great-grandfather got too big for his britches?" I asked.

"Because he was a pain in the ass," Dusty told me. "Before *The Wanderer* went down, he put my great-grandpop in the brig."

"No shit," Sal said, leaning forward. "How come?"

It struck me that Sal and Dusty might make good drinking buddies.

Dusty gnawed at an onion ring. "He accused him of trying to take over."

"The ship?" I asked.

"Yeah." Dusty finished his second burger in one quick bite. "Conners was a greedy SOB. He used to bring chickens on board and eat five-course meals in his cabin while the rest of the men ate shit. He

155

cheated them at their wages, didn't do his fair share of work. Everyone saw his true colors when he ran off with the silver."

"Allegedly," I said.

Dusty jumped. "You a cop?"

"Huh?" I said. "No. Why?"

His eyes became tiny slits. "Cops and lawyers say that sort of thing."

"I'm not a cop."

Sal snorted. "She's not a cop."

"Why's she so interested, then?" Dusty asked.

I glanced at Sal. "Because I—"

"Because she's a treasure hunter." Sal rubbed his thinning hair. "You may as well admit it."

"I am not," I insisted. "I just want proof that the silver is still out there."

A smile gashed through Dusty's face. "So, you *are* trying to find it."

I sighed. "I guess it would help." I took a sip of Coke. "So, your great-grandfather never said anything about it?"

"Nah." Dusty pulled the straw out of his drink and used it to pick at his teeth. "He would have been in on the heist, though, if Conners gave him a chance. The silver or the whiskey."

"The whiskey's still down there," I told him. "It's just too dangerous to get it."

Sal raised his eyebrows. "Yeah?"

Dusty pushed his plate away. "Look, I gotta go. I got to get to the library to teach a class on the Franco-Spanish War."

"You're a teacher?" I said, baffled.

Dusty puffed out his chest. "The old folks call me a walking encyclopedia. You really should interview me for your documentary," he told Sal.

"I might do that."

Dusty gave a loud sniff. "If you find out anything good, let me know." Then he kicked back from the table and lumbered out the door.

"Jeez." I shook my head as he left.

Sal crushed a straw wrapper. "You can say that again."

I was tempted to give Sal a piece of my mind for interrupting my meeting. At the same time, Dusty had only stuck around in hopes of being part of the documentary. If it weren't for Sal, I never would have learned that Dusty's great-grandfather tried to take over the ship. That meant Fitzie had enemies, and there was a strong motive for someone to frame him.

Taking a bite of my chicken sandwich, I looked at Sal. "That was interesting. I didn't know my great-grandmother was serious with anyone before Fitzie."

Sal slid his hand through his hair. "I'm sure it irritated the first mate to have his low-class friend swoop in and get the girl."

"Low-class friend?" I echoed.

He nodded. "Even though Conners became captain, the first mate's family was rich. They lost their money during the Depression. It's interesting that his family blames their failures on your great-grandfather. The easiest scapegoat is one who can't fight back."

Despite my reluctance to talk to Sal, it didn't sound like he was against my great-grandfather. In fact, it sounded like he was for him. But maybe Sal was just skilled at getting people to talk.

"Well, thanks for the information." I signaled the waiter for the check. "I should probably head out."

"Hint taken." Sal got to his feet and slid on his sunglasses. "Sorry to bust in on your meeting, but you and I really should talk sometime. I bet I've got information you'd be interested in."

I hesitated. I only had a few weeks left to answer the insurance company. If I ran out of leads, I might have no choice but to talk to Sal.

"Maybe," I said. "We'll see."

He gave me a sly grin. "I'll look forward to it."

There was still something sleazy about Sal that I didn't like. But maybe he could tell me something that would point me in the right direction. The trick, of course, would be to not tell him anything more than I wanted him to know.

~

I was leaving Towboat when Kailyn called to ask if I wanted to take a walk during her lunch hour. We met on the boardwalk. To my surprise, she couldn't stop complimenting my outfit.

"You look great," she cried. "So casual!"

"Thanks," I said, embarrassed.

Since I hadn't wanted to dress up for the great-grandson of the first mate, I had on a white T-shirt and pair of soft jean shorts, a marked difference from my typical starched dresses.

"This is a really good look for you, Dawn." Kailyn tugged at my shirt. "You're so pretty. This makes you a lot more approachable."

"What do you mean?"

"You're intimidating," Kailyn said. "Especially when you're all dressed up."

Intimidating? That's not how I felt on the inside. In fact, it was pretty much the opposite.

"Dressed like this," Kailyn continued, "you look like you belong on the beach. Especially with that sunburn." She waggled her eyebrows. "You must have been up to something fun. I hope it involved a boy."

I flushed. Should I tell Kailyn? Even though we were getting to be friends, I still didn't know her that well. Besides, I still didn't want to admit I liked Kip.

Before I could make a decision either way, her phone rang.

"Shoot!" She gave me an apologetic look. "Do you mind? It's the showing I just did."

"Go ahead," I said.

It was another beautiful day. The sand underneath my feet was as soft as milled flour. Since it was getting hot, I waded up to my knees.

The water was freezing, as though someone had melted a billion ice cubes and dumped the excess into the lake. I relished the feeling of my calves going numb in contrast to the tight sunburn on my shoulders.

The sun sparkled against the sand at the bottom of the lake like gold. Tourists dotted the beach chairs in the distance, a teenager pulled a white chair into the shallows of the water, and a family sat on a sandbar, their kids splashing happily in the waves.

Was the weather this calm the day *The Wanderer* went down? I imagined Captain Fitzie and his crew relaxing on the ship, enjoying the sunshine. Maybe he even set the course and was in the middle of a poker game when the clouds started to roll in.

I shivered. Before he knew it, he was battling the wind and rain, desperate to survive and save his men. The ship breaking apart beneath him must have sounded like a firing squad.

"Hey," Kailyn shouted.

I turned to see her waving from the shore.

"Hoping to get swept away so you can trick some hot sailor into rescuing you?" she bellowed.

Laughing, I waded back to shore. The second I got there, Kailyn bumped into me with her hip, almost knocking me back in.

"I think I sold another property!" She looked thrilled. "Waterfront. They're going to decide on their offer and call me back tomorrow. They might decide tonight, though. They really want this house." She pulled out her cell phone, checked it, and then grinned. "You are good for business, my friend. Everyone thinks I know what I'm talking about since I sold the ultimate waterfront property to you."

I held out my hand. "Put me on the phone with them. I'll tell them your definition of a fixer-upper."

Kailyn cracked up. "You're the one who placed the bid." Her face got serious. "So, are you excited about the historical society?"

I knew she was going to bring that up.

"I'm nervous," I admitted. "What if they start throwing things at me? Demanding I give the lighthouse back to the people of Starlight Cove?"

"Listen." She stopped walking and gripped my hands. "I would not put you in the line of fire. These women want to help you. Besides, I'll be right there with you."

"Thank you for being so nice to me," I said.

Kailyn cocked her head. "You don't have to butter me up. If you want to get some more half-priced food at the Harbor Resort, say the word."

"I'm being serious," I said, refusing to let her dodge the compliment. "I'm really happy we're getting to be friends."

"Aw." Behind her sunglasses, Kailyn flushed. "You're going to make me cry. This mascara is not waterproof, and, to be honest, I really can't afford to mess up my makeup right now, because there's a chance the client will call me again, and I'll have to skip out on being such a good friend to meet them for paperwork and . . ." Finally, she stopped rambling and gave me her dimpled smile. "I'm glad we're friends, too."

"I was thinking," I said, encouraged. "We could go to Maddie's tomorrow night."

"The bar?" Kailyn cried. "It's not really your type of place."

"What's my type of place?"

She laughed. "*Not* Maddie's."

Hmmph.

"We could have a drink," I said. "Have some fun . . . hang out with the Hendersons . . ."

Kailyn grinned. "Oh, *I* get it," she said. "Someone has a crush on the Hendersons. Am I right?"

I gave an innocent smile. "Something like that."

Chapter Fifteen

Maddie's was a small shack just off Main Street. The front yard was littered with weeds, and a kitschy sign over the front door read **ENTER AT YOUR OWN RISK.** The wood practically shook with the reverberation of a drum set from the band playing inside. The front lawn was deserted, and if it weren't for the noise and a full parking lot next door, the place might have passed for abandoned.

"Don't be fooled," Kailyn said, fluffing her hair. "The back patio opens up onto the sand. It'll be packed. The last time I was in here, I lost an earring, a bracelet, and my dignity, and I didn't even get kissed. Do you think I look okay?"

Kailyn wore a pair of white shorts that showed off tanned and curvy legs, a pair of strappy black sandals, and a black shirt blooming with hot-pink flowers. The flowers matched her lipstick and the scent of her perfume, if such a thing were possible. She looked fantastic.

"Like a supermodel," I said. "I feel ridiculous with my hair like this."

When I arrived at Kailyn's house, she had ripped out my bobby pins and gone to work with a flat iron. By the time she was finished, my hair was perfectly straight and fell just past my shoulders.

I drew the line at her attempts to get me to change from my straight-legged navy pants into one of her flouncy skirts. My white silk top was risky enough. It fell off my right shoulder, revealing the strap of the camisole I wore underneath.

"You sure this place isn't empty?" I asked.

"Trust me," she said, pushing open the front door.

Maddie's was packed. Wall-to-wall people of all ages played pool and darts and danced to the cover band. The back doors were wide open and led right onto the beach. It smelled like beer, burgers, and onion rings.

I wrinkled my nose.

She laughed, watching me. "You hate it! I knew you would."

It was not my type of place. For one thing, the music was much too loud. Some local band played and the drummer whaled away at his drums. The space was claustrophobic, with knickknacks cluttering every surface. Plus, the room teemed with people. I'd lived in a city for years, but had never warmed to crowds.

"Do you want to leave?" Kailyn asked.

If we left, she wouldn't get to hang out with Carter.

"No, I just . . . I never would have pictured this, based on the front."

"We try to keep out the tourists." She winked. "You're one of us now."

I stood up a little straighter.

As we walked to the bar, Kailyn gave a high five to an older man and said something to a woman about vacation property.

"What do you want to drink?" she asked.

"Hmm . . ." I scanned the options posted on the wall. There were a couple of unique creations, like a Beer Float and something called a Sand Doom. "A cider beer. That sounds summery."

The bartender, a kind-looking man with a face as wrinkled as tree bark, reached across the bar and gave a half hug to Kailyn. "Where have you been?"

"Ralph!" She returned the hug. "This crazy codger is an old friend of my dad's," she told me. "Emphasis on *old,* right, Ralph?"

"You're always a charmer," he teased. "What can I get for you?"

Kailyn and Ralph caught up on local news and gossip while I surveyed the bar to find the Hendersons. It didn't take much effort. I could see Carter outside on the porch doing something sporty, but it was hard to tell what.

I hoped the night would be a success. I didn't like surprises, but Kailyn seemed like the type of person who would. I had a feeling she would be thrilled to spend time with Carter, and I hoped I was right.

The second the bartender moved on to help other customers, I said, "We should get some fresh air. It's a nice night."

She looked in the direction I was pointing. "I know what you're interested in!"

"You're wrong," I sang as we walked out to the porch. "We're here tonight because Carter asked about *you.* He said he wanted a rematch in darts because you kicked his ass."

Kailyn stumbled into a nearby chair, almost knocking it over. "You can't be serious," she gasped.

I laughed out loud. "So serious."

"Why didn't you tell me?" she cried. "I would have worn something else. Done my hair different. Gotten plastic surgery. I would have—"

"*Stop,*" I insisted. "You are perfect. Besides, it's no big deal. We're just going to hang out." Outside, we came to a sudden stop. "Look at that."

Carter stood on the sand with a group of guys. It was dark out, and they were in the middle of a volleyball game. He held a glow-in-the-dark ball in his hands, and the net was lined with glow-in-the-dark tape.

Cody stood to the side of the court, shirt off. His muscles rippled in the moonlight, and he rubbed oil across his barrel chest.

"Should someone tell him there's no sun?" I cracked.

Kailyn giggled. "Fifty bucks its self-tanner."

We slipped into the wooden benches lining the outside of the bar to watch the game. Carter headed back to serve. Kailyn could not stop staring at his six-pack. He lifted up his arm to hit the ball, and she gave an appreciative coo.

Cody, on the opposite side, popped the ball up for his team member to spike. Carter's team defended, and the play went back and forth. A tall guy on Carter's team slammed a spike into the glow-in-the-dark line. Some sort of a grunting, chest-bump, cave-manlike ritual followed that left Kailyn fanning herself with a cocktail napkin.

Carter was about to head back to the serving line when he noticed us watching. He gave a shy wave.

"Hey!" he said.

"Hi, Carter," Kailyn called.

"We're rooting for you," I said.

He seemed to strike a pose before giving the ball a strong whack. Kailyn pounded her drink and murmured something unintelligible.

"What?" I whispered.

"I said," she mumbled, *"I like the way you hit it, Henderson."*

I burst out laughing.

It took a few more shirtless plays, but Carter's team won the game. Cody was annoyed, his collection of muscles rippling with irritation. His team made threats and promised a rematch. Then the guys took a break to get drinks.

Cody lifted his hand in greeting but headed inside with his buddies. Carter, on the other hand, walked right over. He kept sneaking peeks at Kailyn, much to my delight.

"What are you two up to?" he asked.

"Enjoying the night," Kailyn said. "It's gorgeous out here."

I stifled a laugh.

Carter nodded, oblivious. "So many stars."

The night was an inky black, but patches of the sky seemed lit with an ethereal glow. A full, white moon hung just over the horizon. I could hear the shadow of the lake as it lapped against the edge of the sand.

"Shoot." I looked down at my drink. "I'm out." Hopping up, I said, "What can I get you guys?"

"I'll get it," Carter said. "Kailyn, what would you like?"

"Sit down." I gave him a gentle shove toward the bench. "I owe you after the work you've been doing for me. I'll grab you a beer."

I rushed off. Once inside, I looked over my shoulder. Carter and Kailyn were talking nonstop.

I ordered the drinks, chatted with Ralph again, and was about to head back outside when a deep voice said, "So, you found our fun little bar."

My skin tingled before I even turned to see Kip. His eyes were a deeper blue than usual, and his hair was rumpled in all the right places. His gaze wandered to my shoulder, where my shirt showed skin. My hands were full, so I made a failed effort to tug it back up with my chin. He reached over and did it for me.

A smile tugged at the corner of my mouth. "Thanks."

I felt shy after our day at the beach. I now considered him a friend, which was a big step. Still, even that made me nervous. I didn't want to read into friendly gestures, if that's all they were.

"What are you doing here?" I asked.

Kip held up a to-go container. "Best chicken tenders in town." He nodded at my armful of drinks. "Drowning your sorrows?"

"I'm here with Kailyn. She's talking to Carter Henderson." Hesitating only for a brief second, I said, "Would you like to join us?"

The noise of the band muted as our eyes met. A slow flush started in my cheeks, but I didn't break eye contact.

He cleared his throat. "Sure."

"Great." I led the way toward the patio, conscious of the fact that my shirt dipped once again. When I walked out with Kip, the look on Kailyn's face was priceless.

"Kip Whittaker," she squealed. "It's so good to see you!"

I had no doubt that if Kailyn had the ability to freeze time, she would have. Then she would have pummeled me for details on how I managed to coerce Kip into joining us.

"Hey," Carter said, giving him a high five. "What are you up to?"

"Grabbing some dinner." Kip settled in on the bench. "I still haven't figured out how to fry a chicken on the houseboat."

"It's that one, isn't it?" Carter pointed at the marina, which was close to the bar and packed with yachts and speedboats. "The log cabin?"

In the dim lights from the dock, I spotted a boat constructed from logs, with a copper-green roof. It was two stories, with a large main floor and a smaller one on top.

"That's your houseboat?" I said, fascinated.

I should have guessed Kip's boat wouldn't be like the others. But I didn't imagine a full-blown log cabin on a mini-barge.

"It's really cute," I added.

Kip's mouth dropped open. *"Cute?"* he demanded. "Try rustic and manly." Everyone laughed, and he opened his box of takeout. "How's business, Carter?"

The two launched into a conversation about the hardware store. Kailyn kept trying to make eye contact with me, but I avoided her gaze. She was clearly dying to ask if anything was going on between us, and I didn't know how to answer.

Yes, I like him, I'd say. *Just like everybody else.*

It might seem significant that Kip came and sat with us, but maybe it wasn't. I still didn't know if he had a girlfriend. Besides, Starlight Cove was a small town. It might be considered rude to decline an invitation. The way he looked at me, though, made me hope there could be something more between us.

The volleyball team came back from the bar and demanded a rematch. They were down one player and, after a round of greetings and high fives with Kip, asked if he wanted to play.

"I have to get back." He raised an eyebrow. "Maybe one of the girls would?"

Cody looked like he'd swallowed a bug. "I don't know . . ."

Carter lit up. "Kailyn's good," he said. "Hey, do you want to play?"

To my surprise, she jumped right up. "Absolutely."

She kicked off her shoes and headed out onto the sandy court with confidence. She was up first to serve, and not only did she hit it overhand hard and fast, but she aced the other team. I started to cheer, whistling and clapping my hands.

"I can't believe that," I said, turning to Kip. "What a lucky shot."

"Don't be fooled," he murmured. "Kailyn is one of the best beach volleyball players around here. That's why Cody didn't want her to play."

I watched as she hit another serve. The other team scrambled but got it over the net. She helped set it up and then hit a perfect spike from the back row.

"Wow." I watched as she high-fived Carter and everyone else on her team. "People never fail to surprise me."

"Clearly," Kip said, in a teasing tone. "You seemed surprised my boat was . . ." He frowned. "What was it? Oh right. *Cute.*"

I laughed. "I can't tell from here. It's hard to make a fair judgment."

The words hung between us for a moment. The thwack of the ball, the music inside, and even the waves against the shore seemed to go quiet.

My stomach dropped as he said, "Well, why don't you come see it?"

The boat was only a few steps from the bar. I could check it out and be back before Kailyn even knew I'd left. Still, there was that tiny, terrifying detail that I would be alone again with Kip.

Letting out a breath, I slid off my shoes and then strolled with him across the sand toward the marina. The further the bar receded, the more I panicked. This was different from the kayaking trip. It was dark out, my shirt revealed way too much skin, and he smelled so good, it was distracting.

"Carter seems pretty interested in Kailyn," Kip said, glancing at me.

I cleared my throat. "Yeah. They'd be a great match."

"I thought you weren't into matchmaking." He raised an eyebrow. "Based on the day we met at the beach."

Was he flirting with me? If he was, I didn't know how to respond. I've never been good at flirting. It makes me feel ridiculous. Instead of commenting, I focused on the feeling of the sand beneath my feet. It was cold and grainy and, for whatever reason, helped me to relax.

We reached the marina, and Kip turned to face me. The dock lights glowed, and the dark stubble on his face seemed more attractive than ever.

"I have a few house rules," he said in a low tone.

"House *rules*?" I echoed.

"They're not optional."

This was the bossy Kip Whittaker I was not too fond of.

I shrugged. "I'll listen. I can't guarantee I'll comply."

"Rule number one: No high heels. I don't need you to poke a hole in the floor of my boat and sink it."

I held up my shoes. "These are pumps. It's different."

"Rule number two: My sister might have left a romantic comedy or two in my home. If you see one, know that it's hers."

I smirked. "Not buying it. But go on."

"Rule number three . . ." His gaze dropped to my lips and lingered there. "If I hear the word *cute*, I'm throwing you overboard."

My breath caught. "Thanks for the heads up."

I followed him onto the dock and was about to walk through the front door, when he said in surprise, "Sami!"

I stopped short. I could tell he had no idea his niece was there. I hung back on the dock looking at the expanse of stars over the water, not sure whether he still wanted me to come in.

"Sorry to crash," she said. "Mom was being annoying, so I came here to watch a movie."

Kip cleared his throat. "Gotcha. I have a visitor . . ." He poked his head outside. "What are you doing out here?"

Quickly, I adjusted the sleeve of my shirt to cover my shoulder.

"Do you still want me to come in?" I whispered.

He gave me a funny look. "Of course."

How mortifying. I must have imagined the whole attraction thing. He probably brought me over just to show me his house. Embarrassed, I tucked my bag over my shoulder to hold my shirt in place.

"I was just looking at the stars," I said, before heading in. "It's such a nice night."

Sami sat on a leather couch in the living room, next to a small stone fireplace. She wore a pair of black stretch pants and an enormous red T-shirt that fit her like a Snuggie. Spotting me, her face scrunched up in confusion.

"What are you doing here?" she demanded.

"Sami!" Kip scolded. "Don't be rude."

"Sorry," she mumbled.

"I wanted to see the houseboat," I said quickly. "Decorating ideas. For the lighthouse."

To back up my claim, I turned to survey the space.

The houseboat was pretty impressive. Wooden walls, exposed beams on the ceiling, and worn leather furniture gave the space a masculine and rugged feel, while cheerful rugs and cozy-looking throws pulled it all together. A small kitchen was just off the main room, along with a bathroom and a closet. I glanced at the wooden staircase that led up to the bedroom and quickly turned my attention back to the door that led to the deck.

I shook my head. "This is cool. It's really . . ."

Kip was down on his knees by the fire, lighting kindling. He gave me a dark look.

"Cozy," I said. "It's perfect." And he smiled.

The houseboat was the type of environment I had imagined the other day, when I dared to think about living in the lighthouse. Small, functional, and brimming with personal details. I was oddly pleased to discover Kip and I had the same taste.

"Are you staying?" Sami asked.

"Dawn and I can sit on the deck and talk," he said easily. "Watch your movie."

Sami tossed the remote control on the couch.

"No, thanks. I'm out." Giving me a cutting look, she stalked to the front door. "I'll go to Rachel's house. She's been texting me all night."

"Let me know when you get there."

Sami swept by me without so much as a look, and the door banged shut behind her.

I cringed. "Sorry. I didn't mean to . . ."

"Teenagers." Kip shook his head. "It's not your fault." He headed to the kitchen area. "What would you like to drink? Chai tea?"

"Sounds good." Then, I realized he was teasing me. "Decaf, if you've got it."

Kip filled up a portable coffeepot with water and coffee, fired up the gas burners, and set it up to boil. When it was ready, he dumped in a generous amount of cream and handed the mug to me. Then he perched on the couch and gave me a serious look.

"There's something I need to tell you," he said. "I hope you don't get mad."

In my experience with Kip, he didn't worry too much about making me mad. He said whatever he wanted. With that in mind, I figured he was kidding.

"How could I get mad when you make me coffee like this?" I asked, holding it up. The creamer was hazelnut and added a bold, nutty flavor.

"You might." His tone was serious. "I haven't been entirely honest with you."

My stomach dropped. "What do you mean?"

Kip got to his feet and walked over to the mantel above the fireplace. The fire crackled and popped as he took something out of a small box. He settled back on the couch and slid three faded pieces of silver across the table.

"Morgan silver dollars," he said. "The imprint is extremely rare. They match the description of the ones lost on *The Wanderer*."

I set down my coffee cup. "Where did you get them?"

"My great-grandfather's coin collection." Kip ran his hand through his hair. "It's the real reason I started comparing his letters to his office records. I wanted to figure out where they came from."

I stared at the coins. Even though I didn't know the exact value, some were worth hundreds, if not thousands, of dollars apiece.

"You had these the whole time?" I asked.

"Yes."

"But . . ." My anger began to mount.

The frustration I felt at my father for keeping secrets from me rushed back to the surface. Come to find out, Kip Whittaker had done the same thing. I had suspected he was hiding something, but I had no idea it would be this.

The fact that Dr. Whittaker had the Morgan coins in his collection made it clear that Fitzie had used the silver for his own benefit. I could imagine them as Exhibit A in the insurance company's case against my family.

"Why didn't you say anything?" I demanded.

"If I would have showed you this that first day, you would have thought I was calling Fitzie a crook."

"You're not, then?"

"No." Kip's handsome face was earnest. "It just proves he was alive."

It was hard to get mad at Kip for hiding this when I was keeping secrets, too. I still hadn't told him what my father said about the night of the wreck, and I didn't plan to. It was too risky to have that information out there until I knew what it meant.

I picked up one of the coins and squeezed it tight. The silver was cool to the touch and heavy in my palm. It was hard to believe that it once passed through my great-grandfather's hand, made it through the torment of the storm, and, somehow, ended up here.

It carried such sadness with it: the men that were lost, the pain of my great-grandmother, the accusations that plagued my family name. It hit me that I didn't know a thing about my great-grandfather.

Yes, I wanted to believe that he was the man he seemed to be in the love letters to my great-grandmother, but how was that possible? My father confirmed he was alive after the ship sank, Kip had a letter clearly penned by his hand, and now here was some of the very silver in question, sitting on the coffee table like a centerpiece.

The news my father gave me that night at the lighthouse shook my confidence. But seeing the silver destroyed it. What was the point in trying to prove Captain Fitzie was innocent, when it was so clear he wasn't?

I couldn't help but feel angry with my great-grandfather. Thanks to the letters between my great-grandparents, I had bought into the idea that a man could love his wife beyond reason. That gave me an excuse to avoid getting close to the men I dated. They could never live up to the Captain Fitzie standard of romance.

Based on these coins, the Captain Fitzie standard of romance did not exist. He claimed to love my great-grandmother above all else, but, clearly, he loved money and power more. That was the only explanation for surviving the crash, hiding out, and walking away with the treasure, never to be heard from again.

"The coins could have washed up onshore," Kip said, as though reading my mind. "Or they could have been part of his payment for captaining the ship. There are a number of ways they could have gotten . . ."

"Into the hands of your great-grandfather?" I said. "Come on."

I dropped the coin back on the table and put my head in my hands. We sat in silence. In the distance, I could hear the music from the bar.

"I should get back to Kailyn," I said, getting to my feet.

Disappointment numbed me. Not only did seeing the coins make it even more difficult to imagine proving Fitzie's innocence, I couldn't get past the betrayal. It was heartbreaking that my great-grandmother loved Fitzie so much, only to have him leave.

Kip got to his feet. "Let me walk you back."

I held up my hand. "Thanks, but I'm fine. I need some time to think."

I stood on the dock and stared at the dark expanse of the water, my heart full of disappointment. I'd gone to Kip's house in the hope that something romantic would happen. Instead, I was walking away with the knowledge that love was as flimsy as a fairy tale.

Chapter Sixteen

I was in a black mood after learning about Dr. Whittaker's coin collection, so it was somewhat annoying to be around my parents. They were as cheerful as the sunshine, making breakfast and getting ready for some antiquing getaway.

My father noticed my mood and ruffled my hair. "What's wrong with you?"

I sat down at the kitchen table, cradling a mug of my mother's chicory coffee. "Kip's great-grandfather had some of the silver coins," I said. "In his collection."

"So?" my father asked, stirring a pan of oatmeal.

"They were Morgan silver dollars."

"Those aren't rare. He could have gotten them anywhere."

"They were the same year and imprint as the ones lost on *The Wanderer*."

My father stopped stirring. "You saw them?"

I gave a glum nod. "So, I guess that pretty much answers that."

My mother breezed to the stove. She dropped dried cherries, blueberries, and a handful of almonds into the pan of oatmeal. "What does it answer?"

"Dr. Whittaker helped Fitzie," I said. "The fact that he paid him off with missing silver means he had access to it. He stole it."

My father tightened his sweater around his shoulders. "That's bunk. They could have paid him in silver."

"It's not like they had direct deposit back then," my mother chirped, patting my father on the shoulder.

I shrugged. But their words gave me hope.

"How many coins did he have?" my father asked, joining me at the table.

"Three." I breathed in the rich scent of the coffee.

My mother poured the oatmeal into ceramic bowls. "Oh come on," she said. "Three dollars is hardly a treasure trove. The dollar was the equivalent to maybe twelve or thirteen dollars back then. So, Fitzie paid the doctor a decent sum to help him out, but it wasn't anything outrageous." She pointed a spoon at us. "I dare you to argue."

My father's booming laugh bounced around the kitchen. "Let's unleash your mother on the insurance company."

She swatted his arm, setting the bowls on the table with a clink. "I mean it. Three coins is hardly a windfall. I wouldn't give up now."

I bit my lip, irritated to see them taking the threat so lightly.

My family had shared so many special moments in this kitchen. Packing sandwiches for Fourth of July picnics with my grandmother, chasing a Pomeranian around the table the summer they babysat their friends' dog, sitting with mugs of tea, listening to my father's latest adventure at sea . . . I wasn't ready to give that up, even if the evidence seemed stacked against us.

"It's not over." I picked a blueberry out of the oatmeal and rolled it between my fingers. "I'm just tired of hitting these roadblocks."

"It's the name of the game, kid," my father said. "If you want to be a treasure hunter, you need a thicker skin."

I dropped the blueberry back into the oatmeal.

"I don't want to be a treasure hunter," I told him.

175

"Too late." He waved his spoon at me. "Besides, the challenge is good for you. You can't stay dry and in one temperature all your life."

I rolled my eyes. "Thanks, Dad. I'll keep that in mind."

∼

The conversation with my parents put me in better spirits, but it didn't solve everything. In some ways, I was back to square one.

I decided to check on the progress of the mold treatments at the lighthouse. I needed to know that something I was doing was working.

I climbed up the ladder, unlocked the door, and cringed at the harsh smell of bleach. It was biting, but I was pleased to note that the disgusting speckles that once lined the walls of the main floor were gone.

"Take that, mold," I muttered.

I went up to the next floor to find the same thing. Encouraged, I went from floor to floor, my steps quickening as I neared the top. The bedroom floor was underway, the mold was almost destroyed, and it looked like things were in much better . . . I walked into the bedroom and came to an abrupt halt.

The window—the one Cody had fixed—was broken.

A small brick sat in the center of the room next to the patch in the floor. I picked my way through the broken glass and crouched down to look at it. A note was attached with yellowed string. In tight, angry letters, it read **GET OUT!!!**

A chill ran up my spine.

I walked over to the broken window, careful not to step on glass. The window wasn't visible from the shore, so the brick had to come from a passing boat. The aim was impressive, unless fifty other bricks just like it sat at the bottom of Lake Michigan.

Turning away from the window, I considered the mess.

It was so ironic. We'd kept this place closed for days. What if the window was broken the whole time?

Birds must have stayed away because of the strong bleach smell, but the mold would have kept growing and festering. The thought infuriated me.

I didn't know if I was fixing up the lighthouse to make it my home or to walk away. But it was my decision. Outsider or not, I did not deserve to have someone make that decision for me.

In the beginning, I was moved to tears by the vandalism. Now, I was moved to action. The lighthouse belonged to me. Its light was operated by the US Coast Guard. The destruction of lighthouse property could very well be a federal offense, which meant I didn't need to put up with this shit.

Turning on my heel, I headed straight for the Coast Guard to file a report.

~

The Coast Guard jumped into action. They communicated the information to beach patrol and the local police. They also spent an unnecessary amount of time discussing my personal safety. I assured them I was just fine—that this was about the lighthouse, not me.

Still, I was nervous.

The person vandalizing the lighthouse obviously had problems. What if I was the next target? I promised to take some precautions.

That afternoon, I decided to go for a bike ride to burn off my nervous energy. I was standing in my parents' garage when my cell phone buzzed in my pocket. I jumped a mile, still on edge from the safety warning.

The caller ID read Kip Whittaker, and I hesitated, thinking about the night before. Finally, I picked up.

"I heard from Beulah," he said, without prelude. "She found her mother's journal."

I sucked in a sharp breath. "Really?"

"Good news, huh? When do you want to meet with her?"

I brushed a spider off the wicker basket on my mother's bike, thinking. The journal meant having something in writing that, if in the wrong hands, could implicate my great-grandfather. That was a risk I wasn't ready to take.

"Kip, I think we should let it go," I said. "I don't want to see the journal."

He sighed. "You're thinking the worst."

"Then what's the best?" I demanded. "I see no good outcome here."

"Captain Fitzie was trying to protect your great-grandmother," he insisted. "The question is, from what? I know you're upset about the coins, but you knew the silver was out there. People have said that for years."

"It's not about that."

I twisted the edges of the tassels on the handlebars, wishing I could tell Kip about the pending investigation. But I still didn't know if I trusted him.

I didn't know if I had it in me to trust anyone.

"You owe it to yourself to find out the truth," Kip said. "You owe it to your family."

"Fine," I finally said. "But I want a guarantee that we won't photograph it, photocopy it, or walk away with a record of information that could hurt my family's reputation. Deal?"

"Deal." Kip's tone was serious. "She wants to meet Monday afternoon."

"That works. And Kip?"

"Yeah?"

Even though he was pushing me past my comfort zone, I was grateful. I needed to find the answer. Maybe this could help.

"Thanks," I said.

I hung up and stared out of the dim garage into the light of the day. Climbing onto the bike, I pushed down on the pedals and headed out to Starlight Cove, with no clear destination in mind.

Chapter Seventeen

I spent the day exploring the hills. On the way home, I stopped by the Henderson brothers' shop. Like always, it was packed with men hunting for that perfect tool and women looking for any excuse to find a repair project.

Cameron grabbed his hair in outrage when he saw me. "Dawn, it's disgusting someone smashed that window! That type of thing doesn't happen around here."

"The Coast Guard's keeping watch," I said. "It should get better."

"Put us on speed dial," he said. "Call day or night. We'd come right over."

A woman in a low-cut sundress overheard. "Ooh, is that standard?" she asked eagerly. "I mean, for repairs?"

I hid a smile and set out to find Carter. He was in the back, talking to a man about a circular saw. He gave a little wave and, once free, came right over.

"That was fun last night," he said. "I forgot how good Kailyn is at volleyball."

The night at Maddie's seemed like a long time ago, thanks to everything that had happened.

"She is," I said. Then, as if the idea just hit me, I added, "Carter, I think you should ask her out."

He scanned the store, as if to make sure his brothers weren't listening. Leaning in, he said, "Do you think she'd say yes?"

"Absolutely."

"Hmm." He fiddled with a box of nails. Then his freckled face lit up. "I have something for you! Cody found a box when we took out the boards in the lighthouse. Under the floor."

My breath caught. "What?"

"Follow me," Carter said, leading me back to Cody's office. "He said to tell you if it's not lighthouse paperwork, but some strange form of currency, he wants a cut."

"Not a chance," I said, following him in.

It felt strange to get a glimpse into the world of Hulk Henderson (as Kailyn called him), but it was everything one would expect. The walls were hung with posters of sports teams, a large jar of protein powder sat on top of a black minifridge, and a small flat-screen was set to ESPN, where sports news played on mute.

Carter handed me a metal box. It was old and rusted and sparked a secret thrill in me—probably what my father felt every time he found a new treasure.

Tentatively, I sat in the chair in front of Cody's desk and opened the box. I half expected triumphant music to play or birds to fly out. Instead, I found myself looking at a sheaf of yellowed papers as thin as parchment.

"Look at that," I said, carefully lifting them out.

They were loose sheets of ledger paper from handwritten logs. One page documented the cost of everything from groceries to kerosene, while another had annotations about the weather, the tide, and shipping. The penmanship was small, neat, and from the year 1920, two years before *The Wanderer* went down.

"It's the same keeper," I said. "The one that knew my great-grandfather."

"Whoa," Carter said. "That's a coincidence."

"Maybe." Steve at Search and Rescue did say the keeper had a drinking problem. "There were rules on how the keepers should document information. This should have been kept in a logbook. Based on some of the things I've learned about this keeper, he seems a bit more . . . freewheeling than that." I turned the pages slowly, as if they might turn to dust in my hands. "I'm going to read them the second I get home."

How cool. I could envision matting and framing the pages to decorate the main floor. The presentation would be a draw for a history enthusiast, if it came time to sell it.

I placed the papers back in the box. "The floor looked like it was on its way."

"He's putting in the new floorboards now. Should be ready tomorrow. It's a bummer he has to fix that window again before you can get to the final round of mold treatments." He cleared his throat. "Dawn, I . . . I think I might ask Kailyn out."

"Really?" I gave him a friendly swat in the arm. "That's great!"

"Yeah." Carter rubbed his face. "I could take her to Olives on Friday. It's a little Italian place that's kind of out of the way, up in the vineyards on the Peninsula. Do you think she'll like it?"

"It sounds perfect," I said.

I couldn't help but think how nice it would be to have someone to plan a date for me. A certain dark-haired, blue-eyed Casanova glowered through my head, but I quickly pushed the thought aside.

Turning my attention back to the box, I hefted it off the desk. It was much heavier than it looked, probably thanks to the old casing.

"Where you headed with that?" Carter asked.

"Where do you think?" I said. "I'm going to go home and read every page."

I walked out of the hardware shop with the box tucked firmly under my arm. Sal was walking through the door at the same time I was headed out, and we crashed into each other. The box dropped with a clatter, and the top few pages fell onto the sidewalk.

"Shoot!" I scrambled to pick them up, but Sal was faster. He skimmed a few pages, his filmmaker brain probably tucking the information away in some mental filing cabinet.

"I'll take that," I said, sticking my hand out.

Reluctantly, he handed the pages over. He watched as I placed them inside the box and examined the exterior for damage. No dents; still in good condition. I clicked the lock tightly shut and tucked the box back under my arm.

In the sunlight, the dark circles under Sal's eyes were pronounced. He seemed less slick than usual, like he hadn't gotten enough sleep. Still, he gave me a cheeky grin.

"Those papers are pretty old," he said, pulling his hat low over his eyes. "Treasure maps?"

I laughed. "Hardly." Then, because he was still eyeing the box, I said, "It has nothing to do with the treasure, Sal. It's just old paperwork from the lighthouse."

He looked disappointed. "Oh."

"What?" I teased him. "You're not interested in history, now? That's supposed to be your shtick."

"I'm interested in history if it fits in with my story."

"The lighthouse fits into the story," I said, before thinking it through.

Sal looked over his shoulder and slid on his sunglasses. "Yeah? How so?"

I couldn't believe I'd let that slip. The last thing I needed was for him to take that information and use it in his documentary. Quickly, I shrugged.

"It's a lighthouse," I said. "There was a shipwreck. It ties in."

Sal didn't look impressed. "Unless it leads to the treasure, I'm not interested."

"What's with you and the treasure today?" I asked. "Did Dusty get you thinking about it?"

He shrugged. "I'm starting to think the treasure might be the only way to prove your great-grandfather didn't do anything wrong."

"Not the *only* way," I said. "But yes, it would help. How's your research going?"

Sal grinned. "Getting sick of me?" He ran his hand through his thinning hair. "Research is taking longer than I anticipated. That's how things go in film. It can move at a glacial pace."

"Got it." I was getting hot standing in the sun. "Well, I should hit the road."

"Where you off to?" Sal asked, looking again at the box. "Want to grab some coffee now?"

I shook my head. "Maybe next week."

"Let me know if you find anything good." With an abrupt turn, Sal headed back down the sidewalk. He'd bumped into me on the way into the hardware shop but now was headed in another direction.

Sal was such an odd bird. Still, he probably had information up his sleeve that could help the puzzle pieces fit together. I made a mental note to contact him at some point next week.

I headed back toward my bike, secured the box in the basket, and headed over to Kailyn's office, hoping to find her there. I couldn't wait to share the news about Carter.

~

Sure enough, Kailyn was at her desk, hard at work. I grabbed a cookie off the tray and rushed in.

"I have great news." I flopped onto the green leather chair and set the metal box on the floor.

"Ooh, I love great news!" Kailyn sat at her desk, with her glasses on and hair pulled back in a neat chignon. She tapped away at her keyboard, deep in concentration.

Brushing crumbs off my hands, I said, "I need your full focus." I waited for her to pull her attention away from the computer, take off her glasses, and look at me. "Guess who has a date with Carter Henderson this Friday?"

Kailyn's eyes widened. "He asked you out?" Hurt colored her features, but she covered with a dimpled smile. "That's why I always liked him. He has great taste!"

"The date isn't for me, you goof," I said. "It's for you."

This time, her face showed everything from shock to delight to fear. "I don't understand."

I couldn't believe someone as kind and hilarious as Kailyn didn't know she was a catch. I was determined to help her figure that out.

"What's not to understand?" I said. "I saw him at the hardware store and he said how fun it was last night, how good at volleyball you are . . ."

Her face lit up. "Really?"

"Yes! He wants to go out on Friday." I gave a dramatic wiggle of my eyebrows. "Looks like you've got a date with Carter Henderson."

Once the magnitude of this hit her, Kailyn was up and out of her chair like a hurricane. She tackled me, and we jumped up and down with glee. In the midst of this, a man dressed for a day on the golf course walked into the office and stared at us in surprise.

Kailyn struck a serious pose. "Yes, sir." She gave him her most professional look. "How can I help you?"

"I have a meeting with Kailyn Barnes? I'm looking for a vacation home. I heard she was the one in town everyone wants to see."

"You can say that again," I murmured.

"Yes, sir." She choked back a giggle. "You've come to the right place."

~

By the time I got back to my parents' house, they'd left for their antiquing trip. I was faced with a few days alone, something I hadn't had in a while. I planned to cook dinner, watch some television, and then review the papers in the metal box.

I headed off to the shower and plugged in my cell on the way. It had died on the bike trip, and I hadn't checked it in hours. When I got out of the shower, I was happy to find a couple of cute texts with giddy emoticons from Kailyn and a voice mail from Kip Whittaker about Beulah.

Monday at two, he said. *Call me if you need to talk.*

I set down the phone, his message ringing in my ears. In all of my history of dealing with men, I never met one who said things like *Call me if you need to talk.* In fact, most of the men I knew did their best to avoid talking.

Kip wasn't like that, which scared me. It seemed that, more and more, he was proving to be the type of man I always imagined falling in love with. But I wasn't going to be in town much longer. Opening myself up to Kip seemed like a one-way road to heartache, considering any type of relationship would be over before it began.

Bummed, I headed to the kitchen to start dinner. I pan cooked a chicken breast with potatoes and rosemary, then whipped up a leafy green salad. I set the meal up on a TV tray in the living room and settled in to watch a scary movie.

Halfway in, I regretted choosing a movie designed to freak me out. The Coast Guard had questioned my personal safety. Why had I thought it would be a smart idea to watch a scary movie when I was home alone? Just as the thought ran through my head, a loud crash outside almost made me hit the ceiling. Pulse racing, I muted the television.

Bang!

It sounded like someone was trying to break in. Leaping up, I grabbed the poker from the fireplace and tore toward the front door. I flipped on the lights and rushed out onto the brick stoop.

"Who's there?" I demanded.

Silence.

My parents' house was one of the larger houses on the street. Their front lawn was at least ten acres. I was in a pretty remote space, and there would be no one close enough to help me if I needed it. Still, I stepped farther out onto the porch. My brain screamed that I was doing something dangerous, but it was too late to back off now.

"What do you want?" My voice rang out cold and steady. "Because if you're mad about the lighthouse, it's too late and too bad."

Silence.

The hair on the back of my neck stood up.

Maybe this wasn't about the lighthouse at all. Like Kip said, thanks to *News Tonight*, some people actually believed my parents had found the treasure. Which meant standing on the porch with only a fire poker for protection was a pretty stupid plan.

I gripped it tightly and took a step back. "Is this about the treasure?" I demanded. "My family doesn't have it. So, get out of here!"

A shadow stretched across the lawn, and a startled scream caught in my throat. Then, a fat opossum waddled his way across the light from the porch.

Relief weakened my legs. "I've gone mad," I whispered. "I just told off a rodent."

The opossum glared at me with beady eyes before scampering toward the hedges.

"That's right," I said, waving the poker. "You'd better run."

With every ounce of remaining dignity, I went back inside. Then, I drew the curtains, set my parents' alarm system, and turned off the television. Even though the perpetrator in my drama was just an opossum, I decided it was not the best idea to watch scary movies alone.

"The lighthouse papers," I mumbled, setting the poker back down on the fireplace. "That's a much better option."

∼

I spent the next hour reading through the papers in the metal box. They were fascinating from a historical perspective, but dry in the way of intrigue. Page after page offered detailed reports on the weather, supplies like acetylene fuel, and the ships passing through. I managed to work my way through every page but felt a vague sense of disappointment when I finished.

I'd expected them to be more interesting. Romantic, somehow, like Fitzie's love letters.

The love letters had been on my mind since I'd arrived in Starlight Cove, but I hadn't read them. I was afraid they wouldn't be nearly as good as I remembered. But now, my main goal was to find information.

"All right." I headed toward the attic. "Let's take a look."

My parents' attic was as big as the Whittaker attic but nowhere near as organized. It was stacked from floor to ceiling with boxes and crates, as well as random mementos from the countries they visited on explorations and dives. I picked my way through musty artifacts and dodged dust bunnies and cobwebs, but had no luck. Finally, I picked up my cell phone and called my mother.

"Hey," I said, after she filled me in on their lodge up north. "I'm trying to find Fitzie's letters. Where did Dad put them?"

There was some fumbling. Then my father got on the phone.

"The safety-deposit box."

"Oh."

My parents weren't due back for almost a week.

"Why?" he asked. "Is it an emergency?"

I brushed some sweat off my forehead. "It's not an emergency. The letters seemed like a good thing to research. Beulah is going to let us see her mother's journal Monday."

My father let out a low whistle. "I'd like to see that."

"Do you want me to wait?" I asked. "We can do it when you're back in town."

"No, but let me know what you find."

Once we said our good-byes, I climbed back down the stairs and lay down on the couch. Staring up at the ceiling, I listened to the sound of the summer night settling around me. It was so different from night in my apartment in Boston.

For a moment, I felt suspended between two worlds—my life in the present, in Starlight Cove, and my life in the past, in Boston. In my half-asleep state, I could admit that I preferred living in Starlight Cove—but that was a given. I was living a grown-up version of summer vacation. Life wouldn't be like this if I stayed here forever.

Besides, living in the lighthouse was completely impractical. Having a relationship with Kip, the same. I needed to get my head back on straight and make a plan to transition back to Boston once I'd proved Fitzie's innocence and finished the lighthouse.

The thought made me feel lonelier than I had in ages.

The pattern of the trees reflected on the ceiling, and I pulled a throw blanket close to my chest. I knew I should do the civilized thing and make my bed with fresh sheets before going to sleep, but, for once in my life, I didn't see the point. Pulling the blanket over me, I closed my eyes and fell asleep.

In the light of day, I laughed out loud at my ridiculous altercation with the opossum. I had a crick in my neck from sleeping on the couch but looked forward to seeing Cody's progress with the bedroom floor.

The new floor looked great, with clean planks of fresh lumber stretched across the room in a hexagon. And he'd already replaced the window. I couldn't help but think how incredible the lighthouse would look when it was fully restored.

What would it be like to live here? I wondered again.

It would be like living in a fantasy world, a notion I refused to entertain. Still, the picture of what the lighthouse had the potential to become lifted my spirits.

I got to work spraying for mold one last time, hitting each area that still seemed suspicious. It was hard, lonely work without my father. I didn't expect to miss him, considering I'd made a habit out of spending so much time away from home.

Yes, my parents were always busy on dives. Still, it would have been easy for me to take a break from number crunching to take a trip or two and visit them. It would have been interesting to see some of the countries where they worked and experience some of their dive sites. I never did that, though, because I felt betrayed by the way I was raised. Now, I didn't see the point of hanging on to that anger.

My parents did the best they could. They lived their life and followed their passion. I could blame them or learn to let it go. Based on the past few weeks we'd had together, blame seemed like a waste of time.

I aimed the bleach gun at a persistent spot of mold. Then I pulled the trigger.

The steady stream battled against the speckles. I watched, satisfied, as the small, angry spores seemed to disintegrate right in front of my eyes.

Chapter Eighteen

By the time Monday's meeting with Beulah rolled around, I was so eager to see the journal that I arrived at Beulah's before Kip did and immediately regretted it. The property was big, and being alone felt creepy. Once again, I remembered the Coast Guard's warning about personal safety and shivered.

As I walked through her yard, the scattered twigs cracked under my feet, and shadows seemed thick in the woods. A dark shape moved across a pine tree, and I stopped, squinting at it. For a split second, it looked like a man, and the hair on the back of my neck stood straight up. But then, it dissipated into nothing.

I flushed, remembering my adventure with the opossum. "You've got to calm down, Dawn," I muttered.

I climbed up the steps and knocked on the door. The brass knocker sounded like gunshots echoing through the woods. I expected Beulah to answer instantly, like last time, but I waited three minutes and still didn't hear footsteps.

I tried knocking again.

Nothing.

Maybe I'd misunderstood Kip's message. He wasn't here yet, and Beulah was nowhere to be found.

I clicked on my phone and listened to it again.

Nope. He'd said two, clear as day.

A new text from Kip popped up: Five minutes late.

Kip still planned to show. So, where was Beulah?

I knocked on the door once again. Then I walked over to the edge of the porch and peered into the thick glass windows, squinting to see through the sheer curtains. A heavy hand landed on my shoulder.

"What do you think you're doing?" a deep voice asked, close to my ear.

I jumped straight up in the air. Of course, it was just Kip.

"Don't do that!" I squealed, punching him in the arm.

He laughed. "Why are you so jumpy?"

He'd gotten a haircut. It made the stubble on his cheek look more inviting than usual, and I felt those darn flutters in my stomach again.

He strolled to the door. "Instead of peeping in the windows," he said, "you could have just knocked."

"I *did*." I followed him, my low pumps clacking against the wood of the porch. "She didn't answer."

He knocked. When she didn't answer, he made a face. "That's weird," he said. "I talked to her last night."

Sweeping past me, he cleared his throat. Then he tried to peek into the windows.

"Exactly," I said.

"Hmm," he mused, looking up at the silent house. "I don't like this."

His somber tone made me think the worst.

"You think she . . ." I couldn't bring myself to finish the sentence.

"It's a possibility." The fact that Beulah was in her eighties meant that anything could have happened overnight. "I'll check it out."

Before I could protest, Kip jumped over the edge of the porch. I stood and waited, fighting against a prickly feeling at the back of my neck. He was gone long enough for me to wonder if something happened to him, too, but he then walked back around the front of the house, brushing dirt off his hands.

"I tried to open the lower-level windows," he said, climbing the front steps. "They're all locked. I'm going to have to make a call."

"Who are you calling?" I asked, dread filling my voice.

But I already knew the answer.

Kip was going to call Maeve Weatherly.

The conversation didn't go well. Maeve informed Kip that her mother had decided to visit a sick relative down in Florida. If the weather agreed with her, she might stay through the winter. When he asked for a number to reach her, Maeve feigned a bad connection.

"She should have said no." I wrapped my arms around myself, looking up at the empty house. "Instead of the charade."

Kip sat on the porch railing. "Maeve Weatherly doesn't say no. It reduces her bargaining power for next time." He drummed his fingers on the railing. "Looks like we're back to square one."

"We're not back to square one," I insisted. "Beulah was going to show us that journal. Now she's in Florida? There's something Maeve doesn't want us to see. I need to know what it is."

Maybe it was something that could prove Captain Fitzie's innocence. Nothing would irritate Maeve more. Especially considering her insistence that he was guilty.

"Dawn . . ." Kip frowned, displaying the attractive lines around his eyes.

"What?" I demanded. "Call her back and tell her I need to see the journal. If you don't, I will."

Kip ran his hand over the stubble on his face. When he didn't make a move toward his phone, I picked up mine.

"Give me her number."

"She'll hang up on you."

"Then I'll just go talk to her."

I stalked off the porch, through the disarray of the yard, and down the driveway. I was so angry I could hardly see. It was bad enough that my family had to suffer because of something that happened years ago, but I couldn't stand the possibility that Maeve Weatherly might be hiding something that could clear my great-grandfather's name.

I was halfway down the hill when I heard the crunch of footsteps behind me. I turned. Kip was jogging toward me.

"I'll come with you," he called, "but this is not going to work."

I shrugged, secretly grateful I didn't have to go alone. "You never know until you try."

Maeve did not look pleased to see us standing at her front door. In fact, she probably would have offered a kinder welcome to a traveling salesperson selling snake oil. Still, she opened the door, which I decided to take as a good sign.

"Kip." She stood up on her tiptoes to kiss his tanned cheek.

I didn't get a kiss or so much as a second glance, which was fine. I was too busy gaping at her home.

The entryway gleamed with cold white marble and gilded mirrors. Morning sunlight spilled through windows showcasing the lake. Silver rays of sun glistened against an enormous crystal chandelier.

"I thought we just spoke," Maeve said.

Kip gave a charming smile. "We hoped for a couple more minutes of your time."

"I have somewhere to be."

He held up his hands. "Ten minutes. I promise."

Maeve frowned. She looked ready to head out, dressed in a tailored pantsuit, designer jewelry, and velvet slippers with some sort of an emblem. Expensive perfume lingered around her like a cloud.

I remembered what my father said about the power of Maeve's family fortune. The fact that she was fighting this so hard could only mean she had something to hide. I stood by in silence, determined not to say a word until we were in.

To my relief, Maeve gave a crook of her finger. We followed her to a front room off the left of the entryway.

It reminded me of the parlor we had sat in at her mother's house but with a contemporary feel. Modern upholstery in bold designs covered the chairs and window treatments, complementing the vibrant art on the walls. Based on her decorating skills, Maeve Weatherly did not miss a detail.

"I know you've met Dawn," Kip said, once we were seated. "I assume you've heard her great-grandfather was involved with the wreck of *The Wanderer*."

Maeve lifted her chin. "I told you I only had a few minutes, Kip. Get on with it."

Kip nodded. "Your mother told us that, when she was a little girl, she overheard her mother mention that Captain Conners was alive after the wreck."

Maeve gave me a cool stare and returned her gaze to Kip.

"She said it was a terrible secret," Kip continued. "One that could put Dawn's great-grandmother in danger. Do you know about this?"

"Yes, I am aware," she said. "This conversation upset my mother a great deal. I suggest if Dawn needs a history lesson, she discuss the matter with her parents."

"That's the thing," Kip said. "They have as little information as we do. Beulah, on the other hand, told us she had a journal with additional information about what happened that night. Maeve, we need to see it."

She shook her head. "That's not possible."

"I think it is possible," he said. "But you're choosing to not allow it."

Maeve gave a pointed look at her watch. "I'm sorry, Kip; I cannot allow my family name to be dragged through the mud over something that happened a hundred years ago. I simply cannot."

"Why would your name be dragged through the mud?" I burst out. "What's in the journal that you don't want us to see?"

Maeve got to her feet. "It doesn't concern you! Now, if this is all—"

Kip followed her lead and stood up. "Thanks for your time, Maeve."

"This meeting is not over," I said, furious. "So you can all take a seat."

Maeve and Kip looked at me in surprise.

"Sorry, but I need to see that journal," I said. "If you won't provide it, I'll ask my father's lawyers to subpoena it from you."

Maeve gave a bitter laugh. "I can assure you, if you do that, you will be disappointed with the journal you receive."

I got the message. Since we'd never seen it, I'd have no way of proving the journal Maeve supplied would be the same one she wanted to hide. The threat infuriated me.

"That's clever." I tried to keep my tone steady. "But the news outlets interested in *The Wanderer* adore intrigue. The moment you try to fight me on this, I will share the fact that you are trying to hide something. The speculation will be much worse than the truth."

Maeve sputtered her outrage.

I held up a finger. "But if you share the journal with me, you have my word that I will keep the information quiet. So please. Let's stop playing games."

Kip gave me a dark look. I couldn't tell if it was tinged with anger or admiration. Either way, I didn't care. I was not about to sit back and let Maeve Weatherly dictate the terms of my life.

Maeve rested her hand on top of a wingback chair. I could see her weighing the options, trying to determine the next move to make. I'd just increased the risk that she would go after my parents' store, but that was the last thing on my mind. I was more worried about keeping our family home.

The air in the room was tense. Even the birds outside the window seemed to have stopped chirping. Finally, she lifted up her hands.

"Fine. I'll show you the journal, but . . ." She shook her head. "I will need you to uphold your word. *No one* can know about this. If word gets out, I think you should know that the Weatherlys also have an impressive team of legal representation."

I sat back in the chair, weak with relief. "I have no doubt you do."

Maeve swept out of the room. The moment she was gone, Kip turned to me in disbelief.

"What was that all about?" he demanded. "Maeve is a family friend. I didn't bring you here to *threaten* her!"

"Sorry." I refused to feel guilty. "I need to know what happened."

"But at this price?" He glowered at the floor. "She's never going to forgive me."

"Kip, she has information that I need," I said. "You have no idea what's at stake for me."

"What?" he demanded. "What's at stake?"

I squeezed my hands. "I can't tell you. I'm sorry."

We sat in silence as birds chirped outside the window. I stared down at my shoes, focusing on the sheen of the polished wood floors.

When Maeve returned, I said, "Kip has nothing to do with this. So you know."

Maeve pressed her lips together but didn't answer. Instead, she swept over and handed me an old-fashioned journal with a pale-pink cover and small gold lock. "Here is Ruth's journal," she said. "I have postponed my meeting. I'm sure you understand that I cannot allow this to leave our house." She sat in a chair next to Kip, crossed her arms, and stared me down as I began to read.

I thumbed through the pages, working my way to April 1922. The passages reflected on the weather, the latest gossip, and how bored Ruth was now that the war was over. Her responsibilities had shifted from running the family's shipping company while the men were away, back to "learning the most popular poems, perfecting my hand at the piano, and trying not to doze off during the majority of social discourse."

"I like her," I told Maeve. "She had spunk."

Maeve didn't answer, but I could tell she agreed.

When I got to the passages about my great-grandfather and Madeline, I went back and read them again, confused. Ruth referred to Fitzie's survival with relief and spoke of the fact that he was injured with great distress. She waxed poetic about longing to wrap him in her arms when he returned.

"Wait. Was she . . . ?" I squinted at the page in disbelief. "I think Ruth was in love with my great-grandfather."

Kip leaned forward. "Really?"

Maeve sighed. "That's how it appears."

Stunned, I kept reading. The wording became even more emotional, especially when Fitzie refused to see anyone but Madeline. I felt sick inside.

"Were they together?" I asked, lowering the journal.

What if Fitzie had been in love with someone else, the entire time?

Maeve shook her head. "If you keep reading, you'll see this was a one-sided fantasy on the part of my grandmother. She was in love with her best friend's husband from the moment they met. However, he did not feel the same."

"Thank goodness," I breathed.

"Personally, I find the whole thing distasteful." Maeve's voice was tight. "Ruth was a strong, admirable woman. By all accounts, she loved my grandfather. This is not something . . ." She frowned. "I did not enjoy discovering this."

I continued to read through the pages. The more I read, the more I realized Maeve's assessment was correct. Ruth was in love with Fitzie, but he only had eyes for her best friend.

I came to the final passage on the topic:

He gave me a message to deliver to his one true love. It seems that, no matter the feelings that fill my days, he refuses to accept my devotion. Well, I will never give another woman the satisfaction of stealing my one true love away. I am not a delivery boy. If he wanted her to receive the message, he should have sent it himself.

"He gave her a love letter to give to Madeline," I said to Kip. "But she never received it."

I kept reading. For weeks, there was no other mention of Fitzie or *The Wanderer*. When it became clear he was never coming back, Ruth was nearly gleeful about the fact that he left Madeline. Eventually, she stopped writing about him altogether.

The information didn't teach me anything new about what happened to Fitzie. But I finally understood why Maeve had fought so hard to hide the information.

"Thank you." I closed the journal and handed it back to her.

She gave a sharp nod and got to her feet. "I'll show you out."

Kip and I followed in silence.

At the front door, I stopped and looked at her.

"I understand that was hard for you," I said. "Thank you for trusting me. I promise you, I will not discuss this with anyone outside of my family. You have my word."

Her eyes held mine. "That best be true."

"Thank you, Maeve," Kip said, kissing her cheek.

"Don't worry," she murmured. "I don't blame *you*."

With that, she gave me another sharp look and shut the door in our faces.

≈

I spent the evening sitting on my parents' back porch, looking out over the woods. The hum of insects was thick, but a citronella candle kept the mosquitoes away. As dusk fell, fireflies flashed like twinkling stars, and I felt sad about the things I'd read in Ruth's journal.

How could Ruth claim to be best friends with Madeline when she was secretly in love with Fitzie? She also held back a letter that might have given a valuable clue as to why he never returned. It could be hidden somewhere in Maeve's paperwork, but I didn't dare ask.

I'd pushed Maeve hard enough.

I reached for the glass of white wine resting on the arm of the deck chair and took a sip. It was smooth and sweet, the opposite of my interaction with Maeve. I was glad I'd seen the journal, but it didn't help Fitzie's case in the slightest.

Time was ticking. The deadline for the insurance company was looming. It was hard to believe that if I couldn't find some sort of proof of Fitzie's innocence, I'd never get to sit on this deck again, take in the view, or feel the familiar comfort of my family home.

That thought, coupled with the reality of the lost letter that Madeline never got to see, made it impossible for me to enjoy the peaceful evening. With a sigh, I blew out the candle and went inside.

Chapter Nineteen

I met Kailyn at a small white building just off Main Street for the meeting at the Women's Chapter of the Starlight Cove Historical Society. The front lawn was freshly mowed and had an American flag on a pole in the center, surrounded by a base of white stones. Cheerful flowers lined the front walkway.

Kailyn beamed at me. She was as cute as ever in a pink dress and an outrageous beaded flower necklace.

"Hi," she called. "They're so excited to talk to you."

I was so nervous, my legs were sweating. I wanted to be a good friend to Kailyn, but at the same time, I was tempted to take off running.

"This is terrifying." I smoothed my hair. Ever since that night at the bar, I'd been experimenting with wearing it down. Now, I wished I could pull it back. "Is Maeve going to be here?"

"Forget Maeve." Kailyn reached out and grabbed my hands. "These women are excited to talk to you. My aunt is a member of this group. They love it that you bought the lighthouse, and they're all super, super nice people. I figured it wouldn't hurt to bridge the gap and invite them to be a part of your journey."

Bud, the GSA agent from that first day, had said the community would want to get involved in the project. Maybe he was right.

"Fine," I whispered. "I will run, though, if they—"

Kailyn squeezed my hand. "They won't."

We headed into the building, taking two steps down into an old-fashioned lodge. The entryway carpet was forest green, and the walls were lined with cream-and-gold-striped wallpaper. Modern and antique photographs of very serious-looking women hung in key positions. For once, I didn't see a picture of my great-grandfather anywhere.

"Isn't this fun?" she asked. "I don't get to come here a lot, but when I do, I can't help but think it's like some secret society." Leaning in, she murmured, "I think this organization was founded before Starlight Cove even existed, so wrap your brain around that."

Kailyn plastered a dimpled smile on her face and led me into the main room, a parlor roughly the size of a ballroom with the same carpet and wallpaper as the entryway. "Toodle-oo," she called, waving at the ladies in the room.

There were twenty or so women who all looked over the age of sixty. I recognized one or two from Henderson Hardware. The group greeted us with curious smiles.

My legs went weak, but Libby's words from that day on the phone gave me strength. *You have fire.* I wanted to believe that. I didn't want to keep running away from things that made me afraid.

A stern-looking woman with shoulder-length chestnut hair swept toward me. She looked like a librarian with money, dressed in a short-sleeved tweed suit with an amber brooch.

"I am Percy Reed," she said. "The current president of the Women's Chapter of the Starlight Cove Historical Society. The title is not hereditary; it was determined by a vote."

That made me smile.

"I'm Dawn Conners," I said. "It's an honor to meet you."

"You, as well. Today, we plan to give a presentation on the lighthouse in Starlight Cove, as well as some other lighthouses in the country." She led me over to a display table. "Would you like to take a look at our lighthouse collection?"

I clasped my hands in delight. The table was full of lighthouse artifacts. It showcased an official keeper's hat, a paraffin vapor lamp, and even a copy of the book my father had given me, *Instructions to Light-Keepers*.

I slid on the white gloves next to it and flipped carefully through the pages. "My father gave me this same book."

"You might be interested to know that this book was the one in your lighthouse," she said. "It belonged to the keeper stationed there."

My mouth dropped open. "We might have to swap."

"Perhaps," she said.

I ran my hand over the book with affection before setting it down.

"I'll have to let you see the papers I found at the lighthouse," I told her. "I'm going to give them to my mother to send to restoration, along with the box they were in, but once they're back, I'll bring them over."

Percy gave an enthusiastic nod. "What a treasure."

Once I'd browsed through the items, she guided me to the group.

"Speaking of treasure," she said, "your parents' antique shop is quite a treat. We enjoy it immensely."

"Thank you." I was glad to hear that business wasn't just coming from tourists, but from the locals, too. "You like it?"

"Like it?" another woman said, bustling forward. She was jolly, with permed white hair and a colorful velveteen scarf around her neck. "We keep it in business."

I don't know what came over me, but somehow, I launched into a clever story about my parents' antiquing adventures on their trip this week. My mother had called me with some good stories, and now I shared them with the women. They laughed, and Kailyn winked at me.

"There's my Aunt Annabelle," she said, waving. "I want you to meet her."

Aunt Annabelle had the same friendly smile as her niece, as well as the same loud fashion sense. She wore a purple velour pantsuit partnered with chunky jewelry. Her hair was perfectly sprayed, like a curly helmet. She giggled like a teenager and gave me a friendly hug.

"We are simply fascinated by the idea of living in a lighthouse," she sang. "Would you like any treats before we get started?"

With a plump hand, she pointed at a small tea tray in the corner. It was stocked with brownies, lemon bars, and what looked like oatmeal-raisin cookies. Silver coffee carafes and pitchers of lemonade and iced tea decorated the table.

"Yes, please," I said, delighted.

I loaded up a plate with one of everything, grabbed a cup of iced tea from a glass dispenser, and followed Kailyn to a seat in the back row. We'd just settled in when Percy swept up and said, "You girls are in the front. You're the guests of honor."

Before I knew it, we were seated at a table below the film screen, facing the audience. Small microphones sat on the table in front of our chairs. My palms went damp, and I wiped them off on my napkin.

"I'm not supposed to give a speech, am I?" I asked Kailyn.

Public speaking was not my forte. In college, I had to give a speech in my language arts class, and I passed out. Libby reenacted the moment for months, blinking like a lost deer and crumpling to the floor.

Kailyn grinned. "It's probably just to help everyone hear us."

Percy called the meeting to order. To my surprise, the women stood up and launched into a song. They got into it, adding motions and interacting with their neighbors. It was really cute. Kailyn and I clapped and cheered along with them when it was over.

Growing up, I had always wanted to join the Girl Scouts, but we were never in one place long enough. If I was still connected to Starlight Cove by the time I was sixty, I'd join the Historical Society, if only to have the opportunity to learn that song.

Percy went through the minutes, caught the group up on business, and started the slide show. It included several of the pictures my mother had e-mailed me, as well as some I'd never seen before, including pictures of all the Starlight Cove lighthouse keepers. I caught my breath as a photograph flashed by of the keeper who helped my great-grandfather.

The picture was taken from far away, but I could tell he was wiry, with a wry smile and bulbous nose. He wore the traditional keeper's uniform that started in the late eighteen hundreds: a sleek navy coat with a required number of brass buttons. My favorite part of the uniform was the hat, with its embroidered golden wreath encompassing a silver lighthouse emblem.

Once the keepers flashed by, the slides explained the uniforms, the evolution of the United States Life-Saving Service, and even details about Fresnel lenses, navigation bells, and fog signals. It was a thorough maritime education. I liked hearing about the US General Services Administration and the process of buying a lighthouse at auction, since I was the only person in the room who had been there, done that.

It must have taken a lot of time and effort to put together the slide presentation, and I was touched. It was the type of information I wouldn't have minded having in a little video on my phone, to whip out whenever someone said, "So, why were you interested in remodeling a lighthouse?"

When the slide show was over, Percy turned on the lights and made her way to the front of the room. She introduced me and Kailyn, before saying, "It is remarkable that Starlight Cove holds yet another piece of history that has lasted through the centuries. We invited Dawn here today to discuss the current status of the lighthouse, as well as her plans for it. Then we'll open the floor for questions."

Discuss the current status of the lighthouse?

That sounded suspiciously like a speech. To make things worse, I suddenly noticed a small figure with sleek, dark hair sitting in the back row: Maeve. She must have snuck in during the video.

"Thanks for having me here today." My voice boomed across the room, and for a moment I felt light-headed and clammy, but I was not about to make a fool out of myself in front of Maeve. Taking a deep breath, I said, "The presentation was wonderful. My father, as some of you might know, is a treasure hunter. As a result, my family spent a lot of time on the lakes and on the ocean when I was growing up. I've loved the lighthouse in Starlight Cove ever since I was a little girl."

I glanced at Kailyn, wondering if what I was saying was boring. She gave an enthusiastic nod, as though to say, "Go on."

"I bought the lighthouse at auction because I'd just lost my job and didn't know what else to do," I continued. "In fact, it went up for auction that very same day."

The crowd murmured.

"The experience has been wonderful at times but painful at others. Recently, there has been vandalism on the lighthouse. I haven't determined who is responsible, but not everyone has wished me well on this venture."

I locked eyes with Maeve. Her face colored, and she looked away.

"The Coast Guard is aware of the issue," I continued. "Because of that, I believe it will stop. I want you all to know that my goal is to restore the lighthouse to honor Starlight Cove. My family has been a part of Starlight Cove's history for well over a century. In fact, if anyone here has information on the history of my family, I would love to hear it."

I paused for a moment, hoping someone would raise a hand. When no one did, I added, "I would also like to invite each and every one of you to come see the lighthouse. I can always use an extra pair of hands. *Especially* when it comes to painting."

The women laughed.

"Most of all," I continued, "I appreciate your trust and your assistance as I restore a place that has always seemed so magical to me."

To my surprise, the women in the room burst into applause. It seemed like a logical stopping place, so I sat back into my seat, embarrassed. It dawned on me to look and see if Maeve was clapping, but her seat was empty.

Kailyn kicked my legs in excitement. "That was great," she whispered.

My palms were wet with sweat. "Do you think it was okay?"

She gave me the thumbs-up. "Perfect."

The applause died down, and Percy opened the floor for questions.

"What type of work have you done so far?" a frail-looking woman asked.

I walked her through the updates I'd made with the Henderson brothers.

"I just finished the final mold treatment," I said. "When that's done, I'm going to paint the interior. It should be a breeze."

This brought another round of laughter.

"Why did you decide to work with Kailyn?" Aunt Annabelle shouted.

Kailyn leaned forward. "That's my aunt, everybody," she said into the microphone. "She's trying to get Dawn to say I'm the best real estate agent in town, but Dawn could have bought the lighthouse without me. I think she wanted the comfort of someone to review the paperwork and . . ." She winked at me. "To tell her she wasn't crazy."

I laughed. "True."

A woman in a pair of red-rimmed glasses raised her hand. "You said you want to honor the community with the lighthouse," she said. "Will you open it to the public?"

The question caught me off guard. Right now, I was focused on getting the lighthouse restored. But the idea of sharing its history didn't seem like a bad idea.

"It might be interesting to open it up to the public or school groups in some way," I said slowly. "That's something I might look at in the future."

At the end of the question-and-answer session, Percy ushered us to the reception area. I shook hands with countless women, listening to their personal experiences. One woman told me that her husband had proposed at the bottom of the ladder fifty years ago, and my mind started imagining crazy things, like inviting her and her husband over for dinner on their anniversary.

When it was all over, Kailyn and I stopped at a tea shop to talk about the meeting. To my delight, the shop carried chai. We sat at a lace-covered table, and I sipped on it, trying to find the words to explain how the women made me feel.

"I came to Starlight Cove with a vague idea that the lighthouse was about more than just me, but this was the first time I really felt it," I said. "Thanks for setting it up."

Kailyn sipped at her lavender tea. "I think you did great, but I did *not* know it would be, you know, us talking on microphones and all that."

"I really didn't mind." I smiled, thinking about the interest on the women's faces. "It was an opportunity to be heard. All this time, I've kind of been this silent person, hiding out by the edge of the water. Now, I've said why I'm here. They can take it or leave it." I took a sip of tea, looking out at the people walking down Main Street. "I have a good feeling. Those women care about the lighthouse, the history presentation was great, and I just . . . I don't know. I feel it was a step in the right direction."

"I'm sorry to hear about the vandalism." Kailyn shook her head. "Why didn't you say anything?"

"It's embarrassing," I admitted. "It was someone telling me I don't belong."

"You do belong," Kailyn said. "You're a part of this community now."

I blinked back unexpected tears.

"Thanks," I said. "You don't know how much it means to me to hear it."

Chapter Twenty

On Thursday, Kailyn and I spent hours on prep work for her upcoming date. We picked the perfect outfit, hairstyle, and even perfume. Friday night, she called me fifteen minutes before Carter was supposed to pick her up.

"Hey," I said, adding grapes to a chicken salad. "Need a pep talk?"

"Can you come over?" she asked. "I'm at the office."

Her voice sounded stuffy, like she had a cold.

"Did something happen?" I asked, spoon poised over the bowl.

"The date is off."

What? Carter didn't seem like the type to break a date, even if he was having second thoughts.

"He cancelled?" I said. "I can't believe that."

"He didn't cancel," she wailed. "*I* did!"

∾

I headed to the real estate office, where I found Kailyn seated behind her desk. The lamp cast a yellow glow over her face, and her fingers flew over the keyboard. If her eyes hadn't been puffy from crying, it would almost seem like a normal day.

"What are you doing?" I asked, standing in the doorway. "You said you couldn't stand living another day without a Henderson brother in your life. That you *loved* him."

I hoped that by bringing in humor, Kailyn would see how ridiculous she was being. That I could get her to pick up the phone, call Carter back, and tell him she'd made a huge mistake. Instead, she looked even more defeated.

"I don't love anybody," she said. "When I love people, they leave me."

I suddenly realized how little I really knew about Kailyn. She was so talkative that it felt like I knew her. Yet, in the midst of all her funny stories and silly observations, she never volunteered personal information.

"What do you mean?" I asked, settling into the green leather chair.

"My mother left us when I was in high school," she said. "She just took off and married some tourist. He owned a karate dojo or something stupid in California. She just up and left."

"I'm sorry," I said. "That's awful."

Kailyn pressed her fingers into the skin under her eyes. "My brother, he couldn't handle it. He started drinking, doing drugs, and basically got sent to reform school. Now, he's living down South, and he won't talk to me or to my dad. It's like he blames us or something." She stared dully at the keyboard. "You know, I kept telling myself that I'd find someone, one day, but . . . I can't abandon my father. He needs somebody to take care of him."

"Kailyn." I reached for her hand. "Honey, I didn't know your father was sick."

"He's not *ill*." She snorted. "But he'd be on his own if I got married. He could barely get out of bed when my mom left. I don't want him to have to go through that again."

The man Kailyn introduced me to the night we ate dinner at the hotel didn't match her description. He was jovial, friendly, and eager to please his guests. Even though it was sweet she wanted to protect her father, I doubted he still needed someone to take care of him. In fact,

Cynthia Ellingsen

I bet he'd be stunned and a little hurt to learn why his daughter was holding herself back in the relationship department.

"Kailyn," I said gently. "I met your father. He wants the best for you. Has he ever said he doesn't want you to date?"

"Not in so many words," she said. "But sometimes he'll talk about when I get married and leave him . . ."

I tossed my hands in the air. "He's joking! Every parent says things like that."

"They do?"

I rolled my eyes. *"Yes."*

She sat in silence, fiddling with a sparkly earring.

"What?" I asked.

"It's not just about my dad," she said. "I like my life. I love where I live, even if it is with my dad, and I love my job, and I love my friends. I want to fall in love and get married, but it freaks me out because it will change things."

"Do you think one date with Carter Henderson will change everything?"

"If we fall in love and I lose him, yes."

"So, that's what you're really worried about." I could relate. Still, I said, "You have to take risks with love if you want it to happen."

"Says the girl who spends the majority of her time denying the fact that she is completely in love with Kip Whittaker."

I practically leapt up from the chair. "We're just working on a project together!"

My cheeks flamed with embarrassment. If it was obvious to Kailyn that I was madly in love with Kip, it must be obvious to him, too. In fact, he most likely assumed every woman was in love with him, since he was the most eligible bachelor in Starlight Cove. He probably saw me as just another girl, hanging on his every word.

"Either way, he has a girlfriend," I grumbled, sitting back down. "It's not like he would be interested in me."

210

"He has a *girl*friend?" Kailyn said. "Who?"

"You told me he has a girlfriend," I said. "Cassie Whoever-she-is."

Kailyn stared at me. "No! I said she's all over him every time she comes back from the Hamptons; but no. That ship has sailed. He's a free man."

That news filled me with relief, even though I wasn't about to act on it. In a few months I'd be back in Boston, and Starlight Cove would be a distant memory.

"Okay, I do like Kip," I admitted. "Right now just isn't the best time to get involved."

Kailyn twirled a strand of hair around her finger. "You know the problem with us, Dawn? We're two brave girls ready to tackle anything but falling in love. Funny, because I thought you were a pretty bold person."

"I'm not bold," I scoffed.

"You are," she said. "Even if you don't know it yet."

"Thanks," I told her. "But I'm still pretty confident I'm going to die alone."

Kailyn got to her feet and walked over to the table with the cookies. Grabbing us a handful, she flopped down on the chair next to me. "Nah," she said. "You can always move in with me and my dad."

Chapter Twenty-One

I was in the middle of dumping cleaner on the floor of the watch room when a loud clang rang out downstairs. I paused, listening. Then, I realized it was my new doorbell.

When Cody and Carter installed the floor, they decided I needed some way to let visitors let me know they'd arrived. I hadn't liked the idea, at first. I wasn't planning to live there, so why spend the money on something so trivial? But now, hearing the bell gave me an unexpected thrill of ownership.

I swept a loose strand of hair behind my ears and clanked down the spiral staircase, mentally running through a list of who it might be. Kailyn was at work, my parents were at the shop, and Carter was scheduled to stop by later. Secretly, I hoped it was Kip, but quickly pushed the thought out of my head.

I was just about to throw the door open when I remembered what the Coast Guard said about personal safety. Even though I didn't think I was in any danger, I pushed open a window.

"Yes, who is it?" I shouted.

"Percy," a voice called.

"Oh!" I threw open the door. Five ladies from the Starlight Cove Historical Society stood on the boardwalk, blinking up at me in the sunlight.

"We're here to help you paint," Percy called. "At the meeting, you said you needed it."

I stared down at the older group of women in surprise. All five of them were dressed in paint-splattered button-up shirts, loose slacks, and canvas deck shoes. The gesture touched me, and I barely knew what to say.

"Great," I finally managed. "Come on up!"

With not a little laughter, the women managed to climb up the ladder and pile into the main room of the lighthouse.

"It's hot out there," said a short, wiry woman named Gladys. "Thanks for letting us in." She brushed her hands off on her pants, looking around. "This is remarkable."

"Let me give you a tour," I said eagerly.

I was self-conscious about the debris still on the floor and the faded scent of bleach, but I'd made a ton of progress since those early days. I was excited to share the lighthouse with people I knew would really care about it. Sure enough, the women appreciated every inch of the structure, admiring everything from the engineering to the windows to the success of the demolding project.

When we got to the bedroom, I showed them the new floor and told them about Cody's discovery of the papers beneath the floorboards. They oohed and aahed. I also told them my plan to hang the papers in the main entrance, and they seemed impressed.

"Can we see the papers?" Gladys asked, adjusting her glasses.

"Eventually," I promised. "I told Percy my mom was going to send them for restoration. I'll show you when they're clean and mounted."

"Well, time's a-wasting," Percy said, clapping her hands. "Let's get to work!"

They watched me expectantly, as though waiting for orders from a general.

"This is so nice of you," I said, my gaze settling on one of the women's perfectly sprayed hair. "But I need to clean today, not paint. It's way too hot in here for you to help with . . ."

A woman with wispy gray hair burst out laughing. "She thinks we're old!"

The rest of them laughed with abandon, as though she'd said the funniest thing in the world.

"I don't think you're old," I stammered. "I just . . ."

"Honey, my name is Frannie Gussie." She stepped forward and shook my hand with a grip that practically crushed my bones. "My husband passed away five years ago, and I shovel my sidewalk every single year. Have you been here during the winter?"

No, but I'd seen the pictures. Snow up to ten feet high.

"I also clean my gutters and weed my garden," she said. "I'm not afraid of a little hard work."

"Betty Sue here just ran a marathon." Percy pointed at a petite blonde with a wiry figure.

Betty Sue made a pshaw sound. "Half marathon."

I drummed my fingers against my lips, thinking. The help would be nice. But there was still one tiny detail to consider.

"The only bathroom is a compost toilet," I warned them. "It's basically a dry porta potty."

They squealed and giggled.

"If anyone doesn't like it," Percy said, "she can use the beach bathroom, like we have our whole lives. Now." Her steely gaze met mine. "Put us to work."

"Who's good with a scrub brush?" I asked.

～

I spent hours scrubbing the floor of the lantern room and the walls of my bedroom. The lantern room took a lot of work, but my bedroom was the worst. The walls still held traces of the birds that had lived there for longer than I cared to imagine. Several corners and crevices needed serious time with the scrub brush, despite the fact that the bleach had demolished the majority of the stains.

Even with the intense cleaning, the space was still grungy and worn. Fresh paint would make a huge difference. But we would have to peel off a lot of the old paint, particularly from the large frame around the window, before putting on the new.

The cleaning process required a ton of water. I pumped it from the sink in the kitchen, hooked the jugs to the pulley, and transported them upstairs. Then I transported them back downstairs for proper disposal.

By one o'clock I was exhausted, and my stomach was growling. I decided to head back downstairs to see if the ladies would let me buy them lunch.

Walking into the kitchen, I said, "I'm thinking it might be time to wrap it up for the . . ."

The words died on my lips. Percy and her two helpers were caught up in gossip instead of cleaning, because nothing was left to clean. The kitchen was spotless.

"What happened in here?" I gasped.

The windows were open, and thin rays of sunlight shined into the room. There was not a speck of dust or dirt anywhere, not even in the reflection of the sun.

Percy lifted her hands. "We buckled down and got to work."

"It's spotless," I said.

Yes, the paint was still peeling off the walls. The areas by the window were still stained with rust, but the room was pristine. Even the stove was shining, and the area housing the animal nest was open and empty.

I put my hand to my mouth, half-afraid I would burst into tears. "Thank you so, so much. This looks incredible."

"It should." Betty Sue patted her hair. "The second you stopped moving all that water, we had a cleaning crew come in and scrub the place within an inch of its life."

The women burst out laughing.

"Let's take a look downstairs," Percy said.

We climbed down the spiral staircase into the living room. Gladys and her helper, Sarah, were lining up dirty buckets of water. The living room was as spotless as the kitchen.

"I think we're all set in here." Gladys brushed her hands off on her pants.

"This has helped so much." I wanted to hug each and every one of them. "Let's go get lunch—my treat."

I looked forward to sitting down with these women and getting to know them. I hoped they didn't already have plans for a bridge game or something.

"We'll go to my house," Percy said. "I have some casseroles in the freezer, and you need to save your pennies. We want this place to be the best it can be."

The women murmured in agreement.

Even though they were invested in the lighthouse, I could tell these women were on my team. Barely able to hold back a smile, I followed them out to the beach.

Carter was full of compliments when he came over to discuss possibilities for rigging a shower.

"It smells so much better in here," he said. "It looks great, too."

"Thanks." I beamed. Instead of mold and must, the air smelled as fresh as the lake. "Can you believe the women from the historical society helped?"

The lunch with the women at Percy's house had been a lot of fun. She reheated lasagna, and the group of women sat around talking, laughing, and exchanging stories. They were eager to talk about the legend of *The Wanderer* but didn't know much about the story other than the typical details. I didn't share the news that Kip and I were researching it but got the distinct impression that many of them already knew that.

The group also discussed the romance of living in a lighthouse. I decided it might be time for me to sleep over. Staying overnight might help me figure out whether to keep the lighthouse or plan to let it go.

"Now that it's clean," I told Carter, "I'm planning to stay over here one of these nights."

He didn't look thrilled at the idea. "Is that safe? With the vandalism?"

I waved my hand. "I'm not worried," I said. "It stopped the second the Coast Guard got involved."

"Good." He brushed his hand against the wall.

"So . . ." I bit my lip. "How are you doing?"

It was the first time I'd seen him since Kailyn cancelled their date.

Carter pulled out his notebook and measuring tape. He fiddled with the tape for a minute and then said, "You mean about Kailyn?"

"Yeah."

"It sucks, but there's not much I can do. If she doesn't like me, she doesn't like me."

"She *does* like you," I told him. "I think she was afraid of ruining your friendship and panicked."

"I get it," he said. "I was scared of that, too."

"I'm sure you guys will hang out again."

He shrugged. "I still want to beat her at darts. More, now that this happened."

I laughed. "That's the spirit."

Even though it didn't work out with Kailyn this time, I had a feeling there would still be a chance for them in the future. They might even do better hanging out in a group, instead of having the pressure of sitting at some table together on a formal date. That was something to think about.

"You ready to figure out where to install this shower?" Carter asked, heading for the basement.

I had no idea why he was headed downstairs. Maybe to check the cisterns or something. Reluctantly, I followed him down to the basement. It was dark, dingy, and still dirty because I was avoiding it. Too many potential critters.

Pointing at a corner, Carter said, "I think we should set the shower up down here."

"Funny," I said.

He looked confused. "I'm being serious."

"There might be mice down here," I said. "No, no. That's a big no."

Shivers ran up my arms. Even though I didn't know if I'd sell the lighthouse or stay here, I still liked to imagine it as my home. The idea of taking a shower in the basement did not fit in with my vision.

"Hear me out," Carter said. "If the shower is upstairs, you'd have to hand pump it, like you do for the kitchen sink. Which would suck."

It would take a ton of effort to pump enough water for a shower. It would suck if it only sprinkled on me.

"Or . . ." He rubbed his hands together. "We could install a basic electrical pump system down here that will let you get in a decent shower without a lot of work."

"Why couldn't we install that upstairs?" I asked. "Based on the humidifiers and fans we set up, this place can take it."

"Water fights gravity when it heads up," he said. "Unless the shower is in the entryway or the living room, you'd have terrible water pressure."

"I can't just pump into the city water supply like a normal person?"

"That wouldn't change the water pressure," he said. "Besides, the city pipes stop at the edge of Main Street. It would be pretty expensive for you to run a water pipe out here. When I say pretty expensive, I mean the cost of a small planet."

He handed me a stack of brochures.

"Do some reading. The majority of these styles should work, but pick out at least three options in case there's something we can't do. I've already marked the ones I think you should pick."

I flipped through the thin booklets. "How soon are we talking?"

He clicked his tongue. "A week? It'll take a few days for the shower to get here, and then I should be able to install it right away."

I couldn't believe how close we were to making this place habitable.

"That's awesome," I said. "Thank you."

"You know I love this stuff." He surveyed the basement walls and frowned. "By the way, are you planning on living out here during the winter?"

I hesitated. "I don't know yet. Maybe."

Carter's freckled face broke into a grin. "O-kay," he sang. "If it's on the table at all, we'll need to sit down and talk about a heating system. Cody has a few ideas."

"Let me guess," I said. "The price of a small planet?"

"You got it."

My parents planned to return from their antiquing trip that afternoon, so I decided to bake them some "welcome home" brownies. My mother was almost out of flour—which I found in the *S* section in her newly organized cupboard, much to my annoyance—so I set out for the corner grocery.

The store was as cute as everything else in Starlight Cove. It smelled like roasted chicken and freshly baked bread. It offered an olive and salad bar, deli options, and even a small display of homemade desserts. Now that I was close to sleeping over in the lighthouse, I also needed to plan my first meal there. It would be fun coming up with a menu.

Turning down one of the small aisles, I stopped short. Maeve Weatherly stood in the center, looking at an assortment of preserves.

I was just about to sneak out of the aisle before she noticed me, when someone behind me trilled, "Maeve!"

Maeve looked up and our eyes locked. My stomach sank.

Now that I had seen her grandmother's journal, I suspected Maeve was angrier with me than ever before. I couldn't slink away, though, because the woman behind me blocked my exit route. I had no choice but to study an assortment of local honey and wait for a chance to escape.

Maeve gave a swift wave to the woman behind me. "How's Herbert, dear?"

"Cantankerous," she said. "See you this weekend at the Summer Fling?"

"I wouldn't miss it," Maeve cooed.

The woman moved past me down the aisle. I tried to do a U-turn with my tiny cart, but Maeve stopped me. "That was an interesting speech you gave at the historical society."

"It was nice of them to invite me."

Maeve lifted her chin. "I was disappointed to hear about the vandalism. Has it stopped?"

"Yes." I tried to spot guilt, but her face was blank. "The Coast Guard has been keeping close watch."

"Well." She sniffed. "I suppose you simply have a gift for making enemies."

I sighed. "Maeve, look. I feel bad about the journal, but I needed to know there wasn't anything in there that could prove my great-grandfather's innocence."

"You still think he's innocent?" she demanded. "He was alive! How could he possibly be innocent?"

"He never would have left my great-grandmother." My voice was firm. "So, I can't help but think someone was after him. Maybe that someone is the person who stole the treasure."

Maeve gave me a flat look. "Blood is thicker than water. You're loyal to a fault."

"You are, too." I lowered my voice. "You did everything you could to protect your grandmother. And once again, I promise I will never say a word about it. Thank you for showing me the journal."

The cash register rang, customers greeted one another, and the butcher discussed the cut of a steak. Maeve didn't speak. Silence, it seemed, was her go-to weapon. It was my chance to walk away, but something made me hesitate.

"Listen," I said. "I know you have it in for me because of the lighthouse. Now you're mad about this. It seems to me like . . ."

My voice trailed off.

My mother said Maeve didn't get along with her mother. Maybe she was unhappy. I was just in her line of fire.

Hit with inspiration, I said, "I know you're interested in the lighthouse. Do you want to come see it?"

"So you can rub it in my face?" she asked.

"No," I said. "I wouldn't mind getting your input on what I could do to make it better."

Maeve gave a little huff. Leaving her groceries behind in the basket, she turned and walked down the aisle. The front door of the store opened with a tinkle of bells, and she walked down the sidewalk.

Once again, my cheeks flushed with embarrassment. The scolding hadn't been public this time, but her reaction left no doubt.

Maeve Weatherly did not like me. It was foolish to try.

～

I refused to let the encounter ruin my day. I went back to my parents' house and baked brownies with a vengeance.

I made three different kinds: chocolate chip, caramel, and even marshmallow fudge. Each pan was better than the last. When they were finished, I packed some up to bring to Kip as an apology.

The meeting with Maeve must have tested his relationship with her. Even though I would do the same thing all over again, a little chocolate could help soften the blow.

I was halfway to Kip's office when my parents pulled up next to me in their antiquing truck. It practically swayed under the weight of furniture, knickknacks, and art, carefully packed and strapped in. My father beeped the horn.

"Hi!" My mother hung out the window, waving. "Meet us at the store," she cried. "I have the most exciting thing to show you."

"It's pretty incredible," my dad called. "You won't believe it."

Their giddy exuberance charmed me. I realized how much I'd missed them in the past week. My parents were definitely crazy, but also a lot of fun.

"I'll be there in a half hour." I held up the plate of brownies. "I have an errand to run."

I was practically on Main Street, less than a block from the store. Still, I wanted to make sure I had a chance to take the brownies to Kip.

"Go afterward!" My father revved the engine and my mother laughed. "You won't believe what we found."

They took off, honking like crazy. Everyone stared, and I gave an embarrassed smile. Since they were so excited, I decided it wouldn't hurt to stop at the antique shop first.

The truck was just pulling into the back alley when I got there. My mother jumped out and kissed both my cheeks.

"It's good to see you," she said. "Now wait until you see this."

My father hopped out of the driver's seat, shot me a wink, and rummaged through the back. With a grunt, he extracted an object covered in cardboard and burlap. I followed him into the storage room, watching with interest as he laid it down on the table.

"You owe your mother big for this one." He wiped a dirty hand across his forehead. "I never would've spotted it."

My mother picked at the edge of the burlap. "It was on the floor in this lady's basement," she said. "I asked her about it, and you won't believe what she said. Take a look, and then I'll tell you."

My father peeled back the burlap. I watched, hoping it was something that I wouldn't have to pretend to be excited about. He pulled off the layer of cardboard, and I actually gasped.

"Is that a painting of my lighthouse?" I asked, rushing forward.

My mother beamed. "Yes! Isn't that the coolest?"

The painting was done in dark, moody colors, and the lighthouse was instantly recognizable. The daymarks were at the top, the door was the same shade of red, and the lake glittered in the background. The scene nestled against a starscape so detailed it could have been a photograph.

"That's beautiful," I breathed.

It was signed and dated in the lower right-hand corner. I couldn't make out the name, but the year was 1877.

"What's amazing," my mother said, perching on the edge of a wooden crate, "is that I told the woman the story of you and the lighthouse. Turns out, her neighbor was the granddaughter of one of the keepers from way back. This painting was done by his wife. It used to hang *in* the lighthouse until their grandchildren tracked it down and convinced the Coast Guard to give it to them. Well, now they're all dead and gone, and nobody was interested in it anymore."

"Except your mother." My father ruffled my hair. "A piece of history, headed back to its rightful home."

I stared at it in reverence. "Thank you so much."

Resting my fingertips against the rustic wooden frame, I imagined it hanging on the wall. The colors in the painting complemented the brick of the second floor. Maybe that's where it used to hang, when it lived there.

"This is the best present you guys have ever given me," I said. "Seriously."

My father grunted. "I told you we should have gotten her a Nintendo that one year."

I laughed. "Dad, you don't even know what that is."

My mother grabbed a bottle of water from the minifridge and took a long drink. "We need to get the painting cleaned and restored. Bring me that box and paperwork Cody found and I'll send it all at once."

I studied the painting. It sparked something in me. Nostalgia, maybe. The feeling of coming home.

"I don't know if I want to send this away," I told my mother. "I just got it."

"It's an authentic piece of Americana," she said. "You need to get it in the best condition possible. Besides," she added, "there's a bunch of stuff written on the back, and it really needs to be cleaned up."

I held up my hand. "What do you mean, a bunch of stuff written on the back?"

My father laughed. "Spoken like a true treasure hunter!"

I turned the painting over. Sure enough, there was writing on the back: a collection of numbers and dashes that reminded me of Morse code.

"Dad," I said, showing it to him. "That's Morse, right?"

He nodded. "Probably needed to take a message, and the painting was the only place to do it."

My mother batted him on the arm. "No one would take a message on a painting."

"Paper wasn't widely available . . ."

She squinted at the dashes. "Do you really think it means something?"

I pulled out my phone and took a picture. "There's only one way to find out."

My father patted me on the back. "Atta girl."

"Well, whatever," my mother said, pulling her hair off her neck. "Either way, the front needs to be cleaned. It's filthy."

Unfortunately, my mother was right. The paint was covered with dirt and dust. It would look a lot better once it was restored.

I took a picture of the front, too, in case something happened to it.

"That's incredibly cool," I said. "I've got to run, though. I'm delivering some brownies across town."

"What?" My mother held her hand up to her ear. "Did you really just say you're going to help us unload the truck?" She turned to my father. "Honey, did you hear that?"

"Indeed! Time and tide waits for no man." He gave me a vigorous pat on the back. "Let's do it."

I groaned. Considering my father was helping me restore an entire lighthouse, it wasn't like I could say no. I shook my head and rolled up my sleeves.

"What do we need to do first?"

~

I was hot and sweaty by the time we unloaded the truck and was tempted to call off the visit to Kip altogether. But it had been a few days since I'd seen or heard from him, and I was starting to get worried. So I dropped by his office with the plate of brownies, hoping I didn't look as disheveled as I felt.

His office was exactly how I pictured it, with masculine furniture and sleek conference tables.

"Kip?" I called. "Are you here?"

He poked his head out of his office.

I was happy to see him. Unfortunately, he didn't look happy to see me.

Crossing his strong arms, he said, "What are you doing here?"

He was clearly upset about the meeting with Maeve, but I didn't expect him to make it that obvious. I held out the plate of brownies. When he didn't take a step forward, I brought them to him.

"Peace offering." I peeled off the plastic wrap so he could get a whiff of dark chocolate and caramel. "What do you think?"

He gave me a familiar glower.

"Look, I know I put you in a bad position with Maeve," I said. "I wanted to say I'm sorry."

He looked down at the plate of brownies. "Did you make these?"

"Yes."

He leaned against the door. "You bake?"

"Of course." I gave him a stern look. "Why do you look so surprised?"

"I didn't peg you as the domestic type."

"I didn't know I was a type," I said. Then, I remembered his *When Harry Met Sally* comment from the first time we met. "Other than uptight. You said that, once upon a time."

He laughed. "I never said that."

"Yes, you did." I stuck my nose in the air. "But you were wrong, like always."

"Like *always*? Funny, considering I am rarely wrong."

"You're even wrong about that," I said. "How sad."

With an extra flounce in my step, I brushed past him into his office.

It was perfectly organized. Bookshelves with neatly categorized books lined the walls, his desk was free of clutter, and his computer was open to a spreadsheet. The room smelled like Kip—that musky combination of cedar and spice.

I placed the plate of brownies on his desk and sat down in the chair across from it. He eyed me with amusement.

"I assume you're staying because you want a brownie."

"Actually, I stopped by because I want to plan our next steps of attack," I said. "But, since you were wrong again, I think I will go ahead and have a brownie."

I reached for the biggest one on the plate.

Kip grabbed for one, too. He took a bite and raised his eyebrows.

"Wow," he said. "Fancy Pants has a lot of hidden talents."

I grinned. "Did you ever have any doubt?"

Chapter Twenty-Two

The next day, I helped my parents clean the pieces from their trip. Everything was covered with dust and cobwebs. Since it was all antique, we couldn't do much more than wipe the items down with dry rags until they were appraised.

"This is gross," I said, once we were finally on a break.

Stacks of furniture, memorabilia, and bric-a-brac cluttered the back room. My mother flitted around, cataloguing the items in some sort of order I didn't understand. My father and I sipped ice-cold water from bottles.

I wiped my hands on a towel and regarded the mess. "There are more cobwebs here than in a haunted house. Dad, your face is filthy."

His white beard was covered in dust. "You'll never find the gold unless you dig through the dirt," he said, wiping his face with a cloth.

"I'm starting to see the benefits of searching underwater," I said. "Instant shower." Perching on the edge of a wooden crate, I stretched. "What else do we need to do?"

My mother shrugged. She'd tied her hair up in a red handkerchief and looked as cute as ever. "I might dust and wipe things down again, but we should be fine." She beamed at me. "Thanks for all your help."

"Don't thank me yet," I said, getting to my feet. "I have to steal Dad again."

My father was fiddling with the pulls on an armoire. "What do you need?"

"Help with the walls on Monday. Carter said there's some sort of mold-resistant paint we can get. I don't want to do it today because I want to sleep there tonight."

He crawled under a massive oak desk with a measuring tape. "It's a date."

"Great!" I said. "And I looked up the Morse code that was on the back of the painting."

"Yeah?" His voice was muffled. "What did it say?"

"It was just a bunch of numbers. I think it was the coordinates of the lighthouse. Or a serial number or something."

My mother laughed. "Oh no. Really?"

I gave a sheepish nod. "For a minute, I thought I was onto something. But nope."

Silence settled over the room. It was like we all realized at once how far we were from clearing my great-grandfather's name and how close we were to the deadline from the insurance company. My father gave a forced laugh.

"Welcome to the world of treasure hunting! A lifetime of false leads and disappointment."

"Did you get those letters?" I asked.

He gave me a blank look.

"Fitzie," I said.

He nodded. "I'll stop by the safety-deposit box today."

"Thanks," I said. "It would be nice to get an idea of where his mind was."

"Arthur Conan Doyle said, 'When people bury treasure nowadays they do it in the Post-Office bank.' Maybe he's on to something."

Whether that was true or not, I looked forward to reading them. Years had passed since I'd seen Captain Fitzie's letters to my great-grandmother. It would be interesting to see them again and to learn how much my perception of love had changed.

~

Since my parents didn't need any more help, I headed over to Search and Rescue to pick up Captain Ahab. I planned to take him to the beach.

Sheila, a plump older woman who giggled after everything she said, was behind the front desk.

"Dawn!" Chuckling, she got to her feet and led me to the bright-green backyard. "Captain Ahab will be so happy to see you. He's been squirrely all day!"

Sure enough, the dog barked with excitement, running in circles and leaping into the air like he hadn't seen me in months.

"Aw," I said, scratching his ears. "I love you, too."

"I tell you what, honey." Sheila put a hand on a round hip. "If men acted like that when they saw us, they'd be much further ahead in their game."

I tried to imagine Kip Whittaker bouncing up and down as I walked into a room.

"Yup," I said. "That would be a sight to see."

Captain Ahab and I ran all the way to the beach. Once we were there, I let him off the leash and threw a ball. He chased it like it was a seagull. I laughed as he tackled it, snorted, and started the swim to shore.

The gulls soared above, letting out their mournful cry. Tourists walked up and down the boardwalk and set their towels up on the beach. A blond kid in purple swim trunks studied the sailboats on the water with a pair of large binoculars.

A loud burst of laughter exploded across the beach. A group of teenagers was playing touch football. Sami, Kip's niece, was throwing the ball.

She looked cute in a red-and-yellow-striped bikini and wore sunglasses with white frames. She had a good arm and seemed to keep up with the guys, laughing hysterically when they missed a catch.

I thought she looked at me, so I waved. Either she didn't recognize me or didn't want to acknowledge me, because she turned away without waving back. I hid a smile, remembering how embarrassing everything was at that age.

Captain Ahab bounded up and shook water all over me. "Good boy." I scratched behind his damp ears, and his fur stood up like a mohawk.

He nudged me with his snout, as though to say, "Come on, lady."

I threw the ball back out to the water. Off in the distance, a boat caught my eye. It was ridiculously large, with sleek black panels and shiny metallic rails. It moved slowly, and, as I watched, it stopped near the wreckage of *The Wanderer*.

I paused.

The kid with the binoculars was on to building a sand castle by the shore. The binoculars sat on the edge of his family's beach blanket. Turning to his mother, I said, "Do you mind if I borrow those for a second?"

"Go ahead."

I lifted them up and peered at the boat. Sure enough, it was a dive ship. A small group stood at the edge of the deck, suited up in dive gear. They slipped into the water like thieves.

I lowered the binoculars, and my heart started to pound. That was the third time I had seen that boat out there this week.

Since the lost treasure was so famous, it was a popular dive site. People were there all the time. But to see someone come back repeatedly was a little weird.

Even though the wreck had been there for almost a hundred years, I still felt a special claim on it. I didn't like the idea of strangers poking at the bones of the ship. It felt like trespassing on a piece of history that, lately, belonged to me.

I took out my phone and called Kip.

"There's a ship that's been at the wreck site at least three times in the past few days," I said. "I don't like it."

Captain Ahab bounded up and dropped the ball on the sand. It was scratchy and wet against my hand. I practically whipped it out to the water.

"It's a public site," Kip said. "They're probably just checking it out."

"What if the silver is there?" I asked. "What if the current changed and it's there, in plain sight?"

"Then Captain Fitzie would regain his honor," he said. "That's why you're doing all this in the first place. Right?"

I didn't answer.

"What are you doing in twenty minutes?" I finally asked.

"Why?" he asked.

"I was thinking we could go on a wreck dive."

It took me ten minutes to return Captain Ahab to Search and Rescue and rush back to the antique shop. My father was busy researching the new pieces on his iPad. His wool sweater was tucked over his shoulders, and it looked less crazy than usual in the air-conditioned chill of the storage room.

"What's wrong?" he asked, glancing up.

"This boat keeps searching the site of *The Wanderer*," I said, tugging at my hair. "I've seen them there three days in a row."

My father made a grunting noise. "Suckers."

"I want to know what they're up to." I perched on the edge of a wooden crate for a second, then stood right back up. "Kip said he'd meet us at the dock. Dad, I know the silver probably isn't out there, but if it is, I don't want strangers to find it."

My mother fluttered into the storage room, her wild hair buzzing around her head. She was eating fresh strawberries out of a carton. "Did I just hear Dawn say she wanted to dive?"

My father reached for a strawberry. "Like music to my ears."

"Great," I said. "Let's go!"

"Another time," my father said. "We need to keep an eye on the store."

"That boat's out there now," I said. "It's a good time for us to show up."

"Brad's running the register," my mother said. "We could go out."

My father hesitated. He hadn't even gotten in the water since his dives were cancelled. He had to miss it, but his frown indicated that he was not about to budge.

"Dad, it will be fun," I insisted. "You're always telling me to have more fun. We haven't gone down there in years."

My mother touched his shoulder. "You don't have to go in. We could just be the old-timers, rocking the boat."

He didn't answer for a long moment. Then, without a word, he got up and headed for the door.

"Progress," I murmured, to my mother.

She nodded. "That's what I like to see."

Thirty minutes later, my parents, Kip, and I raced across the water in a large speedboat—one with sleek white panels and a pointed bow. It had a navy stripe across the side and a sunrise over the words, *A Beautiful*

Dawn. When I was younger, I pretended to be embarrassed when my father named a boat after me, but, secretly, I always liked it.

I also liked the fact that Kip was on the boat with us. His dark hair was windblown, and he wore a pair of aviator sunglasses that made him look even more attractive than usual. He'd brought enough scuba gear for both of us. My father made a big deal out of checking the equipment and, finally, seemed satisfied that Kip came prepared.

Past the breakers, my father opened the throttle. Icy water misted against my sun-scorched skin as we roared toward the site, bouncing over rough waves. My father lowered our speed as we approached the dive boat at the site of *The Wanderer*. We puttered toward it.

A bald man on the deck waved a warning that divers were below.

My father pulled out a bullhorn. Getting to his feet, he cried, "Ahoy, matey!"

"Dad," I hissed, blushing.

He squinted at me. "I want them to know I'm friendly."

Kip grinned.

My father held up the bullhorn. "May we board?" he asked.

To my surprise, the man on the boat agreed.

~

My mother tied our boat to the edge of the dive boat and helped my father reach for the ladder. I made a move to climb up, too, and Kip touched my leg.

"You're going?" he asked.

"Of course." I narrowed my eyes. "I want to see what they're up to."

"Maybe I should go, too," he said, getting to his feet.

My father waved at me. "Come on, Dawn! Don't let the grass grow under your feet. Kip, you man the fort."

"Sorry, Kip." My mother laughed. "Looks like you're stuck here with me."

I reached for the ladder, stretching to reach the wobbly rungs. The waves rocked the boat up and down. It must have been terrifying for Captain Fitzie to climb into a sinking lifeboat in the midst of a storm. Just thinking about it made me lose my balance, and my father yanked me up onto the deck.

From the new vantage point, I stared into the shadow of *The Wanderer*. The dim outline of the stern pointed upward toward the sky. It pained me to think of the grand ship breaking apart, as well as all the lives that were lost.

The man on the deck approached us. He was bald with strong, tattooed arms. I was glad my father was the one doing the talking.

"What can we help you with?" the man asked in a gravelly voice.

"I have a small interest in wreck dives," my father said. "I wanted to show my daughter what it's all about. How long is your boat planning on sticking around?"

"The day."

My father nodded, running his hand over his beard. "Looking for anything in particular?"

The man shrugged. "Just an easy day out on the water."

My father burst out laughing. "Crumbs," he said. "The silver's still out there. You looking for that?"

"What do you know about it?" the man growled.

"I know it's not under the ship. The whiskey's down there, though."

The man narrowed his eyes. "Yeah?"

My father scratched his beard. "Few years back, it was too dangerous to lift the basin of the ship. Now, there's good enough equipment to do it."

The bald man gave a thin smile. "Sounds like some good drinking on a good payday."

"You can't just walk away with it," my father said. "There are laws against that kind of thing."

"What did you say your name was, again?"

235

"Professor Ward Conners." My father extended his hand. "This is my daughter, Dawn."

While I shook the hand of the bald man, a familiar figure climbed up from the deck down below. Sal. Suddenly, the pieces clicked into place.

The bald man wasn't some bad guy out to loot the ship. He had to be one of Sal's partners, doing a day of research for the documentary. No wonder they'd been there so many days in a row. I felt a huge sense of relief.

"Sal," I called, waving at him.

My father sucked in a sharp breath. "Dawn, go back to the boat," he said. "Tell your mother to prepare my fishing rods."

I looked at him in surprise. "What?"

Back when I was little, my parents would sometimes speak in code in front of people on their dives. It had been years since I'd heard their secret phrases, but something about his tone of voice made me certain that *Prepare my fishing rods* meant he wanted my mother to call the Coast Guard because of a dangerous situation.

"Do you mind?" he said. "I really don't think I feel like diving, after all."

I was so confused. Maybe Sal lied about only wanting to talk to me about the documentary, and my father had already turned him down? But I couldn't imagine my father calling the Coast Guard because of that.

I gave an awkward smile to the tattooed man. Sal must not have realized it was me, because he'd ducked below deck again. I headed back over to the ladder and climbed down to our boat, fighting against the roll of the waves.

My mother set down a bottle of water as Kip helped me climb back in. "Where's your father?"

I braced my hand against the back of a seat, the vinyl hot against my hand. "He said to prepare his fishing rods," I said, sitting down. "But I really don't think—"

Without a moment's hesitation, my mother leapt up and radioed the Coast Guard.

Kip sat next to me. "What's going on?"

"I don't know," I said, frustrated. "My father seems to think there's a dangerous situation. But I know the guy on that ship, so I don't get what the deal is."

Just then, my father climbed down the ladder.

"Did you call?" he asked my mother, quickly untying us from the larger boat.

"Yes." She touched his shoulder. "What's going on?"

"They want to steal the Prohibition whiskey," he said. "Forget the fact that the suction underneath the dome is so dangerous it could kill his men."

My father took the captain's chair. Every sinew in his body looked tense. He shifted our boat into reverse and sped away. When we were parked away from the dive site, he called the Coast Guard again, reporting the information about the whiskey.

"They should be here in a minute," he said, hanging up the radio.

Dread settled in the pit of my stomach.

"Dad, I think you're blowing this out of proportion," I said. "I've met that guy. Not the bald one. The other one. His name's Sal Reynolds and he's doing a documentary on—"

"His name is Sal Reed, and he's no documentary maker," my father growled. "He's a pirate."

I blinked. "What do you mean?"

"He's a treasure hunter, and not a good one," my father said. "Fifteen years ago, off the coast of Spain, he and an Italian were competing for the same find. When they got to the dive site where they both believed the treasure to be, Sal beat the man so badly he was hospitalized."

"You're kidding," I said, stunned.

"Why isn't he in jail?" Kip asked.

My father shook his head. "It happened in international waters, and there was no real proof."

No wonder I never felt comfortable around Sal. The thought that he could be so violent was too frightening to consider.

"If there's no proof," I said slowly, "how do you know he did it?"

"He bragged about it," my father said. "To anyone who would listen. He's unscrupulous, and he's dangerous. That's a man who will do anything to make a quick buck."

I fought off a sudden shiver.

"There's the Coast Guard," my mother said, pointing at the speedboat with red bumpers skimming across the water. It came to a stop near Sal's boat.

I stared at the scene, remembering the easy way Sal crashed the meeting with me and Dusty and the fact that I almost met with him in private to compare notes. I flushed hot and cold, scared to think what could have happened. I'd even mentioned the whiskey at Towboat. I wondered if that was how Sal found out about it, or if he already knew it was there.

Kip reached out and squeezed my hand. "You okay?" he murmured.

"Not really," I mumbled. "I told that guy about the whiskey. I thought . . ."

My father gave me a sharp look. "You've been talking to him?"

I nodded. "A little."

My mother took off her sunglasses. The lines around her eyes were tight with worry. "What did you tell him?"

"Nothing," I said. "Other than the whiskey. I did tell him about that."

I couldn't believe I'd let down my guard and trusted someone like Sal. I'd ignored my instincts about him because I was desperate to get information to protect us from the insurance agency. Apparently, I should have been more worried about protecting us against Sal.

The engines fired up on the black dive boat. It sped off moments later, the wake rocking us so that we had to hang on.

"Good," my mother said, waving at the Coast Guard. "He'll stay away now."

"Good riddance," my father said. Getting to his feet, he tossed me a dive suit. "You ready?"

I was so shaken by what happened with Sal that I'd practically forgotten why we were there. Gripping the rubbery fabric, I hesitated.

"You're coming, right?" I asked him.

My father shook his head. "There won't be enough room to swing a cat," he said. "You and Kip go. Your mom and I will be up here, having a picnic."

He fired up the motor and moved our boat back to the dive site. Once we were stationary, I slid into the warm suit and attached the necessary gear and the oxygen tank. Kip did the same, and I tried not to stare at the emphasis the scuba suit gave to the hard lines of his body.

"You sure you're up for this?" he asked.

I hesitated. My emotions were on edge. I didn't know if I was in a place to see a wreck where so much was lost. But we were here, and with so much at stake, I couldn't back out now.

"Yes," I said. "Let's do it."

Kip slid on his mask. I headed over to the edge of the boat, my hands still trembling. I looked down into the vast expanse below.

"Say hi to *The Wanderer* for us," my father called.

I climbed down the ladder and slid in. Taking a last look at the sunshine, I sank into the dark depths of Lake Michigan to explore the wreckage of the past.

Chapter Twenty-Three

The ghost of the ship came into sight about fifteen feet down. I stared at it in awe, forgetting about everything else. Kip was right next to me, and I gestured in excitement.

Look at that, I thought, as the bow loomed into sight. *There are parts that are perfectly preserved. Like days have passed, not years.*

Kip gave me the thumbs-up. We'd practiced a series of hand signals up above to communicate. He reached out and touched my arm and pointed down, indicating he wanted to keep going.

We headed down thirty feet and sat there for a moment, getting oriented. It was dark and spooky, and I could only hear the sound of my breath. Kip and I wore lamps on the top of our heads, and I flipped mine on.

The Wanderer lay at rest, its wooden base nestled in the sand. This section was not preserved, but covered by moss or algae that seemed to sway back and forth in the motion of the water. Fragments of wreckage were strewn about the floor like car parts in a junkyard.

I swam forward and touched the wood on the ship, the algae rough and slick against my hand. Everything looked the same as it did years ago, back when my father and I spent hours diving the site together.

This time, I said a prayer for the men that were lost and, mostly, the struggles my great-grandfather had to face. Then I began to explore.

I swam over the surface of the sand. My lamp cast an eerie light, and I watched closely for the unexpected sparkle of silver. I knew there wouldn't be coins cast alongside the shipwreck, but I couldn't help but look.

Kip came up next to me and pointed to the ship, indicating we should swim inside. I hesitated for only a moment and then led the way. For a second, I nearly panicked, thinking the ship would collapse on top of us, until I turned to look at Kip. Behind his mask, he smiled, and logic set in. The area we swam through was wide open, not a cave. I relaxed and kept going.

The structure of the boat was a marvel of broken pieces. Splintered metal and wood were scattered along the floor like broken bones. Some pieces were so warped it was hard to believe they had once belonged to the ship.

Kip's light bounced alongside mine as we swam. I spotted a rusted ladder, a broken mast, and the skeleton of a wooden bed. Suddenly, we came upon a rusted metal door. The bars on the small window at the top were reminiscent of a jail cell, and a key sat in the lock.

Kip swam forward and touched it. He pointed and I nodded. The key had to be brass, since it was the only thing that wasn't rusted. I tried to turn it and held my breath, waiting for it to snap off in the lock. Instead, it gave an eerie groan, and the door clicked open.

I followed Kip into the dark and gloomy space. He held up some chains with handcuffs attached, indicating they were used for prisoners. This must have been the brig where the first mate was locked up. I hoped no one else was trapped there when the ship went down. I surveyed the area for a skull, but it was clear, and the cuffs were all unlocked.

Kip swam out of the small room, and we continued to explore the skeleton of the ship until we swam out into another section of open water. There, the base rested on the ground like a dome. A section of the wood was in perfect condition with no algae, preserved by the water and protected by the shift of the current.

This could be the area where Sal hoped to find the whiskey. I ran my hand over the smooth wood and shivered. It would take some serious equipment to fight the current enough to flip the dome. I wouldn't want to try it.

Kip and I kept moving. The ghostly sight of the abandoned ship and the rhythm of my breath felt hypnotic. It was so peaceful that I wanted to stay at the bottom of the lake forever. Eventually, though, Kip tapped my shoulder and pointed at his watch.

It was time to go.

Slowly, we rose to the surface of the water, stopping as we went up.

I turned off my light and he did the same. Our eyes adjusted to the dim light, and, as we waited, we looked at each other. It didn't feel strange or awkward. It was a different form of communication—one that didn't exist up above.

When we surfaced, I removed my oxygen mask and took in deep breaths of fresh air.

Kip did the same. This time, he turned to me and smiled. We still didn't speak. The stillness of the water heavy upon us, we climbed the ladder back up to the boat.

When we docked at the marina, my mother tried to convince Kip to join us for a family dinner.

"Thanks," he said. "I already have plans tonight. We'll have to do it some other time."

I was disappointed. On the other hand, I didn't know that I wanted to sit at a dinner with Kip and my parents. I could only imagine the knowing looks my mother would send my way.

To her credit, she didn't say one word about it until we'd said our good-byes, pulled the cover over the boat, and headed back toward town. My father was at least five feet ahead of us, talking to someone on his cell phone.

My mother looped her arm in mine. "Interesting friendship you've developed with Kip Whittaker," she sang. "Did the two of you enjoy your time underwater?"

I flushed. It felt so intimate, floating near the wreckage with only Kip by my side.

"Sure," I said. "It was fun."

"Please." My mother gave me a knowing look. "Since I like being right, I'd like to remind you I'm the one who thought you two would be a good match."

A tiny smile tugged at the corner of my mouth.

She nudged me with her hip. "You don't have anything to say to that?"

"Not one word," I said cheerfully. "Not even a syllable."

"You don't have to say it." She smiled. "It's written all over your face."

Chapter Twenty-Four

The images of *The Wanderer* swirled through my head, connecting me even more strongly with the ship and its history. The rest of the afternoon, I looked forward to my night in the lighthouse. Sleeping on the water as the ships passed by? I couldn't wait.

The anticipation reminded me of the sleepovers Libby and I used to have at her house. We'd bounce off the walls all day in school, act crazy through dinner, and make big plans to stay up all night. Of course, we never made it past eleven.

Staying up all night was not on my to-do list, but the mood was the same. I spent hours prepping, stocking up on everything from water to snacks to a kettle for morning coffee. I also spent an unnecessary amount of time wondering what I would do if I spotted the ghost of the keeper, before finally managing to push that thought far from my mind.

Prepping the bedroom was fun. I brought a rolled-up egg crate mattress from my parents' house and placed it beneath a down sleeping bag. I set up a temporary bedside table using a black crate with a slab of wood on top. The Coleman kerosene camping lamp Kailyn gave me in the gift basket was the perfect addition.

For entertainment, I planned to read the keeper's manual from cover to cover. Now that the women from the historical society were on my side, I had asked Percy to swap my *Instructions to Light-Keepers* book for the one original to the lighthouse. Because she was the nicest person ever, she made me feel I was doing the historical society a favor with the swap.

"This book is marked up," she'd said, handing it to me. "We'd much rather have a clean copy."

"That is not true, and you know it." I hugged her. "Thank you so much."

How I felt about the people of Starlight Cove had changed completely. Yes, some were still rude to me simply because of my family name, but the majority of people were kind, compassionate, and interested in helping out. Maybe it was because of the progress I'd made on the lighthouse, the fact that I was friendly with people like Kailyn, Kip Whittaker, and the Hendersons, or because I was more inclined to smile and be friendly myself.

Whatever it was, my comfort level was much higher than when I first arrived, prompting my desire to sleep in the lighthouse. Months ago, I wouldn't have even considered staying in a place with paint peeling off the walls, birds roosting on the window, and a toilet that didn't flush. But to quote my father, *You can't stay dry and in one temperature all your life*, and I was ready to change it up.

That night, I settled into my soft foam mattress and turned on the lamp next to the bed. The mattress was surprisingly comfortable. Really comfortable, actually, even though I was so far outside of my comfort zone.

Sitting up on one elbow, I opened up my copy of the keeper's manual. I read a section at a time, learning about requirements such as "filling the lamps" and "regulating the flames." The information was in-depth and sometimes complicated.

The more I skimmed, the more I realized Percy was right. The copy from the historical society *was* marked up. In fact, specific letters were underlined in certain starred sections and pages. Eventually, the redundancy became so apparent that I compared a few sections, only to discover the same letters were underlined every time.

I sucked in a sharp breath. I didn't have paper, so I reached for my phone and copied the letters into the notes section:

difnhetoeanotcsird

My heart started to pound.

Was it a code? A secret message?

I gave a small laugh. The romance of staying in the lighthouse was probably getting to me. Still, I couldn't help but let my imagination run wild. This code could have something to do with the lost treasure.

Even though it was a reach, the letters were underlined in the book for a reason. I wanted to believe it was connected to *The Wanderer*, but it was probably some game the keepers played. I imagined them sending secret messages to one another to pass the time. The first one to unscramble the message would win.

If it was a game, it wasn't easy. I tried to unscramble the letters for nearly an hour and finally gave up. Frustrated, I copied down the page and section numbers. I couldn't wait to show my dad. He'd tease me about being a treasure hunter, like he did with the painting, but I was okay with that.

Closing the book, I put my head back against the pillow and stared up at the starlike pattern in the center of the ceiling above me. Even though the room smelled like fresh wood, it was also tinged with the stale odor of bleach. I pushed back the covers and decided to open the window.

In the event of another act of vandalism, Cody had put a temporary cover behind the window, like a metal screen. I opened the window and pulled it out, placing it carefully on the floor of the bedroom. Then, I put my head out the window and breathed in the night.

The breeze from outside was cool and crisp. Stars stretched across the lake as far as I could see, and a ghostlike mist curled above the water. I rushed back over to my bed and slid back between the covers.

To my surprise, the star on the ceiling lit up. It dimmed and lit again. I sat straight up, trying to figure out what was going on.

Then, I burst out laughing.

Of course.

Without the cover on the window, the pulse of light gleamed from the lantern above. I stared at it, hypnotized by the rhythm. Flash flash, pause, flash flash flash flash, pause, flash flash.

The ships that passed by would recognize the light as the port of Starlight Cove. But for me, for the moment, it wasn't just a call sign—it was my home address.

∽

The romance of falling asleep to the rhythm of the lantern light was the exact opposite of getting woken up by a fog signal at four in the morning.

I bolted awake, convinced a train was about to run me over. The low horn blew once more and then went silent. I caught my breath and remembered.

Lighthouse.

I settled back into my pillow, pulling the feather sleeping bag tightly around me. My eyes started to close, and the foghorn gave another sharp warning. I sat straight up and waited.

It did it again.

I flew to my feet and fumbled my way to the window. The lake was now covered in a heavy fog, which would limit the light's arc of visibility. Rain misted through the air, and I reached out my hand to feel the cool moisture. I brought my hand back inside and wiped it against my sweatshirt.

The fog signal sounded again.

I had two options: I could slink back to my parents' house or close the window and go back to bed.

The foghorn blared once more, deep and low.

Its sound reminded me of those nights when I was younger, out on a ship in a strange place, watching for lighthouses in the distance. Some nights, the fog was so thick I believed we would be lost at sea forever. The fear lessened each time that deep, sonorous cry filled the night.

Was anyone on the water comforted by the sound of my lighthouse? I imagined it, and a deep peace ran through me. It might be four o'clock in the morning, and I might be wide awake, but I was sleeping in a lighthouse.

It was the coolest thing I'd ever done.

The fog detector sensors were up on the gallery—small machines that looked like robots. The actual foghorn was located in the basement but capped on the interior, which meant the sound would be muffled if I closed the window. Once it was shut, I could hear the low moan of the foghorn but nothing like the alarm from before.

I climbed back into my bed and decided to pretend the lighthouse was snoring. Like a friendly giant in a fairy tale, sent to protect me. Pulling the extra pillow over my head, I went back to sleep.

After my big night, Kailyn and I met for breakfast at Towboat. The special pancakes were Fresh Strawberries and Whipped Cream. We ordered them to share, along with a double side of bacon.

I was tired but happy. I'd crawled out of bed, gone on my typical morning run, and met her without showering. I felt wild, as if I'd slept out on the sand.

We were discussing one of her new listings when she leaned forward. "Someone is s-t-a-r-i-n-g at you," she whispered.

Excitement rushed through me. Maybe Kip Whittaker was here. But the look on Kailyn's face indicated s-t-a-r-i-n-g was not a good thing.

"It's some weird guy," she murmured. "Rodentlike."

I turned to look.

Sal was seated just a few tables over with two friends. He raised his hand in greeting, and I shivered. The fact that he was still hanging around seemed threatening, somehow. He should have left town the moment we figured out who he was.

I gave him a cold glare and turned back to Kailyn.

She grinned. "Friend of yours?"

"No," I said, in a low tone. "That's Sal and the treasure hunters. They were searching the site of *The Wanderer*."

Her mouth dropped open. "That is *so cool*," she squealed. "I barely knew treasure hunters *existed* before I met you, and now you're, like, throwing it out in a sentence. Sal and the Treasure Hunters. That's a great name for a band."

The busboy arrived with my pot of hot water, and I turned my attention to my travel bag. I riffled through my collection of tea. Settling on licorice, I dropped it into the water and inhaled its sharp scent.

"Smart," Kailyn said, watching me. "You got a bottle of liquor in there, too?"

"No." I glanced back over my shoulder at Sal. "Why, do you need one?"

"Yes." She toyed with a strand of hair. "I walked by the hardware store this morning. Carter was standing in the door, and I didn't know what to do."

"So, what *did* you do?" I asked.

"I darted past him like a streaker." She dabbed at her face with a napkin. "You know, cancelling the date with him seemed like a good call, but I think it ruined my life. I keep imagining everything that could have happened and the fact that, now, it won't."

"It could still happen," I told her. "If you want it to."

Ever since I'd spoken with Carter, I'd had the impression he was willing to give her another chance. I'd even tried to think up some way to get the two in the same room together with other people. That way, they could have a group interaction without feeling pressured.

I waited to bring up the topic until our food arrived. Then I dug my fork into a plump strawberry and said, "It seems like business is pretty busy lately," as a lead-in.

"Best quarter ever."

"So, I was thinking." I took a bite of crispy bacon. "You should—"

"Hello, ladies," said a familiar voice.

I looked up. "Kip!"

I half stood, but quickly sat back down. I hadn't seen him since that day in the water, and I didn't want to make it super obvious I was excited to see him. Based on Kailyn's wide grin, it was too late.

"Hi, Kip," she sang. "Would you like to join us?"

I gave him a hopeful smile. Unfortunately, he held up a to-go cup of coffee.

"I have to get to work." His eyes landed on my licorice tea bag, and he smiled. "Sorry to interrupt. Dawn, I just wanted to let you know I'm going to get Maeve to let us into her mother's barn."

I appreciated his confidence, considering how rude she was to me at the grocery store.

"Good luck." After a pause, I asked, "Why do you want to look in the barn?"

"The final love letter from Fitzie to Madeline has to be somewhere. I can't imagine Ruth would have destroyed it. If she was that obsessed with him, she probably kept it and pretended it was written to her."

"What are you talking about?" Kailyn asked.

"A history hunt," I said quickly. "To learn more about my family."

She clapped her hands in delight. "You mean *The Wanderer*? Kip, we were just talking about treasure hunters. You think something's hidden in Beulah's barn?"

I shushed her, sneaking a peek at Sal. He and his friends seemed engrossed in eggs, hash browns, and the paper dispersed between them. I didn't think he'd heard.

"No," I told Kailyn. "This is about history, not treasure." I shot Kip a warning look. "Let me think about it."

"That's all I can ask." He winked. "Have a good day, ladies."

"Bye, Kip!" Kailyn sang.

We watched him leave in silence.

The moment he was out of earshot, she murmured, "I have so much to say right now, *but* considering we are in his sister's restaurant, I am going to exercise discretion."

"Good," I mumbled.

It was getting impossible for me to ignore the heat between Kip and me. I wanted something to happen but didn't want to face the hurt of walking away. I didn't know what to do.

Kailyn stirred more cream into her coffee. "Before Mr. Dashing showed up, you said you had an idea for me."

My thoughts snapped back to Carter. "Yes," I said. "You should have a party. To let even more people know what you do. A huge marketing-type event."

She chewed her lip. "Where would I . . . ?"

"Your office," I said. "It's big, and it's a darling location."

"That's not a bad idea." She chewed a piece of bacon, scanning the room. "I could showcase my new listings and even ask the Harbor Resort to donate food. What made you think of it?"

I set down the forkful of pancake that was halfway to my mouth.

"Carter," I said, honestly. "I think you should hang out. In a group situation. A way that won't be forced."

Her smile dimmed. "Oh."

"Look, it was just an idea," I said in a rush. "You said walking by the hardware store was weird, and it doesn't have to be like that. The sooner you two get back to normal, the better chance you'll have of staying friends or . . . whatever."

Kailyn dipped her fork into the whipped cream. "It's not a terrible idea," she said. "I wouldn't be throwing a party to see him."

"You'd be doing it to drum up business," I said.

"He can show up or not, no big deal."

"Exactly."

"I might set up a glow-in-the-dark volleyball game." She giggled. "Just in case."

I grinned. "That's my girl."

Kailyn and I finished up breakfast, and she headed off to a showing.

On the way out of Towboat, I ducked into the restroom to make sure I looked okay when Kip stopped by our table. I was tempted to call him under the pretense of talking about Beulah, but he'd see right through that. Still, I was tempted.

I was so busy thinking about Kip that I forgot all about Sal. He was waiting by the stairs as I headed toward the exit. His friends were nowhere in sight.

"Dawn," he called.

I pretended not to hear, determined not to get into a conversation with him. I was halfway up the stairs when a rough hand grabbed my arm. Sal's grip was tight, and I let out a frightened yelp.

"Hey!" I cried, turning to him.

"I think you and I need to have a little chat," he growled.

I tried to jerk my arm away, but he squeezed it even tighter. The slow start of a bruise pulsed beneath his sharp pinch. But the hostile look in his eye scared me more than the pressure on my arm.

"Let go of me." My voice shook. "Seriously, Sal. Let go of me right now or I will make a scene you will regret."

He stared at me, his eyes narrowed to dangerous slits. The restaurant was busy, but everyone was distracted, eating breakfast or caught up in a conversation. Even if I screamed, there was still plenty he could do before anyone would have time to intervene.

Just then, the door banged open, and a family headed in from Main Street. Sal gave my arm one last hard pinch before dropping it to let them pass.

The moment they did, he hissed, "Your father called the Coast Guard on me."

"You don't know that," I said.

He snorted. "Sure, I do. But I've been watching you, Dawn." His tone made me shudder. "I know exactly where you go and what you do."

"What do you want from me?" I asked, glaring at him.

"Information."

"Sal, I don't know anything about the treasure. My *family* doesn't know anything about the treasure. I promise you that."

"I think we both know that's not true."

My head pounded. "It *is* true," I insisted. "Look if we knew where it was, we—"

"You'll find it," he said. "And I'll be right there when you do."

"Is that a threat?" I asked.

Sal reached into the front pocket of his shirt and pulled out his black sunglasses. "Just tell your father to stay out of my way."

"And if he doesn't?"

He sneered. "Do you really want to find out?"

Before I could respond, Sal headed up the stairs and disappeared onto the street. The door slammed shut behind him, and I swallowed hard.

"You okay, honey?" asked a friendly voice at my shoulder. It was one of the waitresses, eyeing me with concern.

It took a moment for me to answer.

"Yes," I lied. "Everything's fine."

Legs shaking, I headed up the stairs and out to the street. I stepped outside, startled by the brightness of the sun after standing so long in the darkness.

~

The antique shop was busy when I walked in.

My father was behind the cash register in a pair of khaki cargo shorts and a gray T-shirt, with a wool sweater draped across his shoulders. I rushed over to hug him, breathing in his familiar smell of Carmex and vanilla-scented tobacco.

"How was your night in the lighthouse?" he asked.

"Pretty amazing." I took a deep breath, trying to recapture the calm of the starry night and the mist that floated over the water. "But I had a bad morning. I just ran into Sal."

My father tensed. "What happened?"

I showed him my arm. The skin was red where he'd gripped it but still didn't display the bruise under the surface. "He cornered me at Towboat and said some stuff about watching us. That he'd be there when we found the treasure."

My father let out some choice cusswords. "He threatened you?"

I shook my head. "He threatened *you*."

That made my father laugh. "Good luck to him, then."

"Dad, I—"

He gave me a look. "Dawn, Sal Reed is not the first person to throw down the gauntlet with me. It's happened many, many times before."

I frowned. In all the years my parents spent out on the water, it never dawned on me that treasure hunting could be considered dangerous.

"He wants the silver and thinks that we have it," I said.

My father shook his head. "Too bad. He can't squeeze blood from a rock."

"But he *thinks* we know something," I said. "I don't want him to—"

"He's not going to risk jail time unless there's something at stake," my father said. "If he bothers you again, let me know. It'll be fine."

Even though my father had put me in a lifetime of situations where things were not fine, I still trusted him. Letting out a slow breath, I surveyed the store.

"Have you been busy?" I asked, forcing Sal out of my mind.

He gestured at a couple in the corner. "They're about to bite."

Stoic and serious, the couple was deep in discussion about an armoire. I recognized it as one of the pieces I helped lug into the back of the store after the antiquing trip. Now that the dirt and dust was removed, it looked great. It was amazing what a little elbow grease could do. It reminded me of the work I'd done on the lighthouse.

I pulled the keeper's manual out of my shoulder bag.

"I have something to show you," I said.

Flipping through the book, I showed him where the letters were underlined in different sections. "It's always the same." I showed him a few examples. "Do you think it was a mariner's game or something?"

My father studied it for a moment. "You've got me."

"Do you think . . . it had anything to do with *The Wanderer*?"

"Doubt it. More likely, the keeper put together codes for his kids to translate."

"Wait." A memory hit me. "Did you do that when I was little?"

He smiled. "Ship scavenger hunts. Kept you on your toes."

I laughed, remembering. My father used to draw me treasure maps with clues. I'd spend the mornings racing around the ship, trying to find the bag of gold-wrapped chocolate coins he'd hidden under clusters of life jackets or fishing poles.

"This keeper could have done the same thing," I said, studying the scrambled letters. "How cool is that?"

My father nodded. "It's interesting when we start to look at history as real people with families and lives," he said. "Not just blank faces on black-and-white photographs."

"Excuse me." The couple looking at the armoire approached us. "Can you tell us a little about this piece?"

My father strolled out from behind the counter and launched into its origins. I watched the professor in him come out as he pointed out the German origin, the unique grain of the wood, and the famed furniture company on the label in the bottom drawer. By the time my father was finished, the husband and wife were at the counter, credit card ready to go.

When they left to bring in a dolly, my father waved off my praise.

"I knew they'd bite. Your mother and I can always spot the ones with a U-Haul waiting out front." His face brightened. "Oh! I got the letters. They're in the back room."

I bolted for the storage-room door. "You don't even know how excited I am about this. Did you look at them?"

He shook his head. "I stopped reading love letters a long time ago."

"Why?"

My father straightened his sweater. "Well, I started writing them instead."

The sentiment surprised me. "For Mom?"

"Of course for your mother!" he boomed. "Who do you think?"

Laughing, I headed into the back room.

There, sitting on a cluttered table, was the same storage chest I remembered. I opened the familiar lock and stared at the collection. I was tempted to start reading right then and there but managed to hold off. I wanted to read the letters in the lighthouse.

I also wanted to read them with Kip. If I read the letters on my own, I might feel sentimental and not see the information that was there. But if he were there, reading them with me, he could help identify information I might not see.

At least, that's what I told myself.

Chapter Twenty-Five

Kip arrived at the lighthouse at eight o'clock on the dot.

I'd spent the evening whipping up dinner in the makeshift kitchen. It wasn't fancy, but I was more than a little proud of my spaghetti, Caesar salad, and loaf of crusty, toasted French bread. I added fresh garlic and basil from my mother's herb garden to the sauce and imagined planting a garden of my own up on the gallery.

"Something smells good up here," a voice called from the stairwell.

Kip stepped into the kitchen, carrying a bottle of red wine.

The sight of him made everything go still. He wore a weathered gray T-shirt that showed off every muscle in his upper body and emphasized the deep hue of his eyes. I took the bottle of wine from him and, as our hands brushed, my stomach fluttered.

"Did you lock the front door behind you?" I asked.

"Secured." He surveyed the room. "The lighthouse looks great."

I beamed. "Doesn't it?" After wiping my hands off on a towel, I set it on the edge of the sink. "Follow me."

I gave Kip a quick tour, showing him all the details I'd fallen in love with: the windows that push out on the bottom floor, the cozy setup I had for a bedroom, and of course, the gallery outside the lantern room.

"What a view." Kip walked over to the edge of the railing and admired the lake. "This would be my favorite spot."

"It's mine." I hesitated before walking up behind him. "You can see *The Wanderer* from here. Isn't that wild?"

He turned to look at me.

My pulse jumped at our sudden closeness. I turned and headed back toward the door.

"It's about to storm," I said quickly. "Is the table in the kitchen okay?"

Kip didn't answer, and I turned back to look at him. Even in the fresh air, I could still smell his spicy scent. The sight of him backlit by the setting sun was so attractive my knees went weak.

"That sounds great," he said, and followed me to the door.

The kitchen was cozy, with its low lights and the fresh scent of garlic in the air. Over dinner, I told Kip that I'd slept in the lighthouse the night before.

"Bold," he said. "You weren't scared the ghost of the keeper would show his face?"

"Don't say that." I shuddered. "The thought of a ghost did not keep me awake. The foghorn, on the other hand . . ." I explained the sudden blast of sound that happened at four in the morning, and he laughed.

The storm hit just as we finished dinner. Rain started to pour outside, slapping against the water with a fury. I loved listening to the sound. It reminded me of the storms I saw at sea when I was younger.

"Should we close the window?" I asked.

"I don't mind it being open." Kip carried our dishes to the sink. "There's something romantic about a storm." He tossed me a smile over his shoulder. "Appropriate, considering we're about to read love letters to each other."

I shifted in my seat. The storm outside, the glass of wine I drank with dinner, and the presence of Kip Whittaker in my kitchen were making me start to think things I shouldn't. Like how broad his shoulders were in his T-shirt, and whether the stubble on his cheek would feel as warm and soft as it looked.

"You okay?" He raised an eyebrow.

"Great!" Snapping back to my senses, I headed over to the sink. "This is the tricky part about this sink . . ." I placed the plug in the bottom of the basin. "Have you ever pumped water to do dishes?"

"I've always wanted to," he said cheerfully.

I watched in amusement as he pressed down on the pump with a casual tap of his hand. "It's going to take a little bit more effort than that."

Kip frowned. He pressed down on the pump and grunted. Then, he spotted the latch on the back and unhooked it.

I laughed.

"Funny," he said, playfully flicking water at me.

Kip washed the dishes and I put them away, trying not to take the intimacy of the situation too seriously.

Last night? I'd tell Kailyn. *Oh, it was just another night washing dishes with Kip Whittaker.*

I chugged some wine.

Kip dried his hands on the kitchen towel when the dishes were complete. "Should we get started?"

"Sure." The metal box was resting on the ancient iron shelves. Carefully, I unhinged it and pulled out a stack of letters. I checked the table one last time for crumbs or spills and then spread out the papers.

"What, exactly, should we be looking for?" I asked.

Kip studied the stack. "Ones that look or sound like they came after the wreck. Maybe Ruth gave her the last letter, after all. It could be here."

I opened the first letter in the stack and squinted at it. The light in the room was dim, and the darkness from the storm outside made it impossible to read the cramped penmanship.

"Hold on," I said.

I climbed back up to my bedroom and retrieved the old kerosene lamp sitting by my bed. I set it on the kitchen table and lit it. The smell of kerosene was sharp and old-fashioned.

I smiled at Kip. "Kind of appropriate, given the time period we're reading about."

He smiled back. "Incredibly appropriate."

We hovered around the lamp, sifting through the letters. Thunder crashed outside as the thin paper passed through our hands. The romantic words pooled in front of my eyes like tears.

> Dearest heart,
> As the ship tosses on the lost waves of the water, I cannot help but feel lost without you. I know my coordinates, the stars tell me my location, but still I am lost. What is the sense of loneliness? The sense of two souls separated in the wind, drifting farther apart until the pull of the earth will draw us together once again. I go about my daily duties hiding a secret: I am not whole. I am half the man you made me. Will these days stifle the breath in our bodies until it can be once again shared? There are moments I look out across the waves, and I think I see you there, waiting for me. Your essence, your ether, your passion hovering like mist over the water. I am lost without you. You are my home.

The words tugged at my heart the way they did when I was a teenager. For some reason, I figured the words would seem less, now that I was older. Instead, they seemed more, knowing a man could love his wife so much.

Practically holding my breath, I kept reading.

Dearest heart . . .
My only love . . .
You are the one who keeps my eyes on the shore . . .

After one particularly romantic passage, I let out a heartfelt sigh.

"What is it?" Kip looked up, a lock of dark hair falling over his eyebrow.

It was hard to explain and, of course, I couldn't explain it to Kip. Back when I used to read the letters when I was young, I believed I would find someone who would love me that much. Kip fit the ideal of the man I imagined, but I didn't dare dream of him saying these things to me.

"It's pretty romantic stuff, isn't it?" he said, when I didn't answer. "Your great-grandfather had a way with words. It's clear that he loved her. Listen to this one."

In a low, serious tone, he read:

Dearest heart,
Tonight, I got in an argument with the moon. It shone over the water, reflecting like silver, its beams dancing on the waves with such a display of beauty that I felt weakened in the knees. The sight was one of pure magnificence, the proof that glory exists in this lonely world. Yet, when the moon tried to wrap its beams around me, I pushed it away and laughed. "Do you think I have never seen a beauty greater than yours?" I cried. "She sits alone tonight, a light on the shore. The magnificence that shines from her face turns your brilliance to dark." Dearest heart, I will fall to sleep tonight with your beauty lighting my way.

I stared down at my hands, trying not to shiver as the romance of the phrases rained down on me. I'd never had a man read me poetry before and had never wanted to, but this changed my mind. I glanced up just as Kip did, and our eyes met. Embarrassed, I looked back down at my hands.

"Man," he said, when he was finished. "I think I just fell in love with him."

I burst out laughing. "So did I."

"I can see why these letters meant something to you. You can hear the influences of the old poets in there. It's really romantic." He got a serious look on his face. "It *is* hard to believe that a man with this depth of passion would abandon his wife."

I could see the moon outside the window. Getting up, I walked over to look at it. I could imagine my great-grandfather sitting in the cabin of his ship, staring out the window before putting pen to page.

Turning away from the window, I said, "Remember what you said about the ghost of the keeper? I also heard there's a legend that my great-grandmother walked the shores, waiting for Fitzie to come home. That she still does that today. I don't like thinking that. I like to believe they're together now."

Kip considered. "I bet he borrowed a lute from an angel. He's been serenading her ever since."

I laughed. "I can see that."

I walked back to my chair. We sat in silence for a moment. Lightning lit the room with an electric glow.

"It's strange sitting in here." I gestured at the old-fashioned kitchen and the lamp burning in front of us. "It feels like stepping back in time. I feel like I'm reading a fairy tale, or something from a poet. It was fun reading these when I was younger, but not so melancholy. Back then, I still believed . . ."

"It was possible to love somebody like that?" Kip's eyes held mine.

I nodded, blushing.

Kip gave me a look that I felt all the way down to my toes. He leaned forward. Suddenly, I realized he was going to kiss me. I quickly picked up another letter.

"They're fascinating, though, aren't they?" I said in a rush. "They're so old and are in such good condition. Don't you think?"

Outside the window, the rain fell in sheets. Thunder crashed, the lightning flashed, and the beam of the lighthouse caressed the water as I avoided Kip's eyes. I wanted to know what would happen if I fell into his arms but couldn't bring myself to do it.

The idea of leaving Kip to go back to Boston hurt me more than the reality of the breakup with Todd.

I stared down at the letters. Poor Madeline. She loved Fitzie so deeply but lost him. Was it worth the heartache, in the end?

Out of the corner of my eye, I could see Kip watching me. I smelled the scent of spice and cedar and felt the warmth of his gaze. Pushing back my chair, I walked over to the stove.

"I'm going to make us some tea," I said, reaching for the kettle.

"Ah, tea." Kip glowered at the love letters. "That's exactly what we need."

~

I tossed and turned that night. Maybe, after Sal's threat, I should have been scared to sleep alone in the lighthouse. But the only thing I could think about was Kip. The ghost of his scent lingered in the room, along with the scent of stale kerosene and red wine.

The egg crate, so comfortable the night before, pushed into my back like little lumps. Every sound I heard, every creaking crack of the water against the base of the lighthouse or whistle of the wind outside, I imagined was Kip, standing outside, planning to ring the bell.

Of course, it wasn't realistic to think that way. The fact that I pulled away when he leaned in spoke volumes. Why would Kip think I had any interest in him at all?

~

My body ached when I woke up. The sleeping bag was hot, and I was sweating and uncomfortable. I was also annoyed that I refused to let myself explore a relationship with Kip because I didn't want to feel the pain of walking away.

Unless, of course, I decided to throw responsibility out the window, move into the lighthouse, and start a life in Starlight Cove. Something I was not brave enough to do.

I made my way down the stairs and climbed down the ladder to the beach. On Main Street, I got a cup of coffee, a muffin, and two bacon biscuits and headed over to the Search and Rescue building for a little TLC. Captain Ahab was excited to see me and, especially, the bacon biscuit.

"We're not going anywhere exciting today," I told the dog, settling in next to him on the grass. It was damp from the rain the night before. "We're just going to hang out."

I buried my face in his fur. His body was warm, and he smelled good, like he'd been groomed. His tail thumped in the grass, and he snorted as he finished his breakfast. Then he sought out my face, licking me as I squealed and pushed him away.

"No kissing," I told the dog. "I just want to cuddle."

Captain Ahab grinned. He snuggled up next to me on the grass, as though he knew what I was talking about.

Resting his head on his front paws, he let out a loud "Rrrumph."

"I know how you feel, buddy," I told him. "I know exactly how you feel."

That night, I made dinner at my parents' house. They were at a barbecue with friends, so I had the house to myself. I'd just loaded the dishwasher and was right in the middle of rereading the letter from the insurance company, trying to spot some indication that the letter was a bluff, when my cell phone rang.

To my surprise, the caller ID showed a picture of Todd and me standing on a sailboat, his arms wrapped around my shoulders. I stared at it, stunned. Finally, I picked up the phone.

"Todd?" I said.

"Dawn." My name came out like a sigh. "It's great to hear your voice."

I didn't know if I felt the same. I was right in the middle of rereading what would happen if the ninety-day deadline from the insurance company wasn't met. The deadline was right around the corner. I was nowhere near able to supply the hard and fast evidence required to prove Fitzie's innocence. With that in mind, I didn't particularly want to talk to someone who wanted nothing to do with my family.

I set the letter down. "Is everything okay, Todd?"

"I made a mistake," he said, in a low tone. "I miss you."

Emotion flooded my system. Resentment was at the top of the list, followed by a faded sense of hope. I rested my hands against the counter and didn't say a word.

"Dawn, I made a mistake," he repeated. "I didn't know how to react, learning all that about your family secondhand. My actions were immature and, I'm certain, very hurtful."

I looked out the kitchen window at the forest behind the house. The shadows and sun made brilliant patterns along the border of the yard.

"I'm calling to apologize," he told me. "I want you to give us another chance."

I gripped the phone like an anchor. Everything about his voice was familiar: the pauses in his sentences and even the sound of his breath. Todd was a piece of the predictable world I'd built for myself before everything fell apart.

Could that world still be rebuilt? The idea made the letter on the counter less frightening.

"Where is this coming from?" I asked.

"It's been a lonely summer," he admitted. "I've missed our weekends together, how much we had in common, the things we talked about . . ."

I bit my lip. In my opinion, he and I didn't have that much in common. We got along well, but I wasn't interested in polo matches, political debates, or hearing about the stock market.

"Todd, I don't—"

"I've missed you, Dawn," he said. "I've missed *you*."

The sentiment behind the words struck me. He wanted our old life back. That, I could relate to. I wanted my old life back, too.

Yes, I fantasized about staying in Starlight Cove. But maybe I was just afraid to go back to Boston and a life that had fallen apart. With Todd, I could piece things back to the way they were. If I tried hard enough, it could be like nothing had changed at all.

"I missed you, too," I said.

He let out a breath. "I'm so glad. Tell me what you've been doing."

I sat down at the kitchen table and told him everything: the insurance company, the search for *The Wanderer*, and the remodeling of the lighthouse. But for some reason, I left out Kip.

"Do you really think you can convince the insurance company your great-grandfather was innocent?" Todd asked. "It sounds to me like you haven't found much to back that up."

I'd forgotten how skeptical he could be.

"I haven't," I told him. "I'm working on it."

"Dawn, I think you should come home," he said. "Your parents can handle this. They don't need you."

I snorted. "They *do* need me," I said. "They can't handle this on their own."

"If they wanted to, they could."

I opened my mouth to explain. But nothing came out. To be honest, I didn't feel the need to explain my parents to him. I didn't think he deserved an explanation.

"I wish you'd come home," he said. "Promise me you'll think about it?"

I fiddled with a dried flower in the vase on the table. "I still have to finish the lighthouse. I won't be back for a few weeks, at least."

"I could come visit," he suggested.

I paused. The idea of having Todd and his starched shirts here in Starlight Cove, quietly judging my parents, did not sound appealing.

Yes, my parents had their faults. The way they raised me was not ideal. But they did their best, and I was not about to let someone from the outside judge them. Right now, my parents and I were a team, along with people like Kailyn, the Hendersons, and Kip Whittaker. I didn't know how Todd would fit into all that.

"Give me some time to think about it, okay?" I said. "We'll talk again soon."

"I love you, Dawn."

"I . . . I love you, too."

Hanging up the phone, I rested my chin in my hands and stared at the wall. The words felt like a betrayal of something. Fitzie's love letters, maybe. Or the idea of what I hoped love could really be.

Chapter Twenty-Six

Now that the lighthouse was clean, I couldn't put off painting. It was going to be a ton of work, but I hoped it would be a good distraction.

I met my father at the hardware store, where we wasted a ridiculous amount of time comparing the paintbrushes, rollers, paint trays, and extenders. My father had logged the measurements of certain angles in the lighthouse. Now he examined each brush, examining the angles and comparing them to the numbers in his notebook.

"Can we just grab a brush and get on with it?" I finally said.

My father slapped his notebook against the shelves. "Why not? Then we'll get a broken compass and hope it works." He glared at me. "Dawn, that lighthouse has stood for more than a century. It's endured wind, weather, and storms. It's not a paint-by-number. We do it right or not at all."

I rolled my eyes. To be fair, doing it right or not at all was my typical attitude, but not today. It was like I'd already bought a compass that didn't work and, as a result, had no idea where I was going.

"I've been thinking . . ." I ran my palm over the rough bristles of a paintbrush. "There were chains at the wreck site. A brig. That matches up with what the first mate's great-grandson said. I think someone had it in for Fitzie and attacked him the night of the storm."

My father glanced up from the brushes. "What do you mean?"

I leaned against a shelf. "In the letter to Dr. Whittaker, Fitzie asked him to watch out for Madeline. He obviously thought she was in danger. Plus, he showed up at the lighthouse with a gash in his head. What if that injury had nothing to do with the storm?"

My father frowned. "You think the first mate attacked him. For revenge."

"I don't know," I said. "But if we could just find something to prove that, maybe it would be enough to convince the . . ." Remembering we stood in a busy shop, I said, "Convince certain people that he had nothing to do with stealing the treasure."

My father scratched his beard. "That's coming up, isn't it?"

"We have three weeks."

His shoulders slumped. "I didn't realize it was so close."

Carter walked up, a friendly smile on his freckled face. "Did you settle on some brushes?"

In a booming voice, my father said, "We did."

He handed Carter his selections, and we followed him to the cash register.

"Do you have scaffolding?" Carter punched in some numbers. "With a job like this . . ."

My father waved his hands. "We'll be fine."

I wasn't so sure about that. The ceilings were high, and I wasn't thrilled at the idea of balancing at the top of some tall ladder. But my father already had his mind set on how we were going to do the project, so I wasn't about to waste time arguing.

He was quiet as we dragged everything to the lighthouse in the wagon. We lifted the paint and the brushes using the pulley system. Once we were in the lighthouse, he walked over to the window and stared out at the water.

"Ready to get to work?" I asked, locking the front door.

"I'd like to go up to the gallery for a minute," he said. "Get my thoughts together."

He seemed upset. It must have been the reminder about the insurance company. Or the idea that someone might have been out to get Captain Fitzie.

I followed him up the stairs to the balcony outside. He sat against the edge of the iron railing, his feet dangling over the side. It was easy to picture him as a small child sitting with his grandmother.

The sun was brilliant, and cotton clouds floated over the pale sky like something out of a dream. I settled in, admiring the view. Finally, he spoke.

"I want you to be prepared," he said. "If things don't go the way you've planned."

I squinted at him in the sun. "Meaning?"

He took a tube of Carmex out of his pocket and dotted some on his lips. The sharp smell carried on the wind. I breathed it in, caught somewhere between the past and present.

"You're doing this research to try to save the house," he said, "and I know you're frustrated with the fact that your mother and I haven't done more. It seems . . ." He let out a deep sigh. "You're probably frustrated with a lot of the things your mother and I have done. You didn't have an easy childhood."

I flushed. Yes, I harbored a ton of blame against my parents for raising me the way they did, but I didn't want to get into some big confrontation about it. That was in the past. It was easier to focus on the present.

"We have lots of work to do." I stood up. "Let's go downstairs—"

"I want you to listen to me!"

"Fine." I sat back down, frustrated. "What?"

"There were times when you were growing up that your mother and I wondered if we should come in off the water," he said. "Get a job. Stay in one place."

The sharp pain of being uprooted was triggered somewhere in the back of my brain. I focused on the cool breeze as it rushed through my hair.

"Okay," I said. "So, why didn't you?"

He adjusted the wool sweater around his shoulders. "We tried it, once. You were in first grade, and your mother and I weren't making a dime. So, we rented a house in Oregon and got jobs." He frowned at the memory. "She worked at a car rental place and I taught extension classes at some bleak local college."

"I forgot about that," I said, pulling my knees to my chest.

In the back of my mind, I could picture a small house with yellowed linoleum floors and the sound of my parents fighting. I spent a lot of time in the backyard, climbing on a rubber tire hanging from the tree.

"There's not much to remember," he said. "We lasted three, maybe four months. Truth be told, normal didn't solve much of anything. We decided it would set a better example if we were happy following our dreams instead of miserable trying to get by. In the end, I think you paid for that, too."

I concentrated on the rhythm of the waves as they rolled into one another.

"Why are you telling me this?" I finally said.

My father took out his pipe but didn't light it. "I wonder if we were wrong. The way we did things. Maybe we should have settled down, let you stay in one place, instead of dragging you from here to there on the hope we'd track down a treasure."

"It wasn't just hope, though," I said. "You found the *San Arabella*."

"That didn't fix anything. Nothing after that was ever enough, because I never . . ." He gestured at the water where the wreck hid below the surface. "I didn't resolve all this."

"*The Wanderer*," I said.

He let out a deep sigh. "I've spent my life chasing something that might never be found. It hurts me to see you getting caught up in the

271

same thing. Blood might be thicker than water, Dawn, but you don't have to live your life like we did."

"It's not like you guys dragged me here," I said. "I decided to do this."

"Did you?" His voice was quiet. "You didn't want to lose the only place you've ever called home. In the end, whose decision was it?"

"It was *mine*!" I insisted. "I didn't have to come here. I could have let the house go. I could have . . ."

My eyes pricked with tears. I couldn't have let the house go without a fight. It meant too much to me.

I glared at him. "Why are you saying all this?"

My father shoved his pipe into his shirt pocket. "Because I'm sorry."

The words hung between us like mist.

"For what?" I whispered.

"All of it," he said. "Those years we dragged you around, the way it hurt you. You're going to feel that hurt again when this deadline runs out and . . . I'm so sorry, Dawn. For all the times we let you down."

I could barely speak over the lump in my throat. "There's still time."

"No, there isn't." Emotion clouded his face. "I've searched for answers my whole life. What difference does a ninety-day deadline make? Dawn, I didn't sit back from this because I didn't want to protect you. It's because I didn't know what else to do." My father turned to me, and his face crumpled. "I didn't know what else to do."

"Dad," I said. "It's okay."

He pulled me into his arms. Tears rolled down my cheeks. I leaned against his shoulder, the wool sweater warm and familiar. Through my tears, I watched the confidence of the herons as they glided over the water, so sure they would find what they were looking for.

For years, I thought my parents didn't care about me. I assumed they didn't understand the sacrifices they asked me to make. As it turned out, they questioned their decisions every day. To me, that made a difference.

It didn't change the past. Nothing would. But with time, maybe it would help heal the hurt I still felt inside.

"Thank you," I whispered into his shoulder.

"For what?" he grunted.

I didn't answer, but I held him tight.

It was hard to move from that conversation into the banality of painting the lighthouse. Everywhere I looked, there were memories of all the times I'd felt abandoned or left behind. I relived how hard I'd worked as an adult to make my life stable, only to end up in Starlight Cove, where I felt more at home than I had anywhere else in my life.

The work my father and I did on the lighthouse helped quiet my mind. We spent the entire morning sealing the edges between the walls and ceiling with painter's tape. Some of the ceilings were at least fifteen feet tall, which meant a lot of ladders and stretching.

I wished we'd taken Carter up on his suggestion about scaffolding. Priming the lower portion of the walls wasn't bad, but when I stepped up on the ladder and lifted my arms to reach the edges along the ceiling, my muscles ached. Five minutes in, they were burning.

I mopped sweat off my forehead and groaned. "This is not as easy as it looks!"

My father chuckled. "I'd have thought you built up some upper-arm strength with all that cleaning. This will do the trick."

I gritted my teeth and pushed through the pain. Twenty minutes later, I tossed my brush on the drop cloths and said, "This is ridiculous. I'm calling for reinforcements."

Carter and Cameron appeared within a half hour, carrying several pieces of sticklike metal. They assembled a puzzle of crisscrossing bars and solid platforms as we watched. The scaffolding complete, the Hendersons headed back to the store.

I climbed up to the top level and set down my primer can and tray.

"This is so much better," I said, relieved.

My father and I got to work. He didn't say much for the first few minutes. Finally, he turned to face me, his legs dangling over the edge of his scaffold.

"Let this be a lesson to you, Dawn," he called.

"What's the lesson?"

"Your old man is not always right."

The words from our heart-to-heart rang through my head. He was apologizing yet again.

"You're not right about some things," I said. "But others? I couldn't do them without you, Dad."

There was some throat clearing and mumbling. I turned back to the wall, but not before I saw him smile.

A week later, I dropped by Kailyn's office with some muffins and coffee. I'd just finished my run and had gotten a late start, so she would already be in the office. Her face lit up when she saw the muffins.

"You are the best," she said. "I'm starving! How does the paint job look?"

"Great!" I slid into a chair. "It's made such a difference."

My father and I were on the final coat. The cream paint caught the light, making the walls fresh and inviting. It also hid years of wear, including rust stains and the evidence of former mold.

"It looks like the inside of a Spanish castle," I said.

"Sounds cool." She took a sip of coffee. "I'm excited to see it."

I bit into a muffin. "So, how's everything going with the party?"

I'd gotten an invitation from her a few days ago, but had been too busy painting to RSVP. The party was next Friday. I was proud of her for making it happen so quickly.

"Take a look." She turned her computer screen toward me and pulled up a board on Pinterest labeled "Marketing Bash." Based on the pins and the invitation, the color scheme was navy and gold, and the decorations had a nautical theme.

"How cute is that?" Kailyn pointed at a lobster with googly eyes made from a red pepper nestled on a plate of pretzels. "He's one of the appetizers. The pepper holds spicy pepper hummus, or whatever type of dip makes sense."

I scrolled down the page. She'd pinned a life ring hanging from the ceiling that read "All aboard," a photo station with pirate patches and hooks, and drinks in mason jars with sails sticking out of them. My favorite was a six-foot lighthouse made entirely out of balloons.

"How cool," I squealed, pointing at it.

"It's the centerpiece of the party," she said. "I'm excited—I've already gotten a bunch of RSVPs. But only one that really mattered."

"I haven't RSVP'd yet, so it must be . . . Carter?"

She grinned. "You know it."

I was happy to hear it. I also looked forward to spending time with Kip at an event where it was all about talking and having fun, instead of doing research.

"It sounds awesome."

"It's a good weekend for it, too, thanks to the Starlight Festival."

"What is that?" I asked.

"You don't know about the Starlight Festival?" she said, in the same tone someone would have said, *You don't know about food?* "It's only the most fun festival *ever*."

I sat up straight. "Wait. I think I do remember this."

It took a minute, but a memory began to form in my brain. Downtown packed with booths, candy passed out from different vendors, dancing to musicians playing in the street . . . The Starlight Festival was something my grandparents would take me to, if our visit during the summer happened to fall on the same week. It hadn't crossed my mind in years.

"It's a fun weekend," Kailyn said. "Town will be packed. It's good for tourism, good for business. I'm surprised your parents haven't roped you into working a booth yet."

I laughed. "I bet they're waiting to spring it on me at the last minute."

"How's it been working with your dad?"

I grinned, remembering the impromptu dance party my father and I shared at the end of the day yesterday.

"Good. We haven't fallen off the scaffolding yet."

Kailyn laughed. "You're not done yet, though, right?"

"Nope. There's still plenty of time."

Kip called two days later, when my father and I were almost finished with the last coat. I considered taking the call outside, but my father was busy singing along with his iPod. Listening to his off-key versions of classic songs was like playing *Name That Tune*. I'd narrowed this one down to "Sgt. Pepper's Lonely Hearts Club Band."

"Hey," I said, picking up on the first ring. "How are you?"

We hadn't spoken since the night we read the love letters.

Kip paused as my father hit a high note. "Where are you?"

"Painting the lighthouse." I watched my father lift his roller pole in perfect rhythm to the song. "It's getting wild over here."

"I can only imagine," Kip said, in a husky tone. "So, I was thinking back to that day we first met and I took you to Towboat."

My pulse quickened as I remembered the way his shirt showed off his arms as he cinched his boat to the dock. It was hard to believe the haughty way I'd acted. Or that I told him I wasn't there for a hookup.

"Yes?" I said, embarrassed. "What about it?"

"Do you remember when you asked about the photo of Captain Fitzie on the wall? I told you they were for the tourists, because—"

"Every small town needs a good outlaw," I said. "One of your most charming moments, to be sure."

"I try," Kip said. "It struck me, though, that I couldn't think of the last time Captain Fitzie's portrait *hasn't* been hung up around here. It might be the whole outlaw thing, yes, but what if it's something more? Who hung them up? Why? I think we should look into it."

The conversation my father and I had about the insurance company had been weighing on my mind. He might not think it was possible to solve anything in two weeks, but I was still determined to try.

Tucking the phone against my shoulder, I dipped my roller back into the tray. "Okay . . ." I drizzled some paint into my pan. It shimmered against the surface. "How?"

"That, I haven't quite figured out," Kip said. "I wanted to run it by you and see if it sounded crazy."

"It doesn't," I said. "I've wondered the same thing."

"So, let's get together and come up with a plan of attack."

I grinned. "Okay. Just let me know when you're free."

When we hung up, I replayed the conversation in my head. Despite the way we left things the other night, electricity seemed to spark between every word. Such a difference from the phone call with Todd.

The comfort in hearing Todd's familiar voice had faded the moment I said *I love you*. Because deep down, those words weren't true. He'd tried to call me again this morning, but I didn't pick up. I wasn't sure that I ever would.

"Is it break time?" my father demanded. "I must have missed something."

I laughed. "Yes, you missed something." I pointed at the part of the wall he hadn't finished. "Less singing, more working."

"My daughter, the tyrant," he cried.

He turned his iPod back on, lifted his paintbrush, and started singing at the top of his lungs. I joined him, even though I couldn't hear the music.

Chapter Twenty-Seven

The final coat of paint was finished by early afternoon. My father headed back to the antique shop, and I walked along the beach, making plans. Even though I'd planned to call Kip the next day, I decided to get takeout from Maddie's and drop by his house now, instead.

The drop-in was something that was part of Starlight Cove culture, but the idea still made me nervous. It seemed a little transparent. Like, *Hi, Kip, I missed you so badly I couldn't wait for our phone call tomorrow. Thought I'd drop by instead.*

I worried about it on the walk to Maddie's, I stressed while waiting for the food, and I practically panicked when I walked across the sand to his house. The sight of the log cabin almost made me do a 360, but I took a deep breath and kept going.

My steps echoed down the dock. I reached up and gripped the tiny ship anchor that served as a knocker and gave three sharp raps. The door opened, and my knees went weak at the sight of Kip.

He was still dressed for work, and I caught a scent of spicy cologne. His face registered surprise, followed by interest, followed by worry. Half shutting the door behind him, he joined me on the dock.

"What are you doing here?" he asked, touching the to-go bags.

My cheeks flamed. He came outside instead of inviting me in. Maybe he was having dinner with someone else.

"I brought food," I said in a rush. "Chicken tenders. I should've called."

I was so embarrassed. I wished a tidal wave would strike Lake Michigan, knock me off the dock, and wash me away, never to be heard from again.

"You're busy," I said. "I'll leave this with you."

I thrust one of the bags in his direction and let go before Kip had time to grab it. Chicken tenders and French fries scattered along the dock, and he burst out laughing.

"You are the worst delivery person I've ever met." He bent down and scooped the food off the dock, putting it back into the container. Taking the other bag out of my hands, he said, "I'm finishing up a consultation with . . . with one of my clients. You're welcome to sit in the kitchen and wait, but I'm afraid the situation will make you uncomfortable."

Before I could ask why, the door behind him opened. Maeve Weatherly stood there, blinking at me in distaste.

"Oh." Her voice was strangled, as though she'd swallowed a stink-bug. "I wondered what was taking so long." Turning, she headed back inside.

I cringed. "Talk about terrible timing."

"You know, it might be good timing," Kip said. "This might be an opportunity for you to get to know each other on neutral ground. Maybe even let her know you've got good intentions with the light-house." When I didn't move, he said, "Dawn, she's a good person once you get to know her. Trust me."

I bit my lip. Making the decision to trust him was the reason I came over. With that in mind, I followed him inside.

❧

Based on the state of the living room, I could see Kip and Maeve were hard at work. Pages of notes rested on the tables, and small easels with posters and printouts were on display. Maeve typed away on a small laptop and didn't look up when I walked into the room.

"Maeve, I apologize." Kip settled in on the couch. "Dawn and I have dinner plans, and it's quite late. I'd still like to finish up here, though, if she can stick around."

She glanced at her gold watch. "It doesn't sound like I have another option."

"Then it's settled," he said cheerfully.

Kip had mentioned they were family friends, which explained why he felt comfortable bringing me into a business meeting. I, on the other hand, felt anything but.

"Back to what we were discussing," he said. "The educational materials are spot-on, but the website needs a little work."

She frowned. "Define 'a little.'"

He laughed. "Okay, a lot. The message isn't there. You want to build the organization on water conservancy, but too many links distract from that."

I settled back in the chair, interested to see Kip at work. The first day we met, he said he was a consultant. I could see how he was successful. His intelligence and charm probably made it easy for clients to listen to his advice.

Still, Maeve looked frustrated. "It's important to educate the public about invasive species, pollution, the role of government, and all of the factors that contribute to the damage of our freshwater supplies," she said. "The information needs to be there."

I was impressed with her passion.

"I don't disagree," Kip said. "But the site needs to be remapped." He turned to me. "Dawn is a fresh pair of eyes. Can I show her? Maybe she'll prove me wrong."

My palms went damp. The last thing I wanted to do was offer advice on something I knew nothing about, especially in front of Maeve Weatherly. She let out an irritated sigh and held out her laptop.

"Go for it," she said drily. "It seems I can't get rid of you."

The next thing I knew, Maeve Weatherly's computer was in my lap. It was compact and in pristine condition. I was half-afraid I'd drop it.

"Okay," I said. "What am I looking at?"

Kip pointed at the screen. "Imagine you researched this organization. You come to this page. What do you see?"

I studied it. The site showcased several pictures of the Great Lakes with expansive blue waters and lush green coastlines. The home page offered a blurb about the importance of the world's freshwater supply and the role of the Great Lakes.

I glanced at Maeve. "I get what you're trying to do, and I like the pictures."

She wrinkled her forehead but didn't answer.

Kip nodded at me. "Try to click on something."

I went to the top of the page and pulled down the links.

Yikes. He was right. The site offered so many options, so many places to look, that I didn't know where to click first.

"It's too much," I said. "I have no idea what to look at."

Maeve took off her glasses and folded them. "What would you be interested in knowing? Specifically."

"Um . . ." I studied the main page. "What your organization does, why it matters, and how I can get involved." I glanced at Kip to see if I was saying too much. He nodded, as though to tell me to continue. "Then, I wouldn't mind an area where I would find links to learn history. Videos are good, too. Maybe a link to a blog so I could understand why this matters to you."

Maeve gave a sharp nod. "Do you know much about water conservancy?"

I blushed. "No."

Obviously, she thought I had no business offering advice.

"Then that's actually very helpful," she said.

Did Maeve Weatherly give me a compliment? For a moment, I thought I'd misheard. I glanced at Kip, who grinned.

"My target audience is people who know little about the cause but want to learn," Maeve continued. "It's an important issue."

"It's good you're fighting for it," I said quickly.

"Well." She got to her feet, taking back her laptop and placing it into its bag. "I will leave you two to your dinner. What are you having? It smells delicious."

"Chicken tenders from Maddie's," Kip said.

Maeve clasped her hands. "You discovered Maddie's?" she said, looking at me. "It has some of the best food in town."

She seemed pleased that I knew about the little dive, rather than affronted someone told me about it.

"It's a cute place," I said.

"Yes." She gave a sharp nod. "It certainly is."

Kip helped her to pack up her posters and walked her to the door. She kissed him on both cheeks. Then she glanced over his shoulder and gave a sharp nod.

"Have a good night," she said.

It was hardly a huge breakthrough. But it was progress.

"You, too," I managed to say.

Kip closed the door. He stood there for a moment, as though deep in thought, before turning around. His midnight-blue gaze locked onto mine.

I almost made small talk about Maeve, but, looking at him, words escaped me. The air in the room was charged with electricity. It felt the same as that night we read the letters in the lighthouse.

I picked up one of the navy-and-white-striped cushions on the couch and pressed it against my chest, as though for protection. Protection from Kip or myself, I wasn't sure.

"Chicken tenders." He walked to the kitchen counter. "Good choice."

The bag rustled as he dug out the container of food. He pulled out two plates from the cupboard. I couldn't help but fast-forward in my mind to a time when it might be typical for us to share dinner.

Dangerous thoughts. Ones I needed to push away. Yes, I'd spent the last few days thinking I wanted to be open and vulnerable, but the reality suddenly seemed like too much.

"Would you like something to drink?" Kip asked. Hesitating for just a moment, he added, "I have a bottle of white wine."

My mouth went dry. "Sounds good."

He set our plates on the coffee table between us and poured the wine into frosted glasses. I wanted to gulp the whole thing to make this night easier. Instead, I sipped at it after he clinked his glass against mine.

"To the best food in Starlight Cove," he said. "And the fun of a surprise visit."

I dipped a chicken tender in honey mustard sauce and took a bite.

"Wow," I said, surprised at the crunch and the spice. "These are great."

"Best-kept secret."

I smiled, happy he'd let me in on it. "So. I stopped by because I want to go over everything we know about *The Wanderer*. And . . . to tell you why it's so important to me to figure this out."

Kip raised an eyebrow. "So, you've been keeping more secrets. Didn't you get mad at me for that?"

"Yes, but this isn't my secret to tell."

I'd decided to let Kip know about the timeline with the insurance company. I wanted to put all my cards on the table, in case he was still holding something back, like he did with the coins.

"I need to know you won't share this with anyone," I said.

"You have my word."

I took a deep breath. Then, I explained to him about the letter. His face darkened with every word.

"The insurance company is planning to take your parents' *home*?" he demanded. "That's outrageous."

I felt a mixture of embarrassment and relief at the confession.

"I'm only telling you because I need you to know how urgent it is for me to figure this out," I said. "Full disclosure: it turns out my father has known his whole life that Fitzie was alive after the wreck. But he has always believed he was innocent."

Kip ate a French fry, thinking about this. "I wonder if that's what drove him to go into treasure hunting in the first place."

I sat in silence, thinking of the conversation with my father on the gallery. It was hard to think that the events of my entire lonely, crazy childhood were set in motion by something that happened nearly a hundred years ago.

"What else?" Kip asked, watching me. "It seems like there's something else on your mind."

I hesitated. "There are some things that don't add up."

He reached out and brushed the pad of his thumb over the corner of my lips. I took in a sharp breath as heat rushed through me.

"Chicken tender," he said. "What doesn't add up?"

It took me a minute to remember. Rather, to remember why it mattered at all. Finally, I said, "I think your great-grandfather could be a suspect."

Kip drew back. "Sorry?"

"Just hear me out," I said, leaning forward. "Captain Fitzie was injured during the wreck. So badly that your great-grandfather was called to help save him. Then Fitzie told Madeline she was in danger and promised to come back for her. He never did. One of the last people to see him alive was your great-grandfather. I'm just wondering . . ."

Kip's expression made me soften my tone.

I let out a breath. "Look," I said. "I don't know if Dr. Whittaker was involved. But I'm here tonight because I need to understand your interest in the story. The other night, I showed you the love letters written by my great-grandfather. They mean a lot to me. I have been open with you in a way I don't feel comfortable being. I . . . I need you to be open with me, too."

I was talking about much more than research. Based on the look on Kip's face, he knew it. The clock on the fireplace mantel sat next to the box with the pieces of silver. It ticked away the seconds, filling the silence between us. I set my glass of wine down, my hand shaking with nerves.

Kip took my hand in his. Tingles rushed through my body at the feeling of his skin against mine.

"I disagree with everything you are saying about my great-grandfather," Kip said. "He was an honorable man and a good friend to Captain Fitzie. There's no evidence to suggest otherwise. If we find some, I'll consider your theory. Not until then."

"So, why are you . . . ?"

"Dawn, I'm investigating the history of *The Wanderer* because I'm interested in the history of Starlight Cove. This took center stage when your parents moved to town and again when that ridiculous news story aired. But there's a reason I continue to search, long past the point of finding anything." His blue eyes darkened as he held my gaze. "It's because I want to spend time with you."

For a moment, I couldn't breathe. Then he pulled me to my feet.

"What are you doing?" I said, trying to laugh.

He stroked my cheek. "What are you so scared of, Dawn?"

I couldn't answer. Words seemed to have left my brain. Reaching up, I could only manage to trace my fingers over his.

"What do you want?" he whispered. "Tell me."

There were so many things I wanted: To feel settled, to understand love, to believe it could happen to me. More than anything, though, I wanted him to kiss me.

My eyes flickered to his lips.

Kip let out a low groan and rested his forehead on mine. I breathed in the smell of white wine, cedar, and a musky scent that was all him. He lowered his lips to mine. I gripped his shirt, pulling him in deeper, lost in the rhythm of our breath.

The kiss was like something I always imagined a kiss should be. It was like one of the love letters come to life, as though the words on the page were feelings that threatened to sweep me away. We kissed for an eternity, until he drew back and, again, rested his forehead against mine.

In a low tone that gave me the shivers, he murmured, "That was some kiss, Fancy Pants."

I pulled him to me once more.

Chapter Twenty-Eight

The chicken tenders were long forgotten when we finally took the bottle of wine out to the deck on the boat. We sat under the stars, holding hands and gazing at each other. Kip leaned in and brushed back a strand of hair stuck against my lips.

"That first day we met . . ." He grinned. "I thought you were going to push me in the lake."

I ran my thumb over the rough skin of his hand. I shivered, thinking about where those hands had been tonight and the things they'd made me feel.

"I *should* have pushed you into the lake." He glowered and I laughed. "To be honest, I was terrified of you. I was not in a good place when I got here, especially with men. I'd just gotten dumped . . ."

"What happened?" Kip asked.

"*News Tonight*." The words came out short and bitter. "He panicked because he didn't know a thing about my family. He was right—I wasn't exactly an open book. Or a book in print, really. The thing is, I don't have an easy time opening up to people."

Kip stroked my hand, and I looked up at the stars. They filled the sky in a blur of white so intense it was almost purple. The breeze made small waves in the marina, and the boats rocked against the dock in a steady rhythm.

"Why, do you think?" he asked.

"We moved around a lot when I was young. My whole life, actually." I'd brought the throw from Kip's bed outside. Pulling it tightly around me, I said, "My parents were determined to find treasure, no matter where that took us, and it took us all over. I never had much of a chance to make friends, and if I did, I just had to leave them behind. Getting close to someone and leaving, it just . . . I've gotten pretty good at walking away."

"What you're describing doesn't sound easy."

"It wasn't." I took a sip of wine. "My parents did the best they could, but I always wished we could have stayed in one place." I waved my hand, thinking of my father's apology. "It was too much loss, too much instability, and at some point I decided not to do it anymore. There was no point in letting people in."

Kip was silent for a long moment. Then, in a low tone, he said, "That's not going to be good enough for me. I want you to let me in. I want to know everything about you."

Pain cut through me. In a few weeks, I would have to walk away from Kip, too. Once the lighthouse was ready to put up for sale, I would be back to my life in Boston. I wouldn't go back to Todd—I'd already decided that—but I'd be back to my old apartment, my friends, and the job hunt. Unless . . . unless I made the decision to stay.

What if I just decided to stay?

I'd toyed with the idea of living in the lighthouse. I'd thought about what it would be like to live in Starlight Cove. I'd even admitted that here, I finally felt at home. Why would I leave? I wasn't a kid anymore. It wasn't like anyone was forcing me to go.

I looked at Kip, stunned to realize I could actually form a relationship with him. Get to know him, without the threat of the end hanging over our heads. I laughed, the sudden sound echoing over the water.

"I missed something," Kip said, confused.

"No," I said, squeezing his hand. "I'm just realizing how much everything has changed."

I didn't think it was possible, but Kip's words managed to keep me talking. I told him about the years at sea, the excitement and embarrassment that came with the *San Arabella*, the regimented life I lived in Boston, and my plans for the lighthouse. Kip told me about the heart and hilarity that came with growing up in such a small town, the pressure to live up to his parents' expectations about family and career, and that he was once engaged. Not to Cassie, the girl Kailyn mentioned, but a tourist who came to town.

"What happened?" I asked, secretly grateful it didn't work out.

"She crushed me," he admitted. "I thought we were the real deal, that I'd found the person I was meant to be with for the rest of my life, but one day, she shut me out." He ran a hand over his face. "I came home to find the engagement ring next to a note on the back of a pizza receipt. It read 'I changed my mind.'"

My mouth dropped open. "That's awful."

"Like she wanted a different topping on her pizza. I tried to talk to her about it, but she had nothing to say. I finally heard the answer from her friends."

Reaching out, I took his hand in mind. "What did they say?"

Kip shrugged. "She didn't like small-town life. Apparently, if I loved her enough, I'd travel the world and be a part of that jet-set scene. The moment she realized Starlight Cove would always be my home, she was done."

"I'm sorry," I said, shaking my head.

All this time, I thought I was the only one with a reason to put up walls. It turned out, Kip had some walls of his own.

"I would have understood if she'd just told me," he said. "But she didn't. That got me more than anything." He brushed a mosquito away from my cheek. "I've kind of stayed away from relationships since then."

I climbed into his lap and pressed up against him, his strong arms wrapped around me. We kissed right there in the harbor, as the water lapped at the edge of the boat.

"I won't shut you out," I whispered. "I promise you that."

Kip's eyes met mine. The strong, aristocratic version of him melted away, replaced by a sweet, vulnerable man I hadn't yet seen. I nestled my head against his chest and held him close.

I'd been searching for this man my entire life. Staring up at the expanse of stars, I couldn't believe I'd finally found him.

Chapter Twenty-Nine

My father and I kicked off the day at the lighthouse with a final round of painting. Carter and Cameron met us there to install the shower in the basement.

As my father and I started the last coat in the bedroom, I ran the brush over the wall, feeling giddy. All this time, I'd fantasized about making the lighthouse my home. Now that I'd made a decision, each coat of paint felt personal. I was no longer getting the lighthouse ready for someone else—I was doing it for me. I'd already talked to my mother about which pieces from the antique shop I could have to create an old-fashioned feel in each room. I couldn't wait to get started decorating.

When my father and I were finished for the day, I headed back to the houseboat to see Kip. He opened the door and pulled me right into his arms. We spent the evening in his bed exploring each other, talking about *The Wanderer*, and telling stories from the past. I fell asleep with his arms around me, the waves lapping gently outside.

The sound of the fog signal woke me first thing the next morning. Kip was fast asleep next to me, warm and snug in the sheets. I kissed his shoulder and walked over to the window, looking outside.

Fog covered the beach in a gray haze. The night before, I'd brought my running clothes, with big plans to take my morning run and cook Kip breakfast. I was tempted to climb back into bed, but I knew I wouldn't be able to go back to sleep if I did.

I pulled on my running shoes and headed for the door.

Out on the sand, I took in a huge breath of fresh air. It was so crisp, my cells practically lit up with excitement. I stretched back and forth, feeling my hamstrings loosen with the effort.

I ran for a couple of miles, heading toward my lighthouse and the public beach, into the area of the beach that turned to swamp. In the remote area, a figure approached in the distance, about a half mile away. I slowed as a prickle of warning ran up my neck. The beach was isolated at this time of day. Who else would possibly be out here?

Don't be silly, I told myself. *It's just another jogger.*

But maybe not. Some people still thought my family knew the location of the treasure. Dangerous people like Sal and his crew.

I know exactly where you go and what you do, Sal told me.

I'd always heard that joggers shouldn't run at the same time every day or take the same route. I never took the warnings seriously. This trek to the wilderness might have been a huge mistake.

Come on, I thought, remembering the incident with the opossum. *It's nothing.*

The dark figure was now only about a quarter mile away, and I came to a complete stop, the water of the lake lapping near my feet. The figure also stopped. It wasn't anyone I recognized, but I could tell it was a man.

I peered at him through the fog. He stared back. Then, he lifted his hand. There was a flash of silver, like the blade of a knife.

Fear shot through my veins.

I bolted around and ran in the other direction as fast as I could, kicking up wet sand with every step. My heart pounded with exertion, the air like steam burning my lungs. Footsteps thundered after me.

I ran faster, feeling the pressure of the man closing in. I was too far down the beach, trapped by the water and the sand dunes, to run into a populated area. What was I thinking running out there all alone? It might have been dangerous, but I was convinced I was perfectly capable of taking care of myself. Big mistake.

My eyes scanned the beach—the waves crashed to my right, the fog swirled in front of me, and the ghostlike figure of the dunes loomed overhead.

Feeling the exertion of muscles nearly pushed to their limit, I forced myself to run faster. My breath became ragged.

The man was so close I could hear the crunch of his shoes in the sand and breath that came in sharp, jagged gasps. I could confront him but wouldn't last in a physical battle. I tensed, wondering if I would feel the slip of a knife against my ribs or the sudden pierce of a bullet.

Tears tugged at the edge of my eyelids.

Keep going, I told myself. *You can't give up now.* Then it hit me.

The water.

The water would give me the advantage. I knew this lake and expected its icy temperature, the rhythm of the crashing waves, and the strength of the undertow in ways a stranger would not. If I was going to do it, I had to do it fast.

My body was close to the point of exhaustion. It could be mere seconds before I stumbled over a piece of driftwood or turned an ankle in the ever-shifting sand. There was a grunt as fingertips brushed against the back of my shirt.

Without hesitation, I made a sharp, ninety-degree turn and ran into the water. The icy waves knocked the breath from my lungs. I dove into the water with a final burst of adrenaline.

Kicking with all my might, I swam out deeper and deeper, using powerful strokes. The waves crashed around me, and I gasped for breath, my shaking limbs ready to give up. I waited in silence, treading water. Relief shot through me as I scanned the foggy shore.

He was gone.

Quietly, I shifted my direction and swam with sure strokes toward the lighthouse. I could hear the foghorn blaring, see the bursts of light. Tourists would be on the beach by now, snuggled up in blankets, waiting for the sun to rise.

I used every ounce of strength I had to make the final swim to the shore, and collapsed on the sand in exhaustion.

~

The police station reminded me of the set of an old television show.

Lopsided window shades hid the chief's office from the view of the main station. Manila folders sat on an ancient utility desk. A single-blade fan rested on a side table, stirring the only air in the stuffy room.

Kip had brought me one of his sweatshirts and a pair of jogging pants. I was also wrapped in a wool blanket with hot coffee clutched in my hand. Still, the icy lake water left me chilled to the bone, and I couldn't stop shaking.

"Can you describe him?" Kip asked me.

We sat at the desk of the police chief, filing a report.

"I don't . . ." I could barely form the words.

"You saw him coming at you through the fog," Kip said. "What did you see?"

I blinked, unable to explain. It had been too foggy to see anything but a vague outline of the guy, but it had to be a guy from Sal's crew. That day in Towboat, Sal had made it perfectly clear that he was watching me.

He probably sent someone to get more information about something he thought I knew. But I couldn't say that to the police chief without some sort of proof.

"I don't know who it was," I said. "But he was running after me—"

"Running on the beach isn't a crime," the police chief said. "Do you want me to post an ordinance saying it is?"

I gripped my cup of coffee, breathing in the steam floating above the surface. For some reason, it seemed like the chief blamed me for what happened.

"He wasn't just a jogger," I said. "He—"

"How do you know the guy was a threat?"

"Henry." Kip's voice was sharp. "If she felt threatened, there was a reason."

"I thought I saw a knife," I told him.

The police chief peered at me over his glasses. "Did you see one? Or didn't you?"

"I . . . I'm not sure."

He sat back in his chair, unimpressed. Nothing had happened to me, and I couldn't identify the suspect. In his mind, I overreacted.

"What am I supposed to do here?" he asked Kip.

Kip glared at him. "Take her seriously."

The police chief turned his sharp gaze to me. "Look, young lady," he said. "This town was built on tourism. We can't have people thinking that it's dangerous to take a run along the beach. I understand you might be a little jumpy, but let's face it. Your family shows up on a national television show and gets people stirred up about the lost silver. Then, you start living in that lighthouse all alone, while asking around like you're trying to find treasure. It might be time you stop causing trouble and start thinking about how your actions affect others."

I stumbled to my feet. "I think we're done here."

Even though my face burned with humiliation, I held my head up high as I walked out the door.

"What the hell is wrong with you, Henry?" Kip shouted. "Her property was vandalized, and you haven't done a thing about that! Now, someone practically attacks her on the beach and you tell her it's her fault? You might have a burr up your ass about her family, but I'll tell you right now, if anything happens to her, you're going to have to deal with me."

"Kip, you have to understand . . ."

"I do understand," he growled. "You've made it very clear."

Kip stormed out of the office. His face was angry, his blue eyes fierce. Gently, he took my elbow. "It's okay," he said. "I've got you."

~

We walked out of the police station in silence. The station was just off Main Street in a commercial area with regular houses, like the one Kailyn worked in.

I scanned the downtown block. It was lush with greenery. The morning air smelled like freshly mown grass. It was all so peaceful and so different from the way I felt inside.

Kip shook his head. "I'm sorry," he said. "Sometimes, the people who grew up here can be so . . ."

"I get it." I'd kept the wool blanket from the station and tugged it tightly around me. It was hot out, but I still wanted its protection. "I know who it was, Kip."

He looked at me in surprise. "Who?"

"One of the guys from the wreck dive that day," I said. "Sal thinks my family knows more than we do about the treasure."

"Why didn't you say anything?" he demanded. "In there?"

"He didn't want to hear it." I mimicked the police chief's gruff voice. "*Getting people all stirred up about the silver.* Besides, I don't have proof. I think it was someone from Sal's crew, but it could have been anyone. Someone mad about the lighthouse or even mad that I'm a woman running on the beach alone. I don't know."

"Let's get breakfast," Kip said, touching my arm. "You should get something in your stomach."

Two hours ago, breakfast with Kip would have been the highlight of my day. Now, all I wanted to do was to find a safe place and stay there.

"I'd like to go to the lighthouse," I said. "I can't face my parents just yet."

I didn't want to worry them or make them think this happened because I was a Conners.

"Why the lighthouse?" Kip asked.

"I . . . I just want to be there."

I pictured the beacon my father described to me when I was little—the white light that promised to lead me safely to shore.

"Dawn, it's not safe," Kip insisted. "If someone broke in, you'd be trapped. The only exit is downstairs."

A hot tear trickled down my cheek. "It's my home. I'm not going to let anyone scare me away."

"Dawn, don't make this about pride." He brushed my tears away. "You need to stay safe."

I shook my head and started to walk.

Kip caught up and walked beside me in silence. The heat of the blanket and the humidity worked their magic, warming me. I took off the blanket and folded it.

At the lighthouse, I climbed the ladder and stepped into the main cavern. The windows were all open, and the smell of the paint had faded. Without a word, I headed up to my bedroom, Kip right behind me.

I pulled the bundled-up egg crate and my sleeping bag out of the storage space and set up my bed. When it was ready, I crawled into my sleeping bag. I wanted to fall into a deep sleep.

I opened my eyes to find Kip watching me.

"You have to go to work," I said. "I'll be fine."

Kip shook his head. He walked over to my makeshift bed and sat down on the floor. The warmth of his hand pressed against my back.

"You're shivering," he said.

"I'm traumatized."

There was a sigh and a clumping sound. To my surprise, Kip took off his shoes and lay down with me. He reached out and pulled me into his arms.

I froze, stunned at the sudden rush of desire that seared the ice coursing through my veins. Then, my body relaxed against his. I breathed in his scent and allowed his warmth to soothe me.

"I'll stay here with you." He kissed the top of my head. "Everything's going to be okay, Dawn. I'm right here."

I melted into his arms and, slowly, fell asleep.

~

When I woke up, Kip was still there, holding me. He was watching me sleep, a tender look on his face. Gently, he brushed his fingers over my lips.

"How are you?" he asked.

I shook my head, stretching. "Starving. I should get a sandwich. Go tell my parents what happened."

"Are you going to be okay?"

I studied his eyes. The deep blue of the irises was offset by the shadow of his thick black lashes. They were clear, honest, and full of concern for me. Even though I was still scared, I felt safe somehow with Kip near me.

I leaned forward and pressed my lips against his.

Kip seemed surprised but then kissed me back. This time, our lips met with greater urgency, and we melded into each other. Gasping, he pulled back and gazed at me with wonder.

"Last night," he whispered, "I got into an argument with the moon . . ."

Something in me broke open.

Pulling him as close as I could, I kissed him until I couldn't breathe.

∼

Kailyn was horrified when she heard about my scare at the beach.

I picked up sandwiches for lunch and brought them to her office because I didn't want to eat alone. We sat at the table by her front window, and I told her what happened. Even though I was still upset, the memory of being in Kip's arms made it easier to talk about.

"People don't get chased on the beach in Starlight Cove," she said, biting into a potato chip like she wanted to hurt it. "That doesn't happen here. That's why people buy properties here!"

"You must be friends with the police chief," I grumbled. "That's pretty much what he said."

I filled her in, and she made a face.

"*Pfft*, Henry. He's one of the die-hard locals. Thinks no one else has a right to live here." She wiped her hands on a napkin. "He's okay once you get to know him. I just wish he took you seriously. It's so scary that happened."

"I doubt it's random, though." I updated her on the rumors about the treasure and the conversation with Sal. "Not to mention," I added, "I bought one of the most beloved landmarks in Starlight Cove." I set down my sandwich. "I think it's time to figure out who lost against me in the auction. Maybe it won't matter, but it's a good starting point."

It would be a nonissue if the second-place bidder were from, say, Connecticut. If the runner-up was from Starlight Cove . . . well, there could be motive to come after me.

Kailyn got to her feet. "I'll make a few calls."

It took about twenty minutes, but she finally slammed down the phone in triumph. "I got it," she said. "I'm not allowed to tell you how, but let's just say I'll have the e-mail in . . ." She clicked at her keyboard and beamed. "Right now." With a few clicks, she printed out the e-mail and slid it across the desk to me. "Here you go."

I studied the printout. It listed the numbers of those who bid, along with the increments that they bid in. I hadn't read a professional printout in ages, and it took me a few minutes to adjust to the codes and abbreviations.

"There I am!" I tapped my fingers against the page, feeling the same thrill as the day I won. "The top bidder."

I blinked when I saw a name on the paper I didn't expect: K. Whittaker.

"That can't be right," I said, confused.

Kailyn covered her eyes. "Don't tell me," she squealed. "I'm already breaking so many rules with this."

Quickly, I matched up the ID numbers of the bidders with the names listed below.

"I can't believe this," I breathed.

It was right there in black and white.

The person who came in second place in the auction, the one who lost out against me, was Kip.

Chapter Thirty

I could hardly breathe. Instead of being hunted by a faceless man, I was all too able to picture the face of the man who betrayed me. I couldn't believe I'd been so naive.

I took in several deep breaths, trying to remain calm. If I broke down in the middle of Kailyn's office, I might never get up.

In a steady tone, I thanked her for the information. Somehow, I managed to make small talk about her party, set up plans for later in the week, and walk out the front door. The moment I made it down the block, I sank onto the grass and buried my head in my hands.

I couldn't believe this was happening. I'd trusted Kip with my family, my history, and my heart. The whole time, he'd told me nothing but lies.

That first day at the restaurant, he made such a big deal about some moron out-of-towner buying the lighthouse. He hoped that whoever it was would take one look and walk away. Once he learned I'd bought it, I'm sure he decided to play nice to get me to continue on with the treasure hunt.

The treasure had to be his true goal. Not history, not family pride, and not—my heart ached—an interest in me.

I should have known.

Kip Whittaker was a liar, just like Sal. He probably knew about the lighthouse and Fitzie from the start. Maybe he suspected the treasure, or a major clue leading to it, was hidden somewhere inside.

That morning, I'd fallen asleep in his arms. I wondered if he stayed with me the whole time or if he sneaked off, searching the basement or the lantern room for clues. I clenched my fist, fighting to stay calm.

I'd made the mistake of falling for Kip Whittaker's charms once, but it wouldn't happen again. The next time I saw him, I would tell him exactly what I thought of him. My only worry was that I wouldn't be able to do it without bursting into tears, because Kip Whittaker's betrayal didn't just hurt me.

It broke my heart.

I sat in the storage room of the antique shop, sipping on lavender tea. I told my parents what happened that morning on the beach and about the vandalism to the lighthouse. My father flew into a rage and stormed off to the police station to have a "conversation" with Henry.

My mother had to go back to the shop, but she brought me more hot water and kept popping her head in and out of the storage room to check on me. She'd just left when my phone buzzed. Chills ran through me.

It was Kip.

"Hello." My voice was as icy as the lake water.

"Hi." Kip's voice was low and intimate. "How are you?"

My stomach twisted into knots. I tried to block out the moment he quoted Fitzie's words to me. The most romantic moment of my life was one of the biggest setups of all time.

"If you're up for it," he said, without waiting for an answer, "I thought we could look through my parents' attic one last time. See if there's anything we missed."

I didn't see the point in some big, dramatic scene. Flatly, I told him I was done with the treasure hunt.

"It's dangerous," I said. "But don't let me stop you."

"Let's have dinner tonight," he said. "Talk about how you're feeling about what happened on the beach."

"I'm good."

Silence.

It's about time he didn't have the perfect line.

"Okay. How about tomorrow, then?" he said.

"Kip, I appreciate your interest," I told him. "But I don't want to go to dinner with you tomorrow or the day after. To be honest, I'm not interested. I think we've taken this far enough."

There was a long silence. "I don't understand," he finally said.

That morning, I'd clung to him while wrapped in his arms. I'd been so open, so willing to trust him, and he betrayed me.

"Dawn. What happened?"

"I changed my mind," I said, and hung up the phone.

I spent the next few days in a haze of depression.

I tried to focus on the lighthouse. I read through the book my father gave me and met with the women at the historical society about decorating ideas. I reviewed each clue I had about *The Wanderer*, but couldn't come up with anything new. I helped Kailyn plan her party, which was approaching quickly. I even went out for jogs, but on public routes, at staggered times during the day. Most of the time, I sat up on the gallery and stared out at the water, wondering how I could have let myself fall for someone like Kip.

The thing that bothered me the most about it was the fact that I fell so hard. In a span of mere weeks, I'd come to care for Kip more than I'd ever cared for anyone. Some moments when we talked and laughed, it was like he understood me in a way no one else did.

I kept going back to that moment when he said *I got into an argument with the moon . . .* It was a moment I would have cherished for the rest of my life.

As it turned out, it meant nothing at all.

I was desperate to take my mind off the situation with some physical activity, but it rained nonstop the next morning. A jog or a bike ride was out of the question, not that I really should have been doing any of that alone anyway. Instead, I helped my parents prep items for the Starlight Festival.

My mother asked me at least ten times if I was okay. She thought I was still upset about the incident on the beach. I wasn't about to tell her it was about Kip Whittaker. Finally, I decided to visit the Search and Rescue building to hang out with Captain Ahab.

Sheila was covering the front desk when I walked in. She gave a cheerful wave, and her tight brown curls bounced with the effort. The smell of acetone hung thick in the air, and I realized she was painting her nails.

I wondered what she'd say if I told her the details of my heartbreak. She seemed like the type of person who would listen to every word and offer the perfect, pithy statement designed to make everything better. Of course, it wouldn't make everything better. Nothing could.

"Ahab's not here, honey." She waved the red tips of her nails in the air. "He's out on a rescue."

"Leave it to a man," I muttered, settling in on the scratchy green sofa in the waiting room. "Never there when you need 'em."

Sheila giggled. "That's the truth. Coffee?"

I shook my head. "No, thanks. What's the rescue?"

"It's a terrible thing." She looked up at the ceiling, as though offering a quick prayer. "Folks went out camping last night, and, honey, one of their kids wandered off. He's still missing. Eight years old. They're scared he'll fall off one of the bluffs or into the water. He can't swim."

The news was terrible. Captain Ahab was a smart dog, though. I'd watched him do tracking exercises, and it was incredible, the things he could find. My father, of course, joked he'd be an asset in a treasure hunt.

"Captain Ahab will find him," I said. Then, because I didn't know anything about search and rescue, added, "Right?"

Sheila gave an enthusiastic nod. "If anyone can help, it's going to be that dog. He's a good leader. They just have to get there before it's too late."

I didn't know whether or not to stay. Sheila solved that problem for me by getting up, grabbing us some sandwiches from the fridge, and asking me to stick around. We flipped on the television and watched an evening news show.

We were halfway through when the phone rang at the front desk.

Sheila rushed to answer it. "Great," she said, giving me the thumbs-up sign. Then, her face went pale. "Oh. Dawn's here. Should I close up shop or . . . right. That's what I thought."

The receiver thumped down. Sheila sat in silence for a moment, staring down at the desk as if in shock.

"What is it?" I asked, confused.

When she gave me the thumbs-up sign, I thought they'd found the kid.

"Sheila," I said. "Did something happen?"

"It's Captain Ahab," she said. "He got trapped down in the water and swept against the rocks. By the time they pulled him out, he had some serious internal injuries. Honey, they . . ." She cleared her throat. "They don't think he's going to make it."

Chapter Thirty-One

I sat in the vet's office, silent.

Even though the office was officially closed, the waiting room was packed. It was full of volunteers and rescue workers who cared for Captain Ahab, desperate for him to come home. I sat next to a man with arms the size of my upper thighs. He kept staring at a magazine without turning any of the pages. Once in a while, he gave a sharp sniff.

Steve walked into the room with his wife and daughter. Everyone greeted him warmly. He put a hand on my shoulder, and I gripped it. His family found some free seats on the opposite side of the room and settled in.

Come on, Captain Ahab, I thought. *You've got to pull through.*

He'd been one of my main companions ever since I moved to Starlight Cove. This week had been hard enough. I couldn't stand losing someone else I loved.

The man next to me gave another sharp sniff. I glanced at him, even though I knew I shouldn't. He caught me looking and shook his head.

"Damn dog," he said. "He just has a way of getting under your skin, you know?"

"I know." My voice cracked at the end of the whisper.

The man wiped his eyes and went back to staring at the magazine. Leaning back in the chair, I stared at the clock and waited. The surgery was going to take three hours.

I planned to be there every second, ready to greet Captain Ahab when he woke up.

~

I was in the middle of a dream about *The Wanderer* when I heard a rustle and a murmur. Shifting to the side, I rested my cheek against my arm.

"It's over," someone said.

I jerked awake.

Over?

The waiting room was hot and crowded. Everyone was talking.

"What happened?" I asked.

No one seemed to know the answer. Apparently, someone saw the vet pass through the back, take his gloves off, and note something in Captain Ahab's folder. So far, he hadn't come out to say anything.

The energy in the room increased until it reached a fevered, buzzing pitch. Someone went up to the front desk and rang the bell. The nurse rushed forward, her face stressed. I doubted the staff was used to having half of Starlight Cove standing in their waiting room.

"I want to see the doctor." The tough guy stood at the front desk, his arms crossed.

"Yes, sir," the receptionist said. "He'll be right out with you."

Just then, the door opened, and a bespectacled guy in his forties stepped into the waiting room. If intimidated by the crowd, he didn't show it.

"I assume you're all here for Captain Ahab," he said.

The group murmured.

I held my breath.

The vet smiled.

"That dog's a fighter," he said. "Looks like you'll have him around for a few more years."

The whoop in the waiting room was deafening. I hugged a bunch of strangers. Then someone started clapping, and we all gave high fives to the doctor.

"All right, then," the tough guy at the front counter kept saying. "All right."

~

I left the vet still devastated about Kip, but grateful Captain Ahab had pulled through. The news lightened my spirits and gave me hope that I, too, would somehow make it.

The tree-lined streets were quiet and dark. I knew I shouldn't walk alone, but earlier that day my father had armed me with an entire collection of personal protection items. The Taser was tempting, but ultimately I settled on the Mace.

Tugging my thin shirt close, I hugged my arms to me. The rain had stopped, and it was a glorious night. Clear and black, the sky was lit by tiny pinpoints of light. It reminded me of that first night when I rode in the dune buggy, gripping the door and staring up at the stars.

That night, I didn't know what to think of Kip Whittaker; but, even then, something had sparked between us. Now, I wished I could go back and stop myself from being such a fool.

Despite what had happened a few days before, I decided to walk to the beach. I was not about to miss a night as beautiful as this one in favor of cowering in the corner, or crying myself to sleep. The fresh air would help heal some of my confusion.

The silver moon hung over water as black as the sky. Mist reflected over the surface. The lighthouse stood at the edge of the shore, its light flashing against the water. It was a lonely figure with . . .

I came to an abrupt stop.

The lighthouse, *my* lighthouse, was not a lonely figure at all. The dark outline of a person stood on my ladder.

He was dressed in black and held something about the size of a can of spray paint. My body went tense with rage.

I knew I should call the police, the Coast Guard, or even my father. But the anger that swept through me was stronger than fear. The lighthouse was *mine*. I'd had it with this.

I crept up the boardwalk and hid behind the public restroom. Pulling out my can of Mace, I put one finger on the trigger. Then, I turned on the flashlight on my cell phone.

"Freeze!" I called, rushing forward.

The bundled-up figure wore a sweatshirt and a pair of jeans. At the sound of my voice, he froze. The moonlight illuminated the message that dripped down my front door.

CONDEMNED!!!

The vandal scrambled down a few rungs and then jumped off the ladder into the sand. I chased after him with everything I had, the beam of the flashlight bouncing on the sand in front of me.

"Stop," I shouted. "The beach is surrounded."

He must have known I was bluffing, because he just picked up the pace, but I wasn't about to let him get away. I pressed closer and closer, his sweatshirt just inches in front of me. Finally, I leapt forward and tackled him by the legs. A tennis shoe glanced against my chin as we went down into the sand.

Pain cut through my jaw, but I didn't care. I grabbed for his arms, buried in the thick sweatshirt, praying he didn't have a weapon. He flailed and scratched at me. I pulled back the hood of the sweatshirt and aimed my can of Mace.

Suddenly, I stopped.

The vandal was not a man at all. It was Sami, Kip's niece.

"Sami?" I said, stunned.

Her body went limp.

In the faded light of the moon, she struggled to catch her breath. There were tears in her eyes but a stubborn tilt to her chin. She turned toward Main Street as if tempted to leap back up and make a run for it.

"There's no point," I said. "I know who you are."

"Please don't tell Uncle Kip," she begged. "He'll kill me."

"Why?" I demanded. "I'm sure he's the one who put you up to it!"

"Yeah, right," she spat. "The last thing he would want is for something to happen to your precious little lighthouse. But it shouldn't be yours in the first place! It was supposed to be mine."

"What are you talking about?" I said, confused.

She glared at me. "My mother was going to turn it into a restaurant on the shore. I would have run it in a couple of years. Then you came along and ruined everything."

I sat back in the sand with a thump. The cold night chilled me through my shorts.

"Kelcee," I said, stunned. "Your mother's name is Kelcee."

This was unbelievable. The moment I saw the initial *K*, I panicked and assumed Kip bid against me. I brought my hand to my mouth, feeling sick.

"I can't believe this," I whispered.

Sami crossed her arms, sniffling. "Believe what?"

I let out a slow breath. "You mean to tell me that you vandalized my property for the past two months because you were mad that your mother didn't win the auction?"

The sweatshirt practically swallowed Sami up as she shrugged. "Depends on your definition of vandalizing."

"Stealing my wagon, getting your friends to help you throw bricks through the window, and putting graffiti on my door."

Based on her expression, she was guilty of all of it.

"Jeez." I shook my head. "What do you do when people eat at a restaurant other than Towboat?"

The girl opened her mouth, but I held up my hand.

"Skip it." I slid the can of Mace back into my pocket. "Look, I don't know if I'm going to report you to the police. But I am going to have to tell Kip."

Her sharp features tumbled into one another. "Please don't," she begged. "I can help you. I'll clean up the mess that I made and . . . and . . . don't you have a lot of work that needs to get done? Kip is always talking about it."

Now that I knew that Kip wasn't secretly working against me, I was happy to learn he talked about me. Of course, that thrill faded the moment I remembered what I'd done.

"I'll call him and ask him to meet us down here," I said. "In the meantime, I have some paint for you to fix my door. I've gotten pretty well stocked, thanks to you."

~

While we waited for Kip to arrive, I retrieved the scrub brush, paint-brush, and can of paint. Sami worked in silence. I sat on the boardwalk, wondering how I could have made such a huge mistake.

"My uncle's never going to talk to me again," Sami said. Her voice sounded small against the waves and the wind.

"Don't worry." I thought about the terse phone call I'd just shared with him. "I'm pretty much in the same boat."

It was quiet, and the beach, deserted. Given everything happening, it wasn't the smartest idea to be sitting outside in the middle of the night. After all, Sami wasn't the one who chased me on the beach that day. Unless . . . I sat up straight.

Sami had been playing football with some pretty big guys. Some of the guys were big enough to be intimidating on a deserted stretch.

311

"Who was it that chased me on the beach?" I asked.

"Huh?" she said.

"He won't get into trouble. I just want to know I'm safe."

"What are you even talking about?" Sami demanded.

A chill settled over me. "You had nothing to do with the guy on the beach?"

She gave me a blank look.

"All right, all right." I shook my head. "I believe you."

Behind me, footsteps echoed on the boardwalk.

I jumped to my feet, gripping the container of Mace.

Kip's tall form came into view. His shoulders were thrown back, and he walked at a steady pace. He seemed rumpled, as though he'd just climbed out of bed.

I tugged my sweater tightly around me. The evening breeze was cool, and I shivered, remembering how cruel I was during our last conversation. What would it take for him to forgive me?

"Kip, I—" I started to say, but he looked right past me to Sami.

His familiar growl cut across the sand. "Sami? Is this true?"

She burst into tears.

The stars were brilliant above the water. They stretched out farther than I could see, lighting the darkness along with the moon. The beam from the lighthouse swept across it all in a steady, ceaseless rhythm.

I was exhausted from the drama of the day. Even though my parents wanted me to stay at their house for safety reasons, I needed the security of the lighthouse. I climbed up the ladder and opened the door, doing my best not to get paint on my hands.

Turning, I tried one last time to catch Kip's eye. "Thanks for coming by," I said. "I hope we can talk . . . sometime."

Kip didn't answer. Instead, he put his arm around Sami and walked away.

The door clanked shut, and I secured the bolt. Then I stacked leftover paint cans in front of the door for added protection. After climbing up the spiral staircase to my bedroom, I flipped on the lamp.

The illumination was a faded yellow, the bulb barely a glimmer compared to the beam of light outside. The bed was in the same condition I'd left it a few days ago, with my sleeping bag on top and my pillow half-lying on the floor. I hoped it didn't still smell like Kip.

I was tempted to crawl straight into bed and hide under my pillow, but now that I was safely inside, I wasn't tired. Crossing the room to the storage space, I found the welcome basket Kailyn put together for me. The bottle of rum was tempting, but I grabbed a box of chocolates instead.

I shined a flashlight on it to ensure it didn't have teeth marks from unwanted houseguests and climbed the rest of the way upstairs. The sudden light of the Fresnel lens was blinding. Pushing open the door to the gallery, I stepped outside into the wind.

The world was silent around me.

I settled in next to the railing and dangled my legs over the edge. Kicking my feet against the smooth stone of the tower, I popped a chocolate into my mouth and it melted on my tongue, sweet as a kiss.

Then, I remembered the pain at seeing Kip—the way his eyes avoided mine on the boardwalk. The worst part? I knew I deserved it.

I'd cut him off. It was up to me to apologize, to make things right, but I didn't know if I had the strength to do it. I couldn't imagine standing in front of someone I cared about so deeply and claiming such a terrible mistake. But I'd been so caught up in my own fears that I shut out the one man I'd ever cared about.

Pushing the box of chocolates away, I stared out at the water. It seemed more than a little ironic that I was sitting on top of a lighthouse and still felt completely lost.

Chapter Thirty-Two

I had no idea what time it was when I woke up in my sleeping bag. The day was still around me, without the sound of a foghorn or rain or seagulls. Everything was silent.

I stared up at the star pattern on the ceiling. Now that the lighthouse was painted, the interior was a clean slate. I could incorporate hundreds of little details to make it historically accurate and authentic, but for the first time since I moved to Starlight Cove, planning the lighthouse restoration didn't excite me—it made me feel tired.

What was the point in staying in Starlight Cove if I couldn't have Kip?

Yes, I'd made friends here. Kailyn, the Henderson brothers, the women from the historical society, Steve, and Captain Ahab all jumped to mind. Plus, my parents and I were closer than we had been in years. But bumping into Kip on Main Street or at the beach, or seeing him out on his houseboat and knowing that, for a brief moment, we'd had a chance . . .

That would hurt too much.

I thought back to the time Kip called me "Fancy Pants" on the beach. The way the sun lit his face as we kayaked, the moment he handed me condiments, and the countless ways he showed me respect and kindness. Then I remembered how I saw the name K. Whittaker and jumped to the conclusion that he bid on the lighthouse and lied about it.

The way I told him I changed my mind.

Tears burned the backs of my eyes, and I squeezed them shut.

For a moment, I thought I belonged in Starlight Cove. Now, I wasn't so sure. I'd never felt so lonely in my life.

The last thing I wanted to do was stay.

~

I spent the day sitting up on my lookout, rereading the letters from my great-grandfather. I was desperate to find something in his words to let me know why he left, but every word I read convinced me he would have done anything to stay. I knew, with every pained breath I took, that the love he felt for my great-grandmother was true. Unfortunately, my feelings would hardly serve as evidence for the insurance company.

We had little time until the ninety-day window slammed shut. A faceless representative would try to take our family home, forcing my parents to start some ridiculous legal battle based on nothing. If the insurance company was successful, my parents' lawyers suspected, it planned to continue going after my parents until the debt against *The Wanderer* was satisfied.

I couldn't stand knowing that the claim was wrong but being unable to prove it. Besides, based on the mistake I'd made with Kip, I'd lost confidence that my opinions were valid. I "knew" Kip Whittaker was the one who tried to buy the lighthouse out from under me. Yet I was completely wrong about that.

What if I was wrong about my great-grandfather, too?

These thoughts plagued me for the majority of the day. When the sun started to dip lower in the sky, I gathered up my things and headed downstairs. I had to go to my parents' house and put on a good face for

Kailyn's party. Somehow, I managed to get dressed and make my way to her office, the can of Mace clutched firmly in my hand.

I could hear the party all the way down the block. Not because loud music was playing, but because it was so crowded that people spilled onto the front porch. The crowd unnerved me. Sal and his thugs could be skulking around, and no one would notice. I doubted they'd be bold enough to come right in, though. Of course, the person I was most scared to see was Kip.

I was tempted to fake a stomachache and head home. I couldn't do that, though. The party was my idea. I couldn't jump ship now.

I walked up the front steps, adjusting the strap of my dress. I'd planned all week to wear a pale-blue sundress that was feminine and pretty. At the last minute, I slipped on one of the stiff, starched dresses I used to wear like armor. It was hot and uncomfortable but offered just the protection I needed.

Inside, the party was in full swing. I recognized several people and noticed the locals had started to look familiar. I spotted Kailyn across the room and pointed at the bar. She winked and I headed over to get a drink.

Sipping on a frozen strawberry margarita, I admired the decor. The lighthouse made of balloons was in the center of the room, showcased with four spotlights. The punch table glowed with blue drinks lit from the bottom of the glass. The food table was half the length of the room, stocked with everything from lamb sliders to raw oysters on ice. A small placard in the middle of the spread read THE HARBOR RESORT.

"Hiiiiii," called Kailyn, navigating through the crowd. She was radiant in a yellow dress with her hair tucked behind her ear and accented by a pink tropical flower. Pulling me into a hug, she whispered, "This is the best idea you've ever had!"

"The only good idea," I said.

Kailyn must have caught my tone. "What's wrong?"

Embarrassed, I said, "I'm fine."

"Did something happen with Kip?" she whispered.

My chin started to tremble. I took a sip of my strawberry margarita to hide it.

To my relief, I spotted Carter on the opposite side of the room. He was with Cody. The two held court in a crowd of women, but Carter's attention seemed focused on Kailyn. He was dressed up, his hair gelled, and he kept sneaking glances her way.

I nodded in his direction. "You should go talk to him."

Kailyn bit her lip. "What should I say?"

"Say thank you for coming to the party," I suggested. "I hope you're having fun. It's not a big deal. Just go do it."

Kailyn hesitated. Then, she straightened her shoulders, took a large swig of her drink, and headed his way. Carter's face broke into a huge smile. It pained me to think of the times Kip had smiled at me like that.

"Those days are long gone," I muttered, taking another sip of my drink.

"What days are long gone?" someone asked.

Maeve Weatherly stood next to me. She held one of the glowing blue cocktails, a contrast to her conservative linen dress. For once, she wasn't looking at me with disdain, which was good, because that would have pushed me over the edge.

"Oh," I said. "I was talking about the party. I'm happy to see such a big crowd. This is good for Kailyn."

Maeve nodded. "She's good at what she does."

It felt strange, but as the summer breeze blew in through the back porch, the two of us managed to make small talk. We started with the weather, then moved on to the decorations, and finally settled on the enormous lighthouse in the center of the room.

Maeve studied it for a moment with a small frown on her face. "I owe you an apology," she said. "I'm sorry for the way I acted when you moved to town."

Cynthia Ellingsen

I would not have been more baffled if Kip Whittaker rushed up and pulled me into his arms.

"Really?" I said.

I wondered what she'd say if I told her I planned to walk away from the lighthouse altogether. Donate it to the city or sell it to the highest bidder.

"Yes." Maeve regarded me with her cool stare. "My behavior was inexcusable. I also appreciated your input on the website."

"Thanks, but . . ." I fiddled with the silver medallion on my necklace. "I didn't really know what I was talking about."

"It was very helpful."

We stood in awkward silence for a moment. Then she said, "I'm also sorry you and Kip didn't get a chance to search the barn. He asked me a week or so ago, but it's not in the best shape at the moment, after what happened."

"What happened?" I asked.

She wrinkled her brow. "Kip didn't tell you?"

I was not about to admit that Kip might never speak to me again.

"No. I've been busy with some things."

"Well, someone broke in," she said. "Tore the barn apart; looking for valuables, no doubt."

The hair on the back of my neck stood up. The robbery had to be connected to Sal. He had been sitting just two tables away in Towboat the day Kip had said he planned to search it. Sal must have believed the barn held a lead on the treasure and tried to beat us to the punch.

"Maeve." I gripped my drink. "I'm so sorry."

"It's fine," she said. "They were scared away by the alarm system, but that didn't stop them from making a mess. There's so much stuff in there, I have no idea whether they had time to take anything or not. I'm just grateful my mother's still in Florida."

I let out a breath. "Yes," I managed to say, remembering Sal's painful grip on my arm. "Me, too."

"Either way." Maeve shrugged. "I see it as a win. My mother won't let me touch her property. This will give me the excuse to do some upgrades, under the guise of home security."

I remembered the weeds growing around Beulah's front porch. "Good point."

Maeve scanned the room as though preparing to move on. I didn't know if it was the connection to Kip that made me want to talk to her, the fact that I was lonely, or that she was finally being nice to me. Either way, I didn't want our conversation to end.

"Would you tell me more about the program you're working on?" I asked.

It was the right thing to say.

Maeve launched into a fifteen-minute description of the charity she was developing and what it was trying to accomplish. I was still asking questions when Kailyn waltzed up, practically swooning.

"That was the best conversation of my life," she said. "You're a genius."

Maeve gave me a friendly smile. "I'll leave you to enjoy the evening." She indicated her empty drink glass. "It was nice talking with you."

"You, too," I said.

The moment Maeve was out of earshot, Kailyn whispered, "I came over to rescue you."

Maeve was so enthusiastic as she discussed the nonprofit, I couldn't help but admire her.

"It was a nice conversation, actually," I said. "She's really passionate about the program she's trying to set up."

Kailyn clinked her glass against mine. "Well, then here's to a night filled with passion."

Just then, Kip Whittaker walked through the front door.

Chapter Thirty-Three

I must have turned pale, because Kailyn grabbed my hand and whispered, "I knew it. Something totally happened between you guys!"

Kip looked better than ever. He wore a white linen shirt and was so tanned, rumpled, and delicious that it was all I could do to not rush across the room and bury my head in his chest.

"Yup," I said, miserable. "It's over, though."

"What do you mean?" Kailyn asked.

"I'm an idiot," I muttered. "That's what I mean."

Kip walked through the room, clapping friends on the back and flashing that familiar smile. He was hardly nursing a broken heart.

"I need to leave," I said, downing my drink. "I can't stay here."

"He's looking right at you," she murmured.

Kip was, in fact, looking right at me. He held my gaze for a brief moment, his eyes as cold as stone. Then, he turned and shook hands with the guy from the barber shop.

"It's over." I gripped my glass like an anchor. "I ruined it."

"You don't know that," Kailyn said, but even she didn't sound so sure. "Whatever happened, you just need to talk to him. Kip's a good guy. It can't be that bad."

I took in the party. It was full of laughing, chatting, happy people. The decorations were vibrant, and the lighthouse practically glowed in the center of the room. I felt like the only one standing in the shadows.

"It's not the right time," I said.

"Well, this room isn't that big," she said. "So, be ready. You'll have to talk to him at some point."

~

The party raged on. I got caught up in a conversation with Jamie, the edgy girl who had made me an espresso milk shake at Chill Out. Her hair was moussed up in ashy spikes. She wore a small diamond nose ring that shimmered when she moved her head.

I hadn't seen her since the day she was so rude to me. Tonight, I was in a bad enough mood to address it.

"We've met before, you know," I said, when she told me how great it was to talk to the girl who bought the lighthouse. "I told you my parents owned the antique shop. You pretty much tried to kick me out of your store."

"I forgot about that." She cringed. "Look, I'm sorry. I'd heard rumors . . ."

I rolled my eyes. "That my great-grandfather gave Starlight Cove a bad name?"

"No." Her nose ring flashed. "That you were spending time with Kip Whittaker."

"What?" I said, in disbelief.

"I know." She gave me an impish grin. "Look, Kip would never be interested in me, but I didn't want some tourist to get him. That was before I knew you bought the lighthouse and planned to become a part of the community." She fingered a spiky strand of hair. "You must think I'm really stupid."

I shook my head, one eye on Kip. He was on the opposite side of the room, talking to some guys that worked at the bait-and-tackle shop. "We're not together."

"It seems like you could be a good fit."

I shook my head. "We're not."

"Well, maybe he'll come to his senses." She took an enthusiastic sip of her blue drink. "Okay, so I have a question. Why is your great-grandfather's picture hanging all over town? It was there when I leased the building and it's, like, a prerequisite to owning a business."

"No clue," I said.

"Did your family put it up?" Jamie asked.

Kip moved away from the bait-and-tackle guys and headed over to the food table. He loaded up a plate with sliders, which made me think of that day after Beulah's house when I opened up to him about my family.

Since Jamie was still looking at me, waiting for an answer, I shook my head. "It was probably organized by the historical society or the chamber of commerce or something."

"Okay, that's so strange." Jamie polished off her drink. "There's a picture of him sitting on one of the tables, and I noticed something. Will you come look?"

The last thing I wanted to think about was my great-grandfather, considering how little time I had to figure out what happened. I didn't want to be rude, though, so I followed Jamie through the crowd. Unfortunately, she led me to a display table right next to Kip.

My mouth went dry. He stood less than six feet away, laughing with some girls I didn't recognize. I adjusted the straps of my dress, wishing I'd worn the light-blue one after all.

Jamie pointed at a table. In the center of a collection of black-and-white photographs of Starlight Cove sat the picture of Captain Fitzie.

"So check this out," she said, picking it up. "There's an inscription on the photograph. I only saw it because I knocked mine off the wall and the frame broke."

"Sorry," I said. "Saw what?"

I wasn't exactly listening because I was busy trying not to care that Kip was laughing with a cute blonde girl in a low-cut pink dress.

"The inscription." Jamie slid the picture out of the frame and handed it to me.

The photograph was printed on thick matte paper. The area that fell just below the frame read:

Death is not extinguishing the light; it is only putting out the lamp because the dawn has come. —Rabindranath Tagore

"It would make sense if your family hung these up, but since they didn't, it's a little strange," Jamie said. "Don't you think?"

I turned the picture over. A stamp on the back read Shutter Capture and had an address with a street name in Starlight Cove.

"Hi, gals," Kailyn bustled up. "What's going on?"

Jamie held up the picture of Fitzie. "History and mystery."

"Sounds fun." To Jamie, she said, "Let's get a refill."

The moment Jamie headed toward the bar, Kailyn pushed me toward Kip. "Talk to him," she whispered. "Now."

I stumbled slightly. Kip looked at me. Since no one stood between us, I had no choice but to say, "Hello."

"Hello," he said. "I'd like to introduce you to some of my former classmates."

I shook hands with the group of girls. Two of them wore wedding rings, but the one in the pink dress was single. She gave me a tight smile, and I wished I could follow Kailyn to the drink table.

Standing so close to Kip, I could smell his familiar scent. I watched his strong profile and the easy way he talked to people. The group of girls barely glanced in my direction. They swapped stories about people I didn't know. The longer I stood there, the more awkward I felt.

I wanted to talk to him, I wanted to apologize, but I couldn't do it. It wasn't the right time or the right place. I made a quick excuse, ducked away from the group, and headed for the bar. As I walked past the display table with the old photographs, my eyes fell on my great-grandfather.

I couldn't help but think he looked disappointed in me.

The beach was more crowded than usual the morning of the Starlight Festival. Main Street was completely blocked off, and every single shop was set up with a table or a booth on the sidewalk. The booths brimmed with handcrafted items, art, and food. The food looked especially delicious.

Vendors offered everything from miniature blueberry pies to hand-stuffed bratwurst. The air was ripe with the scent of roasted onions, homemade fudge, and freshly baked pies. Tourists and locals tried bites of everything, and the long line in front of the Towboat booth made my heart ache.

A loud cheer went up at the Henderson brothers' booth as Cody reenacted a strongman at a carnival. His shirt was off, and his fake tan glistened in the early morning sun. As he demonstrated how to properly hammer in a nail, the crowd oohed and aahed.

Carter stood to the side, assisting. Spotting me, he gave an enthusiastic wave.

I waved back. The night before, Kailyn and Carter talked more than once and were still hanging out when I headed home. I was curious to hear what happened. Based on the smile on his face, something must have.

My parents' tent was set up in front of the shop. They'd put in a lot of work. It didn't look like a booth, but the inside of a store. Turkish knotted and faux Oriental rugs covered the pavement, and an eclectic array of antiques with street-fair pricing was on display.

My father stood at the cash register. He beamed when I walked up. "Look who rolled out of bed," he said. "I almost rang your doorbell this morning. We were out here at five a.m."

I kissed his whiskered cheek. "I'm glad you didn't."

The sudden sound would have scared me. The walk home last night was filled with bumps and shadows. I tossed and turned all night, thinking about Kip and what it would mean to leave town and start over once again.

My mother waltzed into the tent carrying several bottles of water. She could have been an ad for the street fair, dressed in a colorful sheath she probably bought at a booth and wearing an armful of beaded bracelets.

Setting the water behind the cash register, she cried, "What are you doing in here? Go enjoy the fair!"

Wandering around in the hot sun—alone—did not sound appealing. But my mother was insistent.

"Look at this," she said, pushing me through the crowd and out into the street. "Get out there and enjoy."

Since my own parents kicked me out of their tent, I had no choice but to walk around. I bumped into Kailyn about ten minutes in. She wore a pair of gold-framed sunglasses and a cute navy sundress. Grinning from ear to ear, she grabbed my arm in excitement.

"He kissed me!" Her lips puckered over the straw of her cup of homemade lemonade. "It happened at the end of the party and, Dawn . . ." She wrapped her arms around herself, humming. "It was like something out of a romance novel. That Henderson can *kiss*."

I laughed. "I bet they all can. It's a prerequisite to being a Henderson, like having a six-pack and a cleft in the chin."

Cynthia Ellingsen

"It was, like, the best night of my life ever." She adjusted her sunglasses. "Now let's walk around so Carter can see me in my short little skirt."

The morning was a blur of sights, delicious smells, and the nervous jerk of my stomach every time a man with dark hair and stubble came into view. By the afternoon, I was convinced I might not bump into Kip, and I started to relax. I was laughing at something Kailyn said when a sudden flush of heat shot up my neck.

Kip Whittaker was about to walk past. He looked delectable in a light-blue T-shirt and a relaxed pair of white pants. Kailyn must have noticed my expression, because she instantly turned and grabbed his arm, pulling him over to us.

"Kip!" Kailyn beamed. "I am so happy to see you! A client just walked by and I have to go catch up. Do you mind hanging with Dawn for a second?" She gave me an innocent look. "Meet you back here at one?"

She rushed off toward a display of watercolors before I could blink.

I gave Kip a pained look. "Hi."

"Hello," he said, his voice formal. "Enjoying the fair?"

"Yes, it's . . ." The sun beat down on my shoulders, and the crowd squeezed past us. It was hardly the place for a conversation. "I'd like to talk to you. Do you mind?"

"No problem." He slid on a pair of aviator sunglasses. I could see my reflection in the mirrored lenses. Wild hair, flushed face . . . a big difference from the first time we met, when I was so determined to pretend I had my life together. "What's up?"

"Privately," I said.

Turning, I headed down the block toward my parents' store, hoping no one would stop us to talk along the way. Somehow, we made it without interruption. I led him around the back of the building and unlocked the storage room.

The room seemed dim and dusty compared to the bustle outside, but it was ice-cold from the air conditioning. Feeling awkward, I pulled two wooden chairs out of a stack and took a seat. It was a relief to sit down after a morning in the hot sun, but all I could think about was getting through this conversation with Kip.

He took off his sunglasses. "What's up?"

I fidgeted. "How's Sami?"

"Grounded." He shook his head. "My sister is cutting back her hours at the restaurant to spend more time at home. Sami's a good kid—a great kid. But she needs support from her parents."

"Yeah." I nodded. "I know how that is."

We sat in silence for a moment. The room was eerie, filled with so many relics from the past.

"Thanks for not turning her in." He cleared his throat. "I'm sorry for what she did."

"Kip," I said. "Stop apologizing. I owe *you* an apology."

He frowned in that glowering way that made him look so damn sexy. "Yeah?"

I squeezed my hands together. Even though I had practiced this conversation in my head at least a thousand times, the words did not come easily.

"I'm sorry I cut you off," I said. "I stopped talking to you because I saw the list of bidders for the lighthouse, and I panicked."

Briefly, Kip closed his eyes. "Dawn, that . . ."

"I know." I ran my hands over the chilled skin of my arms. "It was your sister."

The guarded expression on his face softened. "I found out a few weeks ago," he said. "She wanted to do something in conjunction with the restaurant. Dining on the water or something, which was a terrible idea."

True. The meal I'd made for Kip turned out, but I couldn't imagine trying to run a restaurant in there. Even if it was just a small, chef's table–type thing.

"I should have told you," Kip said. "I just didn't know how to bring it up."

"I didn't think it was her, though," I said. "I thought it was you."

"Me?" He looked confused.

"The list said K. Whittaker," I told him. "I panicked."

Kip drew back. "I see." Slowly, he got to his feet.

"Wait." I grabbed for his hand, desperate to keep him from leaving. "I made a huge mistake, I know that. But you have to understand—"

"That you don't trust me?" He pulled his hand away. "Yeah. I got that."

"I was scared," I whispered.

"Of what?" he demanded.

"Of . . ." My voice trailed off.

He glanced at the door.

"Kip," I pleaded, "this is the part where I could remind you that we moved around a lot when I was younger and that I never had the chance to learn how to trust people. But that would all be an excuse, because you were nothing but kind, supportive, and"—I took a deep breath—"I was falling in love with you."

He stared at me.

"I know we can't go back. I am begging you, though, to give me another chance."

A muscle pulsed in his cheek. "You told me you changed your mind," he said in a low tone. "One minute we were together, and the next . . ."

"I know," I said. "I'm sorry."

He shook his head. "I can't go through that again."

I swallowed over a painful knot in my throat. "Kip, I didn't mean it."

His dark eyes met mine. "Yeah. You did."

I put my head in my hands. More than anything, I wanted him to say he understood. That he still wanted to try. But Kip was as guarded as me. He'd let me in, and I'd let him down.

"I understand," I said. "I guess it doesn't matter, though. I'm planning to leave Starlight Cove."

For a split second, confusion colored his face. Then his expression went back to being cold and removed.

"What about the lighthouse?" he asked.

"It's pretty much done," I said. "You were right, you know, in the beginning. I planned to fix it up and sell it for a profit. Then, the more time I spent here, I imagined what it would be like to be a part of this community and live in it, but . . ." Kip's dark gaze held mine. "There's no point. I had a life in Boston."

It was a life that seemed small and stilted compared to the time I'd spent in Starlight Cove, but maybe that's how things were meant to be. Bursts of extraordinary, framed by the ordinary. I couldn't expect the extraordinary to last forever.

Kip shook his head. "That life wasn't good for you. You were so uptight when we first met. You seemed miserable."

The words stung. "I didn't come here under happy circumstances," I said. "I'd lost my job, lost the man I thought I was going to marry, and knew the odds were good I'd lose my family home. Being here didn't change any of that."

Kip frowned. "So, you're going to run away?"

"I'm not running away!" I said. "I can't spend the rest of my life on summer vacation. What am I supposed to do here?" I fought to push back the emotion that threatened to unhinge me. "My life in Boston might not be perfect, but at least I wouldn't feel like this."

Kip looked down at his hands. "Look, I know the thing that happened between us hurt, Dawn. I thought we had something, too. I would have bet on it. But . . ." He ran his hand across the stubble on his face. "It's no excuse to run back to a life that made you feel dead inside. You'll be miserable. You belong here," he said. "Even if it's not with me."

I sat in silence, listening to the sounds of the fair. People laughing, talking, and having fun. I didn't know how to be a part of that—not without him.

"You have the lighthouse," he said. "You have your family. You need to solve what happened with *The Wanderer*. Why would you leave all that to go back to sitting in some high-rise, cut off from everything down below?"

He cared about me. That much was clear. Not in the way that mattered, but it still meant everything to me.

Kip got to his feet. I stood, too. I wanted to put my arms around him, but I didn't dare.

"We should get back out there," he said. "Enjoy the fair."

He walked over to the door of the storage room and opened it. I passed by him, and that familiar electricity passed between us. We walked back into the heat of the day in silence.

Outside, Sal and his friends hovered at the bratwurst station down the block. Sal eyed me from behind his sunglasses. Instead of fear, I felt a sharp spark of anger.

"What is he still doing here?" I demanded. "He put someone up to chasing me on the beach; he's the one who broke into Beulah's barn . . ." I turned to Kip. "Maeve told me about that at Kailyn's party."

He gave a grim nod. "It's terrible." He took my elbow and ushered me away. "If that guy ever shows up when you're alone, I want you to call me. No questions asked."

My whole body tingled at his touch. To be honest, I half hoped Sal *would* show up when I was alone, so I'd have an excuse to call.

Kip walked me back to the place where I was supposed to meet Kailyn. He studied me for a moment, as though trying to find something to say. I imagined what it would be like if we could walk around the fair together, looking at art and holding hands.

"Well, have fun," he said.

"Kip, wait." I took a step closer to him as the crowd rushed around us. "I . . . I was thinking about the photographs. I want to know who put them up."

I pulled my hair off my shoulders. It was so hot that, now that we were out of the air conditioning, my hair was damp. I could smell the peach from my shampoo.

"There's an inscription on the picture," I said. "It's so odd. It's mournful. It might not be anything, but I thought we could meet with someone at the shop that printed them. Find out who put them up."

Slowly, he nodded. "It wouldn't hurt."

"Monday?" I said.

He hesitated. "You'll still be here?"

"I can't leave yet," I said, thinking about the insurance deadline. "Besides, we've come this far. We might as well check."

"Okay," he finally said. "We'll look into it on Monday."

It wasn't a date. That part of our relationship was over.

Still, it was a comfort to know I would see him again.

The next day, I helped my parents with their booth at the festival, but I think my mother could tell my heart wasn't in it. I had no doubt she'd guessed something happened between Kip and me. She suggested I do some work on the lighthouse instead.

I left the fair, suited up, and went down to the basement to clean. It was the only room left, and it was disgusting, but it needed to be done. Of course, my thoughts turned to Kip the moment I started to sweep the floor.

He was right—when I arrived in Starlight Cove, I was not happy. I was uptight, miserable, and didn't know what I was doing with my life. The work on the lighthouse was the first time I'd enjoyed myself in years—not to mention the research for *The Wanderer*. I liked the research because I got to spend time with Kip, but learning about my family history was fascinating as well.

Plus, the opportunity to get closer to my parents.

It had been quite the summer, and I had my time in Starlight Cove to thank for it. I didn't know if it would be possible to go back to Boston and pick up my life where I'd left off. Too many things had changed.

The sudden clank of the bell upstairs made me jump. Everyone in town was at the festival, so who would be stopping by? I grabbed the can of Mace and my cell phone and ran up the steps.

Pushing open the window, I demanded, "Who is it?" There was a pause. Adrenaline rushed through me.

"Maeve," a small voice said. "Maeve Weatherly."

I stuck my head out the window in disbelief.

Sure enough, Maeve stood in the sand, shielding her eyes from the sun. She was casually but elegantly dressed and carried a large black canvas bag under her arm.

"Do you mind if I come up?" she called. "I brought something for you."

Even though I enjoyed our conversation at the party, I never in a million years would have expected her to visit me. I couldn't even begin to imagine what she might have brought by.

"Okay," I said, waving her up. "I'll let you in."

Maeve stepped into the main room, brushing dirt off her tailored clothing. "This looks fabulous," she said, setting the bag on the floor. "Can I have the tour?"

"It hasn't been that long since we painted," I apologized. "It might smell."

"That's fine," she said. "Fresh paint smells like new beginnings."

I gave her a brief tour of the lighthouse. She had a lot of knowledge and asked some great questions. I got into sharing the different aspects of the lighthouse and enjoyed talking to her about it.

"You have done such detailed work," she said, when we walked back into the main room. "Now, I stopped by for a reason, so I don't want to take up too much of your time." Bending down, she picked up the bag she'd brought and unzipped it. "I've been using the break-in at my mother's barn as an opportunity to straighten it up. I found something in there that might interest you."

Maeve pulled a large piece of cloth out of the bag. It was the size of a tablecloth, and when she shook it, pieces of dust shimmered in the sun like starlight.

"This flag is original to the lighthouse," she said. "It was something used only for special occasions. I think it's just remarkable."

The flag was a cream-colored cloth with a red border. It appeared to be made of cotton and wool. In the center, embroidery depicted the lighthouse in white, black, and red with a detailed starscape. It also had several embroidered vignettes to the side, including a boat, a seagull, and a cannon, along with a series of numbers along the bottom.

The stitching was meticulous, with the exception of the numbers. I ran my fingers over the material. It was worn but in great condition. I suspected it was extremely valuable.

"This is beautiful," I said. "How did your mother end up with it?"

Maeve shrugged her thin shoulders. "I wonder whether it had something to do with that final message for Madeline?"

"My great-grandmother?" I said, confused.

"Yes, I . . ." She gave a little laugh. "It's silly. I don't . . ."

I leaned forward. "Please, tell me."

"Kip said you wanted to search the barn in hopes of finding the last love letter to Madeline. I confess I looked for it myself because I've become curious about the story, too. I couldn't find a thing." Maeve lifted her hands and shrugged. "However, when I found this, I started thinking. Ruth said a message, not a letter. Could the message have been something like this? Could he have given her the flag? Perhaps it was symbolic of something."

I stared at her. The last person I expected to climb aboard the treasure hunt train was Maeve Weatherly.

She looked embarrassed. "I can see you think I've lost my mind. However, I could not think of any other historical connection my family had to the lighthouse, so I have no idea why we would have it, which is the only reason it crossed my mind. Either way, I brought it as a gift for you."

This news startled me even further.

"To keep?" I said. "No, this is . . ."

I ran my fingers over the material of the flag. It was so old, so intricate in its design, that I couldn't imagine accepting it as a gift.

"Maeve, you can't give this to me," I said. "Please, let me buy it."

She looked offended. "It is a piece of Starlight Cove and should remain here. Consider it my gift to you and the lighthouse. An official welcome."

"Wow." I hugged the flag to my chest. "Thank you."

I couldn't believe the one person insistent on shutting me out of the community was finally welcoming me in. I swallowed over the lump in my throat, more confused than ever. Reaching out, I clasped her hand.

"Thank you," I said. "You don't know what this means to me."

"Yes, I think I do." She took in the pristine walls of the main room. "Based on the work you've done here, I think I know exactly what it means to you."

Chapter Thirty-Four

The seconds seemed to pass much too slowly until my meeting with Kip. We met on Monday morning at ten sharp at the address stamped on the back of Fitzie's photograph. His eyes had never seemed so blue in the midmorning sun, but, once again, he seemed to go out of his way not to look at me. I squeezed my hands, searching for something to say.

"This place is not what I expected," I said, pointing at the shop.

Even though many of the shops in Starlight Cove were ancient, this one looked it. The paint on the window frames was chipped, the front porch sagged, and the roof's last repair must have been decades ago. In the midst of the wreckage, vibrant paintings filled the front windows, and a menagerie of wind chimes sang in the breeze.

"It's an art gallery," Kip said. "I went to school with the owner."

He walked up the steps and opened the old screen door. A fluffy white dog ran out to greet us, followed by a tiny blonde woman about my age.

"Jolene!" Kip hugged her, which seemed totally unfair, considering he'd barely looked at me. "Are we interrupting your work?"

"I work when the muse shows up," she said, giving him a firm pat on the back. "I think he's been off drinking."

Paintings taller than Jolene lined the walls of the shop: the coastline of Northern Michigan during the fall, drifts of snow as high as hanging icicles, a single grape glistening on a vine, and Lake Michigan at sunset. The works represented each of the four seasons. Her work was good enough to make me forget about Kip for a few minutes, which was pretty impressive.

"You're very talented," I said.

"Sometimes." She shrugged. "So, what's up? You two look like you're on a mission."

Kip pointed at the black-and-white photograph of Captain Fitzie hanging behind the register. "I need a favor. I need to know who made so many copies of that photograph."

Jolene pursed her lips. "Doll face, that's a long time ago," she said. "Paper files. They might not even exist anymore."

He flashed a charming grin. "You know your mother never threw anything away. I bet you can find it somewhere in the back."

Jolene tossed her ponytail. "I would only do this for you." She gestured at the fuzzy white dog. "Keep an eye on George Winston."

The dog ignored us the moment she left, opting to curl up in his wicker-basket bed and fall asleep. Kip and I walked around the store, admiring the paintings. I kept thinking of things I wanted to say to him, but matched his silence instead.

One thing I wanted to talk to him about was the gift from Maeve Weatherly. I'd studied the flag, trying to figure out whether it could have been a message from Fitzie to Madeline, but didn't see how. It was an interesting theory, though, that the message was something other than a love letter.

I was staring at a portrait of a starscape when Jolene marched out from the back.

"Kip," she groaned. "This is crazy! We're talking stacks of boxes. I think I'm going to shred everything and turn it into a collage. I can't deal."

Frustration shot through me.

"Jolene, do you mind if I look?" I said, taking a step forward. To Kip, I added, "I know you have to get to work, but I can search for it."

Jolene put her hands on her hips. "The records are private."

Kip walked over to the picture. He took it out of the frame and showed the inscription to Jolene.

She squinted. "That's cheerful."

"I know," Kip said. "We're trying to figure out who printed the photos, because the inscription seems so personal. Don't you think?"

Jolene's face pinched into a frown. "Are you looking for that treasure?" She held up the photograph and pointed at Fitzie. "He took it, you know."

Kip cleared his throat. "This is Captain Fitzie Conners's great-granddaughter."

"Sorry." Her tone was flat. "It's what people say."

The wind chimes sang outside as Jolene studied the inscription on the photo. She let out a huge sigh and pulled out her phone.

"My mom might know," she said. "That woman can't remember yesterday, but she can remember who the first person in town to order color photographs was."

～

Kip and I headed back to his office with the information in hand. In 1972, a woman named Betty Penn reprinted the pictures. She was "one of those love-the-world hippies," according to Jolene's mother, and hung his picture all over town.

Kip suggested we track her down and try to talk to her. He sat at his desk and searched for her online. The information popped up right away. He put the phone on speaker and dialed.

"Hello?" A woman picked up on the third ring. Her voice was brisk.

Kip started to speak, but I leaned forward instead. "Yes, Mrs. Penn?" I said. "My name is Dawn Conners. I have some questions about the photograph you reprinted of my great-grandfather."

"Conners?" she echoed. "Oh! Captain Conners. Goodness. How are you?"

"Fine," I said, fidgeting with one of Kip's business cards. "I'm living in Starlight Cove, and I've been researching the legend of *The Wanderer*. I was curious how Fitzie's photo got in every shop, and some records at the photography shop led back to you. Can you tell us why you put it up?"

Mrs. Penn was silent for a long moment. So long, in fact, I thought she'd hung up. Then she gave a slight sigh.

"It was silly and sentimental," she said. "However, I thought Captain Conners should be honored. I'd be happy to talk to you about it. Would you like to come by?"

"Yes," I said quickly. "How about early tomorrow morning?" Covering the receiver, I looked at Kip. "Is that okay?"

"I wouldn't miss it."

≈

That night at dinner, I sat with my parents around our dining room table. I took in the familiar sight of the Persian rug, dramatic curtains, and paintings from every era scattered on the wall and tried not to think about how few meals we might have left in this room. Once my mother served the meatloaf, I told them about the phone call and appointment with Mrs. Penn.

My father's face flushed red and he slammed down his fork. "I want to meet this woman." He pushed away his plate. "Give her a piece of my mind."

"Why?" I asked. "She put up the pictures to honor Fitzie."

My father shook his napkin at me. "She made a mockery out of him. People come to town and take pictures like he's some type of outlaw? That woman doesn't know the definition of honor."

My mother gave me a worried look. It was clear my father was at the end of his rope.

"Dad." I sighed. "She didn't plan for that to happen. Besides, Kip and I just want to talk to her, to figure out why she's so interested in the story. I bet she's a history buff or something. It's probably not worth your time."

He got up from the table and went to stand by the window. He looked out over the backyard at the expanse of woods behind our home. He didn't speak for so long that I started to doubt he would.

I was just about to take a bite of green beans when he said, "At this point, everything is worth my time. We'll leave at eight in the morning. I'll drive."

He let himself out the French doors and settled in on the back patio to smoke his pipe. I looked at my mom, trying to fight against the helpless ache in the back of my throat. She reached for my hand.

"It'll be okay, honey," she said, as though trying to convince herself. "It's going to be just fine."

∾

Kip and I piled into my parents' antiquing truck for the meeting, and my father drove us the hour up north. I sat in the middle, sandwiched between him and Kip. The wind whipped my hair, and I tried not to notice the way it brushed against Kip's arm. It was a reminder of how close I was sitting to him—a fact I was trying to forget.

Mrs. Penn's house was made of stone and set back in the woods. A small lake rested behind it, and a dream catcher hung on her front porch. She peered out the front windows and, when I waved to her, opened the door.

Behind the screen stood a slight woman with short brown hair. She wore a simple button-up shirt with a pair of khaki slacks. Something about her demeanor reminded me of a college professor.

"I'm surprised you tracked me down," she said, studying us one by one. "And a little embarrassed. The thing I did with the pictures was meant to be a private gesture."

My father gave her an outraged look. "Private! You made a mockery of my family."

"Dad," I started to say, but Mrs. Penn opened the screen door and stepped outside. She took his hands in hers.

"Sir, what happened to your family was a tragedy," she said. "Those pictures were put up to honor your grandfather. If we resolve anything in our time together this morning, I hope you leave understanding that."

My father didn't draw back. He held her hands for a moment, as though uncertain what to do. Then he nodded and gave a sharp huff.

"Now, please," she said. "Come inside."

Whoa. I glanced at Kip. Talk about taming the bear.

Mrs. Penn gave a brief tour of her home, made small talk about the weather, and eventually bustled us out to the screened-in back porch. The portrait of Captain Fitzie sat on a white wicker table.

Mrs. Penn offered us homemade lemonade and a plate of sugar cookies. Finally she settled into a floral-covered chair. When no one spoke, Kip took the lead.

"Thank you for agreeing to talk with us today," he said. "You've made it clear you put up the pictures to honor Captain Conners. But I have to admit, that quote hidden beneath the frame seemed like a private memorial of sorts. Do you have a personal connection to all this?"

"My grandfather survived the wreck of *The Wanderer*," Mrs. Penn said. "He was one of the few who made it. Unfortunately . . ." She shook her head, and the green chain attached to her reading glasses jiggled.

"I've tried ten different ways to pluck that man out of my family tree. It hasn't worked."

"Why did you want to pluck him out?" I asked.

"My grandfather, Aleksander Penn, was not a nice man. He had delusions of grandeur, from what I understand." She pursed her lips. "Oh, he had a lot of problems. He drank, and he was in and out of jail. During the voyage of *The Wanderer*, he led a mutiny."

My father sat up straight. "He was the one in the brig."

I held up my hand. "No, I met another guy with an ancestor in the brig. How many could have been in there?"

Mrs. Penn shrugged. "I imagine quite a few. Aleksander led a small group to take over the ship. He wanted the whiskey, you see. It was pretty valuable during those times." Turning to my father, she gave a kind smile. "Your grandfather took pity on the men, maybe because they were such a pitiful crew. He didn't report the mutiny to shore, or Aleksander would have been in serious trouble. When the ship started to go down, Captain Conners released the men to get them to safety. It was too late for the whiskey, so Aleksander turned his attention to the silver."

My father looked at me.

I sucked in my breath. "He stole it?"

The only sound on the porch was the low hum of insects outside.

"He tried," Mrs. Penn said. "According to the story my father told me, Aleksander attacked Captain Conners from the lifeboat. The captain fought back, gave Aleksander a nice gash of his own, and managed to escape with the silver. He hid it for safe transport and lay low for several days."

"In the lighthouse." I practically jumped up and down in my chair. "That's when he hid in the lighthouse!"

"Why wouldn't the keeper report Aleksander?" Kip demanded.

I wondered the same thing.

"Maybe Fitzie didn't see who it was," I said slowly. "It had to be pitch black, except during the lightning. So he just hid out in the lighthouse, waiting for a safe time to leave."

"Unfortunately . . ." Mrs. Penn spread open her hands. "That time never came. Aleksander ambushed Captain Conners. When he refused to reveal the hiding place of the silver, Aleksander shot him."

My father's mouth dropped open. "Killed him?"

"I'm afraid so." She frowned and adjusted her glasses. "It's a terrible thing. One of those stories that, like I said, I wouldn't mind plucking out of my family history."

My father sat back in his chair. "He was murdered."

I reached for his hand. "Mrs. Penn, why didn't you say anything?"

"Would you?" She took a sip of lemonade, set the glass on the table, and wiped her hands on her slacks. "Besides, I didn't want to believe it."

"Do you have any proof?" Kip asked.

"Unfortunately, yes." She reached under her chair and removed a small, floral-covered storage box. "Aleksander took the few pieces of silver Captain Conners had on him when he died, and the pouch they were in. The silver is long gone, but . . ." She reached into the box and pulled out a small leather bag. Handing it to my father, she said, "This belonged to Captain Conners. It has his name sewn into it."

I held my breath. Sure enough, in the bottom of the bag, the name Captain Fitzgerald Conners was embroidered in faded gold. Most likely the work of my great-grandmother.

My father studied the pouch for several moments. Then he coughed, his throat constricting with the motion. The sudden gleam of tears in his eyes made my heart ache.

I stood up and rested my arms on his shoulders. "Dad," I whispered. "It's okay. He's innocent. This proves it."

My father ran his hand over his beard. "He was a good man. My grandfather knew he was a good man, my father knew he was a good man," he managed to say. "We just needed the proof. I only wish . . ."

I knew exactly what he was thinking. He wished his family were still alive, so he could have the chance to tell them.

"They know," I said. "They've known for a long time."

My dad got to his feet and drew me in for a hug. I had to fight to hold back tears. Finally, my father patted me on the back and reached into his pocket. Pulling out a handkerchief, he sat down and blew his nose. Our group sat in silence for a long moment, absorbing the news.

"Did Aleksander ever find the lost silver?" I thought to ask.

"No." Mrs. Penn shook her head. "He tried. He stayed in Starlight Cove for more than a year, working odd jobs. He never found a thing."

"It's still out there," Kip said.

"Captain Conners hid it well."

Birds chirped in the trees next to the porch. Ice cubes clinked against the glass as Mrs. Penn took a final sip of lemonade. She moved as though to stand, and I held up my hand.

"Mrs. Penn, would you be willing to share this information with the authorities?"

"Is that really necessary?" she asked. "It's been quite a long time and . . ."

"Unfortunately, it is." I glanced at my father. "My family has been facing a legal battle with the insurance company. They are convinced my great-grandfather stole the silver. If we can't submit proof of his innocence, they plan to take our family home as a starting payment. We'll need you to talk with them. Would you do that?"

Mrs. Penn looked like she might say no. I imagined an entire conversation where my father threatened her with lawyers and Kip lectured her on the right thing to do, but all that wasn't necessary. She looked at the picture of Captain Fitzie and, finally, she nodded.

"I'll make a statement," she said. "It's the least my family can do for the harm that was caused to yours."

My father ran his fingers over the embroidery in the leather pouch. "Thank you."

I picked up the picture of Captain Fitzie. I studied his proud posture, the wise glint in his eye. Then, thinking of the sentiment in the letters he'd written to my great-grandmother, coupled with the realization that this was finally over, made me choke up.

Kip came over and put his hand on my shoulder. "You okay?" he murmured.

I turned to him, my eyes damp with tears.

"He loved her," I whispered. "He was always going to come back for her."

Kip held my gaze. "Was there ever any doubt?"

~

My father was quiet as we left Mrs. Penn's house, something completely out of character for him. Kip and I didn't say a word, either. We rode in silence through the long driveway that cut through the woods.

The branches blocked the sun overhead, and shadows darted across the truck. We pulled out onto the highway, and I noticed a black SUV idling on the side of the road. It roared to life and headed down the driveway, scattering dust behind it.

I sat up straight. "Dad."

The seatbelt cut into my shoulder as I turned to squint at the vehicle. It was hard to see through the dirty windows, but I was certain the man behind the wheel of the SUV was Sal. I remembered the moment in Towboat when Sal insisted my family would find the treasure.

You'll find it, he said. *And I'll be right there when you do.*

Sal had been watching us the whole time. He'd probably talked to Jolene at the photography shop and followed us to Mrs. Penn's house. There was no doubt in my mind he wouldn't believe Mrs. Penn when she told him our meeting had nothing to do with the treasure. My blood ran cold remembering the bruise he left on my arm and thinking of what he might do to her.

"Dad," I shrieked. "Stop the car!"

My father jumped, slamming on the brakes.

"Piss of a fish eye, Dawn," he complained. "What in the—"

"Sal Reed was in that SUV," I cried. "It pulled into Mrs. Penn's driveway the second we pulled out."

"What?" He hit the gas, cut across three lanes of traffic to do a U-turn and, in the process, almost hit three other cars, inciting angry horns all around us. The sudden wail of a police siren made him let out a string of cusswords.

"Thank goodness," I cried.

The moment my father came to a stop, I clambered over him and leapt out of the truck. The police car was pulling in behind us, lights flashing. I raced right toward it.

"Dawn," Kip shouted. "You can't—"

But I didn't have a choice.

"Help," I cried. "I need your help!"

The officer was already half-out of the vehicle. He was tall and intimidating, and had an expression like thunder.

"Ma'am, get back in the truck," he ordered.

"Please," I begged, coming to a stop. "I need your help!"

I must have sounded frantic, because instead of arresting me on the spot, the officer looked like he might be willing to listen.

"The woman who lives in the house we just came from is in serious danger," I said. "Put us all in handcuffs and leave us in your car—I don't care—but please, you have to help her. It's an emergency."

The officer hesitated.

"Please!" My voice broke. "Please call for backup."

The police officer spoke into his radio. "Hang tight," he told me, once he'd passed along the message. "We'll see what I can do."

I wanted to hug him. Instead, I said, "I'll go get back in the car."

My legs felt like rubber with every step. I pulled open the side door and crawled over Kip. He grabbed my hand. Exhausted, I leaned against him.

I breathed in his familiar scent and closed my eyes. It didn't cross my mind to think about the fact that we weren't together. Leaning on him made me feel safe.

"That was brave." He brushed his hand over my hair. "Stupid, but brave."

I didn't feel brave. I shook all over, terrified to think what might happen at Mrs. Penn's home. I hoped she hadn't opened the door. Sal might break it down, but maybe she would manage to buy some time before help arrived.

Sirens wailed in the distance, and I sat up straight.

"Thank you," I whispered.

Even though I didn't appreciate the fact that Mrs. Penn had kept her story a secret for so many years, I didn't want anything to happen to her.

Dust from the gravel kicked up, and flashing lights surrounded us. My father shouted the address, and the battalion of cars took off, racing toward Mrs. Penn's home.

My father laughed, honking his horn. "That'll show those pirates," he roared. "Put them all away!"

I shook my head. "It's not over yet."

"She'll be okay, Dawn," he told me. "She's a smart woman."

"I'm sorry about Fitzie," I told him.

"Me, too, my dear girl," he said. "Me, too."

The cars on the highway zipped past. The policeman who pulled us over had instructed us to stay put, but, either way, I knew my father wouldn't budge until Sal and his men were hauled away for good. As we waited, my father connected his phone to the radio and cued up an old mariner's song.

"For Captain Fitzie," he cried. "May you rest in peace, old chap!"

When the song was finished, my father hit the repeat button. He did this again and again until the three of us knew every word. Then, we sang along at the top of our lungs, the music like a foghorn pulling us safely back to shore.

Chapter Thirty-Five

Once Sal and his cronies were taken away in the back of several police cars, the officer let us go. We called my mother on the way home. She was devastated to hear the story of Captain Fitzie but gleeful to learn that our home would be safe.

"Dawn, you're a firecracker," she said on speakerphone. "I've tried to tell you that for years!"

I blushed at the praise but was glad the research Kip and I had done made the difference. The tension of the past few weeks was finally behind me, which was a huge relief. The fact that Sal and his crew were responsible for my scare at the beach, the break-in at Beulah Weatherly's barn, and the constant, uneasy feeling that someone was watching me, meant that I could finally stop looking over my shoulder.

"How soon are you home?" my mother asked.

My father glanced at the clock on the dashboard. "Twenty minutes," he said. "We might pop off for a bite, first."

"I'd hold off on that," she said. "There's something here I want you to see."

"More work!" My father honked his horn as we zipped down the highway. "Your mother has more work for me to do!"

Kip laughed, and I snuck a peek at him. His eyes settled on mine, and I felt those darn stomach flutters. Quickly, I looked back out at the scenery.

"It's not work," my mother said. "Remember the box you gave me to get restored? The one with those records from the lighthouse keeper? It just came back. I think you guys should take a look."

Something in her voice made me sit up straight.

"Mom . . . is there something you want to tell us?" I asked.

"Nope." She sounded cheerful. "It's more of a visual thing."

She hung up, and my father chuckled.

"The lady has spoken," he said. "We're going to have to settle for drive-through."

"Ah, women," Kip said. "What is it about them that makes us do what they want?"

I looked at him once again. This time, he held my gaze and smiled.

Our little group walked into Shipwreck Antiques and Treasures burning with curiosity. It wasn't like my mother to act so mysterious. The moment we walked in, she rushed forward.

"I'm so sorry about Fitzie." She hugged my father and pressed her hand into the back of his white hair. He leaned into her, and the two stood in silence.

For so long, I'd considered the relationship between Captain Fitzie and Madeline as the height of true love. It suddenly dawned on me that my parents were not too far behind—something I hadn't noticed because . . . well, probably because they were my parents.

"It's okay." My father stroked her hair. "I always suspected it was something like this."

My mother held him for another moment. Then, she patted him on the back. Turning to Kip and me, she said, "Ready to see what all the fuss is about?"

"Yes," I said. "I can't believe you made us wait this long already."

She laughed, linked an arm in mine and Kip's, and ushered us to the back room. It was still dusty and dirty, but I could finally see the order in the chaos.

"You're not going to believe this," she sang.

My mother lifted the box up from a bed of tissue paper. It was still obviously an antique, but the rust was gone, and the exterior had a dull, gray lacquer.

"What do you think?" She smoothed the surface with her hand.

"It looks great," I said. "But I hope that's not what you wanted us to see."

She sailed over to stand by my father. "Why don't you open it?"

Because it was only me, my parents, and Kip Whittaker in the storage room, I had the completely irrational thought that Kip had hidden a diamond ring in the box and was about to propose.

I know, I know. Ridiculous.

Pushing the fantasy out of my head, I opened the box. It was empty other than a small metal line that ran along the center. I wrinkled my forehead and touched it.

To my surprise, something gave. Pushing at the line again, the panels separated into two, revealing an opening in the bottom of the box.

"It has a false bottom!"

Kip and my father leaned in. Then we all looked at my mother.

I could barely get the words out. "Something was in there, wasn't it?"

Grinning, she reached into the drawer of a nearby desk and pulled out a leather-bound journal. "You mean, something like this?"

A squeak caught in my throat as my mother handed me the journal. I held it, remembering that the metal box had seemed heavy when I lifted it off Cody's desk. Now I knew why.

The cover was faded brown leather, and the pages were thin and worn. I flipped it open. The neat handwriting on the very first page read:

Property of Luc Cotrele, 1919.

"The keeper." I gripped Kip's arm. "Mom, did you look at this yet?"

"I've been waiting for you."

I pulled out a dusty chair and sat down. My mother sat in a cross-legged yoga pose on a wooden crate. Kip sat on a chair and leaned forward. My father hovered over my shoulder like a music assistant ready to help turn the pages.

With careful hands, I turned to the year 1922 and started to read out loud.

April 29, 1922

Captain Fitzie Conners arrived in the eye of the storm. The waves were still billowing, the wind howling, and the rain still. He pounded on the door, and I let him in, still sick with the drink and the knowledge that my actions may have lost the lives of so many. He was wild-eyed in a way I'd never seen, with a gash that stretched from the top of his head to his chin. I made a kettle and wrapped him in wool blankets. He moaned, and I said I'd find Madeline. He grabbed my hand. "Please," he said. "Don't go near my home. He's looking for me." Then, he whispered my terrible secret: "The light was not lit." I sat, stricken. The knowledge that I smelled of drink . . . What could a guilty man do? I agreed to keep his location secret and fetch Dr. Whittaker.

"Mmm." My mother shook her head. "That poor man."

I ran my finger over the ink. "I know. Steve said the keeper was devastated because the light wasn't lit. It was his fault."

I kept reading.

April 30, 1922

The cove was buzzing with the news of the ship in the harbor. The rescue service is asking questions about the lamp. Fitzie still remains, feverish and shaking. There is word that there are other survivors. They will tell the light was out. I have to make a decision.

I bit my lip. "Fitzie might have caught pneumonia."

"Or an infection," my mother said. "From the cut."

Clearly impatient with our conversation, my father took the journal from my hands.

"There's an additional entry on the thirtieth," my father said.

O how low can a man sink? I broke the window. I came at it with an axe in the night. The wind, I'll say, put out the light. I don't deserve to stand on my own two feet with all those souls lost, but I've found redemption saving one man. Fever has set in, but Fitzie is safe. No one but Dr. Whittaker knows his whereabouts, and I have sent word to town that I am ill to justify Dr. Whittaker's arrival at my home. My words are true, as I feel sick over what I have done. So much shame, it might kill me. Perhaps it is time to sleep.

"Steve said he fell down the stairs," I said. "Was it really an accident?"

"I don't know." My mother twisted her hair around her hand. "It sounds like he's struggling with all this."

"Would everyone please be quiet?" my father roared, pacing the room. "I'm trying to read!"

We all laughed, leaned forward, and listened.

> May 4, 1922
>
> Fitzie is awake and well. Today, he ate two bowls of stew, and if he keeps up this pace, I will have a hard time keeping his presence hidden. He refuses to report the attack. He wants his crew to believe he is dead, out of fear for Madeline's safety. He went out last night, in the dead of night. I don't know where he has gone, but he returned covered in sand and muttering. The blow to his head might have affected his mind . . .

My father stopped. He rubbed his hand against his whiskers and seemed to skip ahead.

"Not fair," I cried, leaping to my feet. "What does it *say*?"

Smiling, he held up the book. In a booming voice, he read:

> He is speaking of a treasure he has hidden that I must protect. It is the silver from the ship, carefully hidden so the man that attacked him cannot steal it. When Fitzie is well, he plans to bring word to the financiers in person, along with an escort to extract the silver. In the meantime, he wants me to promise I can protect the bounty.

The three of us leapt from our chairs, clapping and cheering.

My mother rushed over to my father and kissed him on the lips. "This says it," she cried. "Written documentation!"

"You can print it in an article," Kip said, slapping my father on the shoulder. "Share it with the historical society . . . this clears the Conners family from all accusation!" He turned to me, his blue eyes sparkling. "He went to see Madeline that night. The night he came back covered in sand. He went to see her first, don't you think?"

"Yes," I whispered. "He wouldn't tell her anything in case Aleksander was still around. Which . . ." My mood sobered. "He was."

My father handed me the journal. "Go ahead, Dawn." He sat in a chair next to my mother, his arm looped around her shoulders. "Tell us what happens next."

> May 7, 1922
>
> Fitzie plans to leave today. He has his health back, and Dr. Whittaker is confident he will encounter no trouble on his return journey south. Fitzie refuses to tell me the location where he hid the silver, for my own protection. He knows I am an honest man but knows my troubles with drink. He feels it is safer for me to have little knowledge. Yet, he has left information about the location in the lighthouse in the event something does happen to him on the journey. He's asked me not to follow the star unless that happens.

"Follow the star?" I said.

My father groaned. "I bet we painted right over it."

I flipped to the next page, skimming the words.

"This is strange," I said, reading a few sentences. "This . . . oh no."

May 8, 1922

I fear for my safety. Fitzie left in the night; he is on
his journey down south. Two hours past, I heard
a banging at the door and rushed down, certain it
must be him. There was shouting outside, a man
determined to make his way indoors. I created a
barricade and now I sit here, alone. The man has
left. I have weapons. I am unafraid. Yet, I worry for
my friend. The man must have seen him leave, or
he would not know to come here. There is nothing
to do but wait.

"It's the last entry." I held up the book as though to prove it.

"He was murdered," my father said.

"No," I said. "He got drunk and fell down the stairs."

Kip shook his head. "I think Aleksander broke into the lighthouse
and made it look like the keeper fell down the stairs. It did him no
good, though, because the keeper knew nothing, and he was smart
enough to keep his journal hidden."

"Unless the code was obvious," my father pointed out. "Aleksander
could have cracked it."

"No." My mother shook her head. "How on earth would he know
to look for a code, without reading this? I bet he went in there, tried to
get information, and when he couldn't get it, gave up."

"Mrs. Penn said he stayed in town for a year," I said. "If he found
it that night, he wouldn't have stuck around. I bet he went to Madeline
to find out if she knew anything."

"I'm sure he kept an eye on her," my father said, "to see if Fitzie gave
her any of the money, but Fitzie was smart. He didn't tell her anything.
It kept her safe."

"Then why was she obsessed with the lighthouse?" I asked.

My mother got up and walked over to the minifridge. She pulled out a bottle of water and took a thoughtful sip. "Because she loved him. It was connected to him."

"Madeline knew Fitzie stayed in the lighthouse to recover," my father said. "He didn't tell her anything else. He only promised he'd come back for her."

I blinked back a tear. "It's all so sad."

My father stared off into space. Sorrow filled the room. For a brief moment, I smelled the faded scent of tobacco smoke and whiskey.

"Is it possible we're missing something?" I asked. "Maybe there's some sort of map in here, in invisible ink."

My mother laughed. "You're starting to sound like your father."

"Oh come on." I grinned. "He's probably thinking the same thing."

My father got up from his chair and stretched. "No, I'm thinking about the star. What that could mean. Have you seen any stars in the lighthouse?"

"Nothing jumps to mind."

He headed for the door.

"Where are you going?" I asked.

"Where do you think?" he said. "It's time to take another look."

He didn't have to say it twice.

∽

The lighthouse felt alive when we walked inside. It was as though it had a secret that it wanted to tell us, if we could only be smart enough to figure it out.

I stood in the main entryway, thinking.

"We're looking for anything with stars," my mother said, as if anyone could forget.

"When you look out the window, you see stars," I suggested.

"I'll look at the windows and see what I can find." She started searching the windows in the room, quickly gave up, and headed upstairs.

"You see the stars when you sit outside," Kip said, and went off to look.

My father stood by the door, jamming his fingers against his lips. "There's a star on the ceiling of your bedroom."

I remembered that first night in the house, when I opened the window and watched the pulse of the light against the star. "You're absolutely right."

My father and I raced up the stairs. We stood in the bedroom and looked up at the ceiling. "Well, we have two options," he said. "Get one of the Hendersons over here to cut into that or—"

"No," I said. "Let's not rip out the ceiling unless we have to. It's not like there's going to be a bunch of silver hiding up there. Or that floor would've come crashing down a long time ago. Maybe he meant it's pointing to something."

I studied the design. My father sat on the bed, resting his chin in his hands. It'd been a long two days. Even though my hands were practically shaking with nerves, he seemed perfectly calm.

I didn't know how he could be so patient. I wanted to find the answer today, right now. My father seemed content to take his time searching.

I sat next to him on the bed, trying to adopt his demeanor. "Do you think—"

My father hit the bed. "Hand me that book," he said.

"What book?"

He lunged across me in a burst of Carmex and vanilla tobacco, grabbing the keeper's manual from my bedside table. My pulse started to race with excitement.

"The sections were starred," I said.

"Exactly." He flipped through the book at a lightning pace. "Give me your phone."

He bellowed for my mother and Kip to come join us. They came racing down the stairs, their faces lit as though expecting the treasure to be sitting on the floor.

"What is it?" My mother rushed over to the bed.

My father summed up what I'd found in the book. "We need to descramble those letters," he said. "D-i-f-n-h-e-t-o-e-a-n-o-t-c-s-i-r-d. I'll need everyone's brainpower on this. Dawn, do you have paper and pencils?"

I tore some pages out of a loose-leaf notebook and tracked down some pens.

"I'll head out to the beach and try to get the Internet," Kip said. "I think they have descramblers online."

He raced down the stairs.

The three of us bent over the page and worked frantically. The door clanked a moment later, and Kip came rushing back into the room. We all looked up in expectation. He shook his head, settling in next to me on the bed.

"It didn't work," he murmured. "How's it going?"

The feel of his breath next to my ear gave me chills. I tried to focus on the letters, but they seemed to swim in front of me.

"Not good," I said. "I've tried this before and came up with nothing. I think it's imposs—"

"I've got it!" My mother threw down the tiny pencil. She pulled her hair off her neck and grinned. "You can all thank me later."

"Hot dog," my father said. "What does it say?"

"It says . . ." She got to her feet, took center stage in the room, and cleared her throat. "Find the coordinates."

There was a brief silence. Then the four of us leapt to our feet.

"Find the coordinates," I cried, looking at the jumble of letters. "Why couldn't I figure that out?"

It was easy to see, now that I knew what it said.

"What coordinates?" Kip asked.

"Why, latitude and longitude, of course," my father said.

Kip grinned. "Of course."

I laughed.

My father opened the keeper's manual and noted the sections where the letters were found. "I bet the pages are the numbers," he mused. "But it would be a whaler to unscramble them to figure out the latitude and longitude. We could determine a close approximation to which one starts the sequence, but it would get tricky from there. They have to be written out somewhere else."

"Dawn, have you seen numbers anywhere?" my mother asked.

My breath caught. "Yes," I said. "Remember? On the back of the painting and on the . . . oh my gosh." I put my hand to my mouth. "The flag."

Everyone stared at me. "What flag?"

I explained the flag Maeve Weatherly had dropped off. "She said she couldn't think of one reason it would be in their family," I said, my hands shaking with excitement. "Unless it was the message Ruth was supposed to give to Madeline."

My mother's eyes widened. "Where is it?"

"Downstairs," I said. "There's also the sequence on the painting. The Morse code."

"How do we know it's the right—"

"Stars," I said. "There's a starscape on both the painting and the flag. Plus, the flag is perfectly embroidered, but the numbers look sloppy. I bet the two sequences are a match."

Our group stood in stunned silence.

My father was the one to finally leap into action. "Well, come on," he shouted. "The flag's downstairs. Where's the painting?"

My mother looked stricken. "I sent it away," she breathed. "To get cleaned, and it's still not back. I bet they wiped the numbers off and . . ."

"I took a picture with my phone," I said. "Let's go see if the numbers match."

My father, my mother, and I raced down the stairs. I stopped, suddenly, noticing Kip wasn't there. I climbed back upstairs and found him in the center of my bedroom, a thoughtful look on his face.

"What is it?" I asked.

"Is this what it's like to hang out with a treasure-hunting family?" he said. "I mean, long term?"

"Yes," I whispered.

"I wouldn't mind being a part of that."

I rushed forward and threw myself into his arms. He pulled me into a kiss, and the world exploded like starlight behind my eyes.

By the time we raced downstairs, my parents were calculating the coordinates of the numbers on the flag.

"Do these match the numbers on the painting?" my father asked.

I read off the series of numbers from my phone, my lips still tingling from Kip's kiss. "Yes."

My mother clapped her hands in excitement. "We know where that is."

My father beamed. "The boat graveyard."

Turning to Kip, I said, "Have you been there?"

He nodded. "It's that part of the beach that turns into swampland, where people sank dugout canoes when they didn't need them anymore."

My father practically did a jig. "The water is cold enough and the current weak. A lot of the boats are still preserved. It's the perfect place to hide a treasure." He stopped, suddenly, and looked at my mother. "My grandmother used to take me there. I wonder if she knew the whole time."

"No," she said, shaking her head. "Madeline never saw the flag with the coordinates. It was probably a special place they used to go to. Maybe it wasn't all swamp back then."

"It's not swamp now," I said, thinking of the route of my run. "The sunken boats are in a runoff area, but it's separate from the swamp. The water's ice cold in that section."

Kip shook his head. "You were right next to it the whole time."

Sunlight streamed through the window. I rushed to the door.

"Let's go," I said.

My parents exchanged worried looks.

"Dawn," my mother said. "Calm down. It's been almost a century. Someone certainly has found it by . . ."

I held up my hands. "Mom, I have spent my entire life trying to keep things calm. I'm done with that. It's not likely we'll find anything, but I think it's okay to get a little fired up."

I yanked open the door and scrambled down the ladder.

"Now, if you'll excuse me," I called, "I have a treasure to find!"

The lake looked peaceful, the caps of the water white and shimmering. Birds flew overhead, and tourists dressed in bright colors strolled along the shore. I sat on the edge of my seat on the boat, gripping Kip's hand in excitement.

My father settled in behind the wheel, a captain's hat perched at an angle on his head. "I've been to this boat graveyard a thousand times and never once thought to look. Come on, Fitzie! Don't let me down." He let out some sort of battle cry, slapping his hand against the steering wheel.

My father was just about to open the throttle when my mother leaned over and whispered something in his ear. He grunted. Getting to his feet, he took off his captain's hat and slid it on my head.

"Be our leading light, Dawn," he said. "You earned it."

I settled in behind the wheel of the boat and took in a deep breath.

Kip shot me a sexy smile. "Show us what you've got, Fancy Pants."

The boat raced across the lake as tiny droplets of water pelted against us like rain. I drove at a steady pace, my mind skipping from the wreck of *The Wanderer* to Aleksander to the image of Fitzie sneaking away and burying the coins in a place no one would think to look.

When we finally approached the right latitude and longitude coordinates, I slowed to a putter. I got as close to the boat graveyard as possible without catching the motor. After dropping the anchor, I leaned over the edge. The outline of abandoned canoes shimmered beneath the water.

"What do we do now?" I asked.

"What do you think?" my father cried. "We dive!"

My father stripped off his shirt and sweater, and dove off the edge of the boat with a tremendous splash. When he surfaced, his hair was plastered against his head, and he had a cheeky grin on his face. My mother leapt in after him, her turquoise dress turning navy in the water. They tugged on face masks, and I tossed one to Kip.

He held it for a moment, looking at me. "You up for this?"

I didn't know if he meant diving into the water or the fact that he took his shirt off. The sight of his tanned, built upper body practically made me forget what we were doing there in the first place.

"Come on," he called, reaching for my hand.

Kip and I dove down around the ghostly figures of the canoes, as if the coins would be hiding out in plain sight. The dugout canoes were about ten feet deep. They were flipped over, creating small domelike shapes in the sand. Our group dove again and again to get a better look, kicking hard to stay low.

The water was cloudy, and it was hard to see much of anything. I surfaced, fighting against my chattering teeth. The four of us treaded water, studying the impressive stretch of sunken canoes.

"What should we do?" I asked. "We can't flip all these to find it."

My father hooted and started swimming back toward our boat. "Lesson number one in being a treasure hunter," he called. "Expect treasure to be hidden in plain sight, but always bring a magnifying glass to see it."

I looked at my mother. "What does that even mean?"

She pushed a strand of wet hair out of her eyes. "I don't . . ." Then, at the same time, we said, "Metal detector."

Turning to Kip, I said, "He loves them."

My mother groaned. "More than life itself."

While we waited, I dove down and ran my hand over the furry algae that covered the slick base of a dugout canoe. I imagined my great-grandfather dropping the heavy bags of silver and positioning a canoe to sink over them. It was the perfect hiding place until the danger had passed.

I surfaced to see my father approach, a portable metal contraption slung across his back. "Let's see what we can find," he said.

My mother ruffled his wet hair, and water splashed in silver droplets all around us.

"Thanks, Dad," I said, shivering.

"Don't thank me," he said. "Thank Fitzie."

I thought of the man in the black-and-white photograph: the kindness on his face and the sense of adventure in his eyes. He'd be proud of us for coming this far.

"For Captain Fitzie," Kip said.

I nodded. "For Captain Fitzie."

My father flipped the switch on the metal detector and dove down into the water.

Chapter Thirty-Six

Finding the treasure was one of those rare moments that proved the impossible was possible. The metal detector had started beeping somewhere in the middle of the boat graveyard. The alert pointed to an old-fashioned dugout canoe, half-buried beneath the sand. It sat below the bridge of the sandbar, protected from the wear of the current.

We dove down as a group to try to dig it out, but the suction made it impossible. With limited breath, we couldn't stay down long enough to pry it from the sand. We needed the right equipment to dig it out and see what was hidden underneath.

By that time, my father felt confident enough to radio the Coast Guard for assistance. Even though Sal and his crew were behind bars, he didn't want to take any chances. He also contacted Steve at Search and Rescue and asked him to bring some excavation equipment to the site.

We sat in our boat wrapped in towels and shivering while we waited for help to arrive. I nibbled at my chilled fingernails, desperate to see what was under the canoes. I knew the treasure was there. It had to be.

The Coast Guard pulled up in a boat with red bumpers and signaled to my father. Steve arrived moments after, with Captain Ahab perched in the front of the boat. Spotting me, the dog wagged with excitement. I reached over to pet him as my father climbed into Steve's boat to evaluate the equipment he brought.

"This will do it," he cried.

My parents both slid back into the water, balancing some sort of high-tech crowbar between them, attached to a long rope. Kip and I jumped in. We swam toward the canoe, but my father shouted for us to stay back.

"It's attached." My mother pointed to the line, connected to Steve's boat. "He's going to try to pull it up."

My father dove down and shoved the crowbar beneath one side of the canoe. He swam over to our group and gave the thumbs-up to Steve. The motor gunned, and the boat lurched a few feet.

The water in the graveyard gurgled, and my father let out a shout. "Here she comes!"

The dugout canoe surfaced with a *blurp* and floated in the direction of the current. Our group swam forward. The sand was settling in a swirling cloud. I grabbed Kip's hand and held my breath.

As the water stilled, three worn, decomposing sacks sitting on the bottom of the lake came into sight. The sun cast light down on them. The sight brought to mind the stars, the beam of the lighthouse, and the belief in the impossible, all at the same time.

From there, it came down to logistics. The bags were each about two feet tall and packed tight with Morgan coins. Our group worked steadily to transfer the ancient burlap bags into reinforced bags to haul up onto our boat. When the three bags were finally on board, the boat sat a few feet lower than it had before.

Steve insisted that Kip and I hop on board with him, which we were happy to do. He had blankets and hot coffee waiting. Captain Ahab licked my face in excitement, as though congratulating me on a successful search.

By now, plenty of boats on the lake had gotten curious. They started to pull in closer to see what was happening. It made me nervous, but with the Coast Guard present, I knew the incredible history resting in my parents' boat was safe.

"You ready to get out of here?" Steve shouted.

"Take her home!" my father called back.

Steve looked over his shoulder. "Hang on," he said. "Captain Ahab will start barking if I don't catch the wind." He opened up the throttle, and the boat roared to life.

I laughed as the Lab scampered up to the front of the boat and put his feet on the bow, his pink tongue flapping.

Kip put his arm around me. I turned to him with a smile, but he was frowning.

"What is it?" I asked.

"Now that our treasure hunt is over, I don't know how I'm going to get you to search an attic with me again."

I reached for his hand. "Oh?"

"Or ride in a dune buggy with me, call me when you get stuck in the floor, or"—he gave me his signature glower—"ignore me while reading love letters during a rainstorm."

I laughed. "You might be right about all that. There is one thing, though, that you'll have no problem getting me to do."

"What's that?" he asked, brushing his fingers over my lips.

"I'll never stop saying I love you."

The light in Kip Whittaker's eyes shone brighter than the beam at my home address. He leaned forward and kissed me.

Chapter Thirty-Seven

With Kailyn's assistance, I set up an emergency meeting of the Women's Chapter of the Starlight Cove Historical Society. The meeting was open to the public and kicked off with a brief luncheon at Towboat.

By now, of course, the entire town knew the Conners family had found the treasure. The news hit the local grapevine, followed by the local media, and rapidly spread online. Reporters and news programs were hours away from descending upon Starlight Cove, so we planned to tell our story before the frenzy set in.

Towboat was packed. The entire town must have shut down to attend the meeting, and I hoped we wouldn't run out of food. I walked around with Kip, shaking hands and greeting people. To my delight, Kailyn sat with the Henderson brothers, looking pleased as pink punch.

"I think we're going to start a band," she called. "Dawn and the Treasure Hunters. What do you think?"

Kip laughed. "It has a nice ring to it."

My father sat at the table of honor, looking distinguished as ever and slightly amazed at the turnout. My mother sat beside him, her hair flying around her head and dusted with silver sparkles. They told me they didn't want to make a formal speech, but since they knew everyone, they ended up chatting nonstop, telling their version of the story to this local or that at least a hundred times.

The lunch was delicious—a simple chicken dish served with mashed potatoes and green beans, and foil-wrapped chocolate coins for dessert. Sami helped to serve, and when she set down my plate, she seemed nervous. She stopped and touched my arm.

"I'm so sorry about the lighthouse," she said. "I can't tell you how sorry I am."

I got to my feet to hug her. "It's okay. It was just growing pains for both of us. Don't worry, okay?"

She beamed at Kip. "I like her," she said, and scampered away.

I sat back down, and Kip squeezed my hand.

Halfway through lunch, I finally had the opportunity to meet his sister. She had the same captivating eyes and friendly demeanor as Kip. He squirmed in his chair as we swapped stories about him, laughing hysterically.

"Oh, he loves romantic comedies," she assured me. "He's seen them all."

Kip turned as red as the tomato in his salad. Kelcee and I laughed so hard, I cried.

When lunch was over, I went up to the microphone and gave a presentation on *The Wanderer* to the packed house. I didn't get nervous, and I even included the pieces of the story we hadn't planned to share with the media, like about being chased on the beach and how Sal and his crew followed us to Mrs. Penn's house. The ladies oohed and aahed at the story of the swapped keeper's books, the hidden coordinates, and the moment we put it all together.

When I mentioned the flag Maeve gave to me, she flushed prettily. I was careful not to mention her grandmother. There were murmurs of approval in the room when I said she gave me the flag as a gift, and she waved off the praise.

"I did what anyone here would have done," she called. "I kept the history of Starlight Cove right where it belonged."

"Speaking of history," Kip said, getting to his feet. "We would like to invite everyone to join us at the lighthouse. There's one more thing we'd like to share."

My parents linked their arms with mine as our group headed down to the beach. The sun was shining, and the lake gleamed in the distance.

"What do you think?" my mother asked. "Do you think you made the right choice coming here?"

"To Starlight Cove?" I nodded. "I feel like I finally made it home."

We walked down the boardwalk and stood in front of the lighthouse, waiting for the large crowd to settle. Kip stepped up to the microphone the Henderson brothers had rigged for the occasion and cleared his throat. The crowd quieted, and the seagulls chattered in the sand.

"First of all," he said, "thanks to all of you for taking the time out of your busy day to learn the truth about the legend of *The Wanderer*. Personally, I will never forget the diligence and passion demonstrated by the Conners family in bringing the story to light."

On cue, I unveiled a poster-size version of the black-and-white photograph of Captain Fitzie. The crowd applauded long and loud. My father stood next to it, looking proud, and my mother held his hand.

"These photographs will be for sale after the meeting," Kip joked. "In case there is someone who still doesn't have one." He passed the microphone to me. "Go get 'em."

I stood up in front of the crowd, relishing the moment and the feeling of the sun shining down on my shoulders.

"It was a great reward to discover the truth about my family's history," I said. "To learn that the love my great-grandfather felt for my great-grandmother was not only true, but enduring. That was the biggest treasure of all."

My parents nodded.

"Receiving an additional reward for finding the silver was completely unexpected," I continued, "as we assumed the coins would belong to the state. However, the original insurance company is still in business. They were kind enough to give us a generous reward for our find."

I still couldn't believe it. We'd contacted them with the information to clear Fitzie's name, to remove the lien from the house. Of course, we also had to report that we'd found the treasure. The insurance company not only lifted the lien, they issued a formal apology and presented us with a reward that had been set aside for nearly a century.

My father was still furious at them, so he almost refused the money. I convinced him to accept it to invest in Starlight Cove.

"After much debate," I said into the microphone, "my family decided this money would best serve our community by being passed on. Therefore, the Conners family has decided to fund a project that will do great good here in Starlight Cove." Squinting in the sunlight, I looked out at the crowd. "Maeve? Would you mind joining me up here?"

I swear, there was so much chest grabbing and gasping from Maeve that I considered calling for medical attention. Or, at the very least, asking a Henderson brother to administer mouth-to-mouth.

When she made her way to the stage, I said, "Maeve, on behalf of the Conners family, please accept this donation to the water conservancy program. With these funds, we trust your program will do great work to educate the public and protect our wildlife and our Great Lakes."

Cameras from the local paper snapped pictures as Maeve accepted the check with a stunned look on her face. Then, she hugged me so tight that she practically lifted me off the ground.

"Just like a Conners," she said, beaming. "Always making waves."

With a delighted laugh, Maeve pulled my parents and Kip into the hug. Then she waved the check in the air. Kip handed her the microphone, and Maeve answered questions about the program and what it could do to help the local community.

I stepped out of the limelight and stood next to the boardwalk with Kip. I remembered the feeling of watching him wade through the water, his hair windblown and his cheeks rough with stubble. The smile he had given me, the one that made me tingle all the way down to my toes.

"This is where we first met," I said, turning to him. Kip was silhouetted against the lighthouse in the bright sunlight. "Who knew where that would lead?"

"I did." He smiled and pulled me in close. "From the very first moment I saw you, I knew."

ACKNOWLEDGMENTS

First, thank you so much to my readers—I am so grateful to each and every one of you. Writing is such a joy, and you make it possible.

Lake Union Publishing, your team is incredible—sales and marketing, editing, design, and everyone who brought *The Lighthouse Keeper* to life. Special thanks to my developmental editor, Marianna Baer. Your sharp eye and suggestions were invaluable. Major confetti and applause to Miriam Juskowicz, my brilliant acquisitions editor. You made this book happen, and I am forever grateful.

Huge thanks to Triada US—home to the one and only Brent Taylor, Super Agent. Brent, you are bold, brave, and hilarious, and it is an honor to work with you.

To my writers' group: Frankie Finley, Jennifer Mattox, and Stephanie Parkin. Starlight Cove shines because of you. Thank you for sharing your talent and insight.

To my family and friends: Carolyn Fitzgibbon, thank you for talking about *The Lighthouse Keeper* with me in its earliest form. Search and Rescue and the dog are all thanks to you. Uncle John, thank you for the perfect day of lighthouse research. Uncle Tom and Aunt Molly, this book wouldn't be the same without the great popcorn, terrible movies, and research efforts that October. Aunt Linda, thanks for the writing dates. Kathy and Butch Ellingsen, for the prayers. And, as always, my mother, for believing and encouraging me every step of the way.

Finally, to my incredible husband, Ryan Ellingsen. Every day with you is a dream come true. I am so blessed to share my life with you. You are the best husband, father, and friend. Everything is possible because of you. I love you.

About the Author

Photo © 2010 Brian McConkey

Cynthia Ellingsen lives in Lexington, Kentucky, with her husband and is the author of two previous novels: *The Whole Package* and *Marriage Matters*. She loves connecting with readers through her website, Facebook, and Twitter. Visit her at www.cynthiaellingsen.com.